ROGER LANGRIDGE'S

Snarked!

BOOK ONE

FORKS AND HOPE

ROSS RICHIE Chief Executive Officer • MATT GAGNON Editor-in-Chief • WES HARRIS VP-Publishing • LANCE KREITER VP-Licensing & Merchandising • PHIL BARBARO Director of Finance
BRYCE CARLSON Managing Editor • DAFNA PLEBAN Editor • SHANNON WATTERS Editor • ERIC HARBURN Assistant Editor • ADAM STAFFARONI Assistant Editor • CHRIS ROSA Assistant Editor
STEPHANIE GONZAGA Graphic Designer • EMILY MCGUINESS Marketing Coordinator • DEVIN FUNCHES Marketing & Sales Assistant • JASMINE AMIRI Operations Assistant

kaboom!

SNARKED Volume One — April 2012. Published by KaBOOM!, a division of Boom Entertainment, Inc., 6310 San Vicente Boulevard, Suite 107, Los Angeles, CA 90048-5457. Snarked is Copyright © 2012 Boom Entertainment, Inc. and Roger Langridge. Originally published in single magazine form as SNARKED 0-4. Copyright © 2011, 2012 Boom Entertainment, Inc. and Roger Langridge. All rights reserved. KaBOOM!™ and the KaBOOM! logo are trademarks of Boom Entertainment, Inc., registered in various countries and categories. All characters, events, and institutions depicted herein are fictional. Any similarity between any of the names, characters, persons, events, and/or institutions in this publication to actual names, characters, and persons, whether living or dead, events, and/or institutions is unintended and purely coincidental. KaBOOM! does not read or accept unsolicited submissions of ideas, stories, or artwork.

A catalog record of this book is available from OCLC and from the KaBOOM! website, www.kaboom-studios.com, on the Librarians Page.

BOOM! Studios, 6310 San Vicente Boulevard, Suite 107, Los Angeles, CA 90048-5457. Printed in China. First Printing.
ISBN: 978-1-60886-095-1

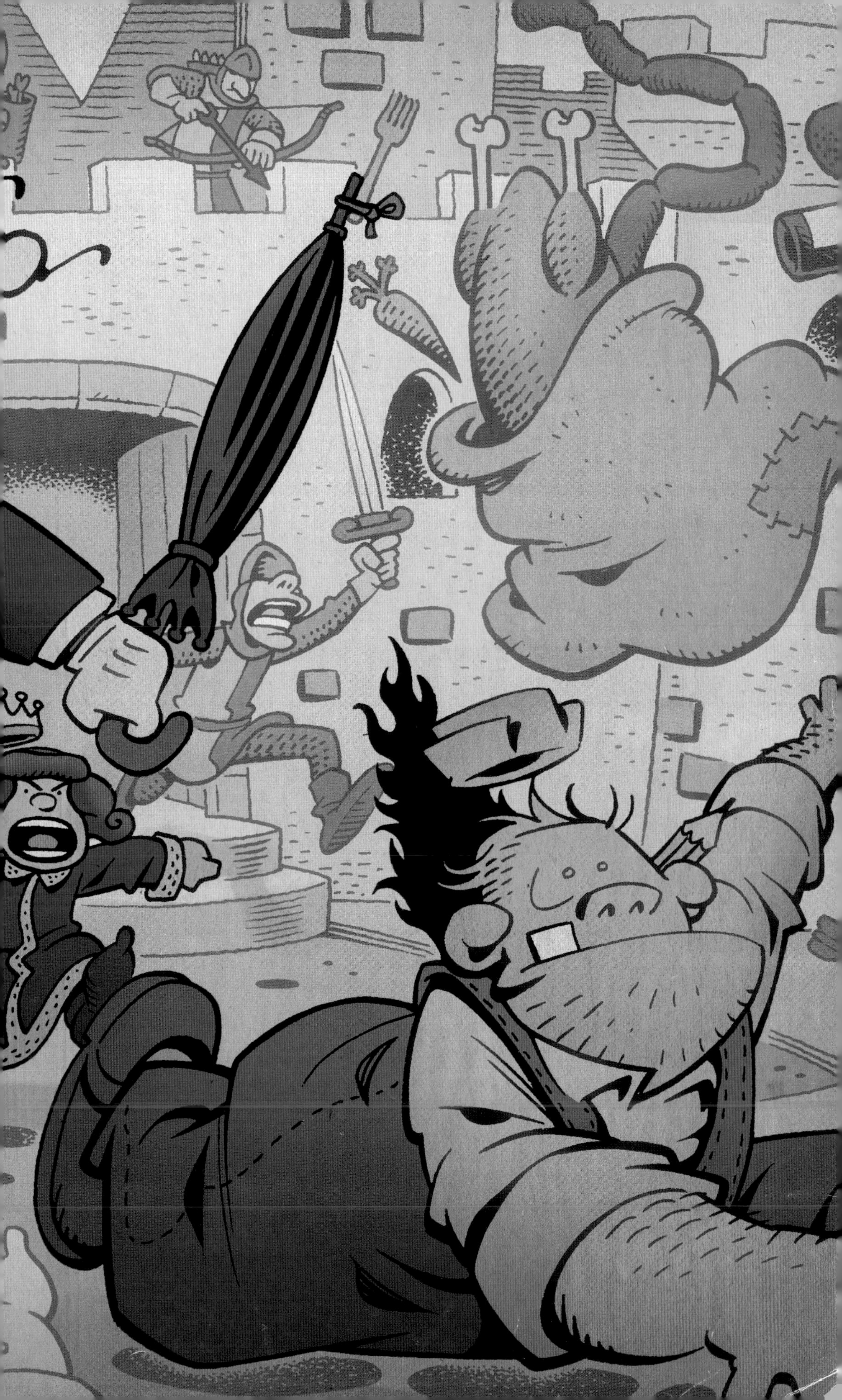

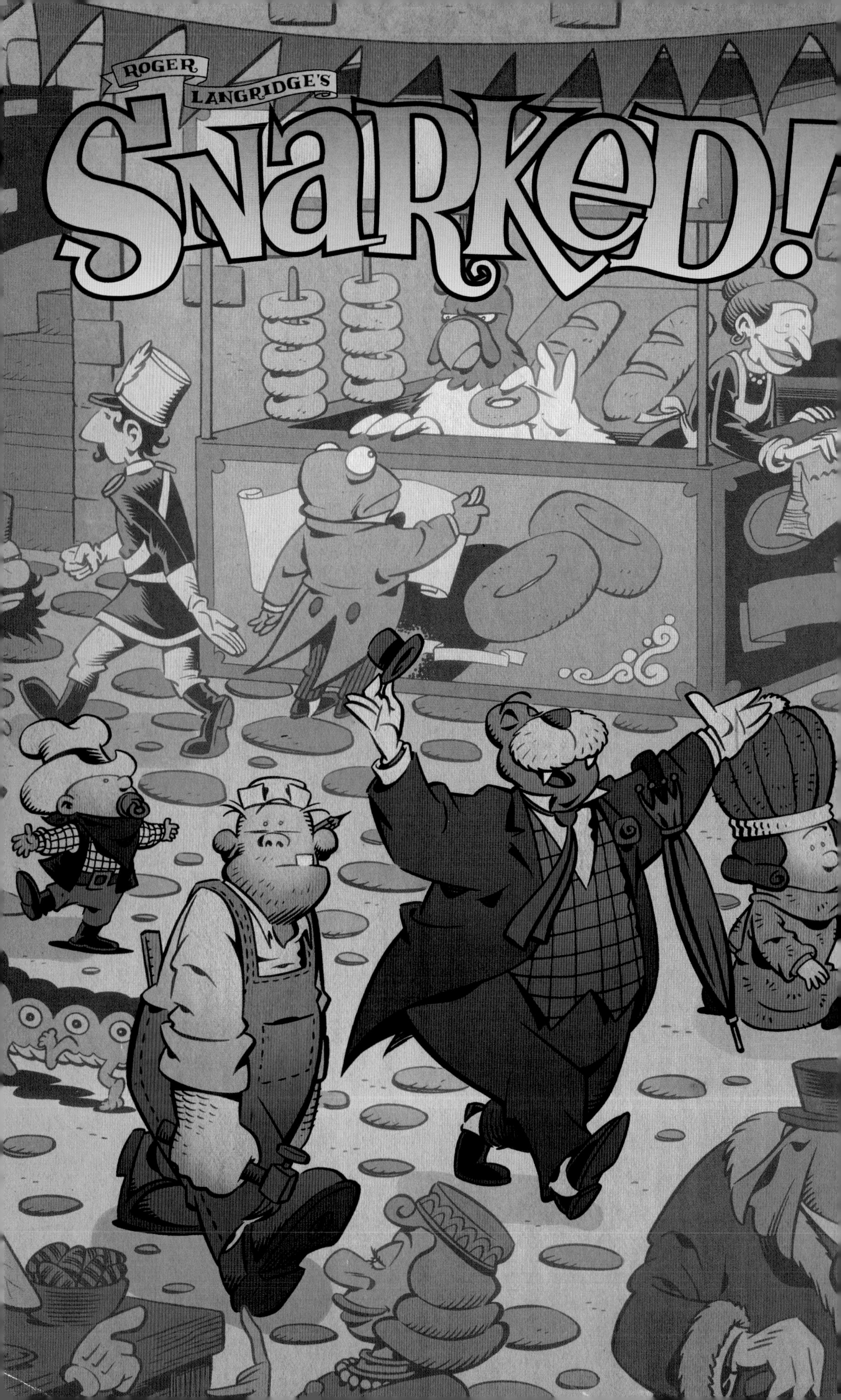
ROGER LANGRIDGE'S
SNARKED!

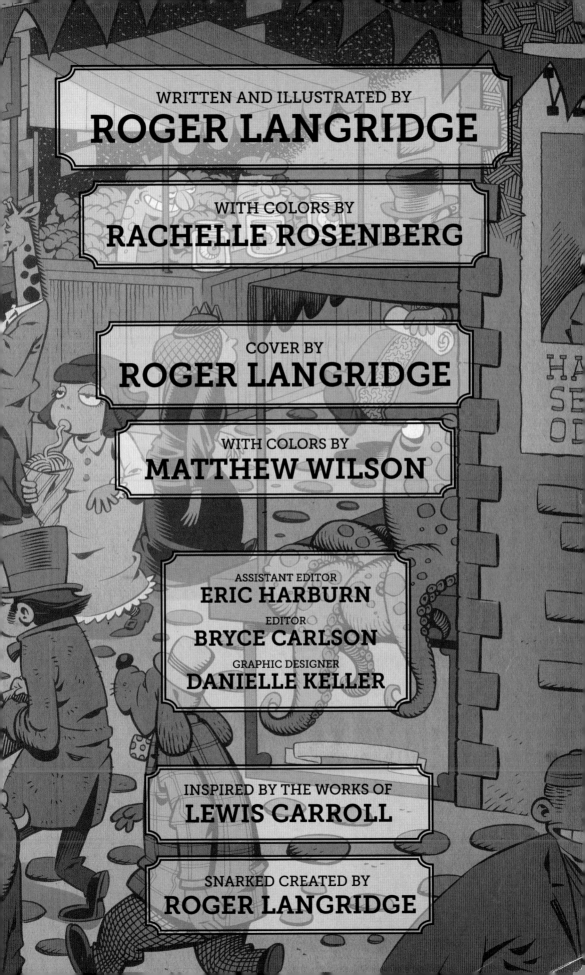

WRITTEN AND ILLUSTRATED BY
ROGER LANGRIDGE

WITH COLORS BY
RACHELLE ROSENBERG

COVER BY
ROGER LANGRIDGE

WITH COLORS BY
MATTHEW WILSON

ASSISTANT EDITOR
ERIC HARBURN
EDITOR
BRYCE CARLSON
GRAPHIC DESIGNER
DANIELLE KELLER

INSPIRED BY THE WORKS OF
LEWIS CARROLL

SNARKED CREATED BY
ROGER LANGRIDGE

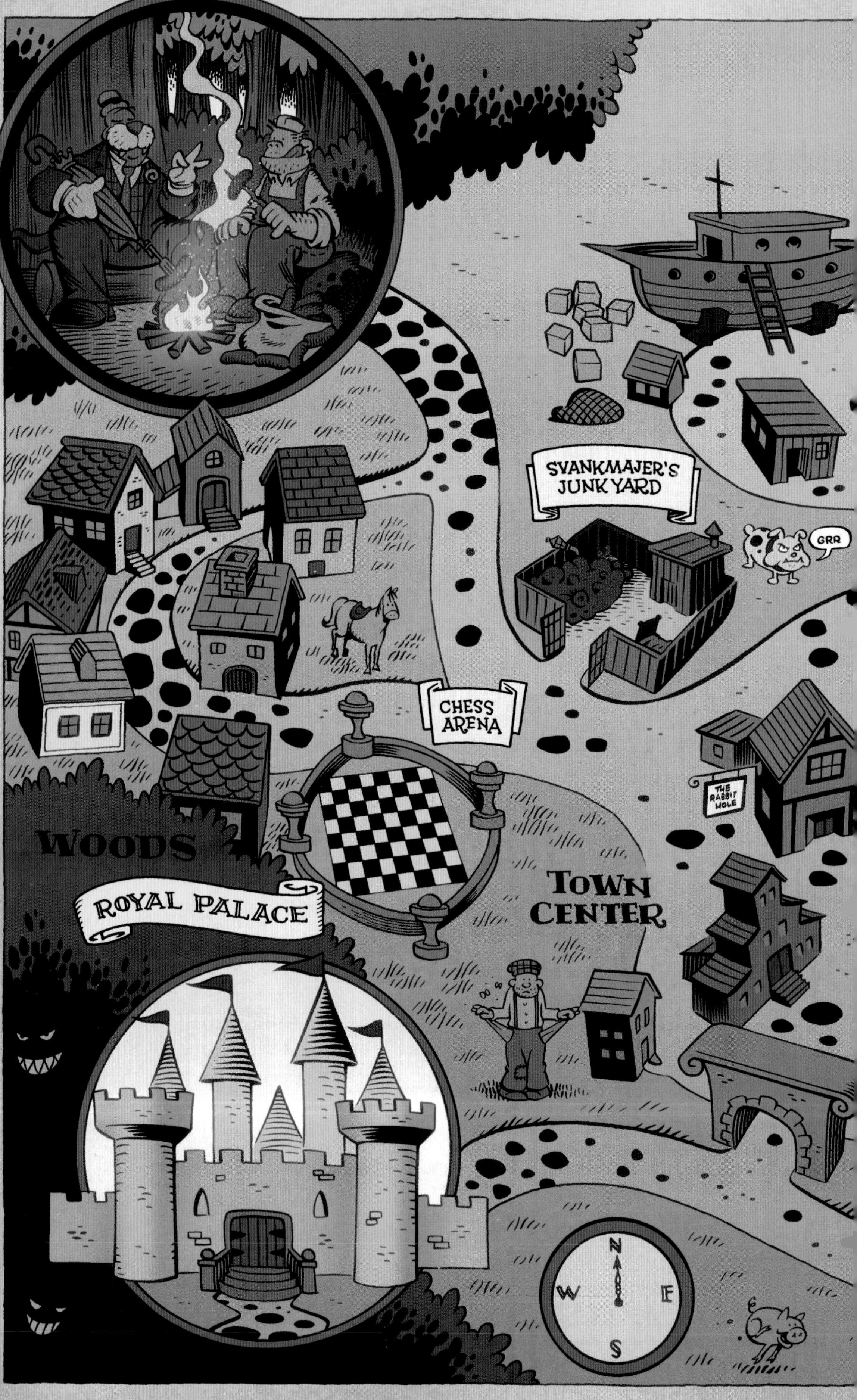

SVANKMAJER'S JUNKYARD
GRR
CHESS ARENA
THE RABBIT HOLE
WOODS
TOWN CENTER
ROYAL PALACE
N
W
E
S

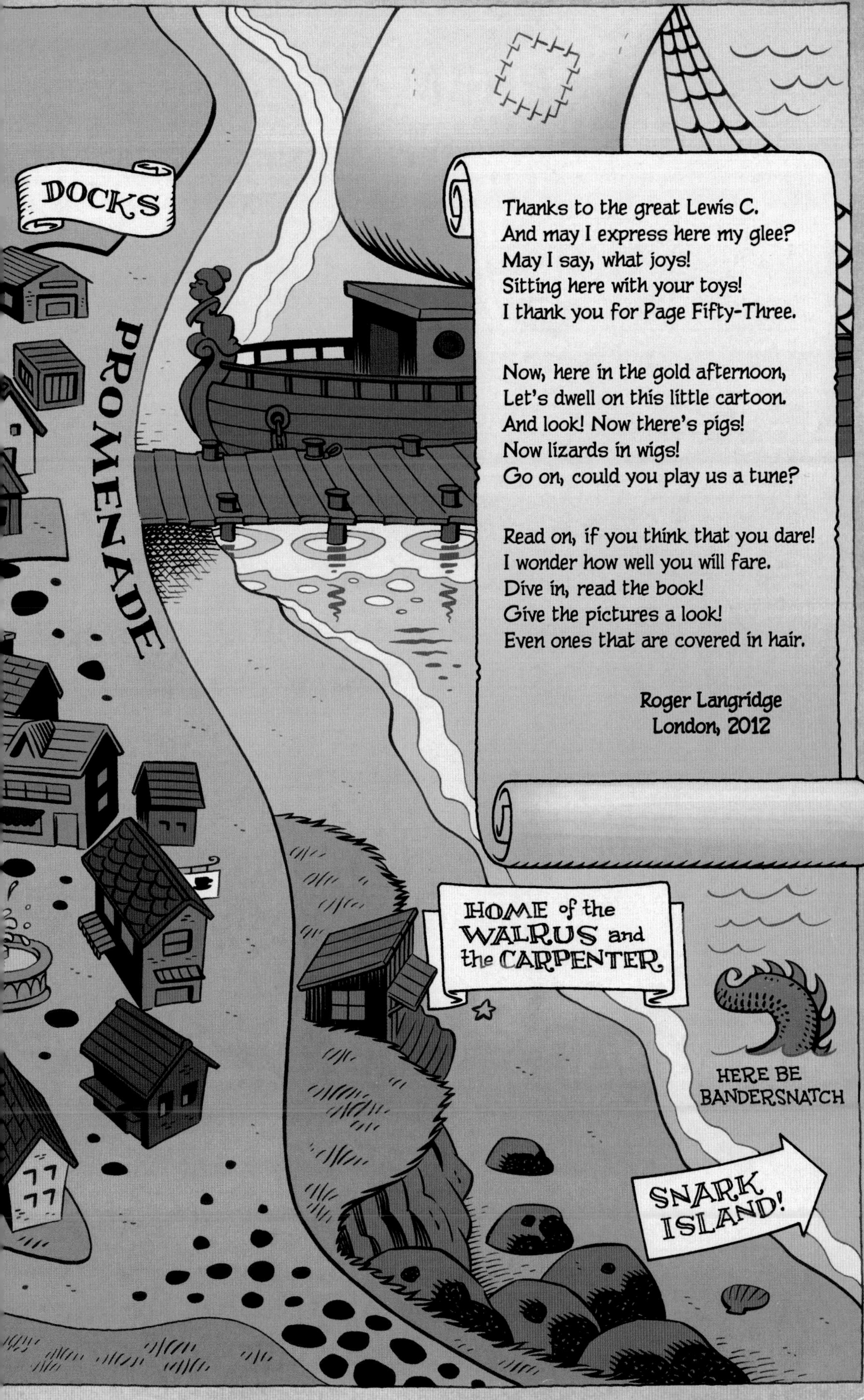
DOCKS
PROMENADE
Thanks to the great Lewis C.
And may I express here my glee?
May I say, what joys!
Sitting here with your toys!
I thank you for Page Fifty-Three.

Now, here in the gold afternoon,
Let's dwell on this little cartoon.
And look! Now there's pigs!
Now lizards in wigs!
Go on, could you play us a tune?

Read on, if you think that you dare!
I wonder how well you will fare.
Dive in, read the book!
Give the pictures a look!
Even ones that are covered in hair.

Roger Langridge
London, 2012
HOME of the WALRUS and the CARPENTER
HERE BE BANDERSNATCH
SNARK ISLAND!

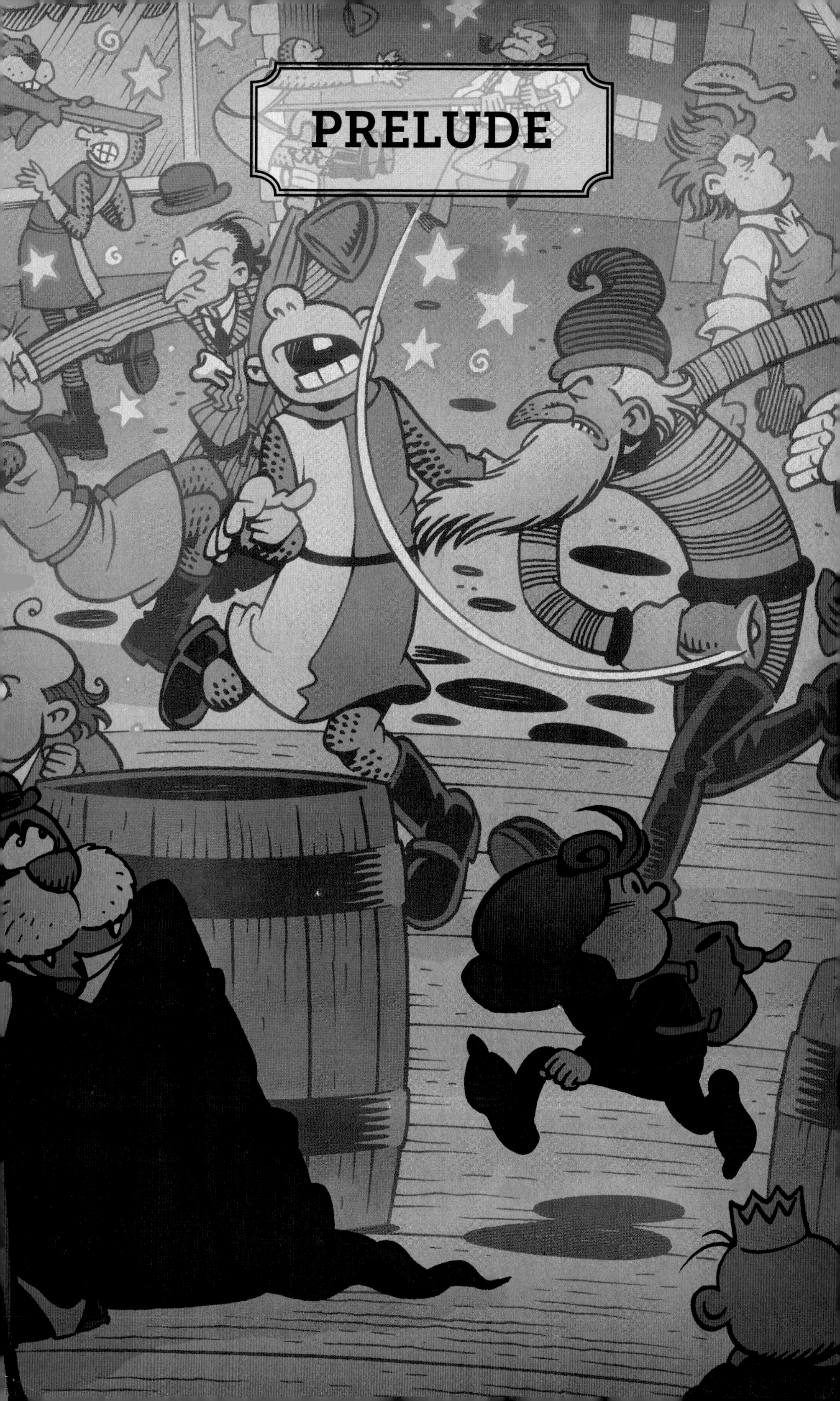
PRELUDE

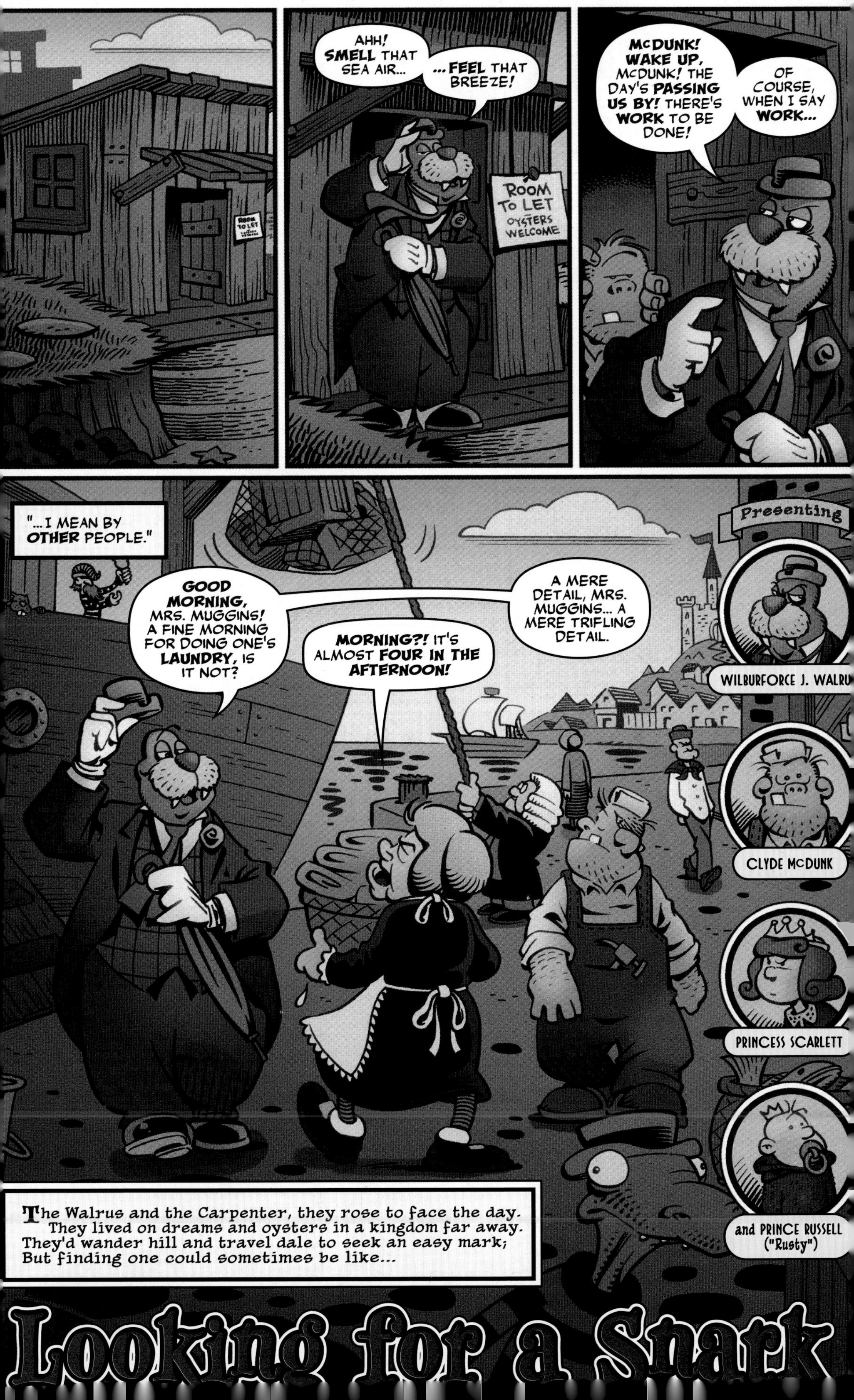
AHH! SMELL THAT SEA AIR...
...FEEL THAT BREEZE!
ROOM TO LET OYSTERS WELCOME
McDUNK! WAKE UP, McDUNK! THE DAY'S PASSING US BY! THERE'S WORK TO BE DONE!
OF COURSE, WHEN I SAY WORK...
"...I MEAN BY OTHER PEOPLE."
GOOD MORNING, MRS. MUGGINS! A FINE MORNING FOR DOING ONE'S LAUNDRY, IS IT NOT?
MORNING?! IT'S ALMOST FOUR IN THE AFTERNOON!
A MERE DETAIL, MRS. MUGGINS... A MERE TRIFLING DETAIL.
Presenting
WILBURFORCE J. WALRU
CLYDE McDUNK
PRINCESS SCARLETT
and PRINCE RUSSELL ("Rusty")
The Walrus and the Carpenter, they rose to face the day.
They lived on dreams and oysters in a kingdom far away.
They'd wander hill and travel dale to seek an easy mark;
But finding one could sometimes be like...
Looking for a Snark

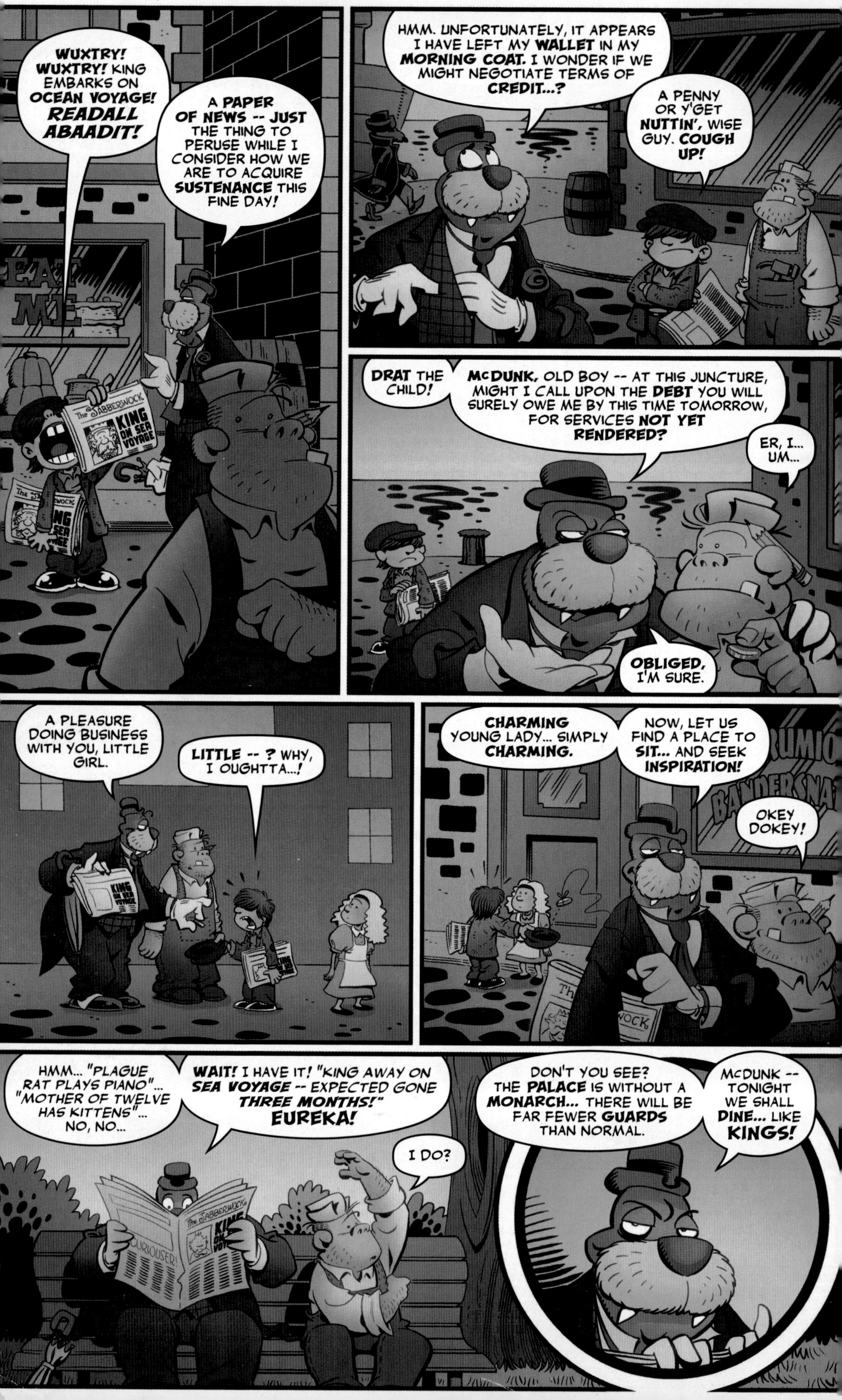
WUXTRY! WUXTRY! KING EMBARKS ON OCEAN VOYAGE! READALL ABAADIT!
A PAPER OF NEWS -- JUST THE THING TO PERUSE WHILE I CONSIDER HOW WE ARE TO ACQUIRE SUSTENANCE THIS FINE DAY!
The JABBERWOCK KING ON SEA VOYAGE
EAT ME
HMM. UNFORTUNATELY, IT APPEARS I HAVE LEFT MY WALLET IN MY MORNING COAT. I WONDER IF WE MIGHT NEGOTIATE TERMS OF CREDIT...?
A PENNY OR Y'GET NUTTIN', WISE GUY. COUGH UP!
DRAT THE CHILD!
McDUNK, OLD BOY -- AT THIS JUNCTURE, MIGHT I CALL UPON THE DEBT YOU WILL SURELY OWE ME BY THIS TIME TOMORROW, FOR SERVICES NOT YET RENDERED?
ER, I... UM...
OBLIGED, I'M SURE.
A PLEASURE DOING BUSINESS WITH YOU, LITTLE GIRL.
LITTLE -- ? WHY, I OUGHTTA...!
CHARMING YOUNG LADY... SIMPLY CHARMING.
NOW, LET US FIND A PLACE TO SIT... AND SEEK INSPIRATION!
OKEY DOKEY!
HMM... "PLAGUE RAT PLAYS PIANO"... "MOTHER OF TWELVE HAS KITTENS"... NO, NO...
WAIT! I HAVE IT! "KING AWAY ON SEA VOYAGE -- EXPECTED GONE THREE MONTHS!" EUREKA!
I DO?
CURIOUSER!
DON'T YOU SEE? THE PALACE IS WITHOUT A MONARCH... THERE WILL BE FAR FEWER GUARDS THAN NORMAL.
McDUNK -- TONIGHT WE SHALL DINE... LIKE KINGS!

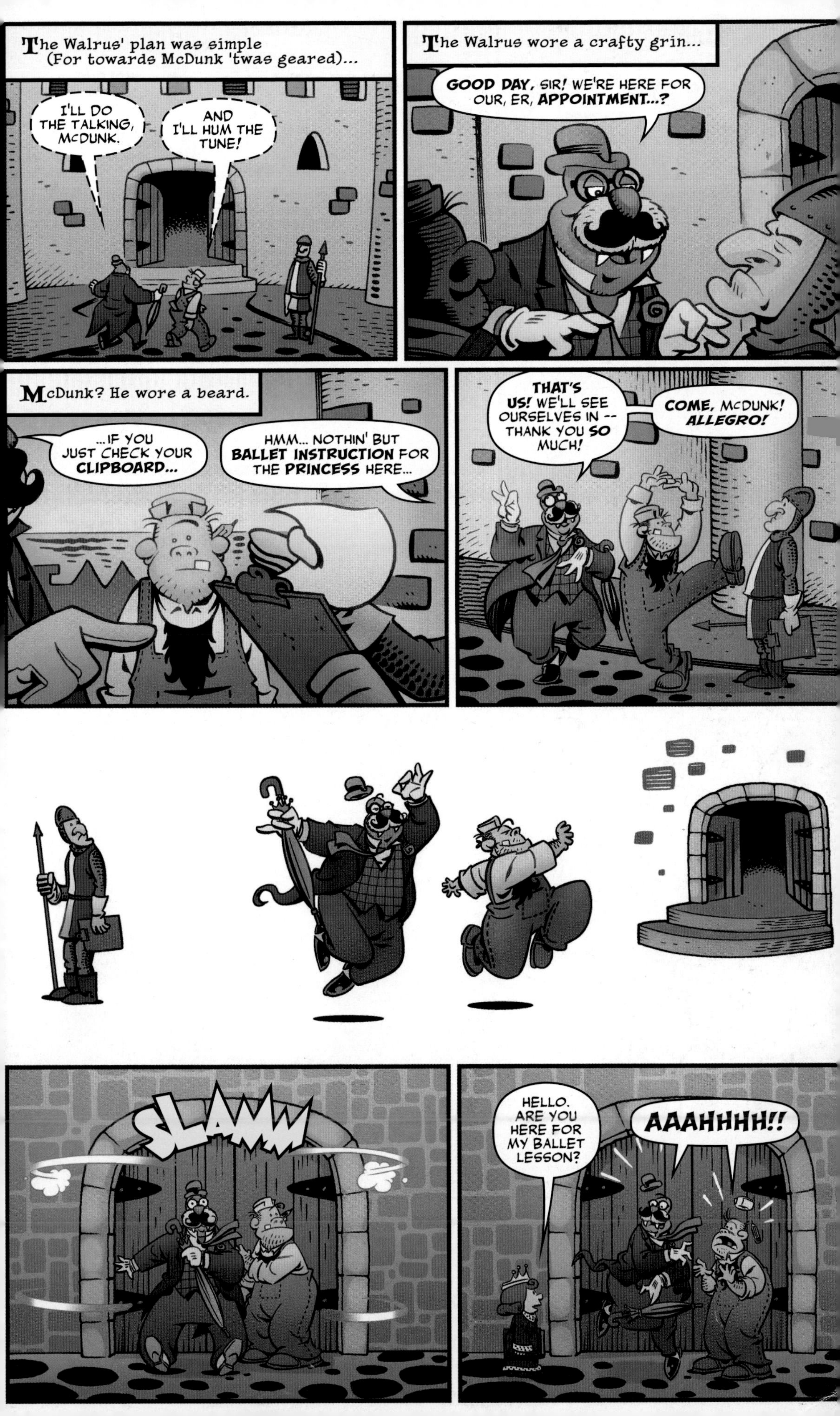
The Walrus' plan was simple
(For towards McDunk 'twas geared)...
I'LL DO THE TALKING, McDUNK.
AND I'LL HUM THE TUNE!
The Walrus wore a crafty grin...
GOOD DAY, SIR! WE'RE HERE FOR OUR, ER, APPOINTMENT...?
McDunk? He wore a beard.
...IF YOU JUST CHECK YOUR CLIPBOARD...
HMM... NOTHIN' BUT BALLET INSTRUCTION FOR THE PRINCESS HERE...
THAT'S US! WE'LL SEE OURSELVES IN -- THANK YOU SO MUCH!
COME, McDUNK! ALLEGRO!
SLAM
HELLO. ARE YOU HERE FOR MY BALLET LESSON?
AAAHHHH!!

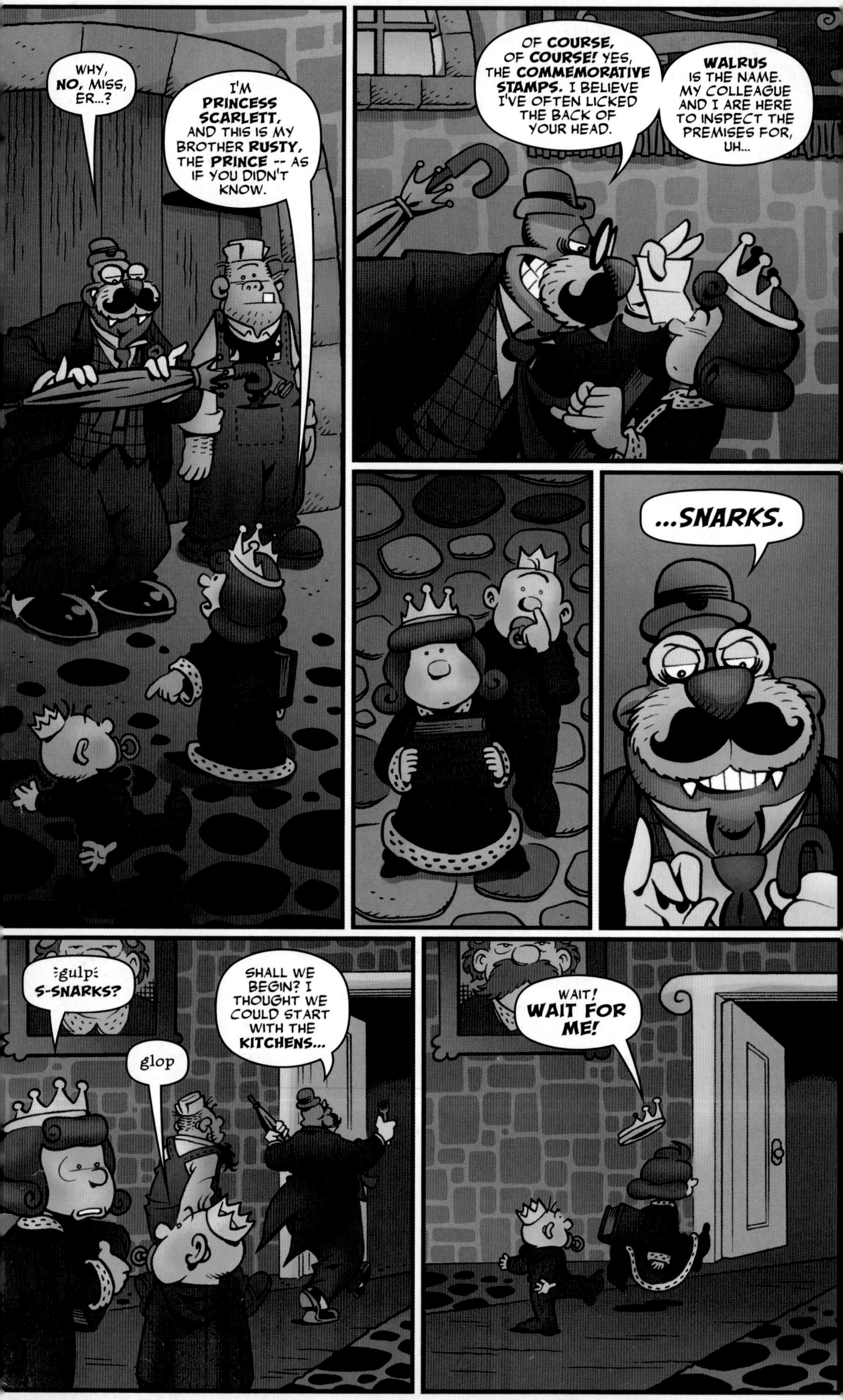
WHY, NO, MISS, ER...?
I'M PRINCESS SCARLETT, AND THIS IS MY BROTHER RUSTY, THE PRINCE -- AS IF YOU DIDN'T KNOW.
OF COURSE, OF COURSE! YES, THE COMMEMORATIVE STAMPS. I BELIEVE I'VE OFTEN LICKED THE BACK OF YOUR HEAD.
WALRUS IS THE NAME. MY COLLEAGUE AND I ARE HERE TO INSPECT THE PREMISES FOR, UH...
...SNARKS.
gulp S-SNARKS?
glop
SHALL WE BEGIN? I THOUGHT WE COULD START WITH THE KITCHENS...
WAIT! WAIT FOR ME!

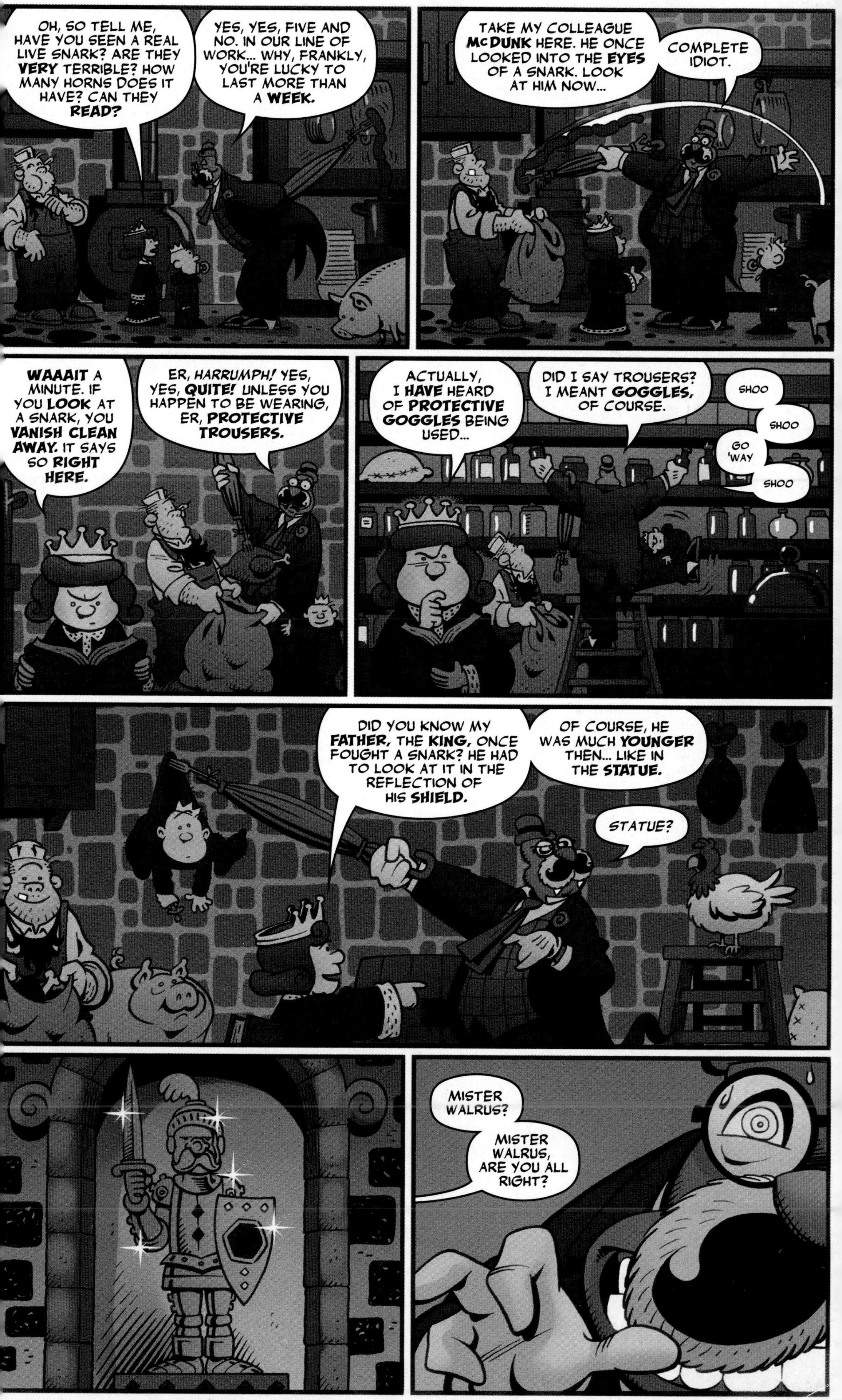
OH, SO TELL ME, HAVE YOU SEEN A REAL LIVE SNARK? ARE THEY VERY TERRIBLE? HOW MANY HORNS DOES IT HAVE? CAN THEY READ?
YES, YES, FIVE AND NO. IN OUR LINE OF WORK... WHY, FRANKLY, YOU'RE LUCKY TO LAST MORE THAN A WEEK.
TAKE MY COLLEAGUE McDUNK HERE. HE ONCE LOOKED INTO THE EYES OF A SNARK. LOOK AT HIM NOW...
COMPLETE IDIOT.
WAAAIT A MINUTE. IF YOU LOOK AT A SNARK, YOU VANISH CLEAN AWAY. IT SAYS SO RIGHT HERE.
ER, HARRUMPH! YES, YES, QUITE! UNLESS YOU HAPPEN TO BE WEARING, ER, PROTECTIVE TROUSERS.
ACTUALLY, I HAVE HEARD OF PROTECTIVE GOGGLES BEING USED...
DID I SAY TROUSERS? I MEANT GOGGLES, OF COURSE.
SHOO
SHOO
GO 'WAY
SHOO
DID YOU KNOW MY FATHER, THE KING, ONCE FOUGHT A SNARK? HE HAD TO LOOK AT IT IN THE REFLECTION OF HIS SHIELD.
OF COURSE, HE WAS MUCH YOUNGER THEN... LIKE IN THE STATUE.
STATUE?
MISTER WALRUS?
MISTER WALRUS, ARE YOU ALL RIGHT?

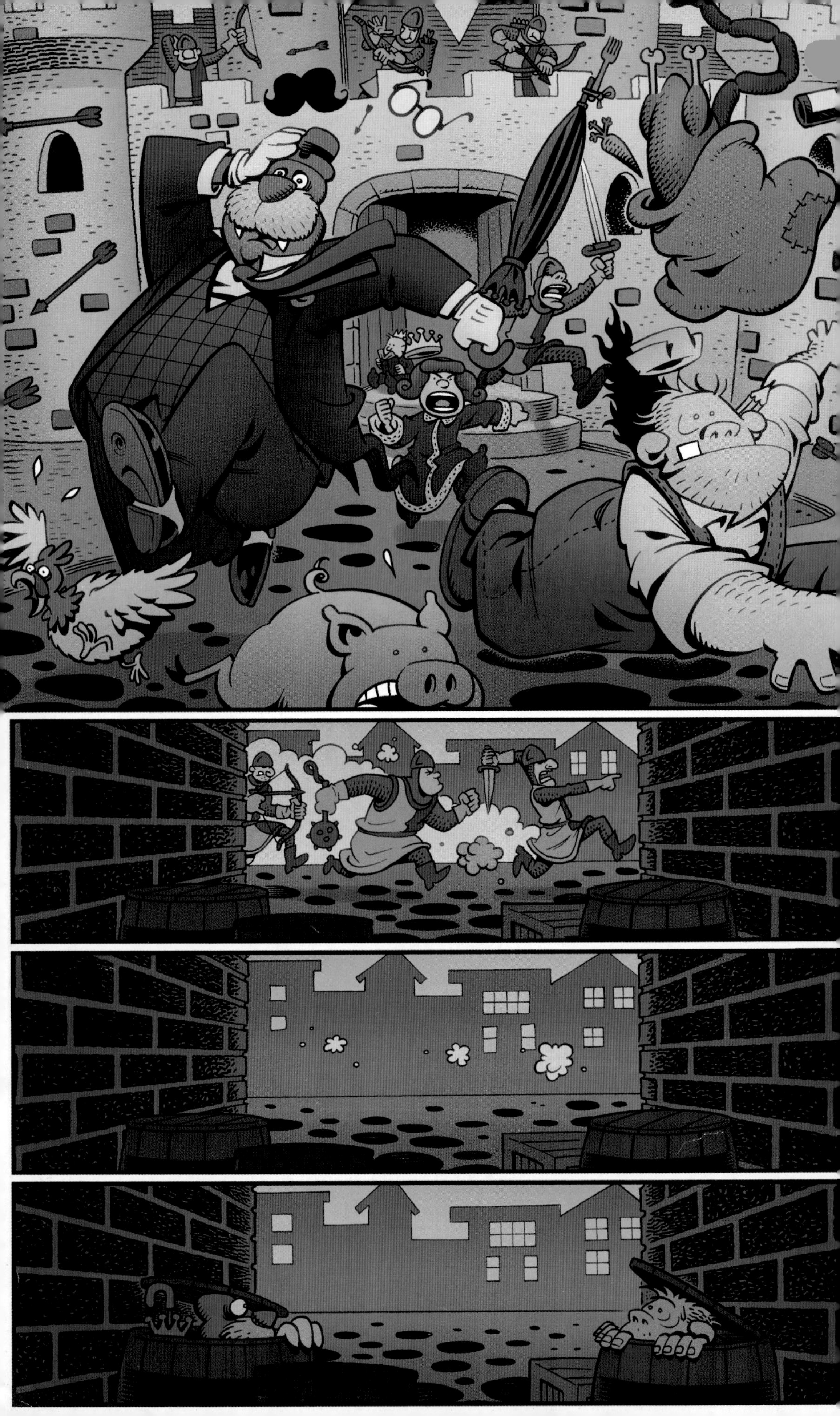

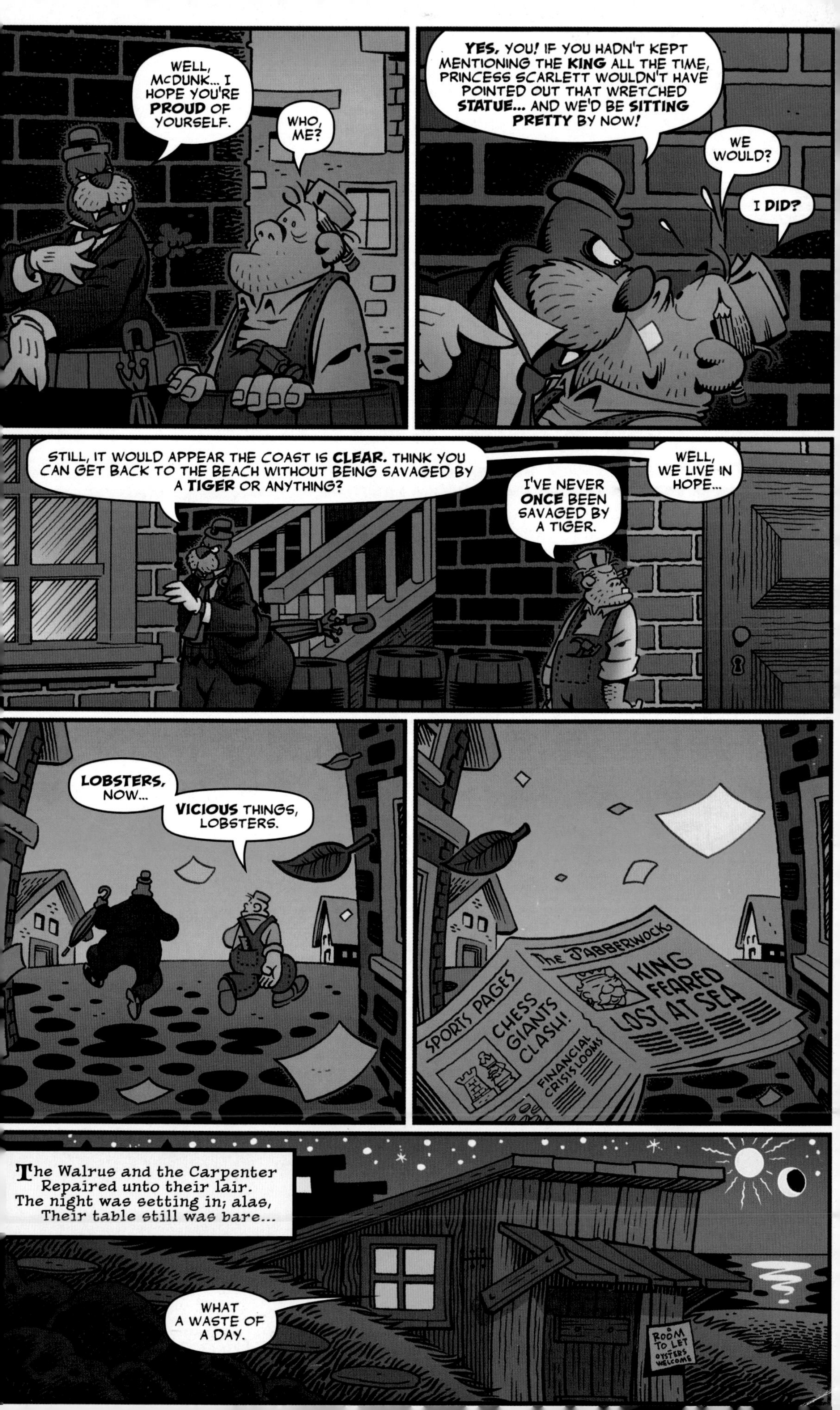
WELL, McDUNK... I HOPE YOU'RE **PROUD** OF YOURSELF.
WHO, ME?
YES, YOU! IF YOU HADN'T KEPT MENTIONING THE **KING** ALL THE TIME, PRINCESS SCARLETT WOULDN'T HAVE POINTED OUT THAT WRETCHED **STATUE...** AND WE'D BE **SITTING PRETTY** BY NOW!
WE WOULD?
I **DID?**
STILL, IT WOULD APPEAR THE COAST IS **CLEAR.** THINK YOU CAN GET BACK TO THE BEACH WITHOUT BEING SAVAGED BY A **TIGER** OR ANYTHING?
I'VE NEVER **ONCE** BEEN SAVAGED BY A TIGER.
WELL, WE LIVE IN HOPE...
LOBSTERS, NOW...
VICIOUS THINGS, LOBSTERS.
THE JABBERWOCK
KING FEARED LOST AT SEA
SPORTS PAGES
CHESS GIANTS CLASH!
FINANCIAL CRISIS LOOMS
The Walrus and the Carpenter
Repaired unto their lair.
The night was setting in; alas,
Their table still was bare...
WHAT A WASTE OF A DAY.
ROOM TO LET
OYSTERS WELCOME

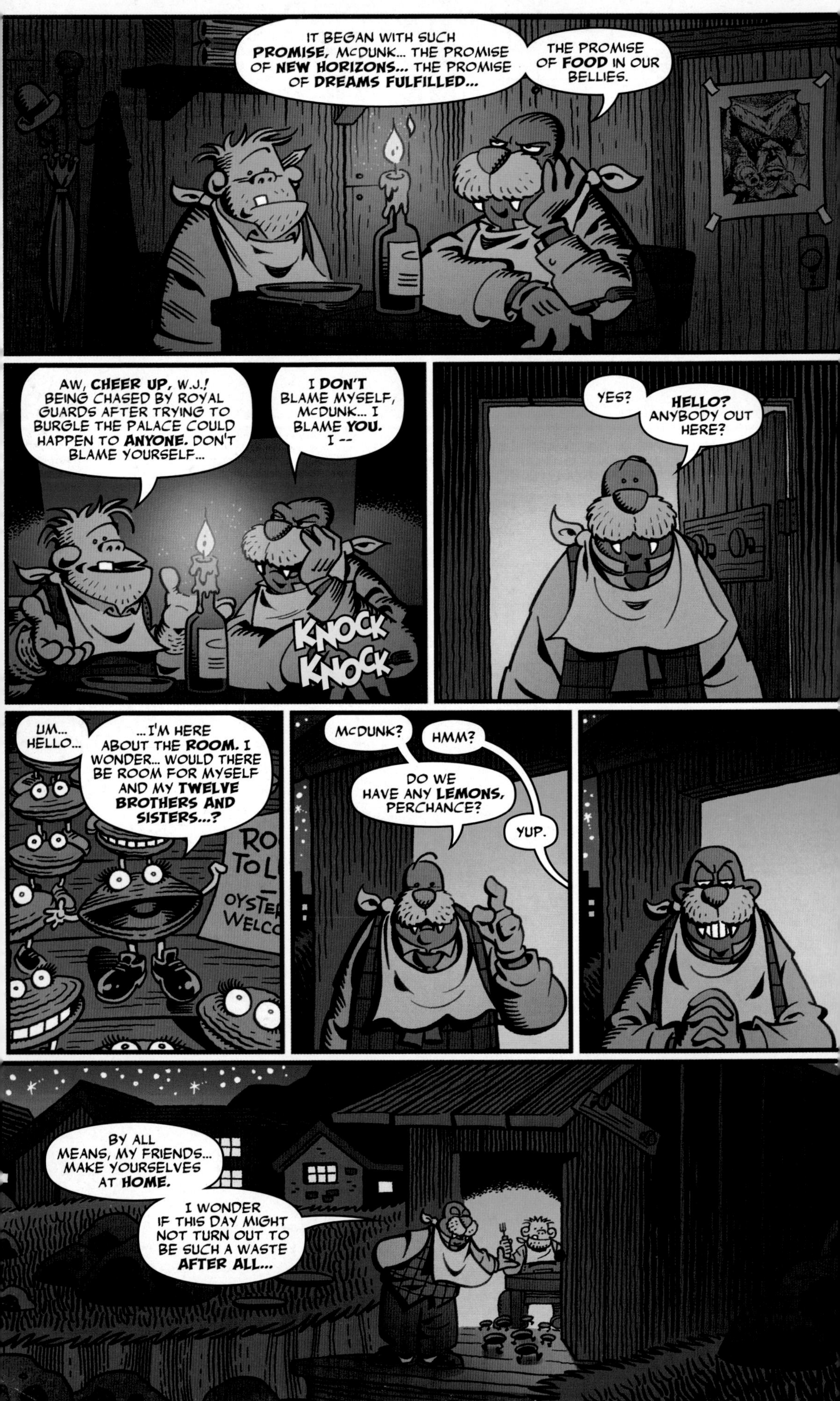
IT BEGAN WITH SUCH PROMISE, McDUNK... THE PROMISE OF NEW HORIZONS... THE PROMISE OF DREAMS FULFILLED...
THE PROMISE OF FOOD IN OUR BELLIES.
AW, CHEER UP, W.J.! BEING CHASED BY ROYAL GUARDS AFTER TRYING TO BURGLE THE PALACE COULD HAPPEN TO ANYONE. DON'T BLAME YOURSELF...
I DON'T BLAME MYSELF, McDUNK... I BLAME YOU. I --
KNOCK KNOCK
YES?
HELLO? ANYBODY OUT HERE?
UM... HELLO...
...I'M HERE ABOUT THE ROOM. I WONDER... WOULD THERE BE ROOM FOR MYSELF AND MY TWELVE BROTHERS AND SISTERS...?
McDUNK?
HMM?
DO WE HAVE ANY LEMONS, PERCHANCE?
YUP.
BY ALL MEANS, MY FRIENDS... MAKE YOURSELVES AT HOME.
I WONDER IF THIS DAY MIGHT NOT TURN OUT TO BE SUCH A WASTE AFTER ALL...

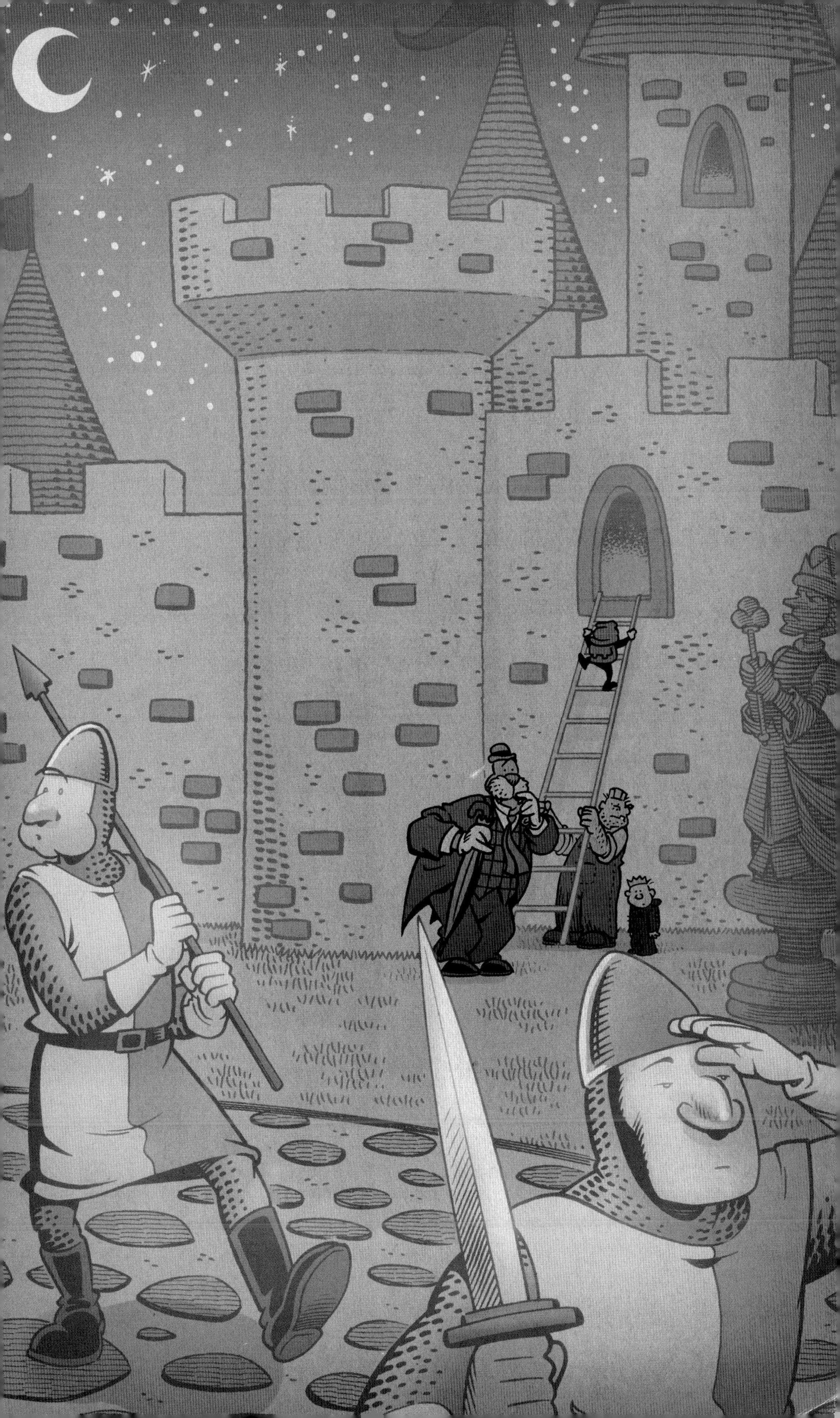

FIT THE FIRST

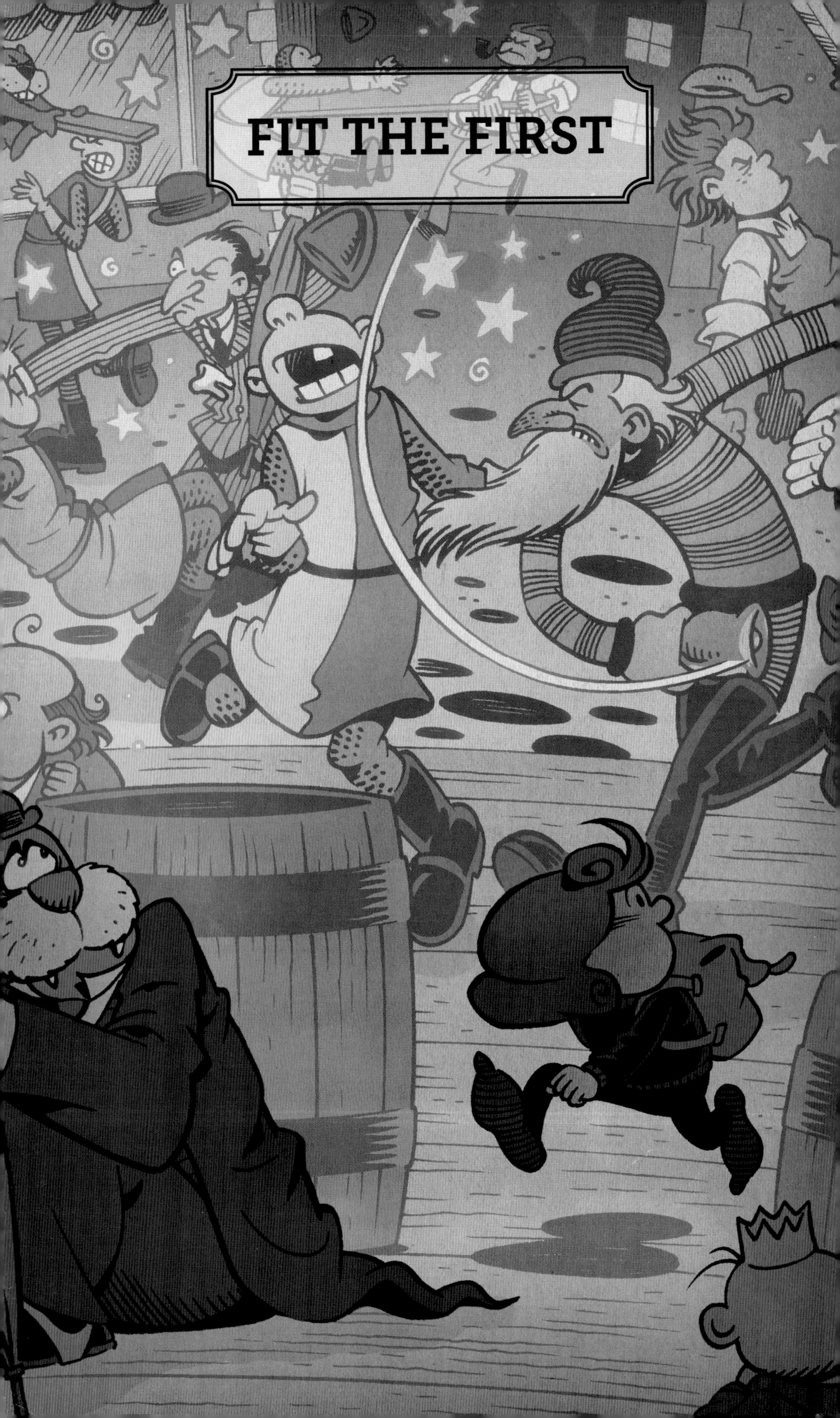

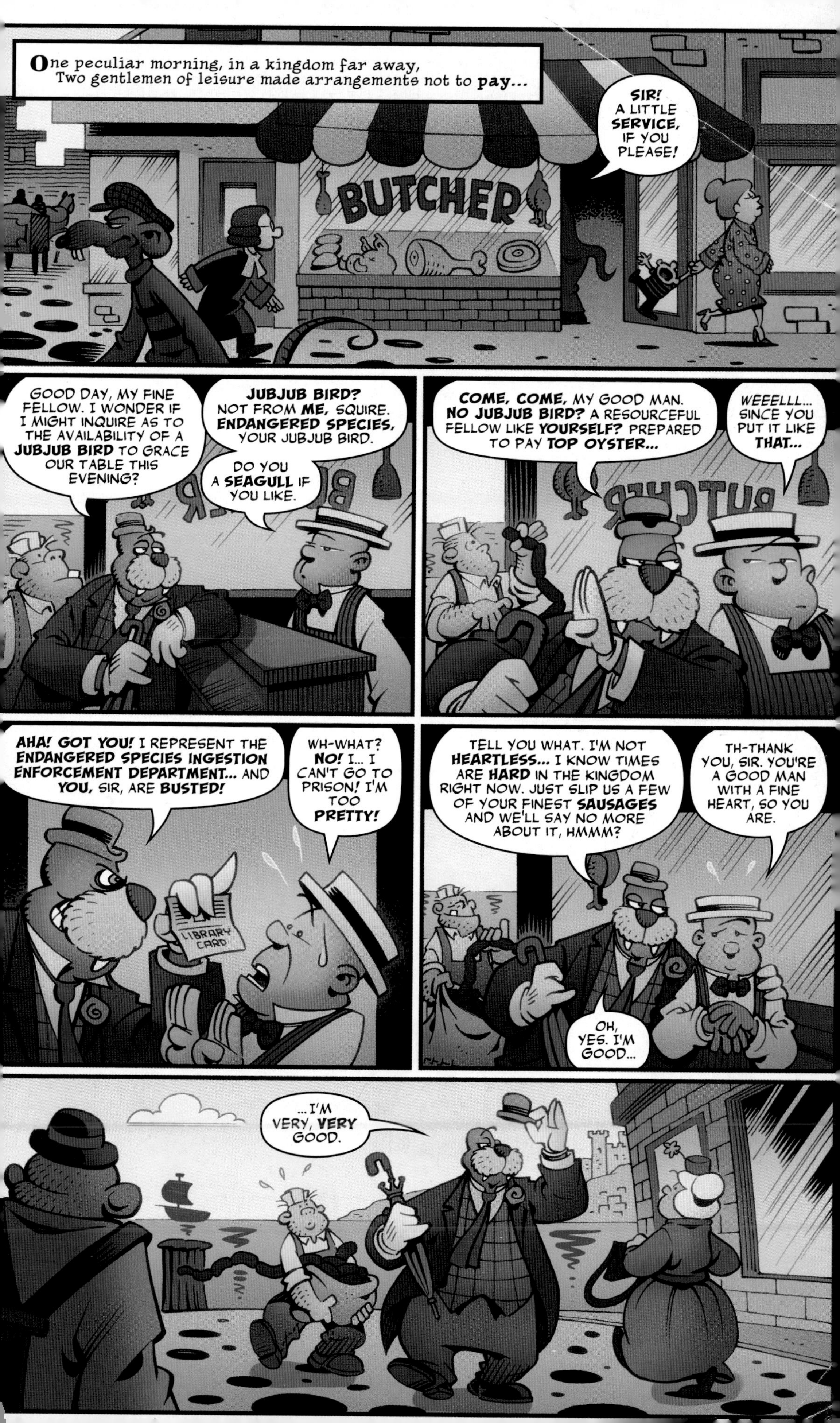

One peculiar morning, in a kingdom far away,
Two gentlemen of leisure made arrangements not to pay...
SIR! A LITTLE SERVICE, IF YOU PLEASE!
BUTCHER
GOOD DAY, MY FINE FELLOW. I WONDER IF I MIGHT INQUIRE AS TO THE AVAILABILITY OF A JUBJUB BIRD TO GRACE OUR TABLE THIS EVENING?
JUBJUB BIRD? NOT FROM ME, SQUIRE. ENDANGERED SPECIES, YOUR JUBJUB BIRD.
DO YOU A SEAGULL IF YOU LIKE.
COME, COME, MY GOOD MAN. NO JUBJUB BIRD? A RESOURCEFUL FELLOW LIKE YOURSELF? PREPARED TO PAY TOP OYSTER...
WEEELLL... SINCE YOU PUT IT LIKE THAT...
AHA! GOT YOU! I REPRESENT THE ENDANGERED SPECIES INGESTION ENFORCEMENT DEPARTMENT... AND YOU, SIR, ARE BUSTED!
WH-WHAT? NO! I... I CAN'T GO TO PRISON! I'M TOO PRETTY!
LIBRARY CARD
TELL YOU WHAT. I'M NOT HEARTLESS... I KNOW TIMES ARE HARD IN THE KINGDOM RIGHT NOW. JUST SLIP US A FEW OF YOUR FINEST SAUSAGES AND WE'LL SAY NO MORE ABOUT IT, HMMM?
TH-THANK YOU, SIR. YOU'RE A GOOD MAN WITH A FINE HEART, SO YOU ARE.
OH, YES. I'M GOOD...
...I'M VERY, VERY GOOD.

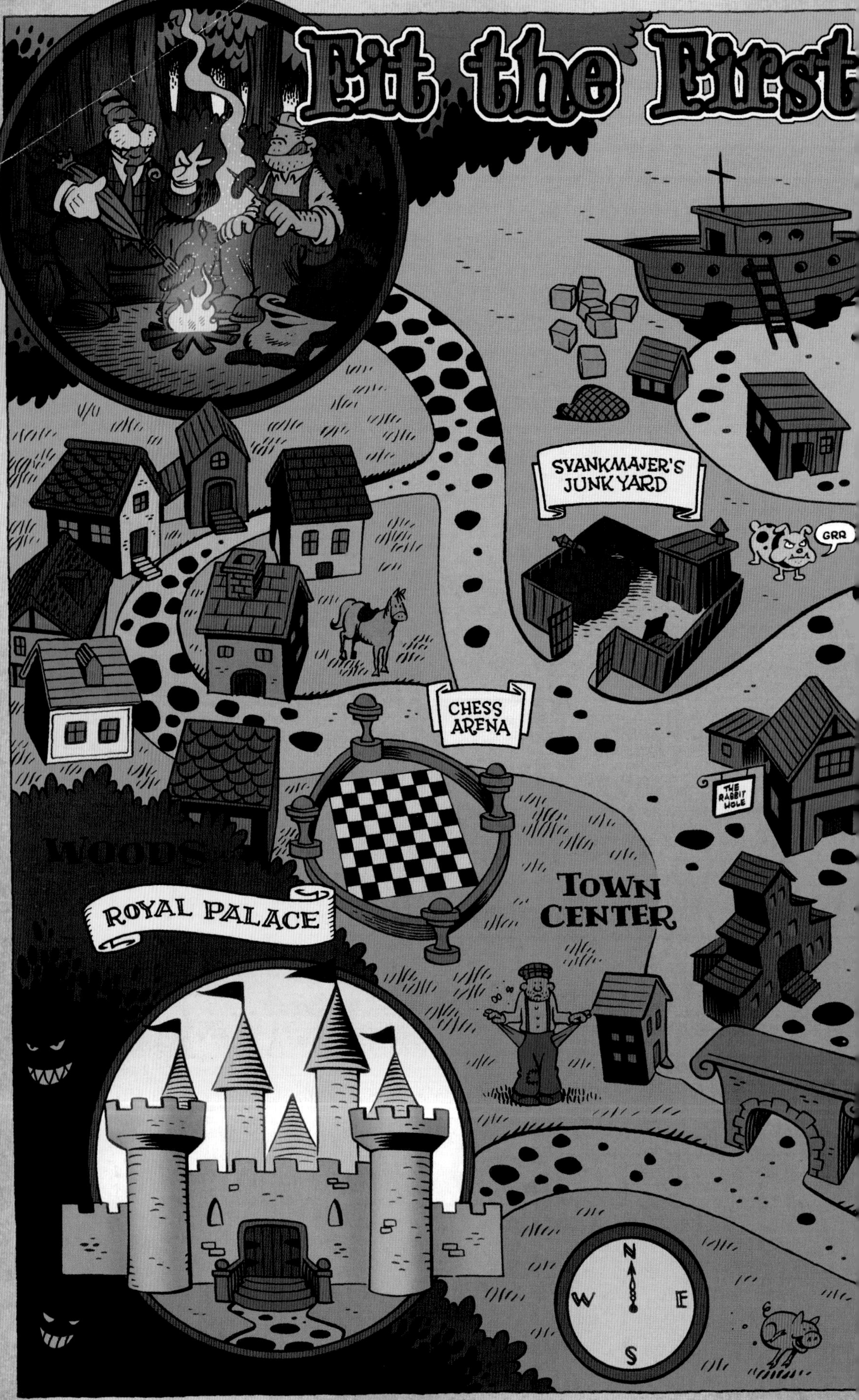
Fit the First
SVANKMAJER'S JUNK YARD
GRR
CHESS ARENA
THE RABBIT HOLE
TOWN CENTER
ROYAL PALACE
N
W
E
S

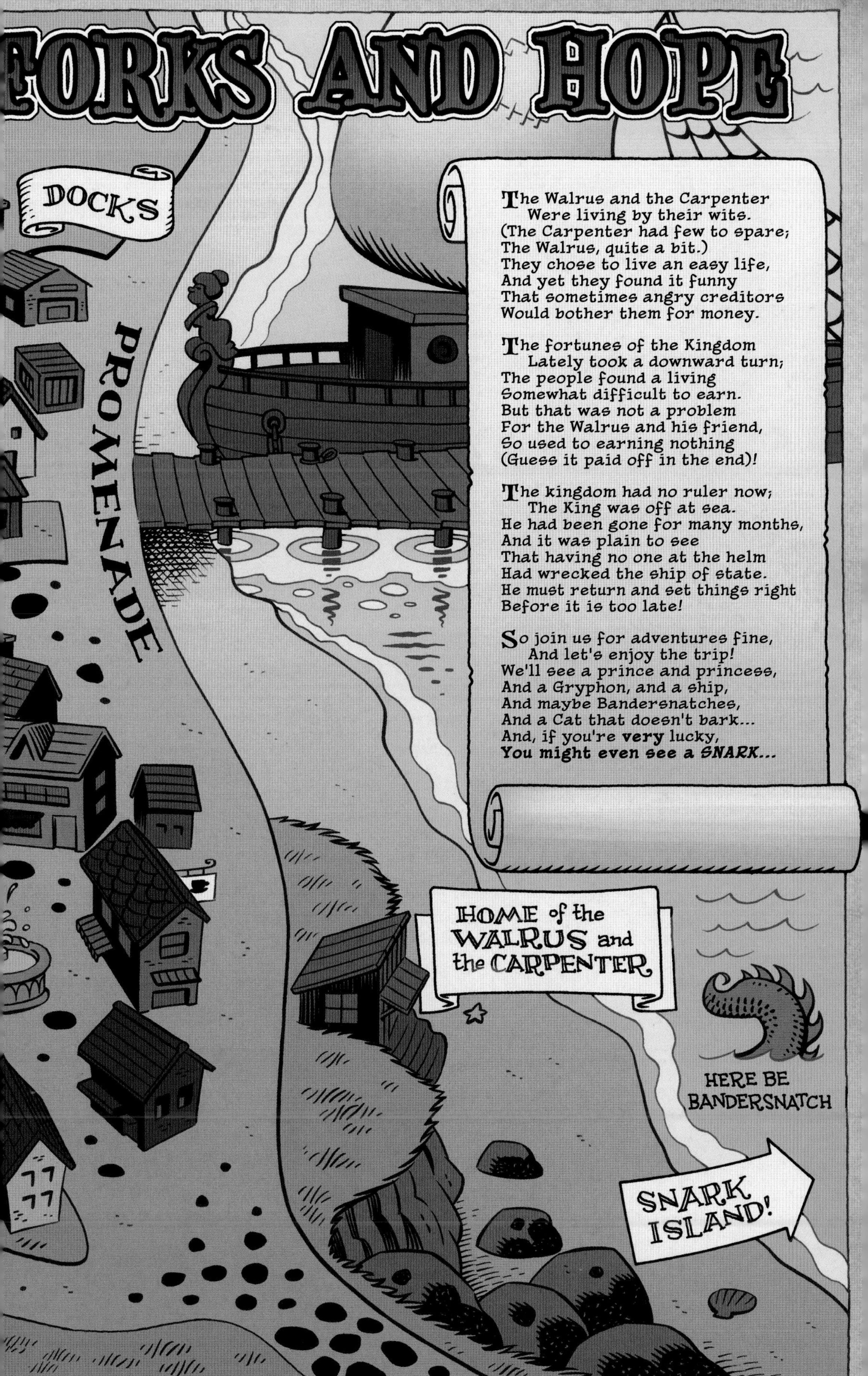
FORKS AND HOPE
DOCKS
PROMENADE
The Walrus and the Carpenter
Were living by their wits.
(The Carpenter had few to spare;
The Walrus, quite a bit.)
They chose to live an easy life,
And yet they found it funny
That sometimes angry creditors
Would bother them for money.
The fortunes of the Kingdom
Lately took a downward turn;
The people found a living
Somewhat difficult to earn.
But that was not a problem
For the Walrus and his friend,
So used to earning nothing
(Guess it paid off in the end)!
The kingdom had no ruler now;
The King was off at sea.
He had been gone for many months,
And it was plain to see
That having no one at the helm
Had wrecked the ship of state.
He must return and set things right
Before it is too late!
So join us for adventures fine,
And let's enjoy the trip!
We'll see a prince and princess,
And a Gryphon, and a ship,
And maybe Bandersnatches,
And a Cat that doesn't bark...
And, if you're **very** lucky,
You might even see a *SNARK*...
HOME of the WALRUS and the CARPENTER
HERE BE BANDERSNATCH
SNARK ISLAND!

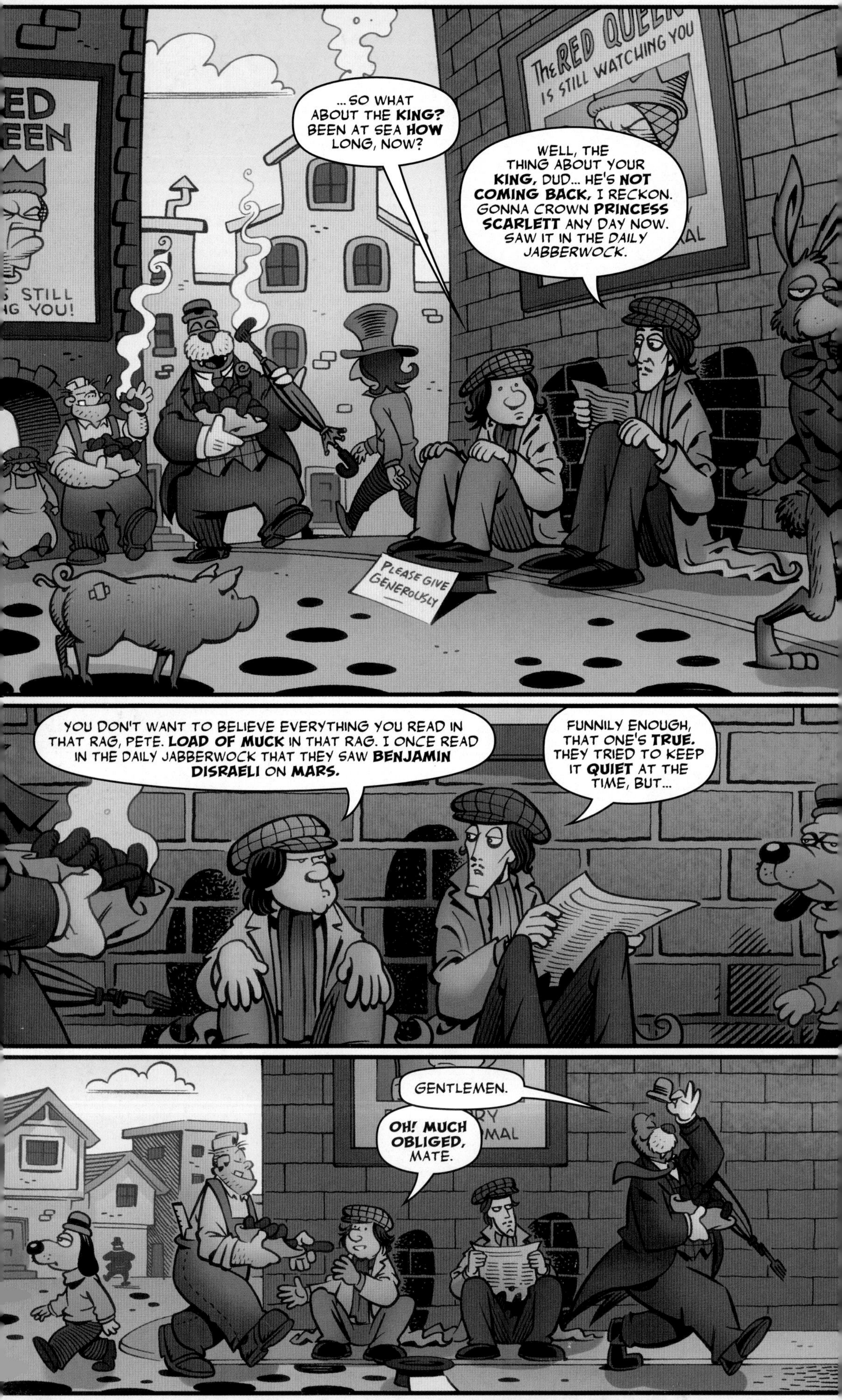

The RED QUEEN IS STILL WATCHING YOU
PLEASE GIVE GENEROUSLY
...SO WHAT ABOUT THE KING? BEEN AT SEA HOW LONG, NOW?
WELL, THE THING ABOUT YOUR KING, DUD... HE'S NOT COMING BACK, I RECKON. GONNA CROWN PRINCESS SCARLETT ANY DAY NOW. SAW IT IN THE DAILY JABBERWOCK.
YOU DON'T WANT TO BELIEVE EVERYTHING YOU READ IN THAT RAG, PETE. LOAD OF MUCK IN THAT RAG. I ONCE READ IN THE DAILY JABBERWOCK THAT THEY SAW BENJAMIN DISRAELI ON MARS.
FUNNILY ENOUGH, THAT ONE'S TRUE. THEY TRIED TO KEEP IT QUIET AT THE TIME, BUT...
GENTLEMEN.
OH! MUCH OBLIGED, MATE.

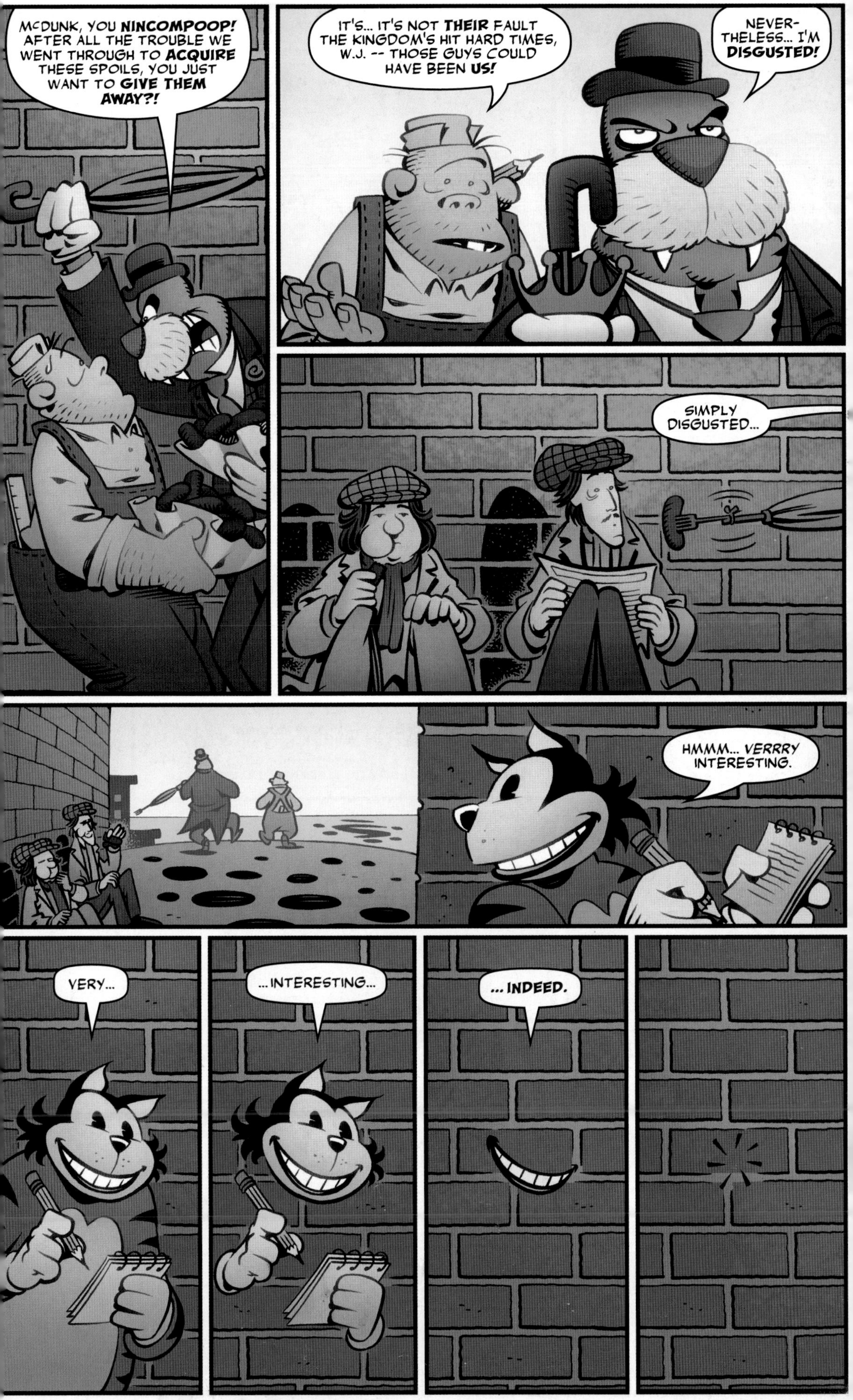
McDUNK, YOU NINCOMPOOP! AFTER ALL THE TROUBLE WE WENT THROUGH TO ACQUIRE THESE SPOILS, YOU JUST WANT TO GIVE THEM AWAY?!
IT'S... IT'S NOT THEIR FAULT THE KINGDOM'S HIT HARD TIMES, W.J. -- THOSE GUYS COULD HAVE BEEN US!
NEVER-THELESS... I'M DISGUSTED!
SIMPLY DISGUSTED...
HMMM... VERRRY INTERESTING.
VERY...
...INTERESTING...
...INDEED.

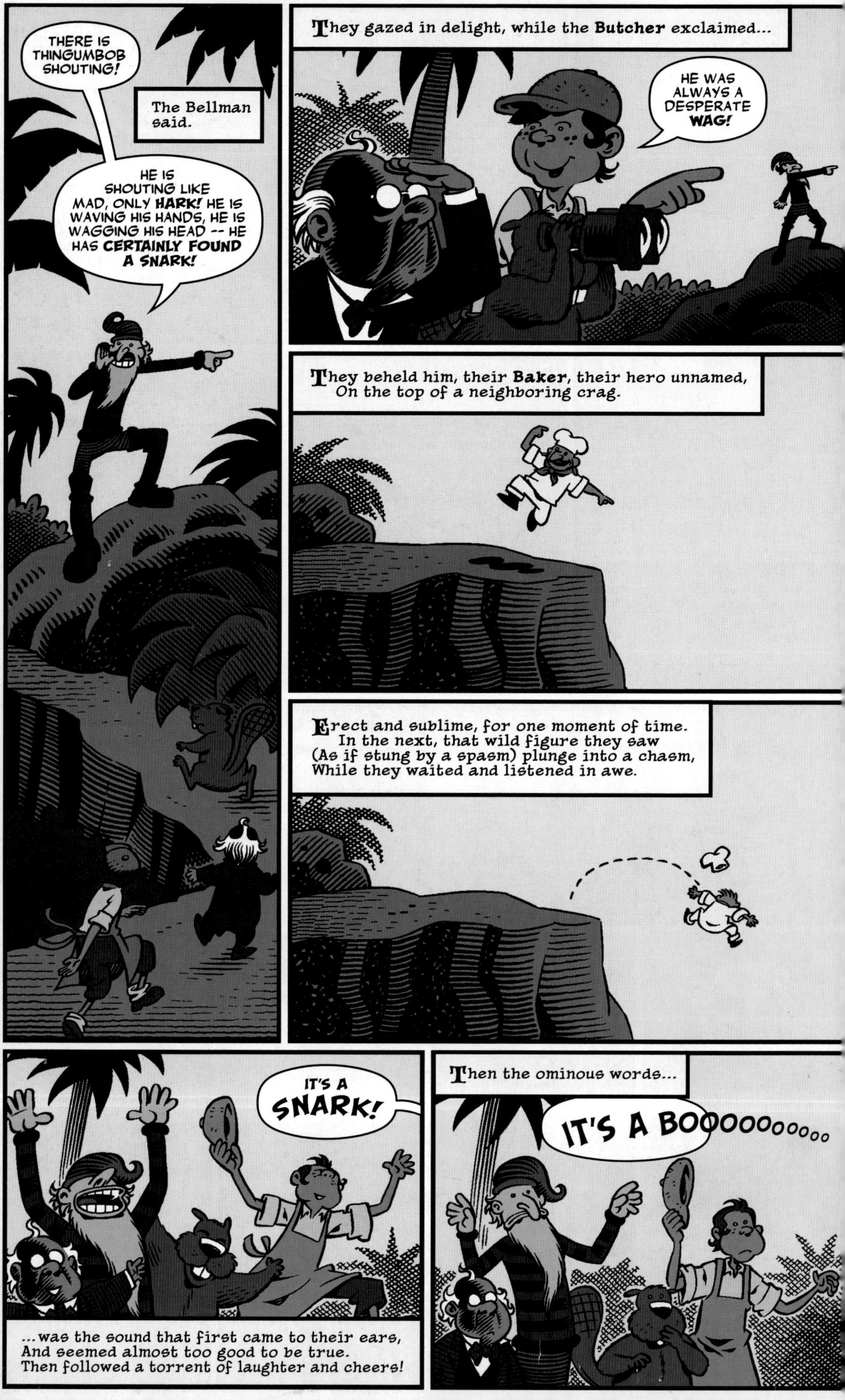
THERE IS THINGUMBOB SHOUTING!
The Bellman said.
HE IS SHOUTING LIKE MAD, ONLY HARK! HE IS WAVING HIS HANDS, HE IS WAGGING HIS HEAD -- HE HAS CERTAINLY FOUND A SNARK!
They gazed in delight, while the Butcher exclaimed...
HE WAS ALWAYS A DESPERATE WAG!
They beheld him, their Baker, their hero unnamed,
On the top of a neighboring crag.
Erect and sublime, for one moment of time.
In the next, that wild figure they saw
(As if stung by a spasm) plunge into a chasm,
While they waited and listened in awe.
IT'S A SNARK!
...was the sound that first came to their ears,
And seemed almost too good to be true.
Then followed a torrent of laughter and cheers!
Then the ominous words...
IT'S A BOOOOOOOOOOO

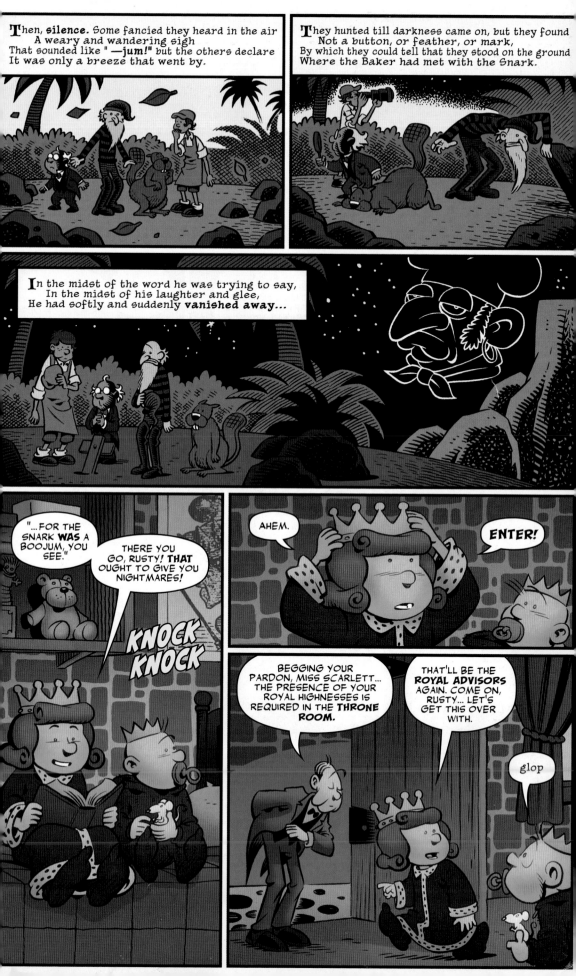

Then, **silence.** Some fancied they heard in the air
 A weary and wandering sigh
That sounded like "—**jum!**" but the others declare
 It was only a breeze that went by.

They hunted till darkness came on, but they found
 Not a button, or feather, or mark,
By which they could tell that they stood on the ground
 Where the Baker had met with the Snark.

In the midst of the word he was trying to say,
 In the midst of his laughter and glee,
He had softly and suddenly **vanished away...**

"...FOR THE SNARK **WAS A BOOJUM,** YOU SEE."

THERE YOU GO, RUSTY! **THAT** OUGHT TO GIVE YOU NIGHTMARES!

KNOCK KNOCK

AHEM.

ENTER!

BEGGING YOUR PARDON, MISS SCARLETT... THE PRESENCE OF YOUR ROYAL HIGHNESSES IS REQUIRED IN THE **THRONE ROOM.**

THAT'LL BE THE **ROYAL ADVISORS** AGAIN. COME ON, RUSTY... LET'S GET THIS OVER WITH.

glop

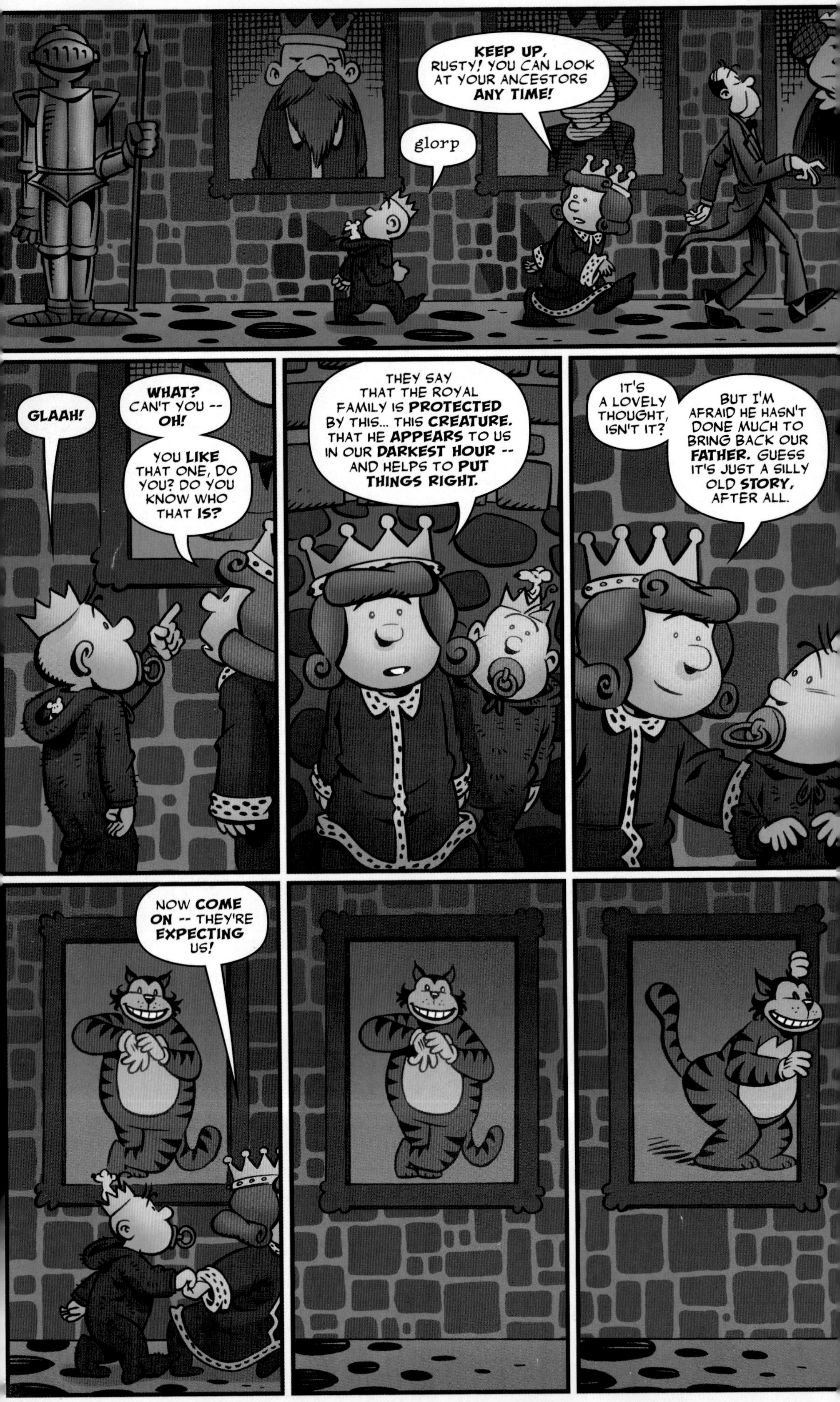
KEEP UP, RUSTY! YOU CAN LOOK AT YOUR ANCESTORS ANY TIME!
glorp
GLAAH!
WHAT? CAN'T YOU -- OH!
YOU LIKE THAT ONE, DO YOU? DO YOU KNOW WHO THAT IS?
THEY SAY THAT THE ROYAL FAMILY IS PROTECTED BY THIS... THIS CREATURE. THAT HE APPEARS TO US IN OUR DARKEST HOUR -- AND HELPS TO PUT THINGS RIGHT.
IT'S A LOVELY THOUGHT, ISN'T IT?
BUT I'M AFRAID HE HASN'T DONE MUCH TO BRING BACK OUR FATHER. GUESS IT'S JUST A SILLY OLD STORY, AFTER ALL.
NOW COME ON -- THEY'RE EXPECTING US!

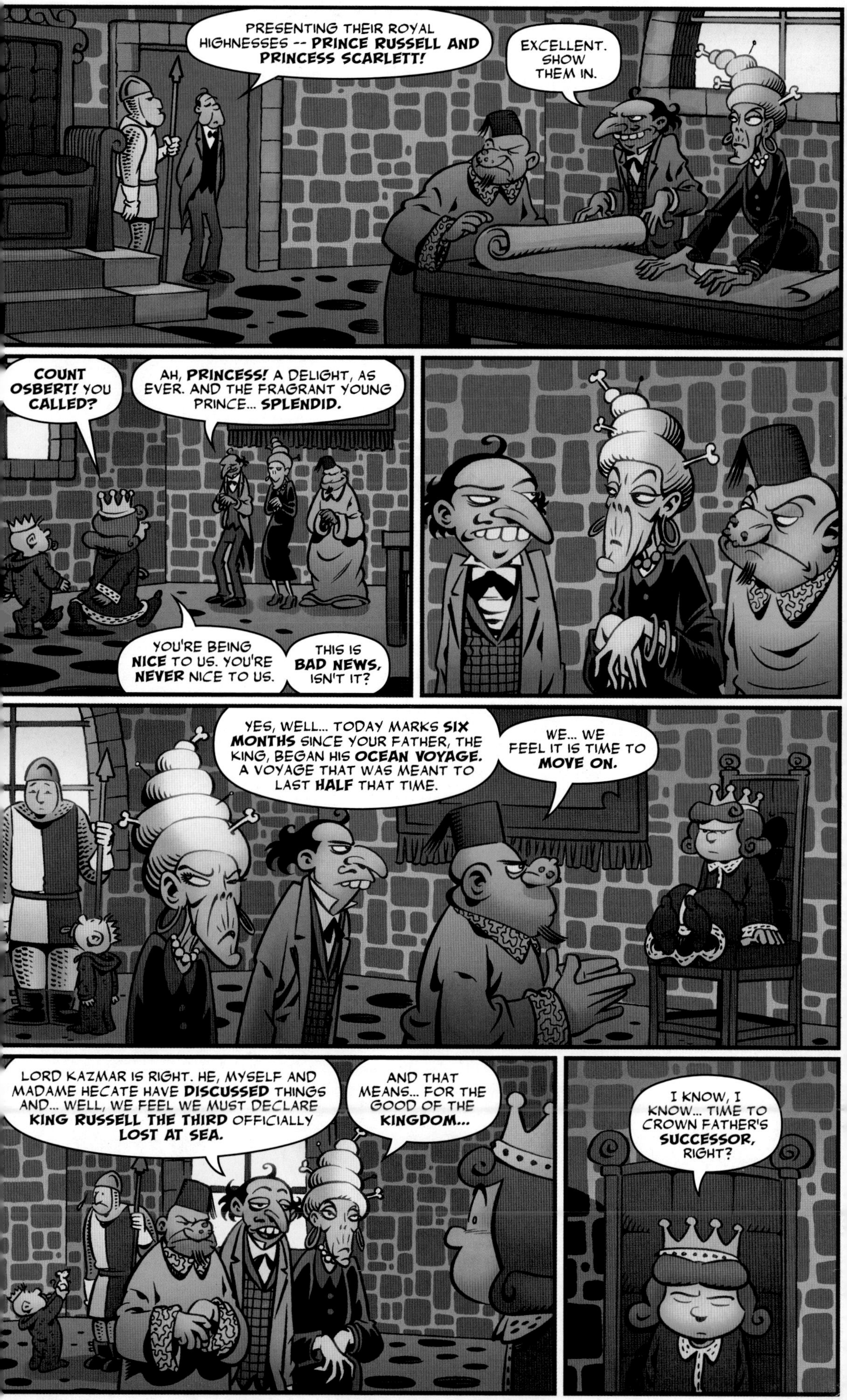

PRESENTING THEIR ROYAL HIGHNESSES -- **PRINCE RUSSELL AND PRINCESS SCARLETT!**
EXCELLENT. SHOW THEM IN.
COUNT OSBERT! YOU **CALLED?**
AH, **PRINCESS!** A DELIGHT, AS EVER. AND THE FRAGRANT YOUNG PRINCE... **SPLENDID.**
YOU'RE BEING **NICE** TO US. YOU'RE **NEVER** NICE TO US.
THIS IS **BAD NEWS,** ISN'T IT?
YES, WELL... TODAY MARKS **SIX MONTHS** SINCE YOUR FATHER, THE KING, BEGAN HIS **OCEAN VOYAGE.** A VOYAGE THAT WAS MEANT TO LAST **HALF** THAT TIME.
WE... WE FEEL IT IS TIME TO **MOVE ON.**
LORD KAZMAR IS RIGHT. HE, MYSELF AND MADAME HECATE HAVE **DISCUSSED** THINGS AND... WELL, WE FEEL WE MUST DECLARE **KING RUSSELL THE THIRD** OFFICIALLY **LOST AT SEA.**
AND THAT MEANS... FOR THE GOOD OF THE **KINGDOM...**
I KNOW, I KNOW... TIME TO CROWN FATHER'S **SUCCESSOR,** RIGHT?

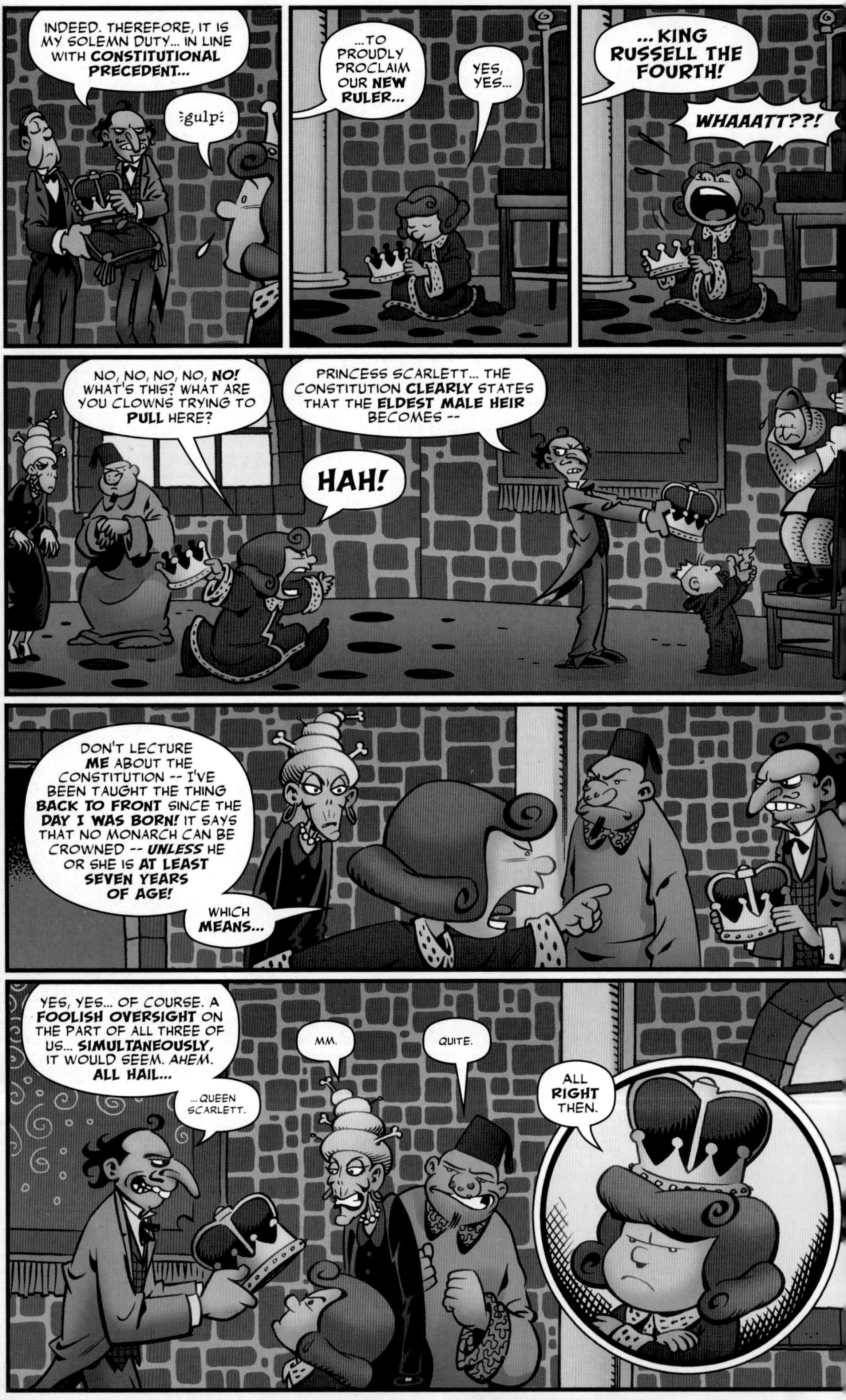
INDEED. THEREFORE, IT IS MY SOLEMN DUTY... IN LINE WITH CONSTITUTIONAL PRECEDENT...
gulp
...TO PROUDLY PROCLAIM OUR NEW RULER...
YES, YES...
... KING RUSSELL THE FOURTH!
WHAAATT??!
NO, NO, NO, NO, NO! WHAT'S THIS? WHAT ARE YOU CLOWNS TRYING TO PULL HERE?
PRINCESS SCARLETT... THE CONSTITUTION CLEARLY STATES THAT THE ELDEST MALE HEIR BECOMES --
HAH!
DON'T LECTURE ME ABOUT THE CONSTITUTION -- I'VE BEEN TAUGHT THE THING BACK TO FRONT SINCE THE DAY I WAS BORN! IT SAYS THAT NO MONARCH CAN BE CROWNED -- UNLESS HE OR SHE IS AT LEAST SEVEN YEARS OF AGE!
WHICH MEANS...
YES, YES... OF COURSE. A FOOLISH OVERSIGHT ON THE PART OF ALL THREE OF US... SIMULTANEOUSLY, IT WOULD SEEM. AHEM. ALL HAIL...
...QUEEN SCARLETT.
MM.
QUITE.
ALL RIGHT THEN.

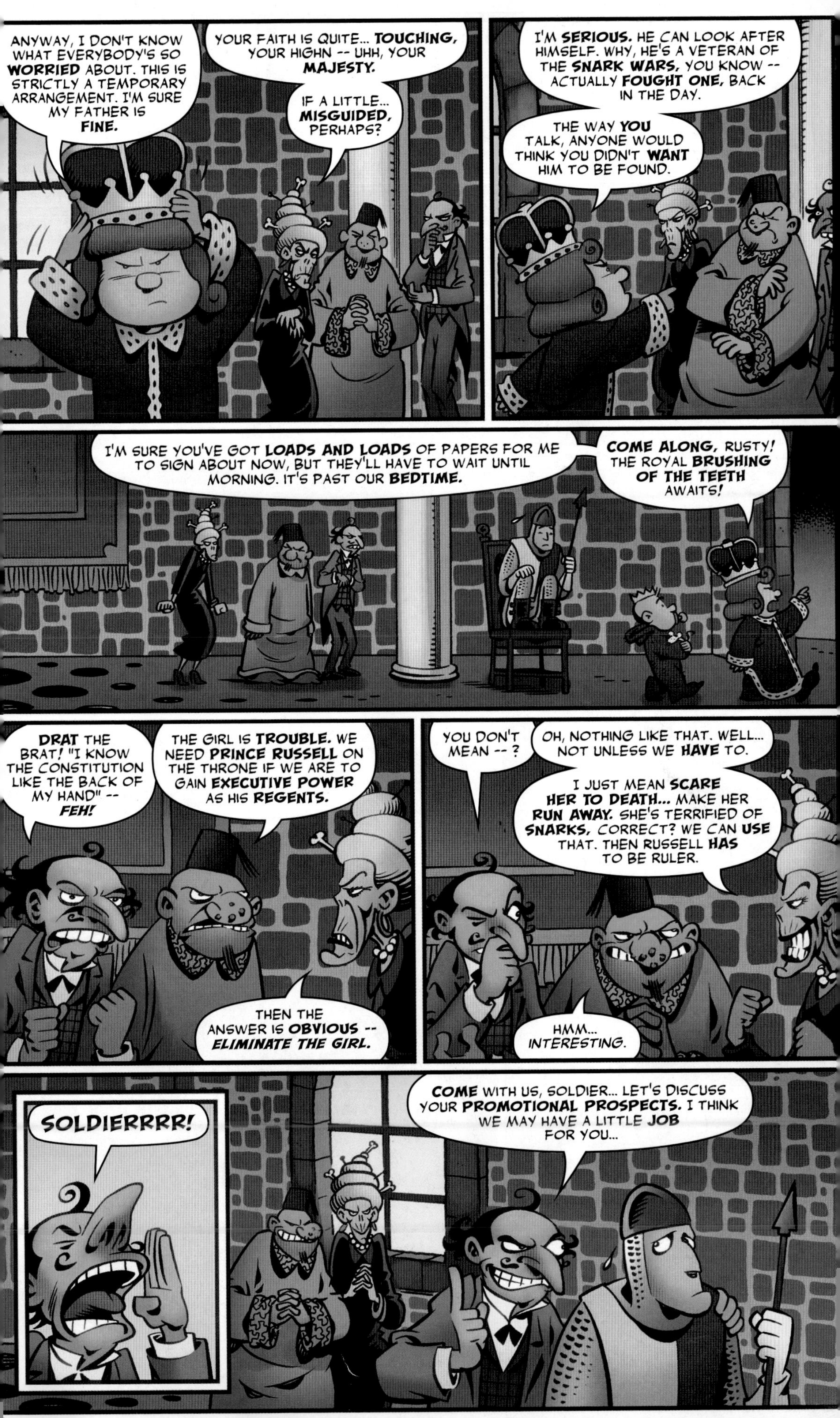
ANYWAY, I DON'T KNOW WHAT EVERYBODY'S SO **WORRIED** ABOUT. THIS IS STRICTLY A TEMPORARY ARRANGEMENT. I'M SURE MY FATHER IS **FINE.**
YOUR FAITH IS QUITE... **TOUCHING,** YOUR HIGHN -- UHH, YOUR **MAJESTY.**
IF A LITTLE... **MISGUIDED,** PERHAPS?
I'M **SERIOUS.** HE CAN LOOK AFTER HIMSELF. WHY, HE'S A VETERAN OF THE **SNARK WARS,** YOU KNOW -- ACTUALLY **FOUGHT ONE,** BACK IN THE DAY.
THE WAY **YOU** TALK, ANYONE WOULD THINK YOU DIDN'T **WANT** HIM TO BE FOUND.
I'M SURE YOU'VE GOT **LOADS AND LOADS** OF PAPERS FOR ME TO SIGN ABOUT NOW, BUT THEY'LL HAVE TO WAIT UNTIL MORNING. IT'S PAST OUR **BEDTIME.**
COME ALONG, RUSTY! THE ROYAL **BRUSHING OF THE TEETH** AWAITS!
DRAT THE BRAT! "I KNOW THE CONSTITUTION LIKE THE BACK OF MY HAND" -- ***FEH!***
THE GIRL IS **TROUBLE.** WE NEED **PRINCE RUSSELL** ON THE THRONE IF WE ARE TO GAIN **EXECUTIVE POWER** AS HIS **REGENTS.**
THEN THE ANSWER IS **OBVIOUS** -- ***ELIMINATE THE GIRL.***
YOU DON'T MEAN -- ?
OH, NOTHING LIKE THAT. WELL... NOT UNLESS WE **HAVE** TO.
I JUST MEAN **SCARE HER TO DEATH...** MAKE HER **RUN AWAY.** SHE'S TERRIFIED OF **SNARKS,** CORRECT? WE CAN **USE** THAT. THEN RUSSELL **HAS** TO BE RULER.
HMM... INTERESTING.
SOLDIERRRR!
COME WITH US, SOLDIER... LET'S DISCUSS YOUR **PROMOTIONAL PROSPECTS.** I THINK WE MAY HAVE A LITTLE **JOB** FOR YOU...

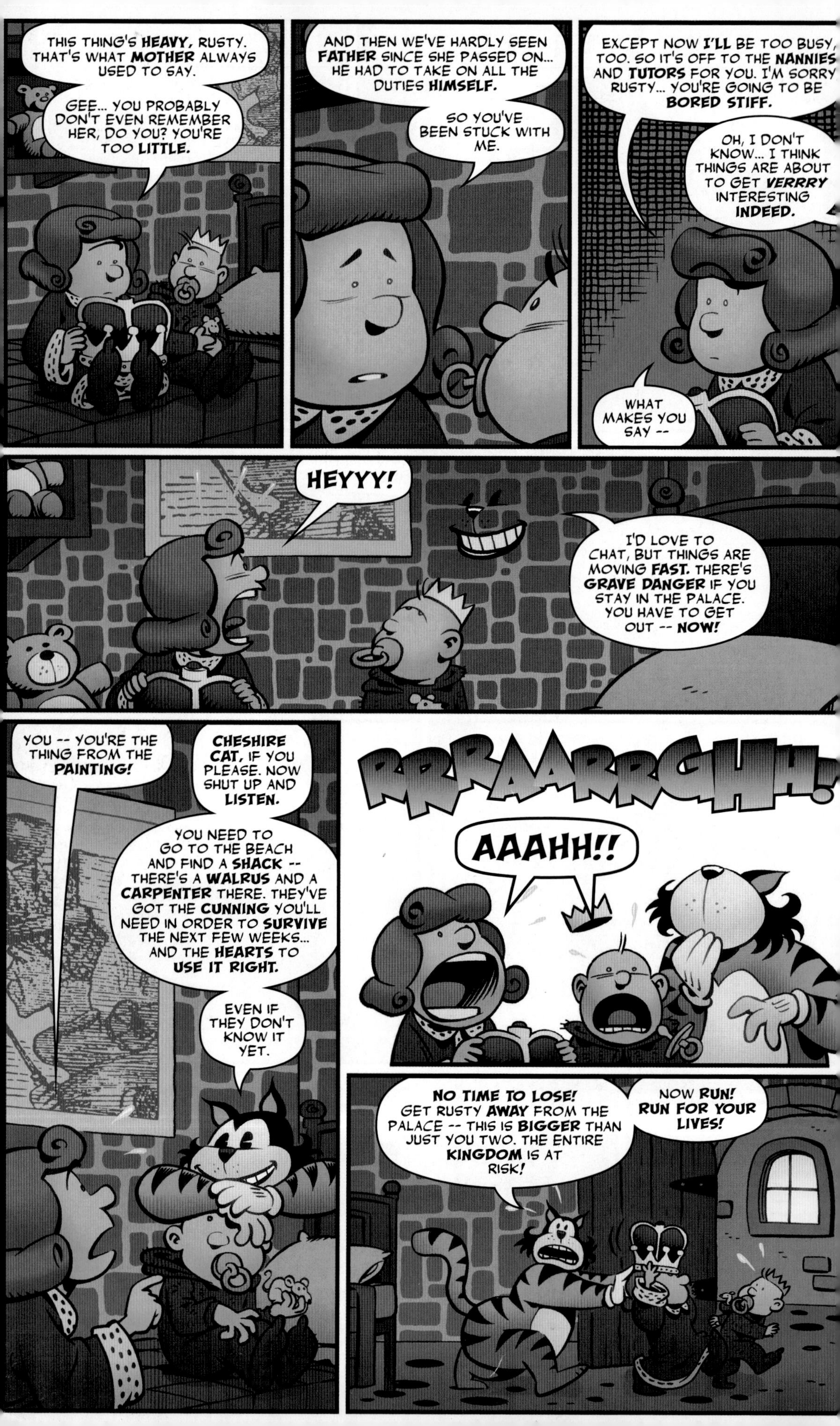

THIS THING'S HEAVY, RUSTY. THAT'S WHAT MOTHER ALWAYS USED TO SAY.
GEE... YOU PROBABLY DON'T EVEN REMEMBER HER, DO YOU? YOU'RE TOO LITTLE.
AND THEN WE'VE HARDLY SEEN FATHER SINCE SHE PASSED ON... HE HAD TO TAKE ON ALL THE DUTIES HIMSELF.
SO YOU'VE BEEN STUCK WITH ME.
EXCEPT NOW I'LL BE TOO BUSY, TOO. SO IT'S OFF TO THE NANNIES AND TUTORS FOR YOU. I'M SORRY RUSTY... YOU'RE GOING TO BE BORED STIFF.
OH, I DON'T KNOW... I THINK THINGS ARE ABOUT TO GET VERRRY INTERESTING INDEED.
WHAT MAKES YOU SAY --
HEYYY!
I'D LOVE TO CHAT, BUT THINGS ARE MOVING FAST. THERE'S GRAVE DANGER IF YOU STAY IN THE PALACE. YOU HAVE TO GET OUT -- NOW!
YOU -- YOU'RE THE THING FROM THE PAINTING!
CHESHIRE CAT, IF YOU PLEASE. NOW SHUT UP AND LISTEN.
YOU NEED TO GO TO THE BEACH AND FIND A SHACK -- THERE'S A WALRUS AND A CARPENTER THERE. THEY'VE GOT THE CUNNING YOU'LL NEED IN ORDER TO SURVIVE THE NEXT FEW WEEKS... AND THE HEARTS TO USE IT RIGHT.
EVEN IF THEY DON'T KNOW IT YET.
RRRAARRGHH!
AAAHH!!
NO TIME TO LOSE! GET RUSTY AWAY FROM THE PALACE -- THIS IS BIGGER THAN JUST YOU TWO. THE ENTIRE KINGDOM IS AT RISK!
NOW RUN! RUN FOR YOUR LIVES!

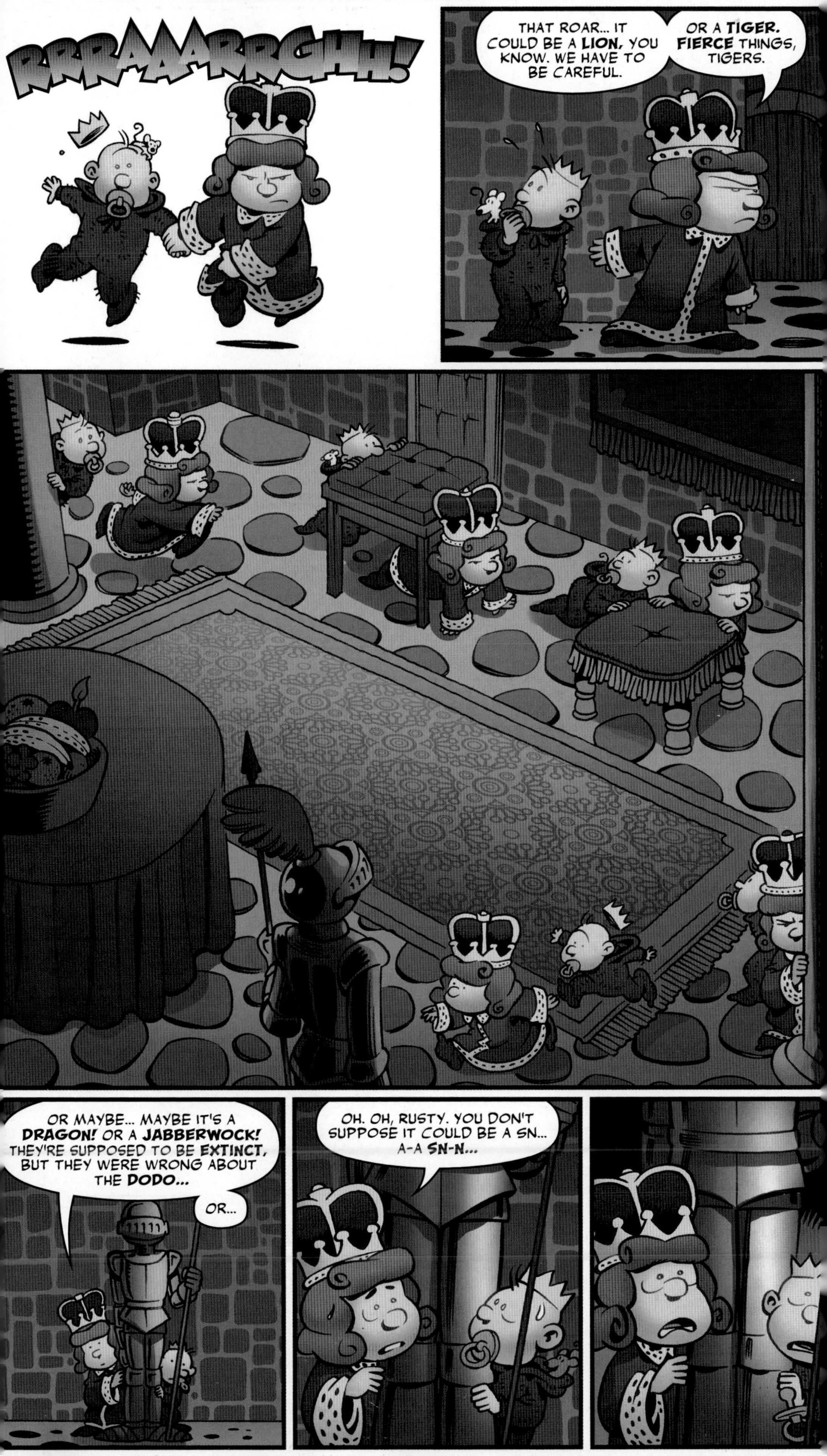
RRRAAARRGHH!
THAT ROAR... IT COULD BE A LION, YOU KNOW. WE HAVE TO BE CAREFUL.
OR A TIGER. FIERCE THINGS, TIGERS.
OR MAYBE... MAYBE IT'S A DRAGON! OR A JABBERWOCK! THEY'RE SUPPOSED TO BE EXTINCT, BUT THEY WERE WRONG ABOUT THE DODO...
OR...
OH. OH, RUSTY. YOU DON'T SUPPOSE IT COULD BE A SN... A-A SN-N...

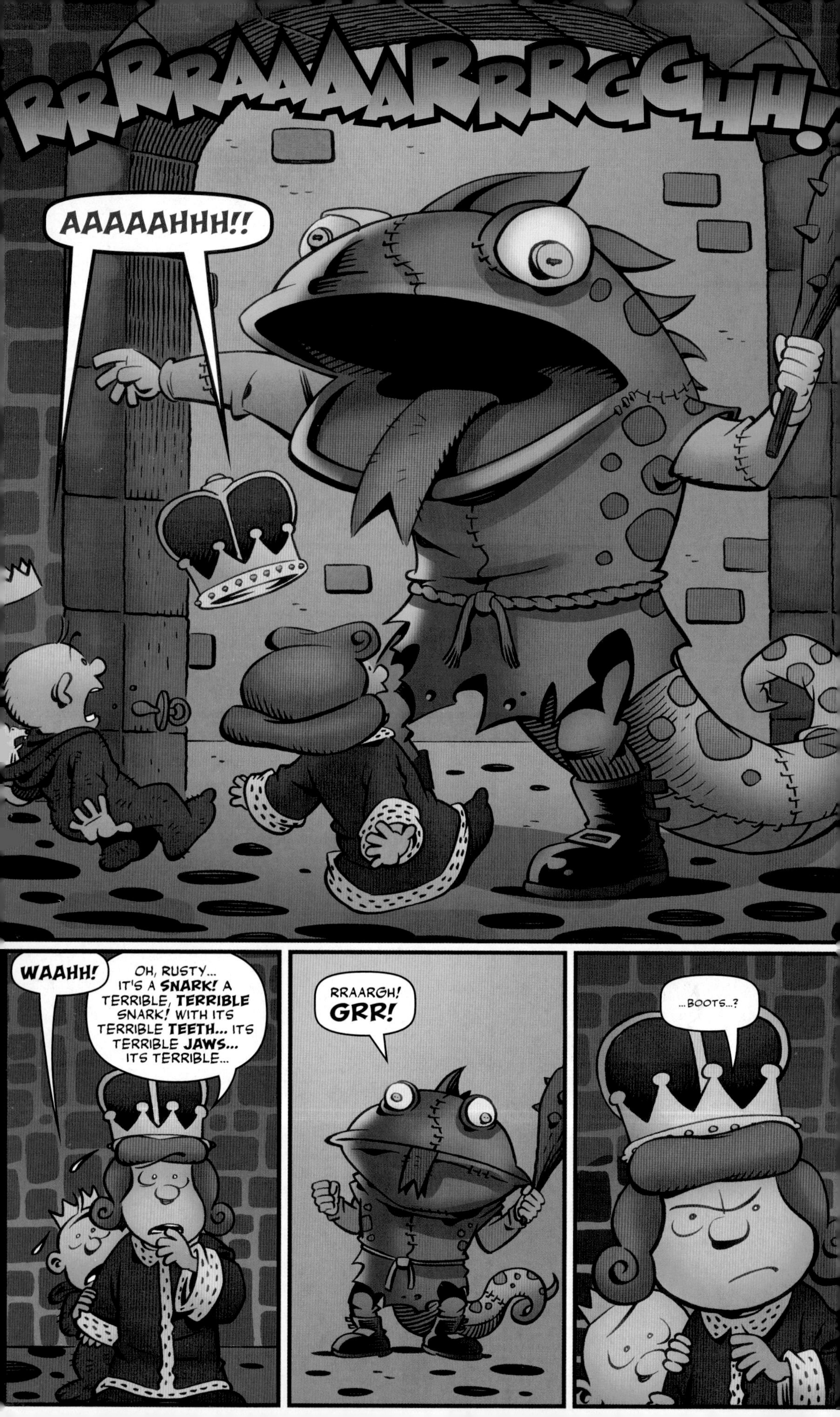
RRRRAAAARRRGGHH!!
AAAAAHHH!!
WAAHH!
OH, RUSTY... IT'S A SNARK! A TERRIBLE, TERRIBLE SNARK! WITH ITS TERRIBLE TEETH... ITS TERRIBLE JAWS... ITS TERRIBLE...
RRAARGH! GRR!
...BOOTS...?

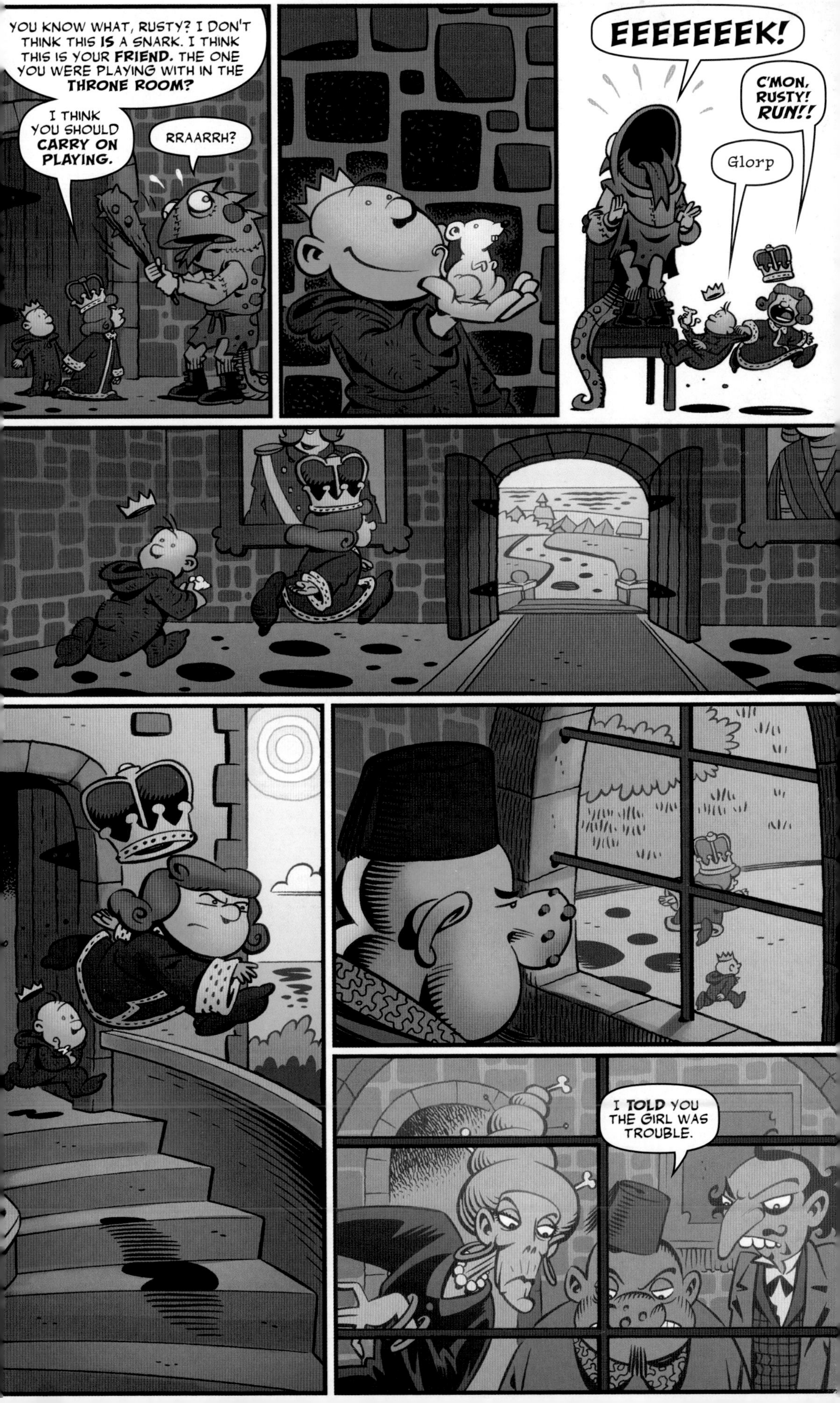
YOU KNOW WHAT, RUSTY? I DON'T THINK THIS **IS** A SNARK. I THINK THIS IS YOUR **FRIEND.** THE ONE YOU WERE PLAYING WITH IN THE **THRONE ROOM?**
I THINK YOU SHOULD **CARRY ON PLAYING.**
RRAARRH?
EEEEEEEK!
Glorp
C'MON, RUSTY! *RUN!!*
I **TOLD** YOU THE GIRL WAS TROUBLE.

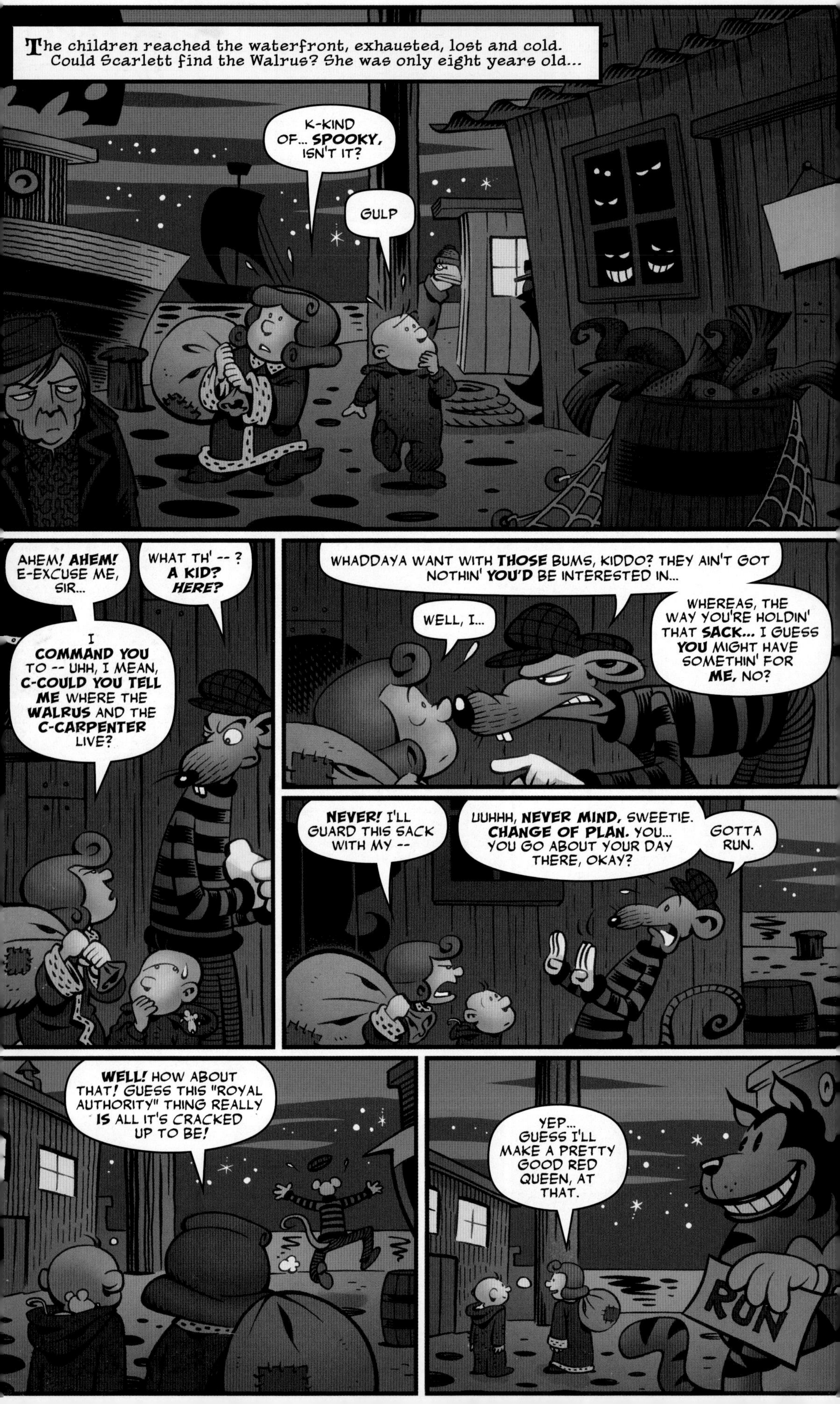
The children reached the waterfront, exhausted, lost and cold. Could Scarlett find the Walrus? She was only eight years old...
K-KIND OF... SPOOKY, ISN'T IT?
GULP
AHEM! AHEM! E-EXCUSE ME, SIR...
WHAT TH' -- ? A KID? HERE?
I COMMAND YOU TO -- UHH, I MEAN, C-COULD YOU TELL ME WHERE THE WALRUS AND THE C-CARPENTER LIVE?
WHADDAYA WANT WITH THOSE BUMS, KIDDO? THEY AIN'T GOT NOTHIN' YOU'D BE INTERESTED IN...
WELL, I...
WHEREAS, THE WAY YOU'RE HOLDIN' THAT SACK... I GUESS YOU MIGHT HAVE SOMETHIN' FOR ME, NO?
NEVER! I'LL GUARD THIS SACK WITH MY --
UUHHH, NEVER MIND, SWEETIE. CHANGE OF PLAN. YOU... YOU GO ABOUT YOUR DAY THERE, OKAY?
GOTTA RUN.
WELL! HOW ABOUT THAT! GUESS THIS "ROYAL AUTHORITY" THING REALLY IS ALL IT'S CRACKED UP TO BE!
YEP... GUESS I'LL MAKE A PRETTY GOOD RED QUEEN, AT THAT.
RUN

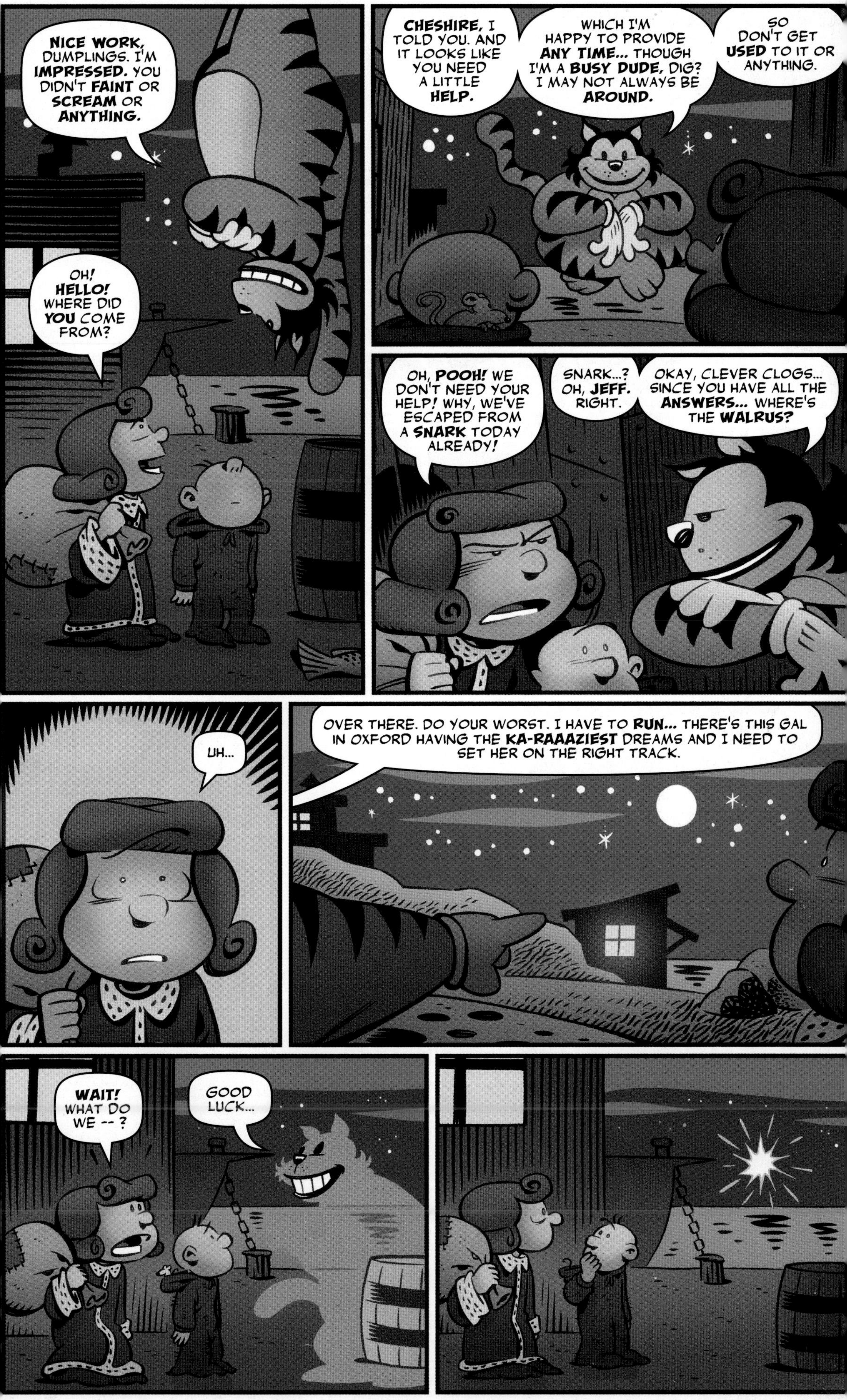
NICE WORK, DUMPLINGS. I'M IMPRESSED. YOU DIDN'T FAINT OR SCREAM OR ANYTHING.
OH! HELLO! WHERE DID YOU COME FROM?
CHESHIRE, I TOLD YOU. AND IT LOOKS LIKE YOU NEED A LITTLE HELP.
WHICH I'M HAPPY TO PROVIDE ANY TIME... THOUGH I'M A BUSY DUDE, DIG? I MAY NOT ALWAYS BE AROUND.
SO DON'T GET USED TO IT OR ANYTHING.
OH, POOH! WE DON'T NEED YOUR HELP! WHY, WE'VE ESCAPED FROM A SNARK TODAY ALREADY!
SNARK...? OH, JEFF. RIGHT.
OKAY, CLEVER CLOGS... SINCE YOU HAVE ALL THE ANSWERS... WHERE'S THE WALRUS?
UH...
OVER THERE. DO YOUR WORST. I HAVE TO RUN... THERE'S THIS GAL IN OXFORD HAVING THE KA-RAAAZIEST DREAMS AND I NEED TO SET HER ON THE RIGHT TRACK.
WAIT! WHAT DO WE -- ?
GOOD LUCK...

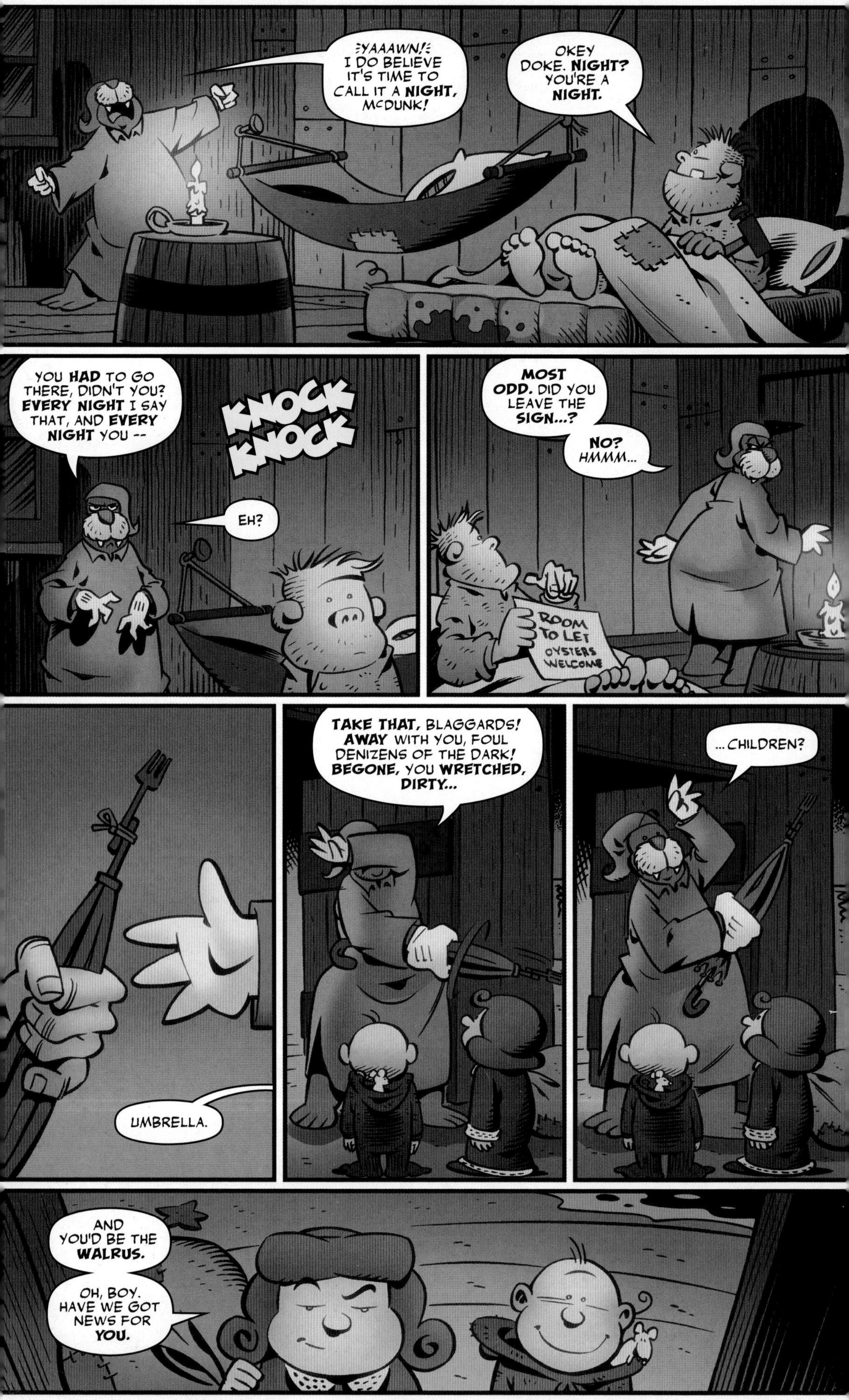

YAAAWN! I DO BELIEVE IT'S TIME TO CALL IT A NIGHT, McDUNK!
OKEY DOKE. NIGHT? YOU'RE A NIGHT.
YOU HAD TO GO THERE, DIDN'T YOU? EVERY NIGHT I SAY THAT, AND EVERY NIGHT YOU --
KNOCK KNOCK
EH?
MOST ODD. DID YOU LEAVE THE SIGN...?
NO? HMMM...
ROOM TO LET
OYSTERS WELCOME
UMBRELLA.
TAKE THAT, BLAGGARDS! AWAY WITH YOU, FOUL DENIZENS OF THE DARK! BEGONE, YOU WRETCHED, DIRTY...
...CHILDREN?
AND YOU'D BE THE WALRUS.
OH, BOY. HAVE WE GOT NEWS FOR YOU.

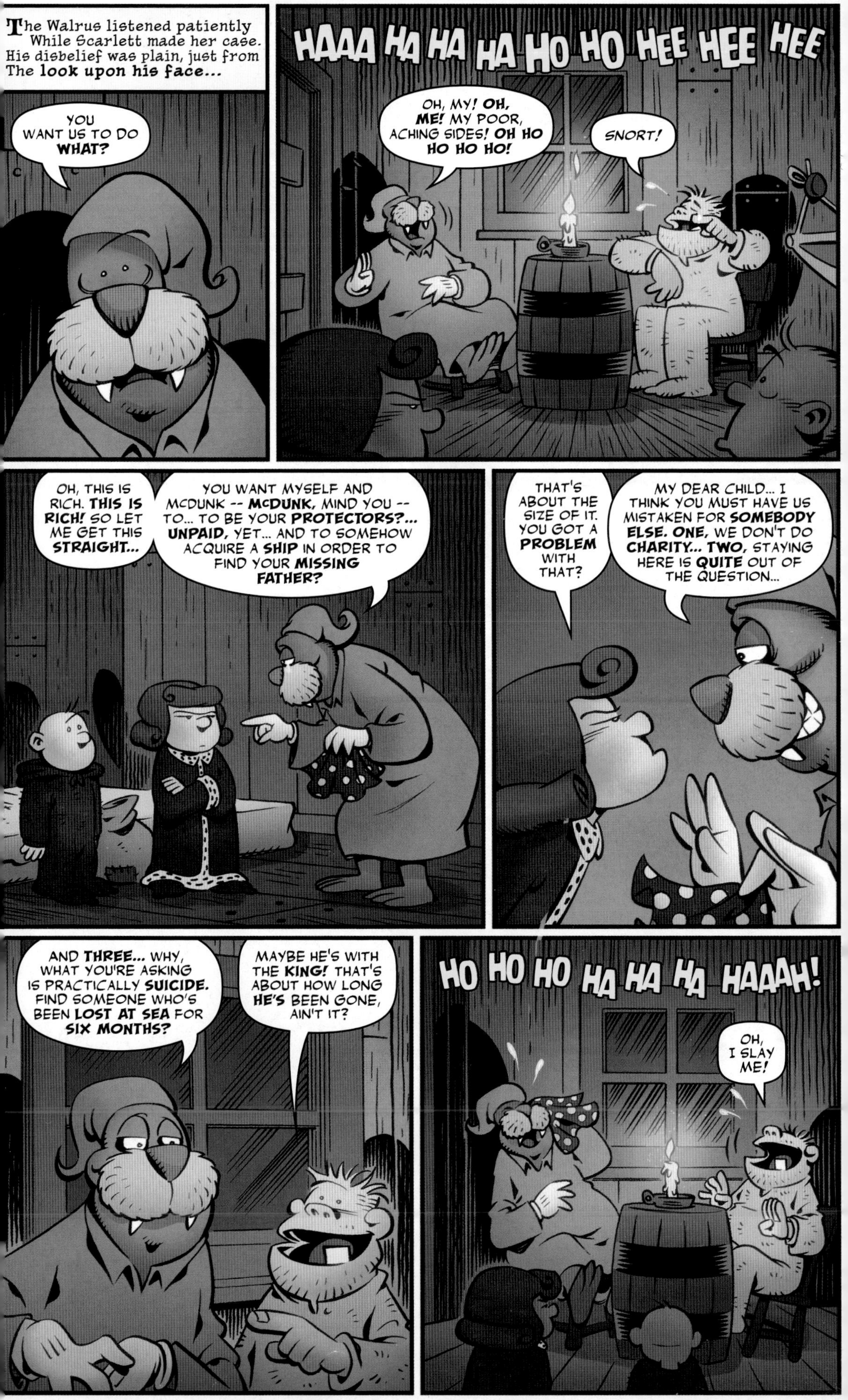

The Walrus listened patiently
While Scarlett made her case.
His disbelief was plain, just from
The look upon his face...
YOU WANT US TO DO WHAT?
HAAA HA HA HA HO HO HEE HEE HEE
OH, MY! OH, ME! MY POOR, ACHING SIDES! OH HO HO HO HO!
SNORT!
OH, THIS IS RICH. THIS IS RICH! SO LET ME GET THIS STRAIGHT...
YOU WANT MYSELF AND MCDUNK -- MCDUNK, MIND YOU -- TO... TO BE YOUR PROTECTORS?... UNPAID, YET... AND TO SOMEHOW ACQUIRE A SHIP IN ORDER TO FIND YOUR MISSING FATHER?
THAT'S ABOUT THE SIZE OF IT. YOU GOT A PROBLEM WITH THAT?
MY DEAR CHILD... I THINK YOU MUST HAVE US MISTAKEN FOR SOMEBODY ELSE. ONE, WE DON'T DO CHARITY... TWO, STAYING HERE IS QUITE OUT OF THE QUESTION...
AND THREE... WHY, WHAT YOU'RE ASKING IS PRACTICALLY SUICIDE. FIND SOMEONE WHO'S BEEN LOST AT SEA FOR SIX MONTHS?
MAYBE HE'S WITH THE KING! THAT'S ABOUT HOW LONG HE'S BEEN GONE, AIN'T IT?
HO HO HO HA HA HA HAAAH!
OH, I SLAY ME!

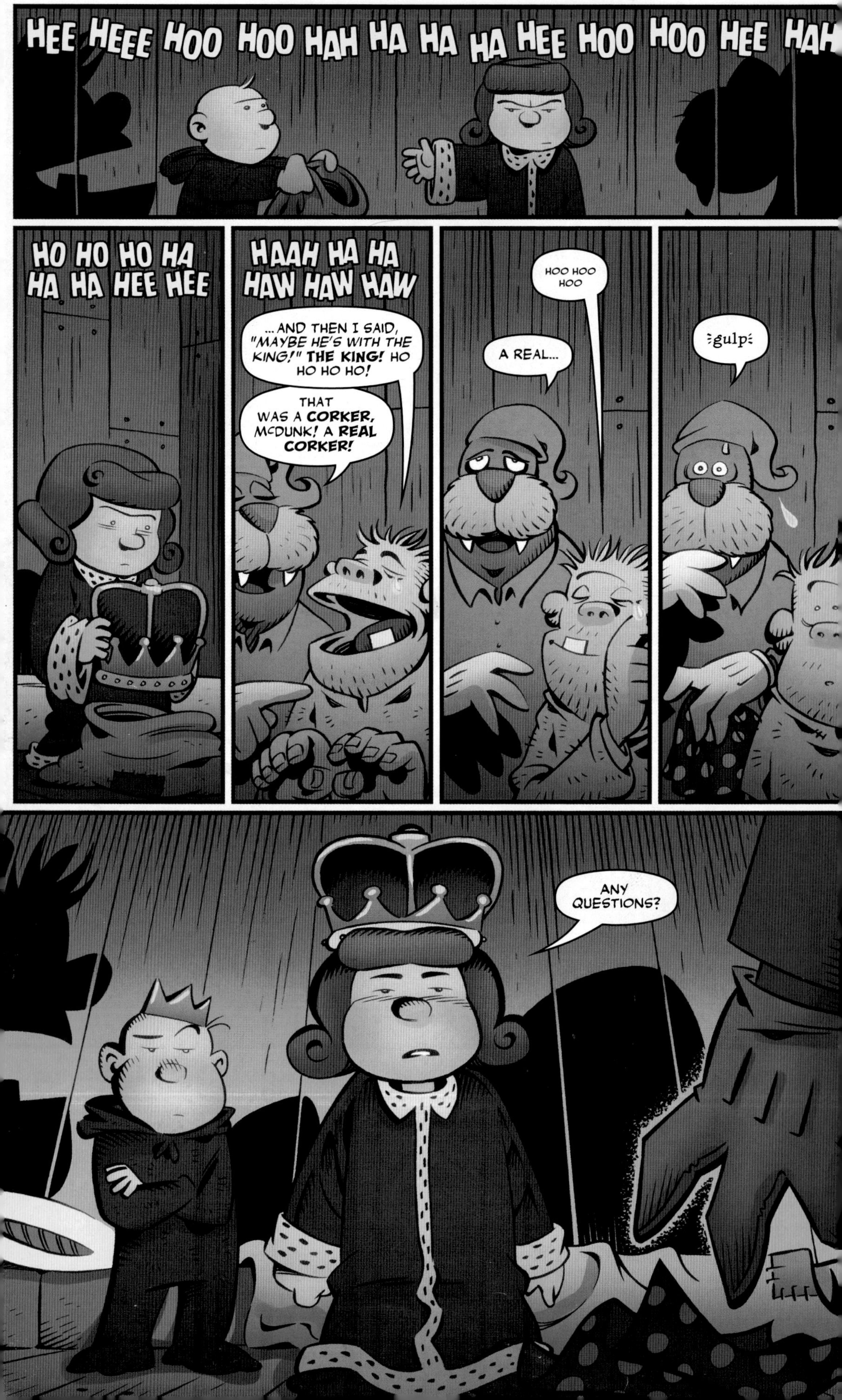
HEE HEEE HOO HOO HAH HA HA HA HEE HOO HOO HEE HAH
HO HO HO HA HA HA HEE HEE
HAAH HA HA HAW HAW HAW
...AND THEN I SAID, "MAYBE HE'S WITH THE KING!" THE KING! HO HO HO HO!
THAT WAS A CORKER, McDUNK! A REAL CORKER!
HOO HOO HOO
A REAL...
gulp
ANY QUESTIONS?

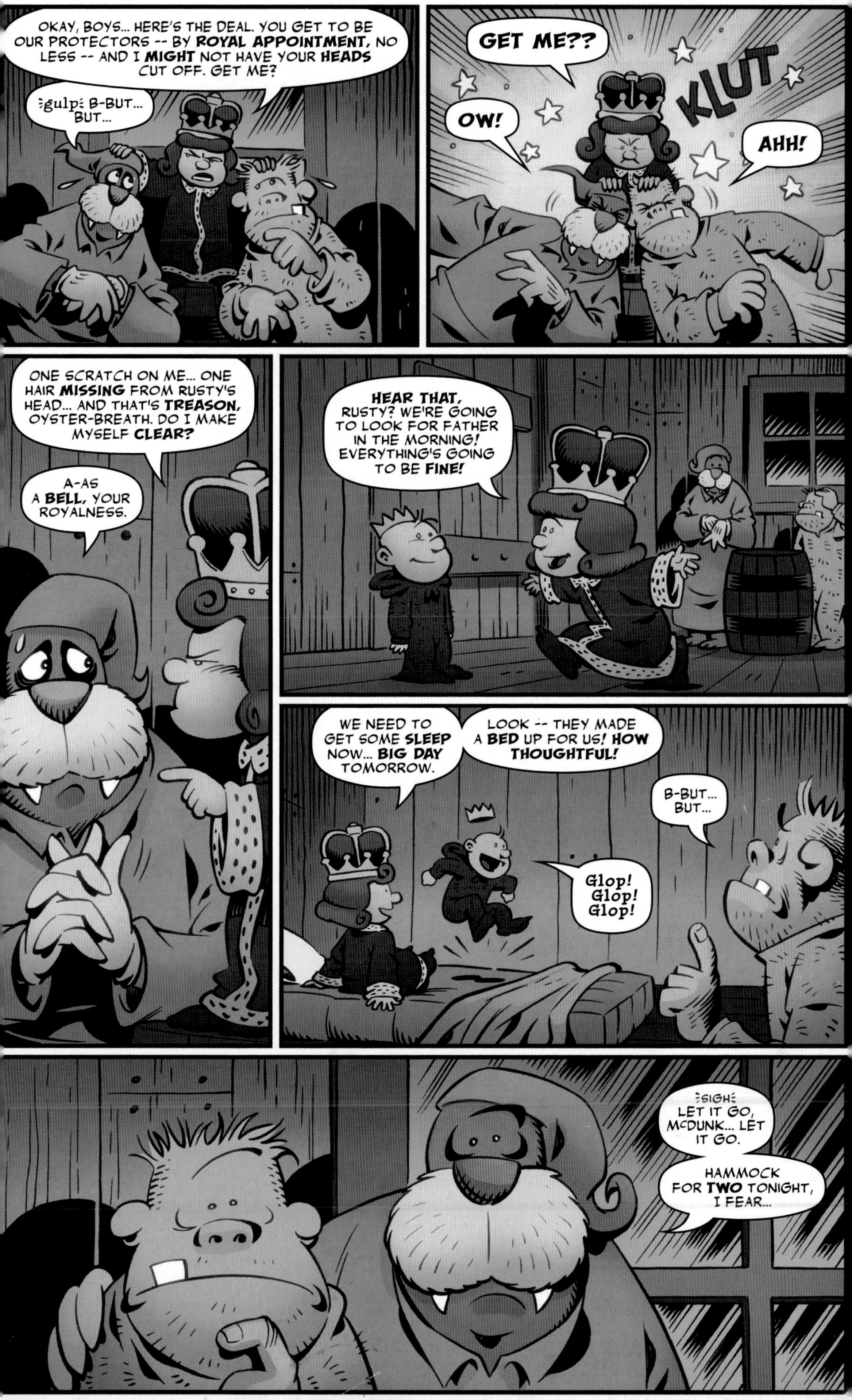

OKAY, BOYS... HERE'S THE DEAL. YOU GET TO BE OUR PROTECTORS -- BY **ROYAL APPOINTMENT,** NO LESS -- AND I **MIGHT** NOT HAVE YOUR **HEADS** CUT OFF. GET ME?
:gulp: B-BUT... BUT...
GET ME??
KLUT
OW!
AHH!
ONE SCRATCH ON ME... ONE HAIR **MISSING** FROM RUSTY'S HEAD... AND THAT'S **TREASON,** OYSTER-BREATH. DO I MAKE MYSELF **CLEAR?**
A-AS A **BELL,** YOUR ROYALNESS.
HEAR THAT, RUSTY? WE'RE GOING TO LOOK FOR FATHER IN THE MORNING! EVERYTHING'S GOING TO BE **FINE!**
WE NEED TO GET SOME **SLEEP** NOW... **BIG DAY** TOMORROW.
LOOK -- THEY MADE A **BED** UP FOR US! **HOW THOUGHTFUL!**
B-BUT... BUT...
Glop! Glop! Glop!
:SIGH: LET IT GO, McDUNK... LET IT GO.
HAMMOCK FOR **TWO** TONIGHT, I FEAR...

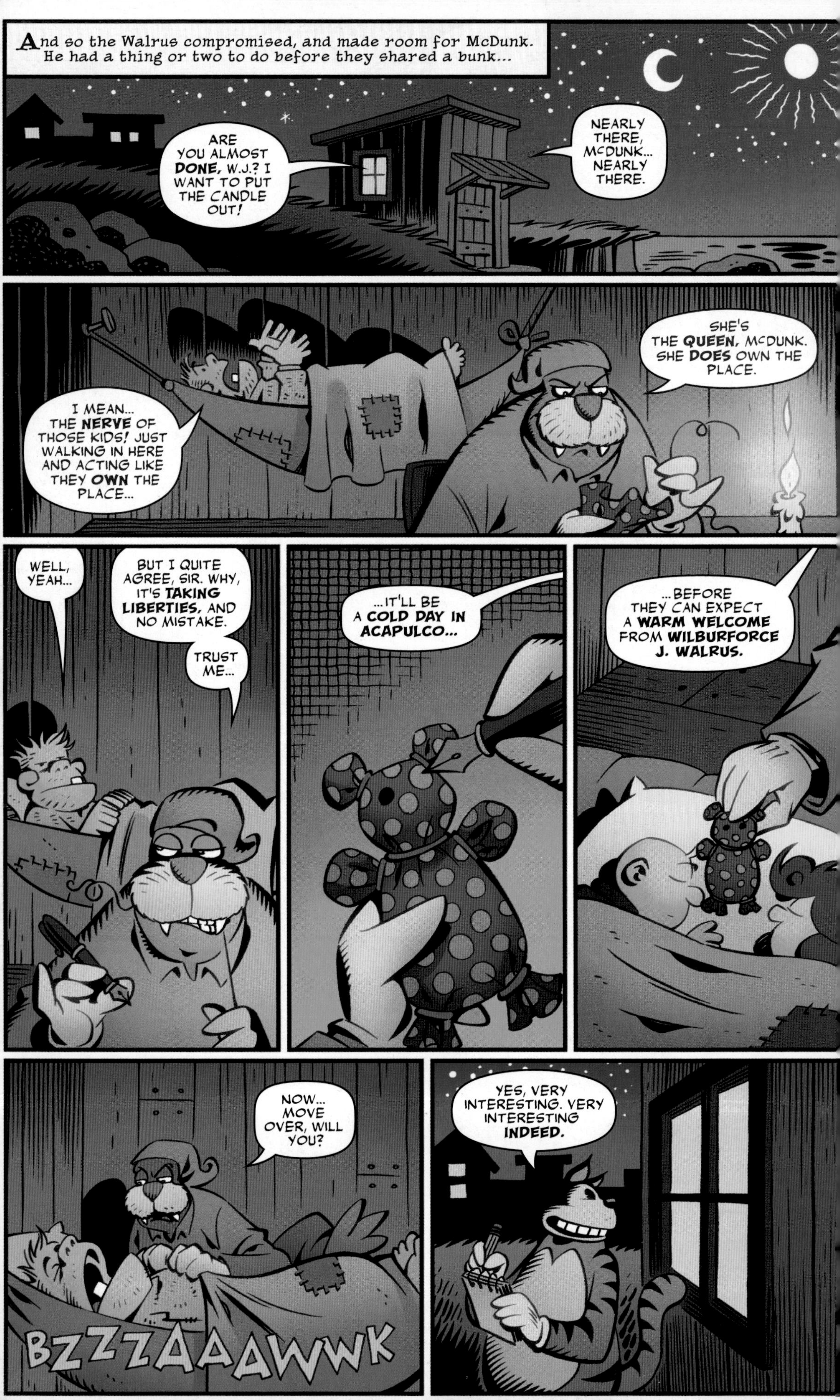
And so the Walrus compromised, and made room for McDunk. He had a thing or two to do before they shared a bunk...
ARE YOU ALMOST DONE, W.J.? I WANT TO PUT THE CANDLE OUT!
NEARLY THERE, McDUNK... NEARLY THERE.
I MEAN... THE NERVE OF THOSE KIDS! JUST WALKING IN HERE AND ACTING LIKE THEY OWN THE PLACE...
SHE'S THE QUEEN, McDUNK. SHE DOES OWN THE PLACE.
WELL, YEAH...
BUT I QUITE AGREE, SIR. WHY, IT'S TAKING LIBERTIES, AND NO MISTAKE.
TRUST ME...
...IT'LL BE A COLD DAY IN ACAPULCO...
...BEFORE THEY CAN EXPECT A WARM WELCOME FROM WILBURFORCE J. WALRUS.
NOW... MOVE OVER, WILL YOU?
BZZZAAAWWK
YES, VERY INTERESTING. VERY INTERESTING INDEED.

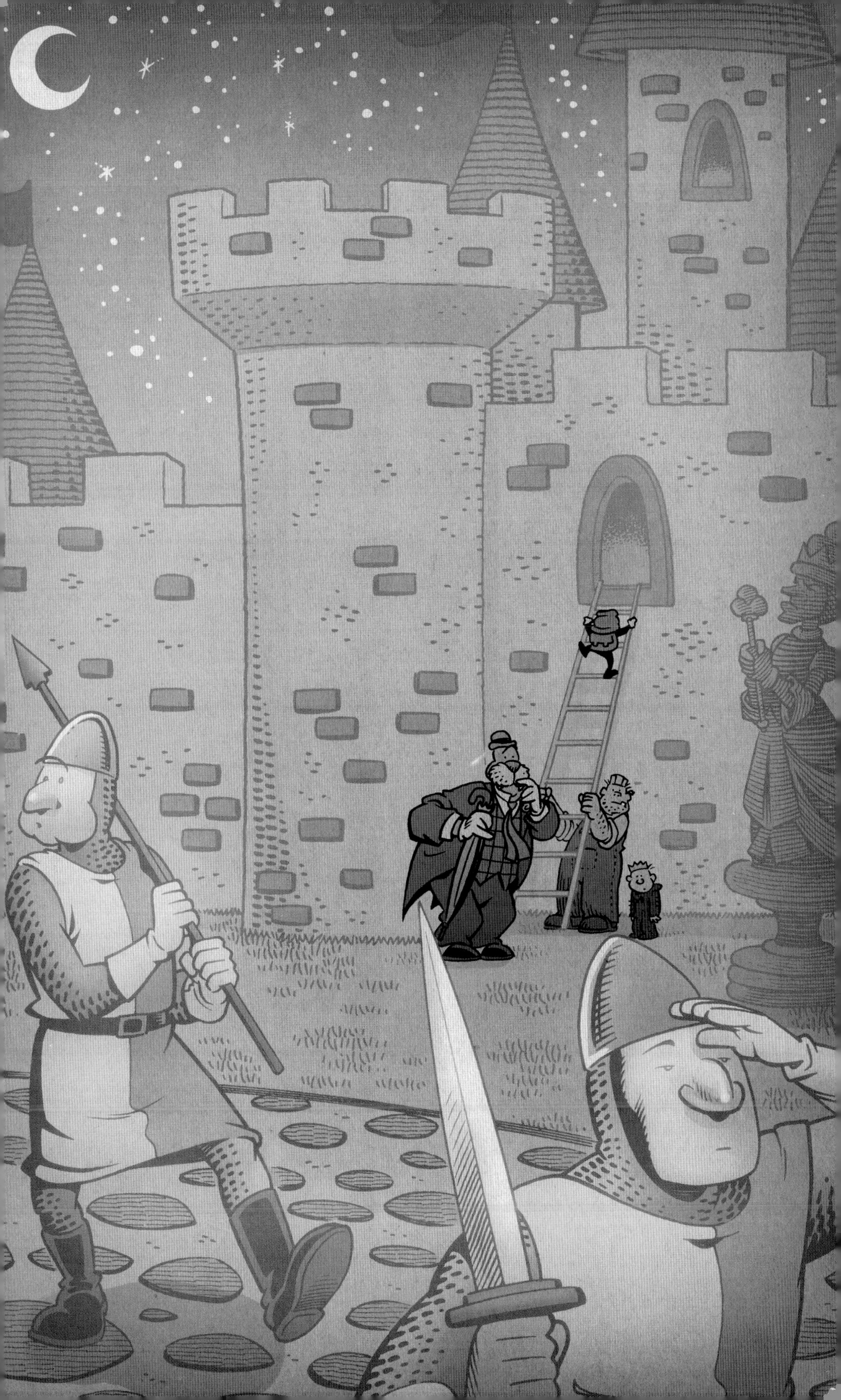

FIT THE SECOND

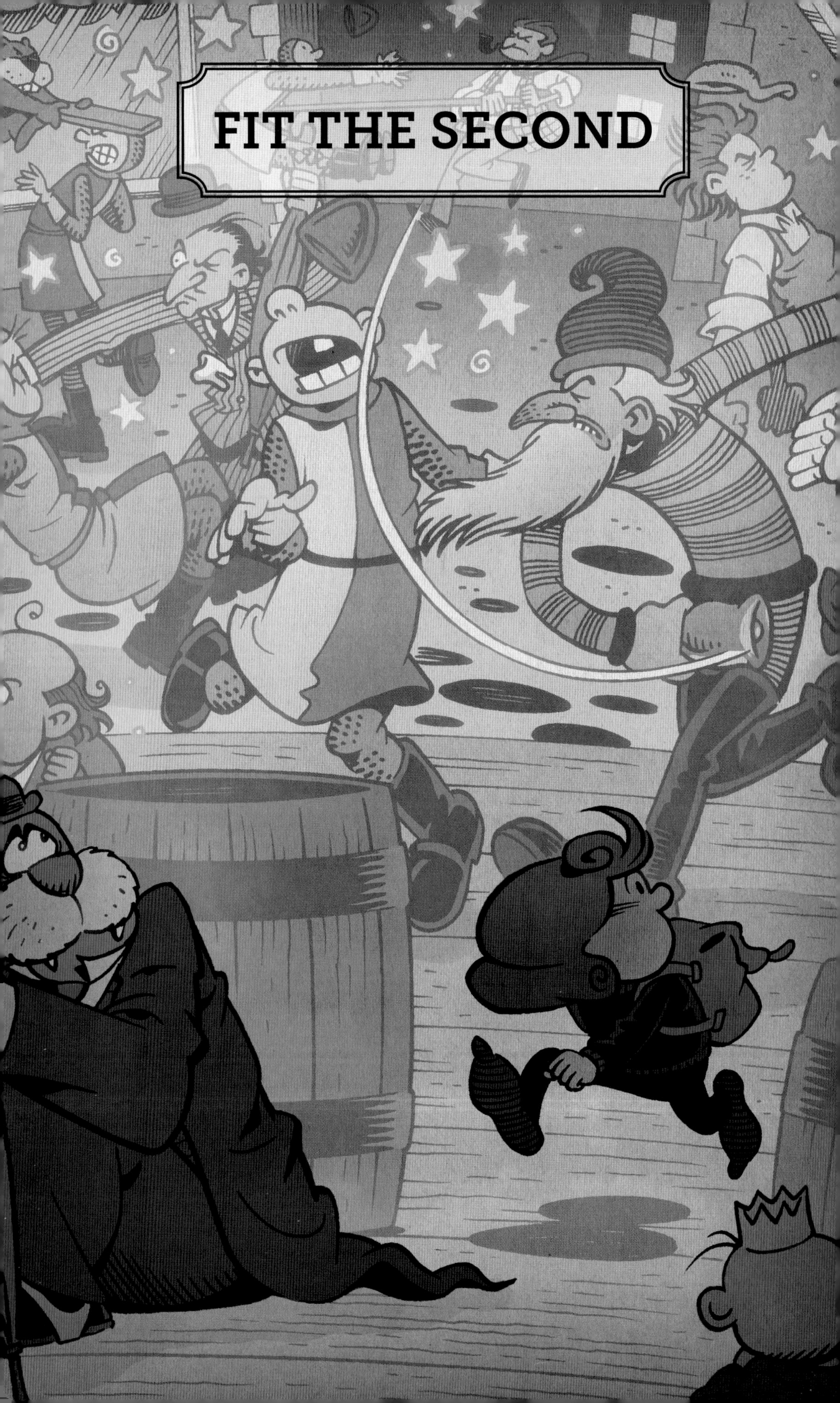

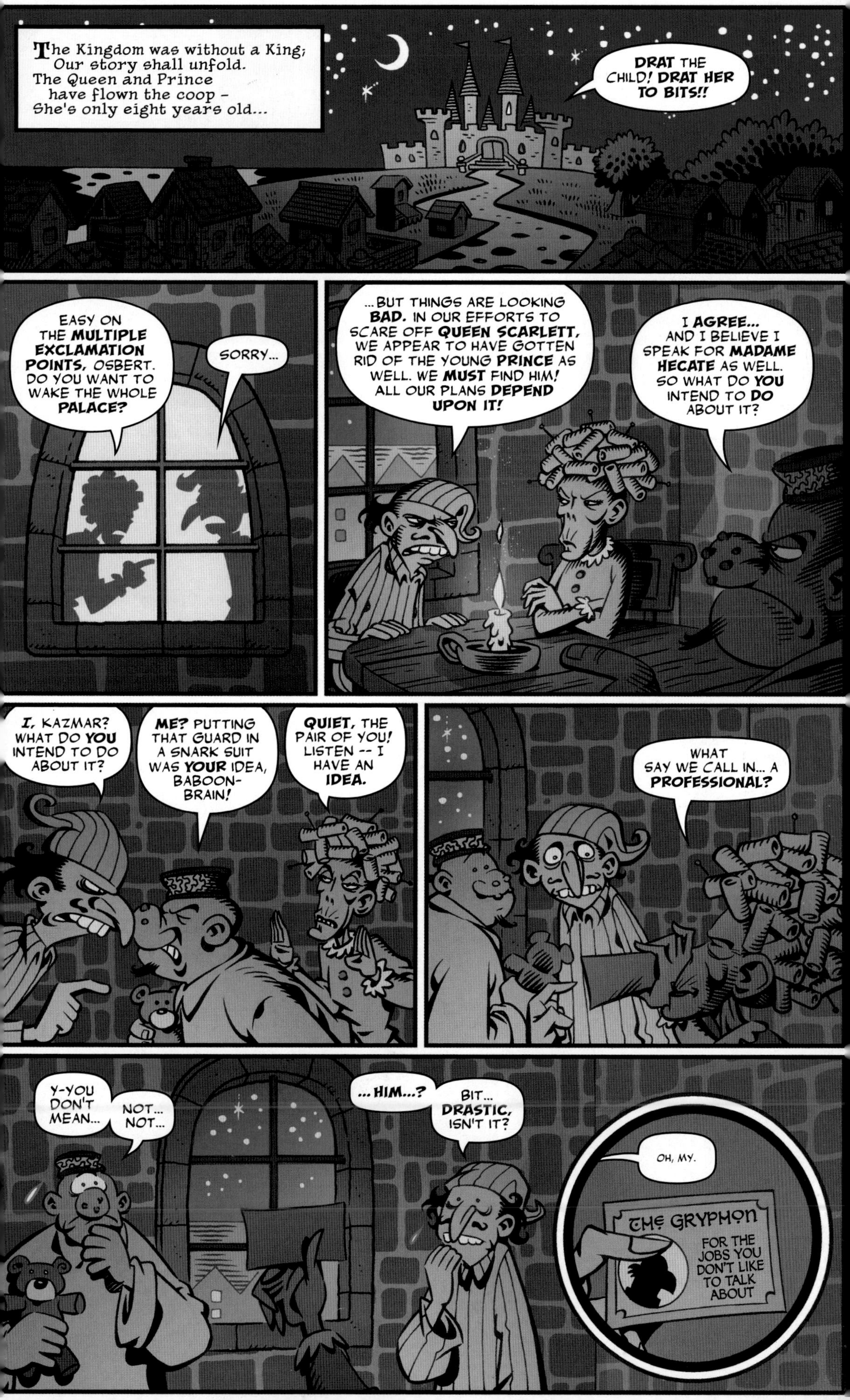
The Kingdom was without a King; Our story shall unfold. The Queen and Prince have flown the coop - She's only eight years old...
DRAT THE CHILD! DRAT HER TO BITS!!
EASY ON THE MULTIPLE EXCLAMATION POINTS, OSBERT. DO YOU WANT TO WAKE THE WHOLE PALACE?
SORRY...
...BUT THINGS ARE LOOKING BAD. IN OUR EFFORTS TO SCARE OFF QUEEN SCARLETT, WE APPEAR TO HAVE GOTTEN RID OF THE YOUNG PRINCE AS WELL. WE MUST FIND HIM! ALL OUR PLANS DEPEND UPON IT!
I AGREE... AND I BELIEVE I SPEAK FOR MADAME HECATE AS WELL. SO WHAT DO YOU INTEND TO DO ABOUT IT?
I, KAZMAR? WHAT DO YOU INTEND TO DO ABOUT IT?
ME? PUTTING THAT GUARD IN A SNARK SUIT WAS YOUR IDEA, BABOON-BRAIN!
QUIET, THE PAIR OF YOU! LISTEN -- I HAVE AN IDEA.
WHAT SAY WE CALL IN... A PROFESSIONAL?
Y-YOU DON'T MEAN...
NOT... NOT...
...HIM...?
BIT... DRASTIC, ISN'T IT?
OH, MY.
THE GRYPHON
FOR THE JOBS YOU DON'T LIKE TO TALK ABOUT

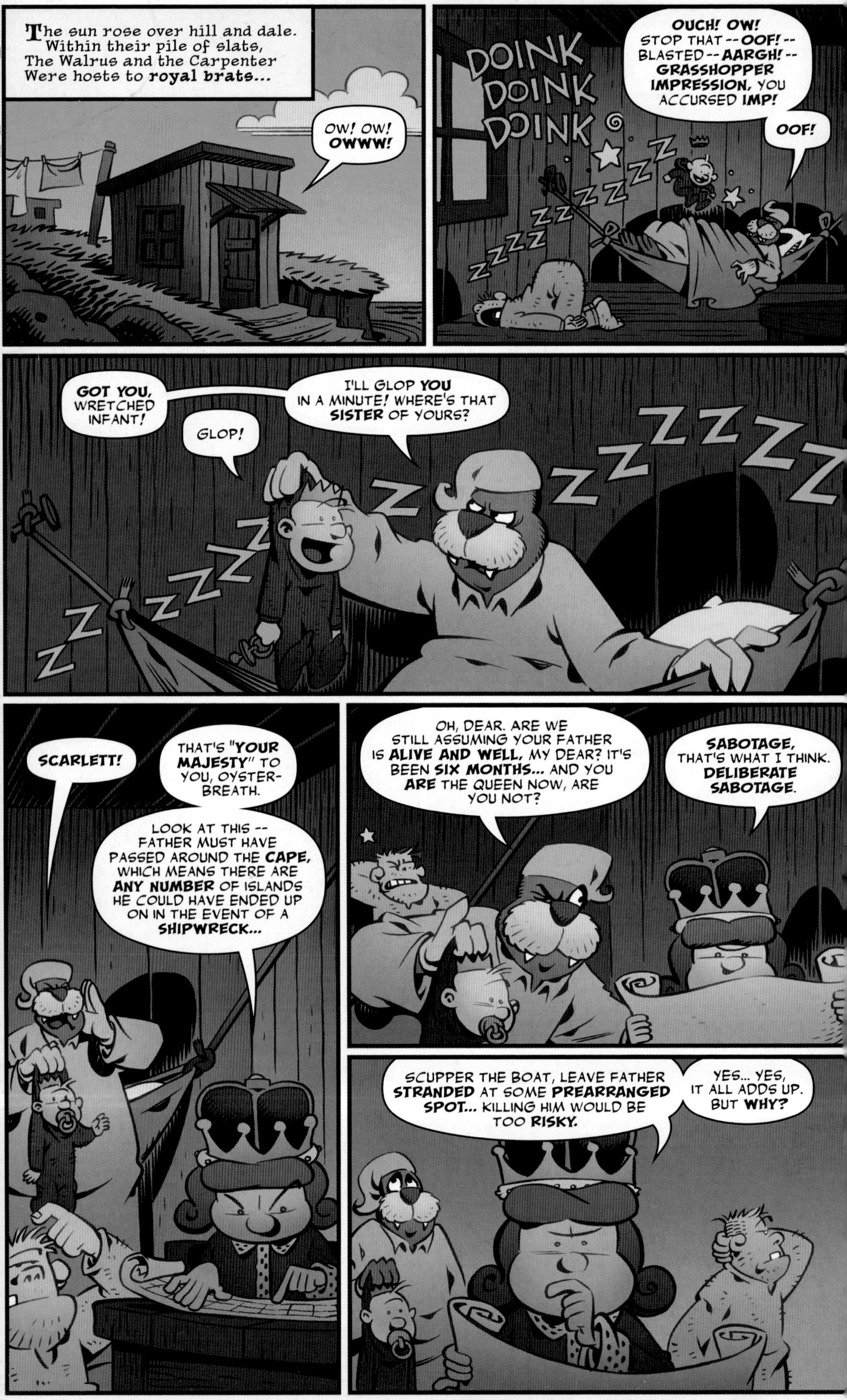
The sun rose over hill and dale. Within their pile of slats, The Walrus and the Carpenter Were hosts to **royal brats...**
OW! OW! **OWWW!**
DOINK DOINK DOINK
OUCH! OW! STOP THAT -- **OOF!** -- BLASTED -- **AARGH!** -- **GRASSHOPPER IMPRESSION,** YOU ACCURSED **IMP!**
OOF!
GOT YOU, WRETCHED INFANT!
GLOP!
I'LL GLOP **YOU** IN A MINUTE! WHERE'S THAT **SISTER** OF YOURS?
SCARLETT!
THAT'S "**YOUR MAJESTY**" TO YOU, OYSTER-BREATH.
LOOK AT THIS -- FATHER MUST HAVE PASSED AROUND THE **CAPE,** WHICH MEANS THERE ARE **ANY NUMBER** OF ISLANDS HE COULD HAVE ENDED UP ON IN THE EVENT OF A **SHIPWRECK...**
OH, DEAR. ARE WE STILL ASSUMING YOUR FATHER IS **ALIVE AND WELL,** MY DEAR? IT'S BEEN **SIX MONTHS...** AND YOU **ARE** THE QUEEN NOW, ARE YOU NOT?
SABOTAGE, THAT'S WHAT I THINK. **DELIBERATE SABOTAGE.**
SCUPPER THE BOAT, LEAVE FATHER **STRANDED** AT SOME **PREARRANGED SPOT...** KILLING HIM WOULD BE TOO **RISKY.**
YES... YES, IT ALL ADDS UP. BUT **WHY?**

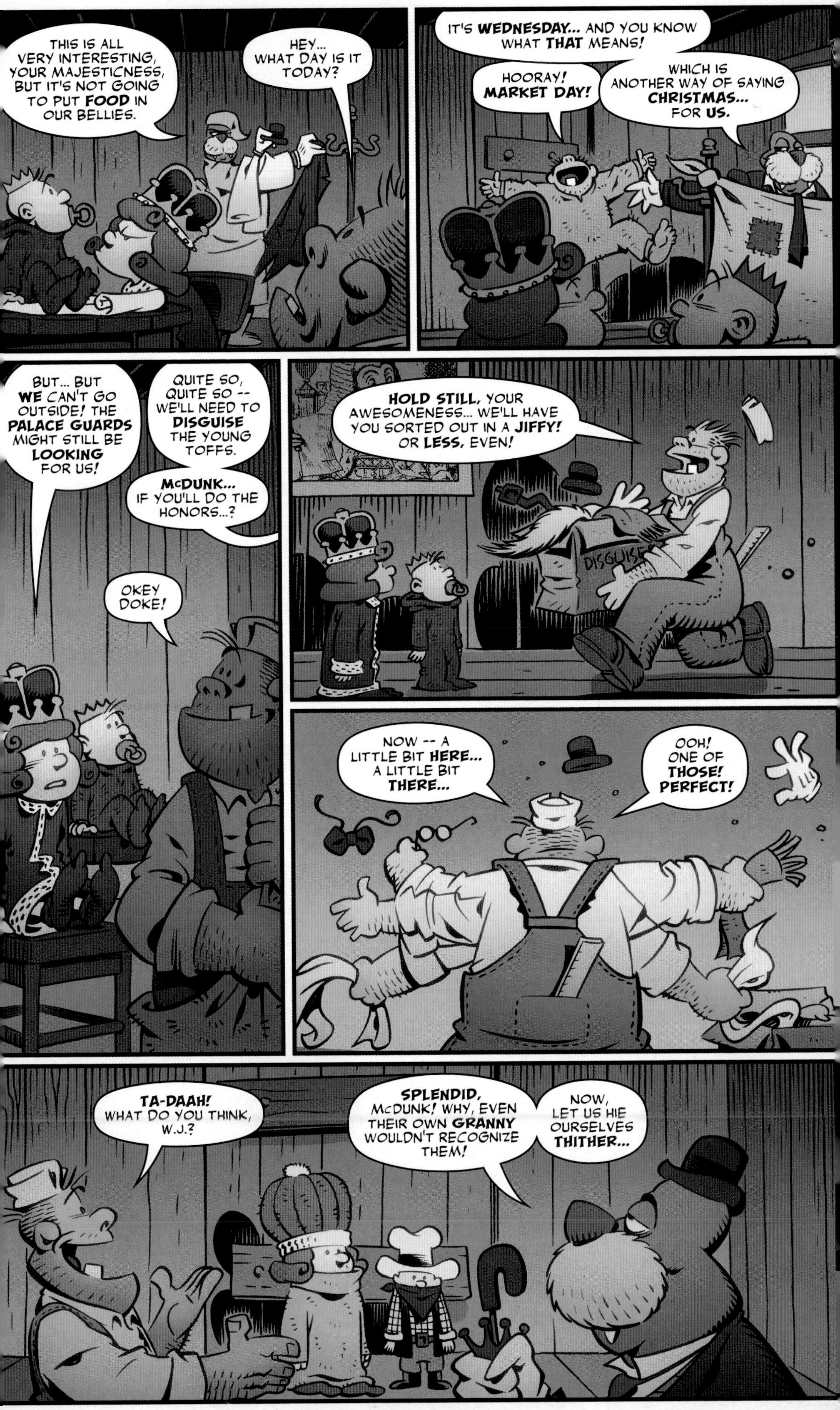
THIS IS ALL VERY INTERESTING, YOUR MAJESTICNESS, BUT IT'S NOT GOING TO PUT FOOD IN OUR BELLIES.
HEY... WHAT DAY IS IT TODAY?
IT'S WEDNESDAY... AND YOU KNOW WHAT THAT MEANS!
HOORAY! MARKET DAY!
WHICH IS ANOTHER WAY OF SAYING CHRISTMAS... FOR US.
BUT... BUT WE CAN'T GO OUTSIDE! THE PALACE GUARDS MIGHT STILL BE LOOKING FOR US!
QUITE SO, QUITE SO -- WE'LL NEED TO DISGUISE THE YOUNG TOFFS.
McDUNK... IF YOU'LL DO THE HONORS...?
OKEY DOKE!
HOLD STILL, YOUR AWESOMENESS... WE'LL HAVE YOU SORTED OUT IN A JIFFY! OR LESS, EVEN!
DISGUISE
NOW -- A LITTLE BIT HERE... A LITTLE BIT THERE...
OOH! ONE OF THOSE! PERFECT!
TA-DAAH! WHAT DO YOU THINK, W.J.?
SPLENDID, McDUNK! WHY, EVEN THEIR OWN GRANNY WOULDN'T RECOGNIZE THEM!
NOW, LET US HIE OURSELVES THITHER...

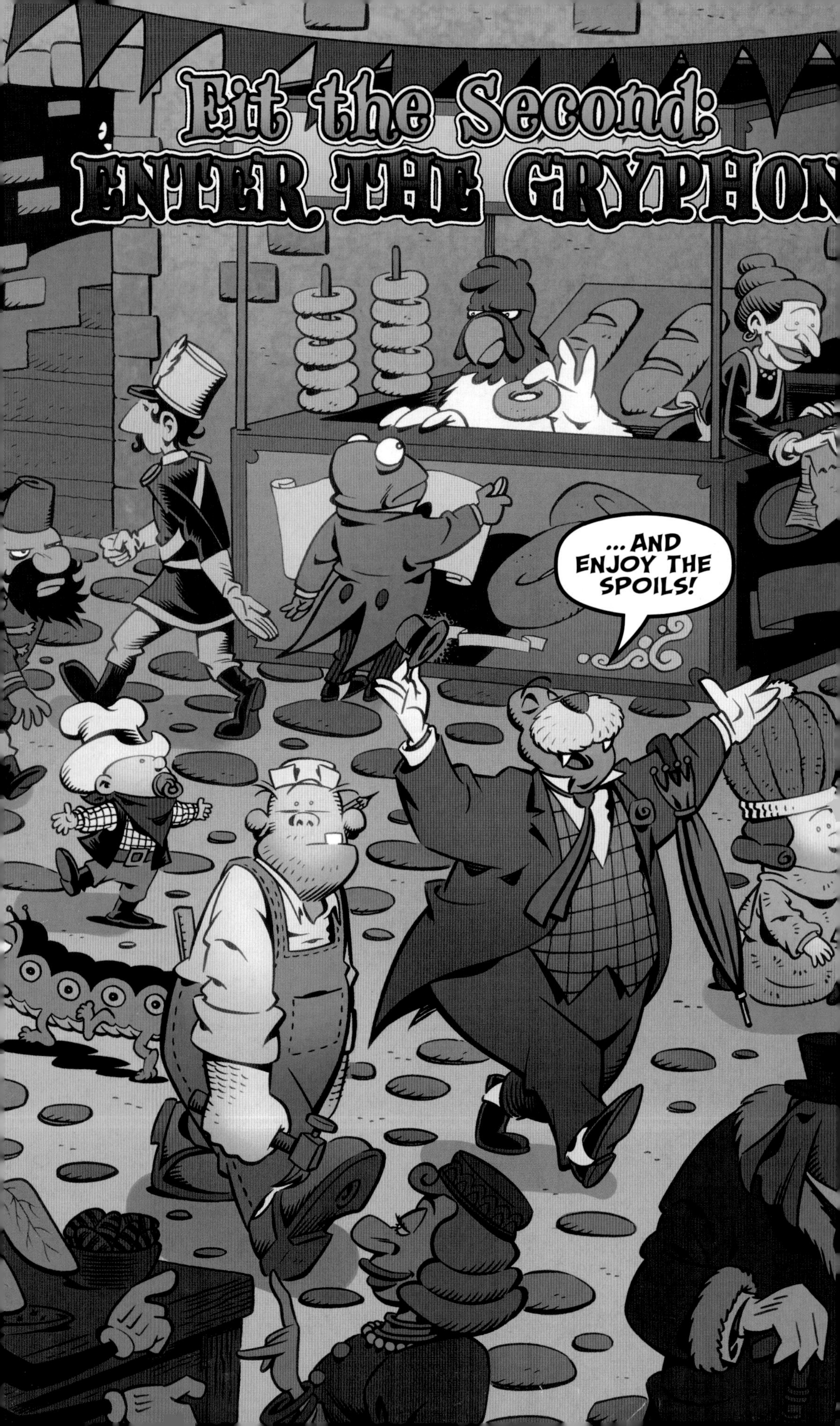
Fit the Second:
ENTER THE GRYPHON
...AND ENJOY THE SPOILS!

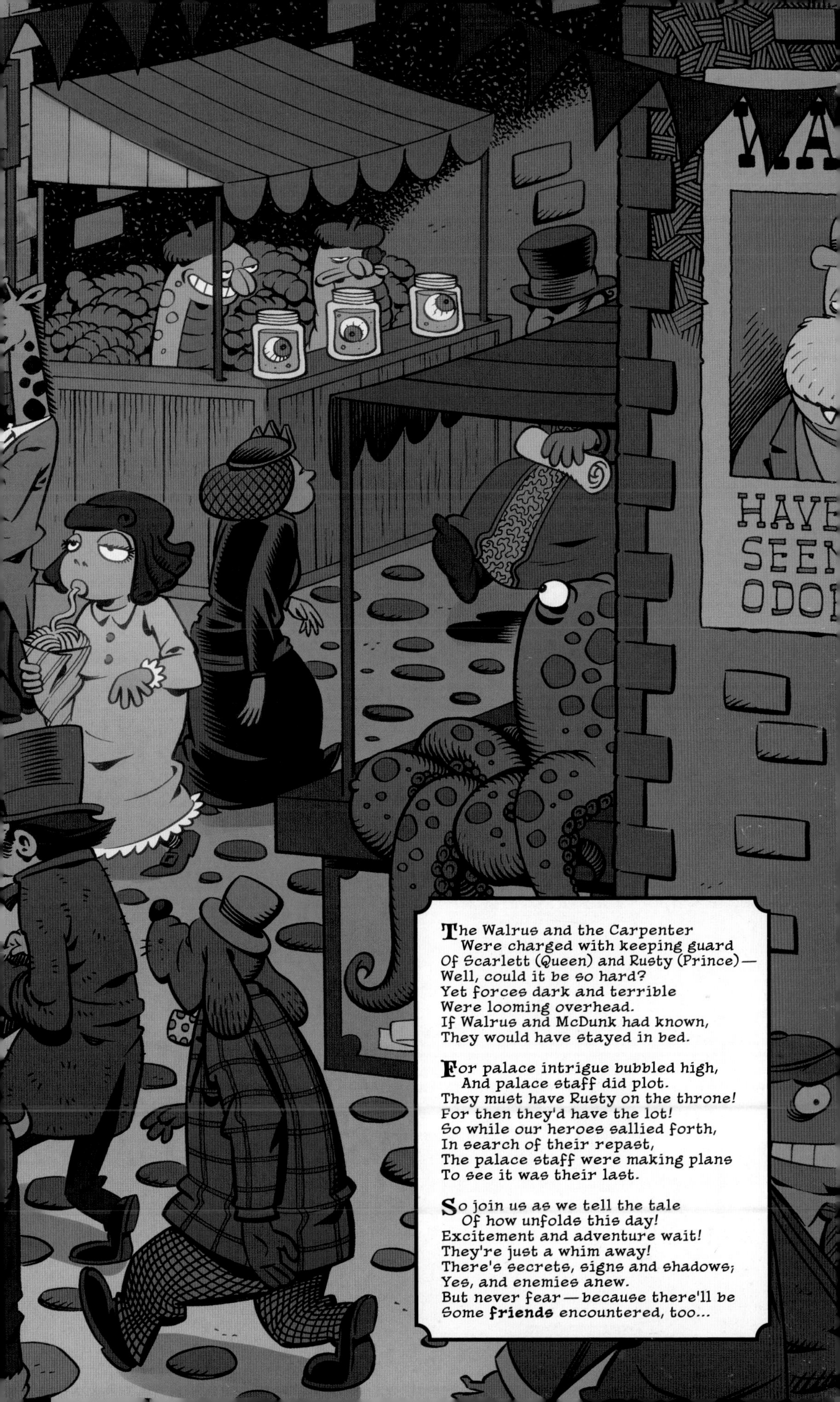
The Walrus and the Carpenter
Were charged with keeping guard
Of Scarlett (Queen) and Rusty (Prince)—
Well, could it be so hard?
Yet forces dark and terrible
Were looming overhead.
If Walrus and McDunk had known,
They would have stayed in bed.

For palace intrigue bubbled high,
And palace staff did plot.
They must have Rusty on the throne!
For then they'd have the lot!
So while our heroes sallied forth,
In search of their repast,
The palace staff were making plans
To see it was their last.

So join us as we tell the tale
Of how unfolds this day!
Excitement and adventure wait!
They're just a whim away!
There's secrets, signs and shadows;
Yes, and enemies anew.
But never fear—because there'll be
Some **friends** encountered, too...

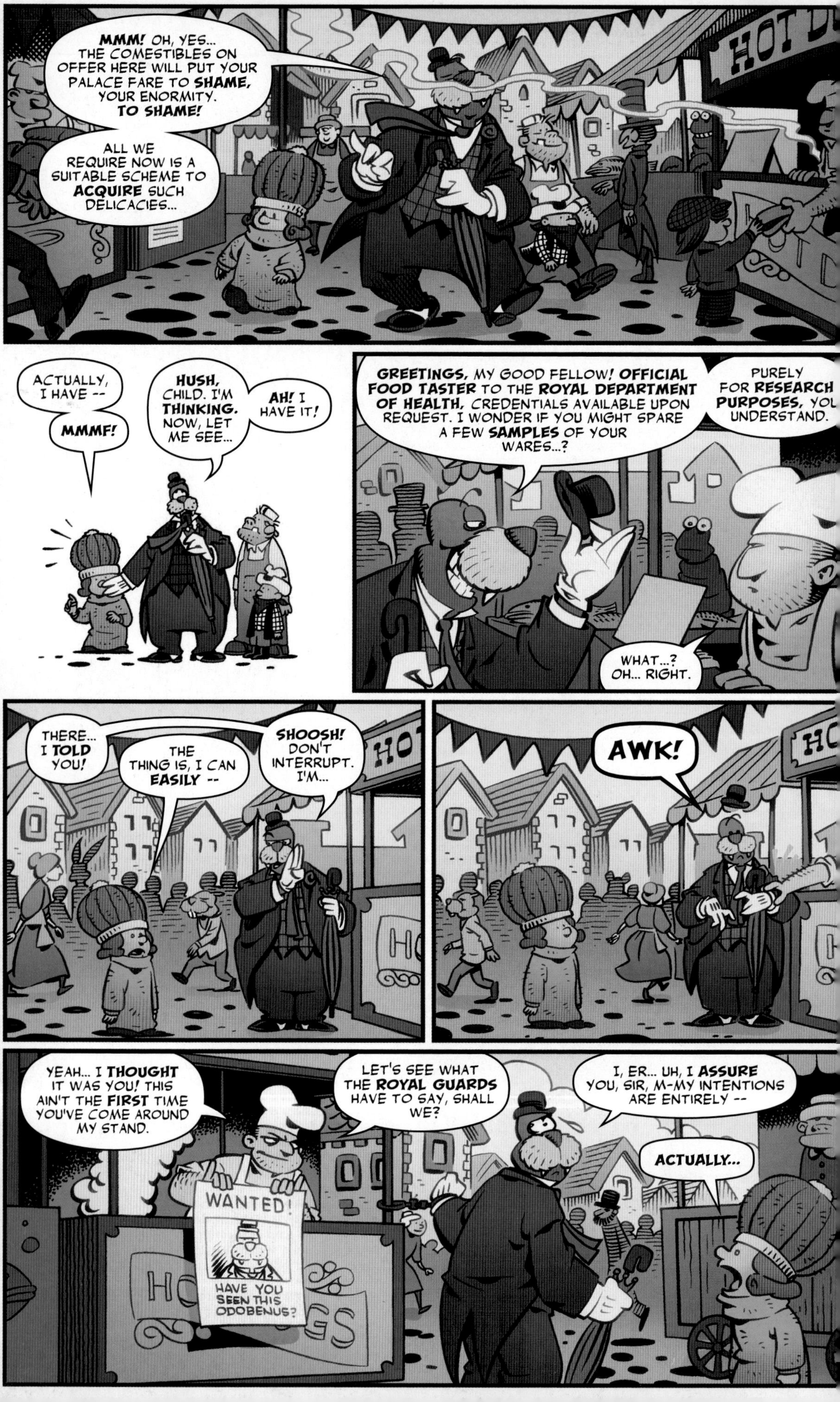

MMM! OH, YES... THE COMESTIBLES ON OFFER HERE WILL PUT YOUR PALACE FARE TO SHAME, YOUR ENORMITY. TO SHAME!
ALL WE REQUIRE NOW IS A SUITABLE SCHEME TO ACQUIRE SUCH DELICACIES...
ACTUALLY, I HAVE --
MMMF!
HUSH, CHILD. I'M THINKING. NOW, LET ME SEE...
AH! I HAVE IT!
GREETINGS, MY GOOD FELLOW! OFFICIAL FOOD TASTER TO THE ROYAL DEPARTMENT OF HEALTH. CREDENTIALS AVAILABLE UPON REQUEST. I WONDER IF YOU MIGHT SPARE A FEW SAMPLES OF YOUR WARES...?
PURELY FOR RESEARCH PURPOSES, YOU UNDERSTAND.
WHAT...? OH... RIGHT.
THERE... I TOLD YOU!
THE THING IS, I CAN EASILY --
SHOOSH! DON'T INTERRUPT. I'M...
AWK!
YEAH... I THOUGHT IT WAS YOU! THIS AIN'T THE FIRST TIME YOU'VE COME AROUND MY STAND.
WANTED!
HAVE YOU SEEN THIS ODOBENUS?
LET'S SEE WHAT THE ROYAL GUARDS HAVE TO SAY, SHALL WE?
I, ER... UH, I ASSURE YOU, SIR, M-MY INTENTIONS ARE ENTIRELY --
ACTUALLY...

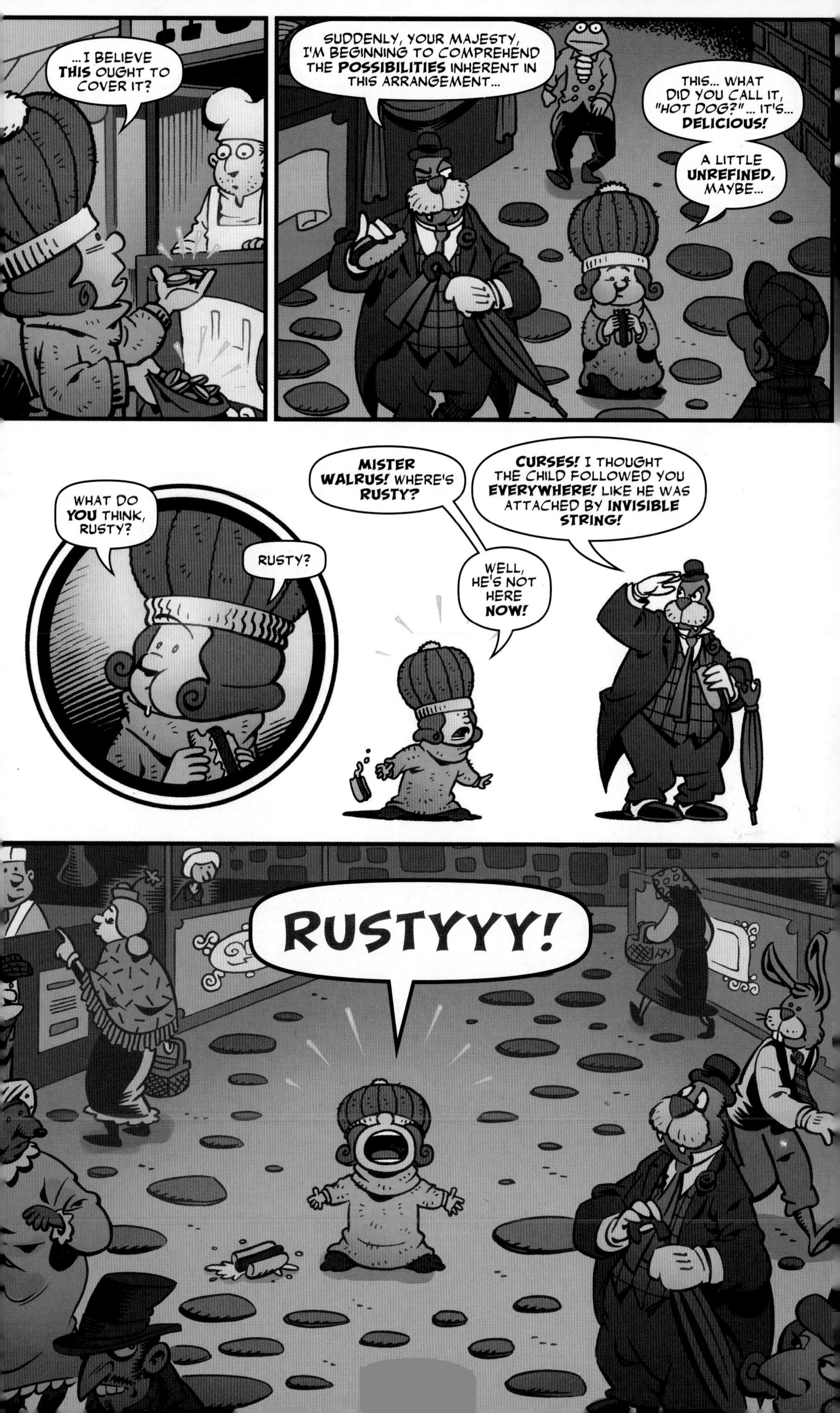
...I BELIEVE THIS OUGHT TO COVER IT?
SUDDENLY, YOUR MAJESTY, I'M BEGINNING TO COMPREHEND THE POSSIBILITIES INHERENT IN THIS ARRANGEMENT...
THIS... WHAT DID YOU CALL IT, "HOT DOG?"... IT'S... DELICIOUS!
A LITTLE UNREFINED, MAYBE...
WHAT DO YOU THINK, RUSTY?
RUSTY?
MISTER WALRUS! WHERE'S RUSTY?
WELL, HE'S NOT HERE NOW!
CURSES! I THOUGHT THE CHILD FOLLOWED YOU EVERYWHERE! LIKE HE WAS ATTACHED BY INVISIBLE STRING!
RUSTYYY!

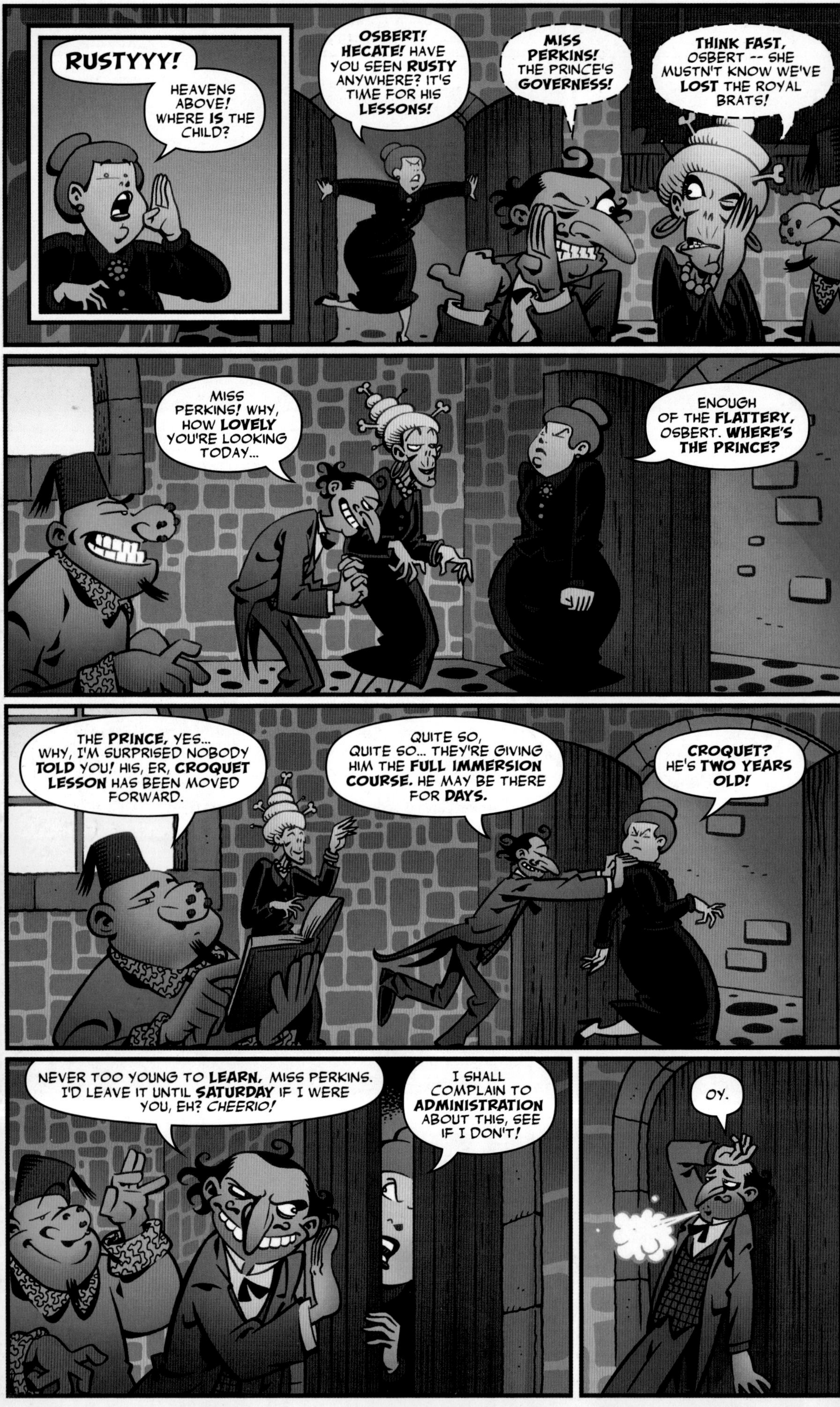
RUSTYYY!
HEAVENS ABOVE! WHERE IS THE CHILD?
OSBERT! HECATE! HAVE YOU SEEN RUSTY ANYWHERE? IT'S TIME FOR HIS LESSONS!
MISS PERKINS! THE PRINCE'S GOVERNESS!
THINK FAST, OSBERT -- SHE MUSTN'T KNOW WE'VE LOST THE ROYAL BRATS!
MISS PERKINS! WHY, HOW LOVELY YOU'RE LOOKING TODAY...
ENOUGH OF THE FLATTERY, OSBERT. WHERE'S THE PRINCE?
THE PRINCE, YES... WHY, I'M SURPRISED NOBODY TOLD YOU! HIS, ER, CROQUET LESSON HAS BEEN MOVED FORWARD.
QUITE SO, QUITE SO... THEY'RE GIVING HIM THE FULL IMMERSION COURSE. HE MAY BE THERE FOR DAYS.
CROQUET? HE'S TWO YEARS OLD!
NEVER TOO YOUNG TO LEARN, MISS PERKINS. I'D LEAVE IT UNTIL SATURDAY IF I WERE YOU, EH? CHEERIO!
I SHALL COMPLAIN TO ADMINISTRATION ABOUT THIS, SEE IF I DON'T!
OY.

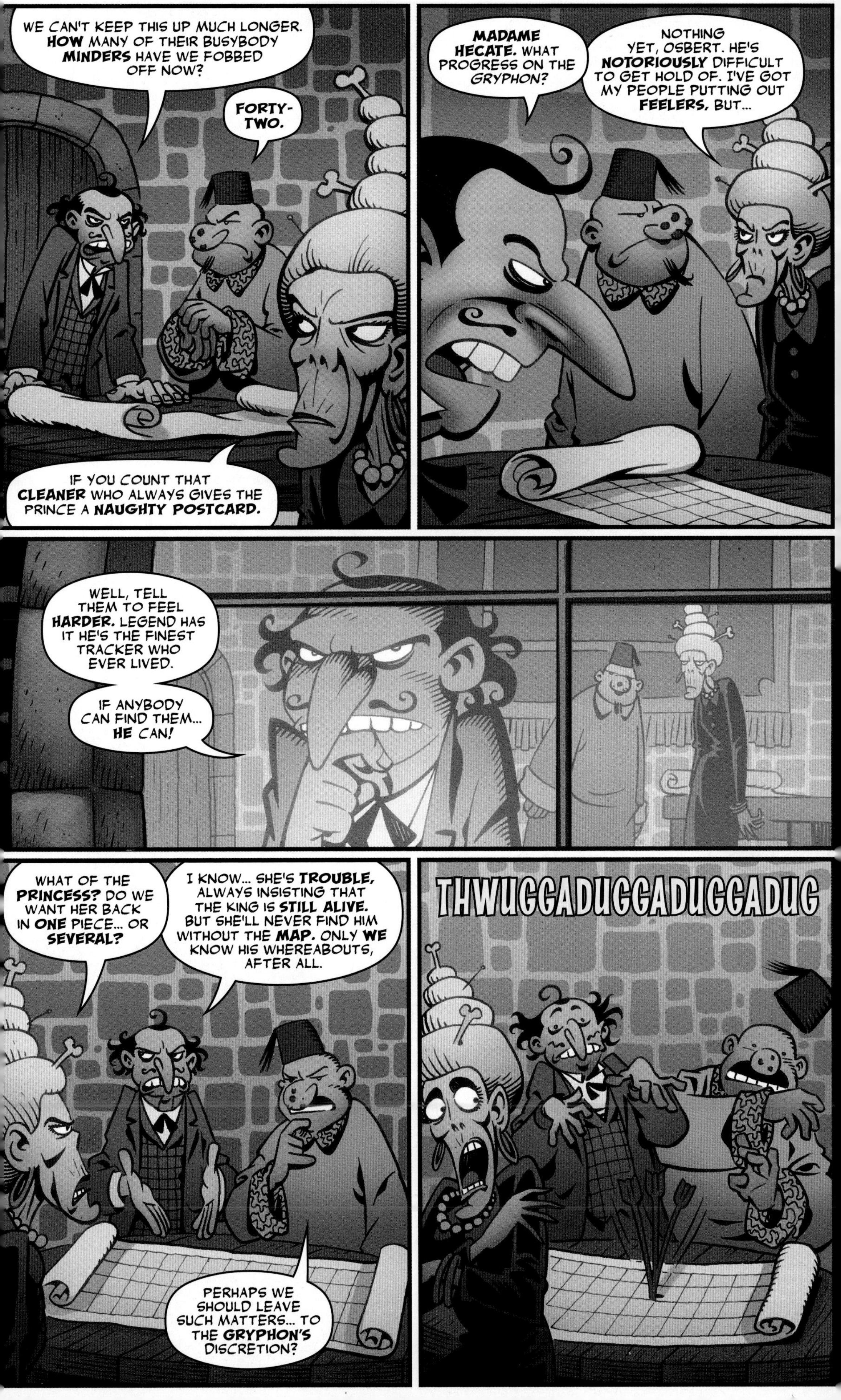
WE CAN'T KEEP THIS UP MUCH LONGER. **HOW** MANY OF THEIR BUSYBODY **MINDERS** HAVE WE FOBBED OFF NOW?
FORTY-TWO.
IF YOU COUNT THAT **CLEANER** WHO ALWAYS GIVES THE PRINCE A **NAUGHTY POSTCARD.**
MADAME HECATE. WHAT PROGRESS ON THE GRYPHON?
NOTHING YET, OSBERT. HE'S **NOTORIOUSLY** DIFFICULT TO GET HOLD OF. I'VE GOT MY PEOPLE PUTTING OUT **FEELERS,** BUT...
WELL, TELL THEM TO FEEL **HARDER.** LEGEND HAS IT HE'S THE FINEST TRACKER WHO EVER LIVED.
IF ANYBODY CAN FIND THEM... **HE** CAN!
WHAT OF THE **PRINCESS?** DO WE WANT HER BACK IN **ONE** PIECE... OR **SEVERAL?**
I KNOW... SHE'S **TROUBLE,** ALWAYS INSISTING THAT THE KING IS **STILL ALIVE.** BUT SHE'LL NEVER FIND HIM WITHOUT THE **MAP.** ONLY **WE** KNOW HIS WHEREABOUTS, AFTER ALL.
PERHAPS WE SHOULD LEAVE SUCH MATTERS... TO THE **GRYPHON'S** DISCRETION?
THWUGGADUGGADUGGADUG

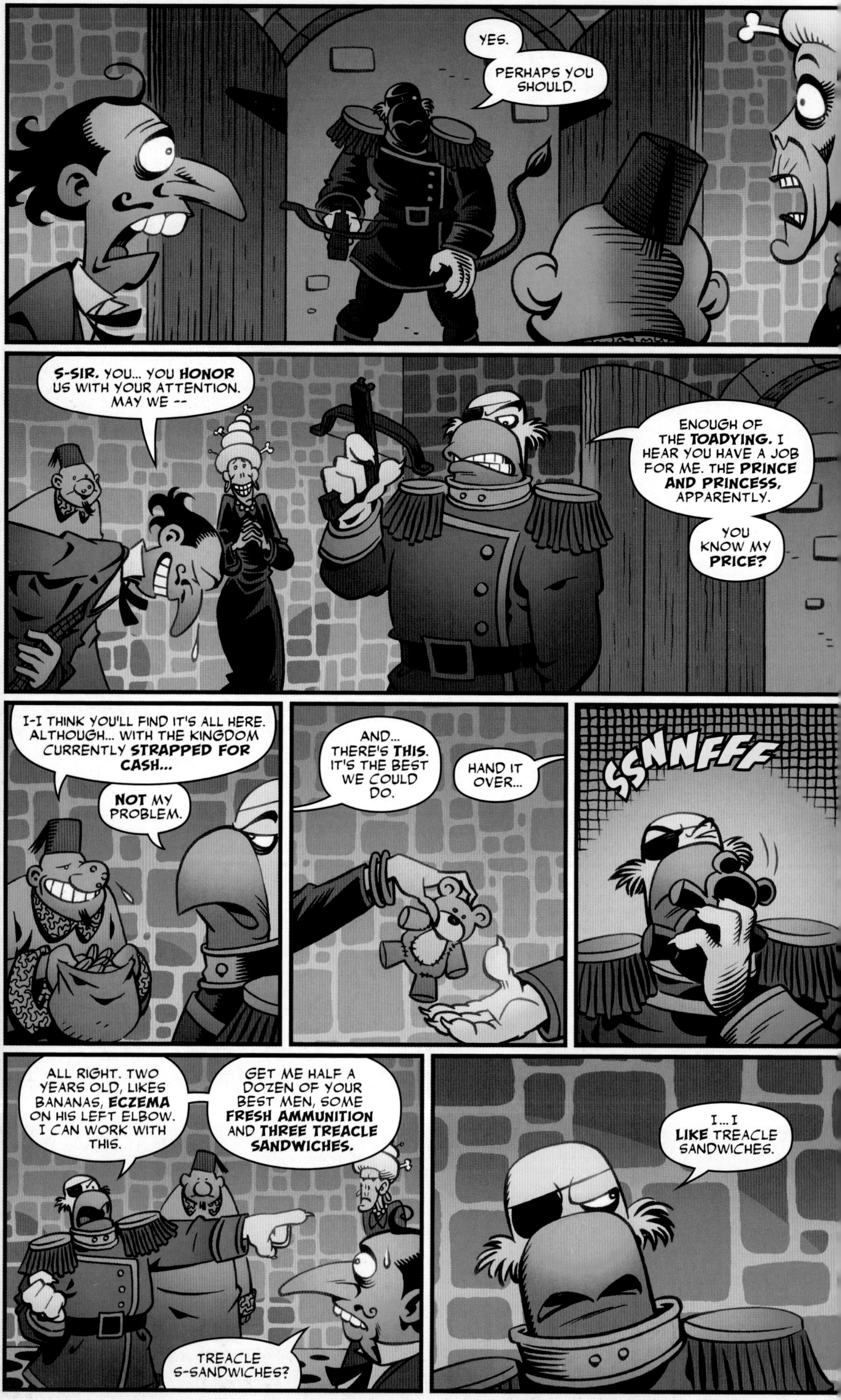
YES.
PERHAPS YOU SHOULD.
S-SIR. YOU... YOU HONOR US WITH YOUR ATTENTION. MAY WE --
ENOUGH OF THE TOADYING. I HEAR YOU HAVE A JOB FOR ME. THE PRINCE AND PRINCESS, APPARENTLY.
YOU KNOW MY PRICE?
I-I THINK YOU'LL FIND IT'S ALL HERE. ALTHOUGH... WITH THE KINGDOM CURRENTLY STRAPPED FOR CASH...
NOT MY PROBLEM.
AND... THERE'S THIS. IT'S THE BEST WE COULD DO.
HAND IT OVER...
SSNNFFF
ALL RIGHT. TWO YEARS OLD, LIKES BANANAS, ECZEMA ON HIS LEFT ELBOW. I CAN WORK WITH THIS.
GET ME HALF A DOZEN OF YOUR BEST MEN, SOME FRESH AMMUNITION AND THREE TREACLE SANDWICHES.
TREACLE S-SANDWICHES?
I... I LIKE TREACLE SANDWICHES.

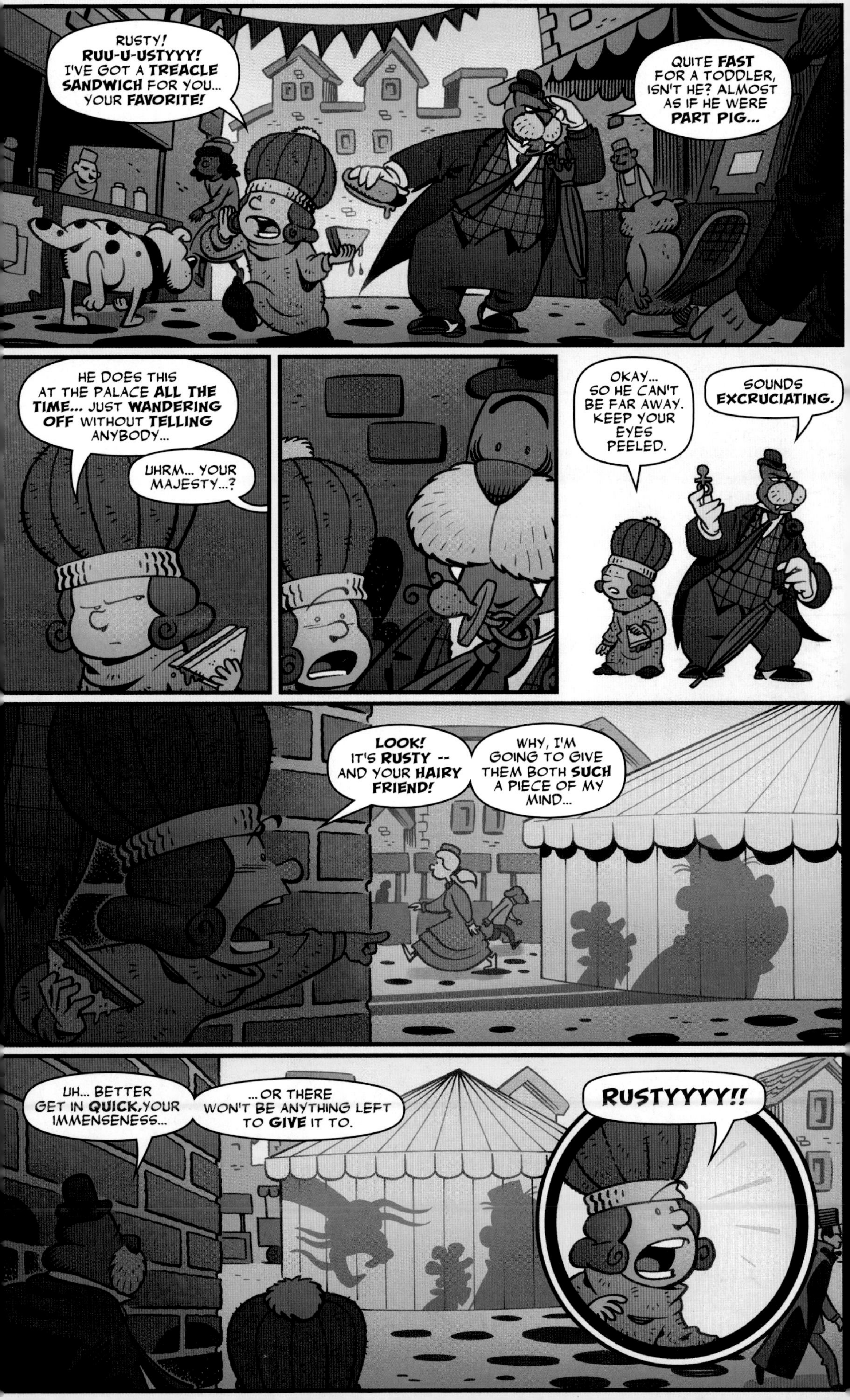
RUSTY! RUU-U-USTYYY! I'VE GOT A TREACLE SANDWICH FOR YOU... YOUR FAVORITE!
QUITE FAST FOR A TODDLER, ISN'T HE? ALMOST AS IF HE WERE PART PIG...
HE DOES THIS AT THE PALACE ALL THE TIME... JUST WANDERING OFF WITHOUT TELLING ANYBODY...
UHRM... YOUR MAJESTY...?
OKAY... SO HE CAN'T BE FAR AWAY. KEEP YOUR EYES PEELED.
SOUNDS EXCRUCIATING.
LOOK! IT'S RUSTY -- AND YOUR HAIRY FRIEND!
WHY, I'M GOING TO GIVE THEM BOTH SUCH A PIECE OF MY MIND...
UH... BETTER GET IN QUICK, YOUR IMMENSENESS...
...OR THERE WON'T BE ANYTHING LEFT TO GIVE IT TO.
RUSTYYYY!!

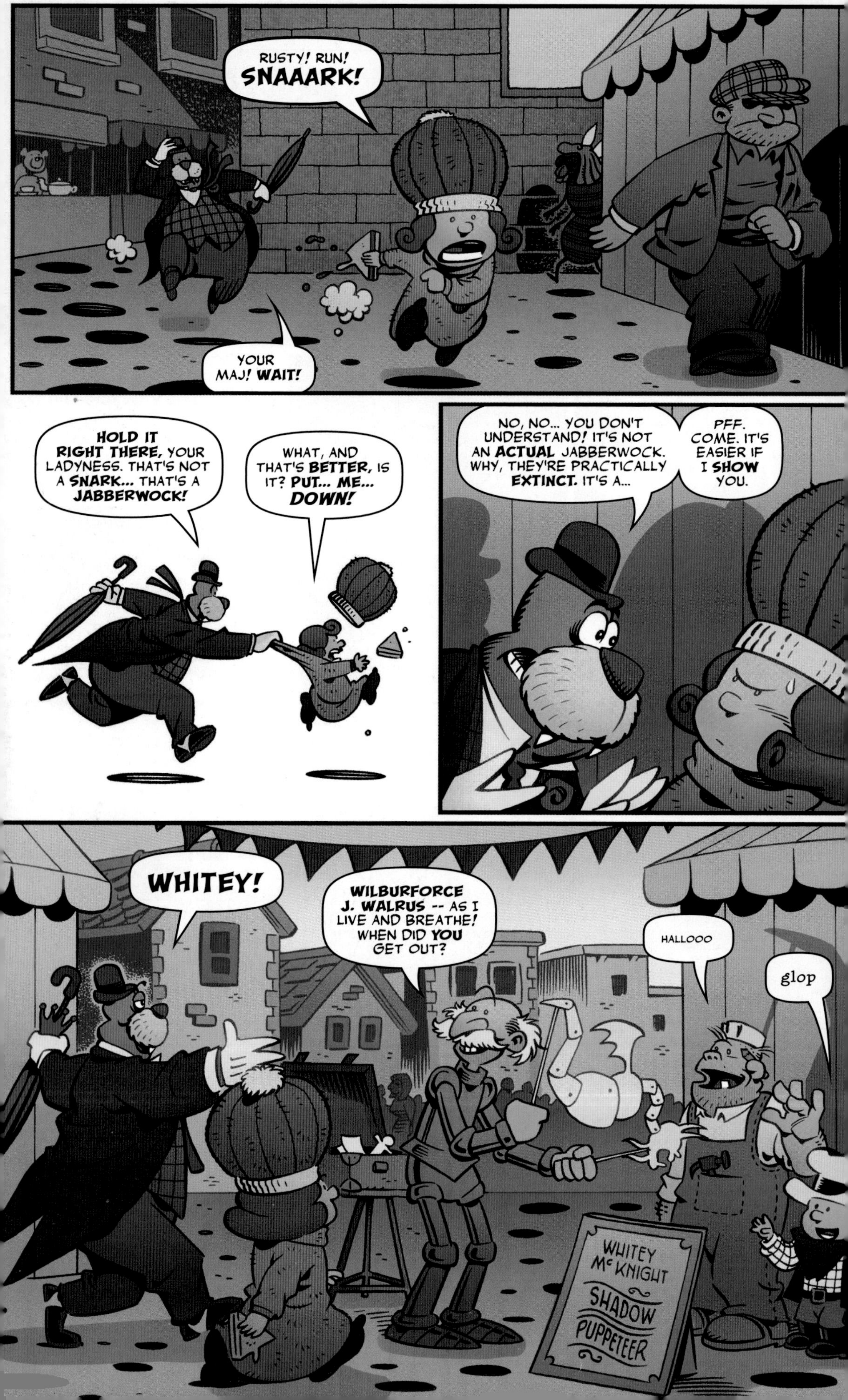
RUSTY! RUN! SNAAARK!
YOUR MAJ! WAIT!
HOLD IT RIGHT THERE, YOUR LADYNESS. THAT'S NOT A SNARK... THAT'S A JABBERWOCK!
WHAT, AND THAT'S BETTER, IS IT? PUT... ME... DOWN!
NO, NO... YOU DON'T UNDERSTAND! IT'S NOT AN ACTUAL JABBERWOCK. WHY, THEY'RE PRACTICALLY EXTINCT. IT'S A...
PFF. COME. IT'S EASIER IF I SHOW YOU.
WHITEY!
WILBURFORCE J. WALRUS -- AS I LIVE AND BREATHE! WHEN DID YOU GET OUT?
HALLOOO
glop
WHITEY McKNIGHT
SHADOW PUPPETEER

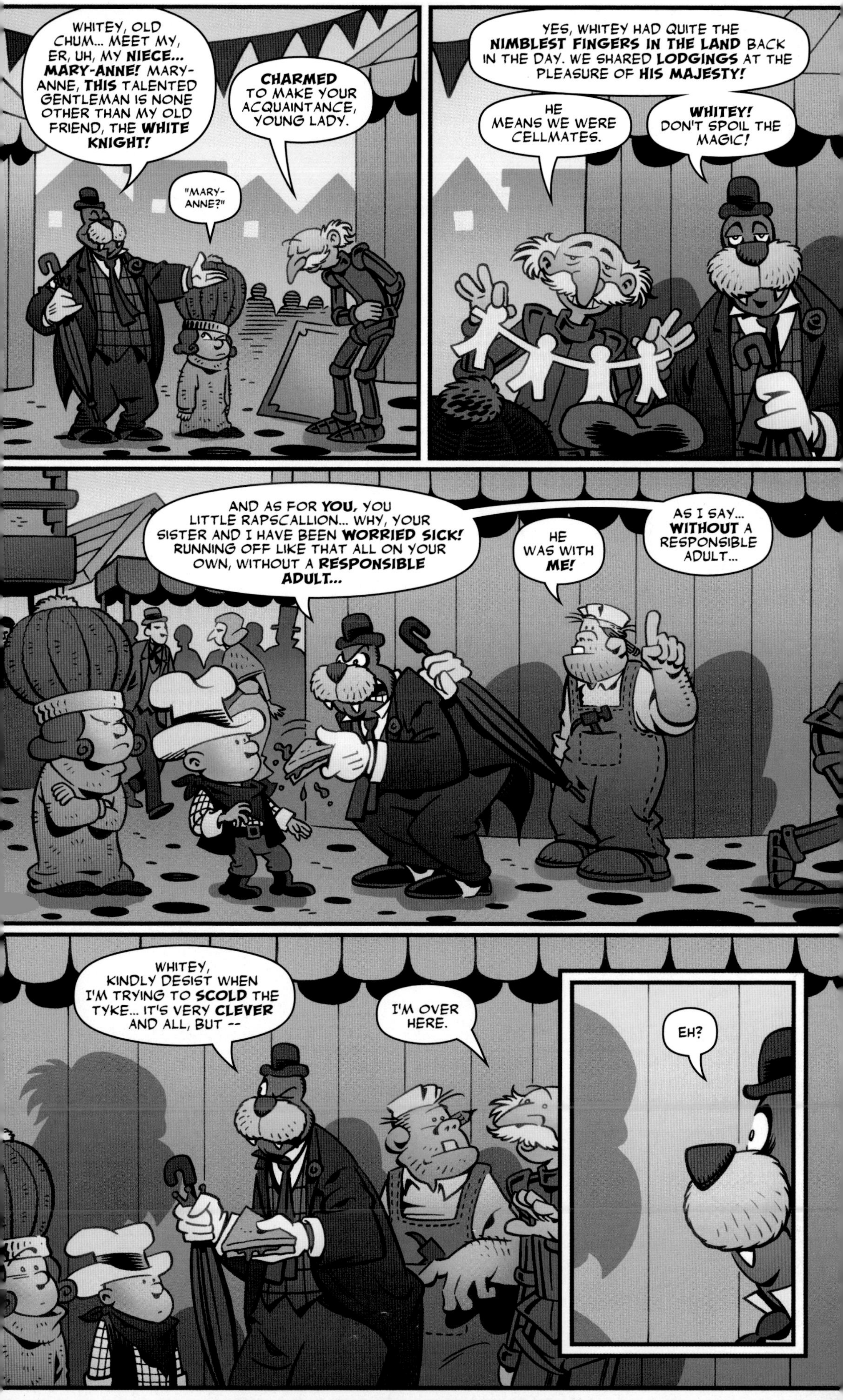
WHITEY, OLD CHUM... MEET MY, ER, UH, MY NIECE... MARY-ANNE! MARY-ANNE, THIS TALENTED GENTLEMAN IS NONE OTHER THAN MY OLD FRIEND, THE WHITE KNIGHT!
CHARMED TO MAKE YOUR ACQUAINTANCE, YOUNG LADY.
"MARY-ANNE?"
YES, WHITEY HAD QUITE THE NIMBLEST FINGERS IN THE LAND BACK IN THE DAY. WE SHARED LODGINGS AT THE PLEASURE OF HIS MAJESTY!
HE MEANS WE WERE CELLMATES.
WHITEY! DON'T SPOIL THE MAGIC!
AND AS FOR YOU, YOU LITTLE RAPSCALLION... WHY, YOUR SISTER AND I HAVE BEEN WORRIED SICK! RUNNING OFF LIKE THAT ALL ON YOUR OWN, WITHOUT A RESPONSIBLE ADULT...
HE WAS WITH ME!
AS I SAY... WITHOUT A RESPONSIBLE ADULT...
WHITEY, KINDLY DESIST WHEN I'M TRYING TO SCOLD THE TYKE... IT'S VERY CLEVER AND ALL, BUT --
I'M OVER HERE.
EH?

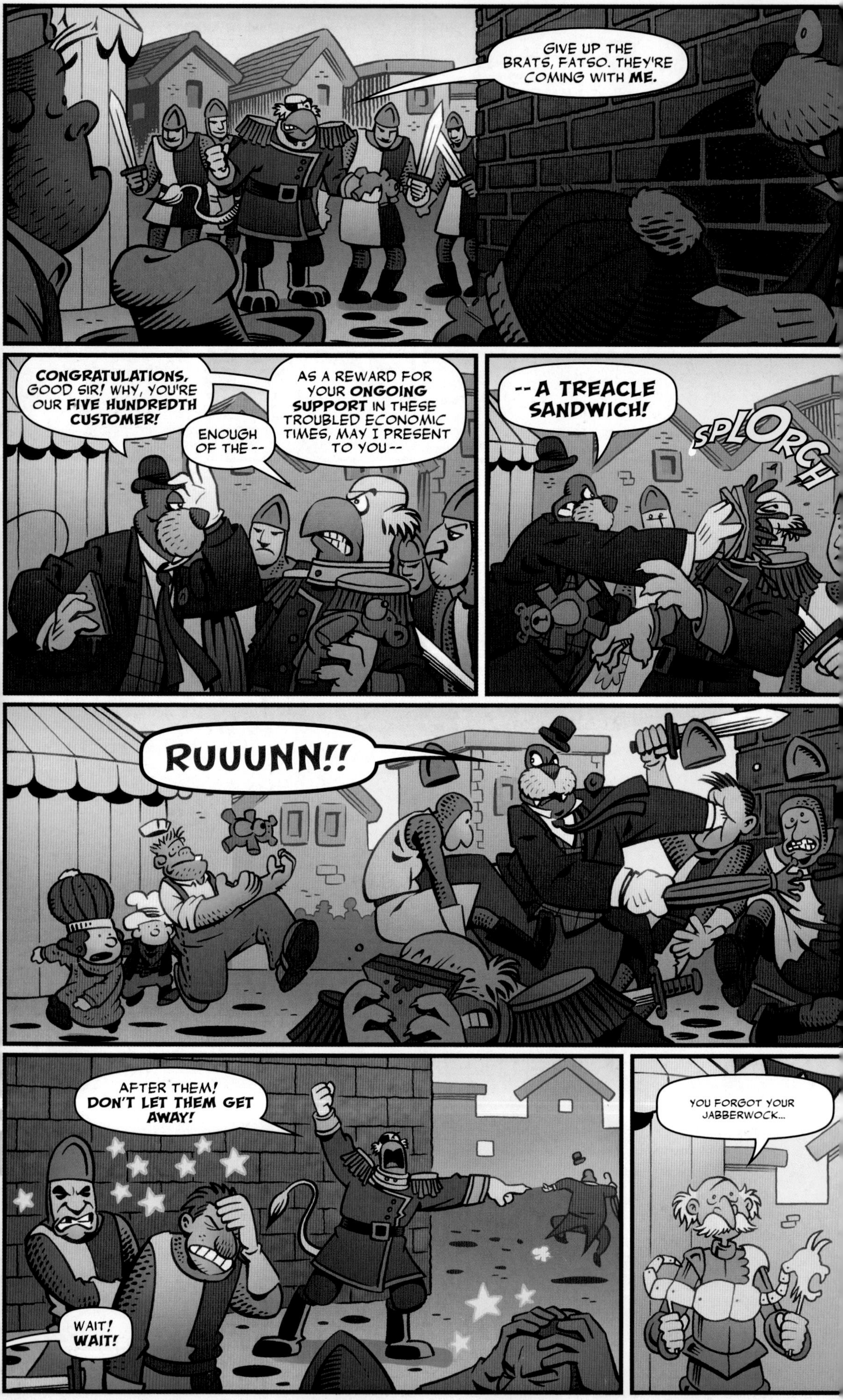
GIVE UP THE BRATS, FATSO. THEY'RE COMING WITH ME.
CONGRATULATIONS, GOOD SIR! WHY, YOU'RE OUR FIVE HUNDREDTH CUSTOMER!
AS A REWARD FOR YOUR ONGOING SUPPORT IN THESE TROUBLED ECONOMIC TIMES, MAY I PRESENT TO YOU--
ENOUGH OF THE--
--A TREACLE SANDWICH!
SPLORCH
RUUUNN!!
AFTER THEM! DON'T LET THEM GET AWAY!
WAIT! WAIT!
YOU FORGOT YOUR JABBERWOCK...

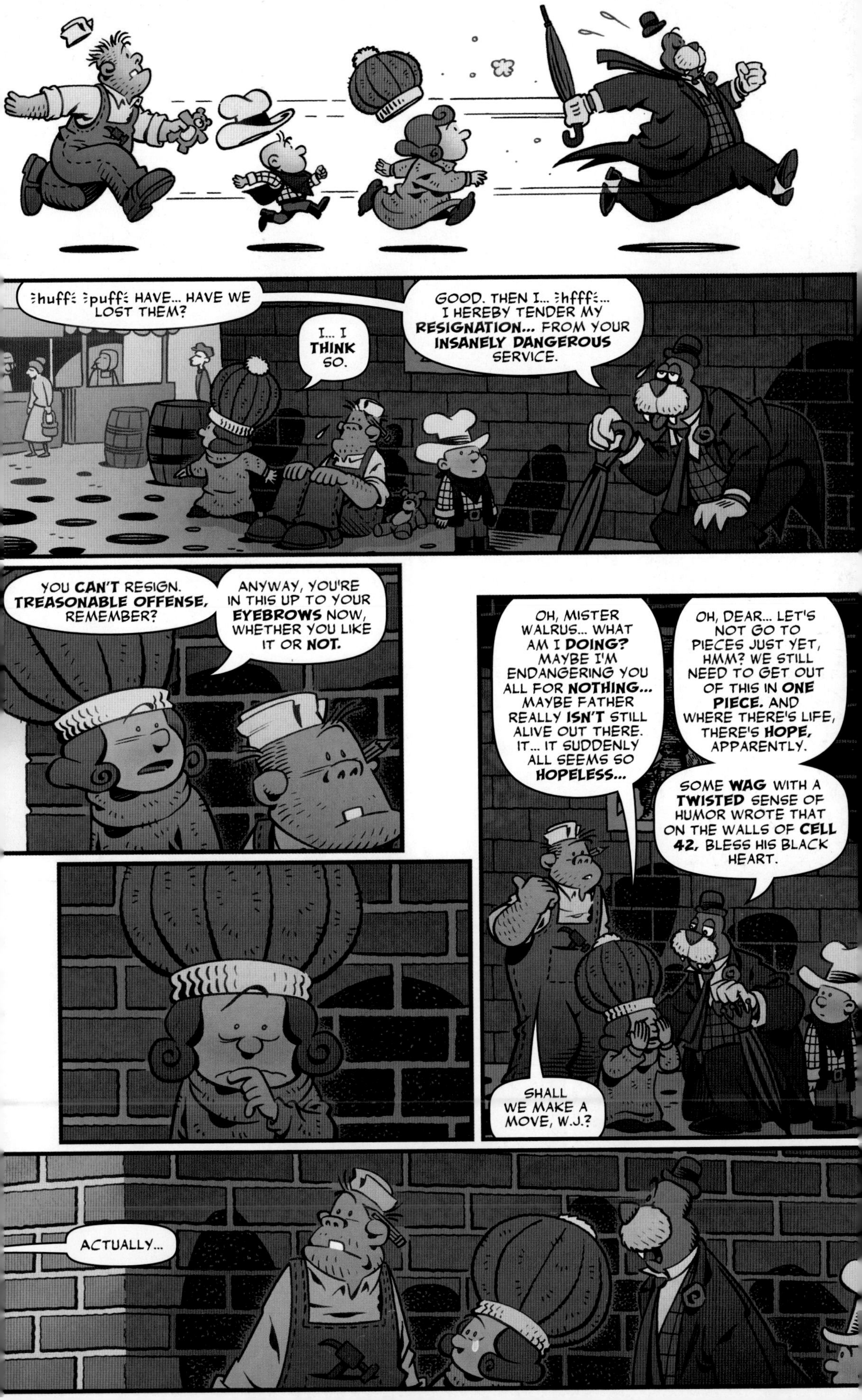

≈huff≈ ≈puff≈ HAVE... HAVE WE LOST THEM?
I... I THINK SO.
GOOD. THEN I... ≈hfff≈... I HEREBY TENDER MY RESIGNATION... FROM YOUR INSANELY DANGEROUS SERVICE.
YOU CAN'T RESIGN. TREASONABLE OFFENSE, REMEMBER?
ANYWAY, YOU'RE IN THIS UP TO YOUR EYEBROWS NOW, WHETHER YOU LIKE IT OR NOT.
OH, MISTER WALRUS... WHAT AM I DOING? MAYBE I'M ENDANGERING YOU ALL FOR NOTHING... MAYBE FATHER REALLY ISN'T STILL ALIVE OUT THERE. IT... IT SUDDENLY ALL SEEMS SO HOPELESS...
OH, DEAR... LET'S NOT GO TO PIECES JUST YET, HMM? WE STILL NEED TO GET OUT OF THIS IN ONE PIECE. AND WHERE THERE'S LIFE, THERE'S HOPE, APPARENTLY.
SOME WAG WITH A TWISTED SENSE OF HUMOR WROTE THAT ON THE WALLS OF CELL 42, BLESS HIS BLACK HEART.
SHALL WE MAKE A MOVE, W.J.?
ACTUALLY...

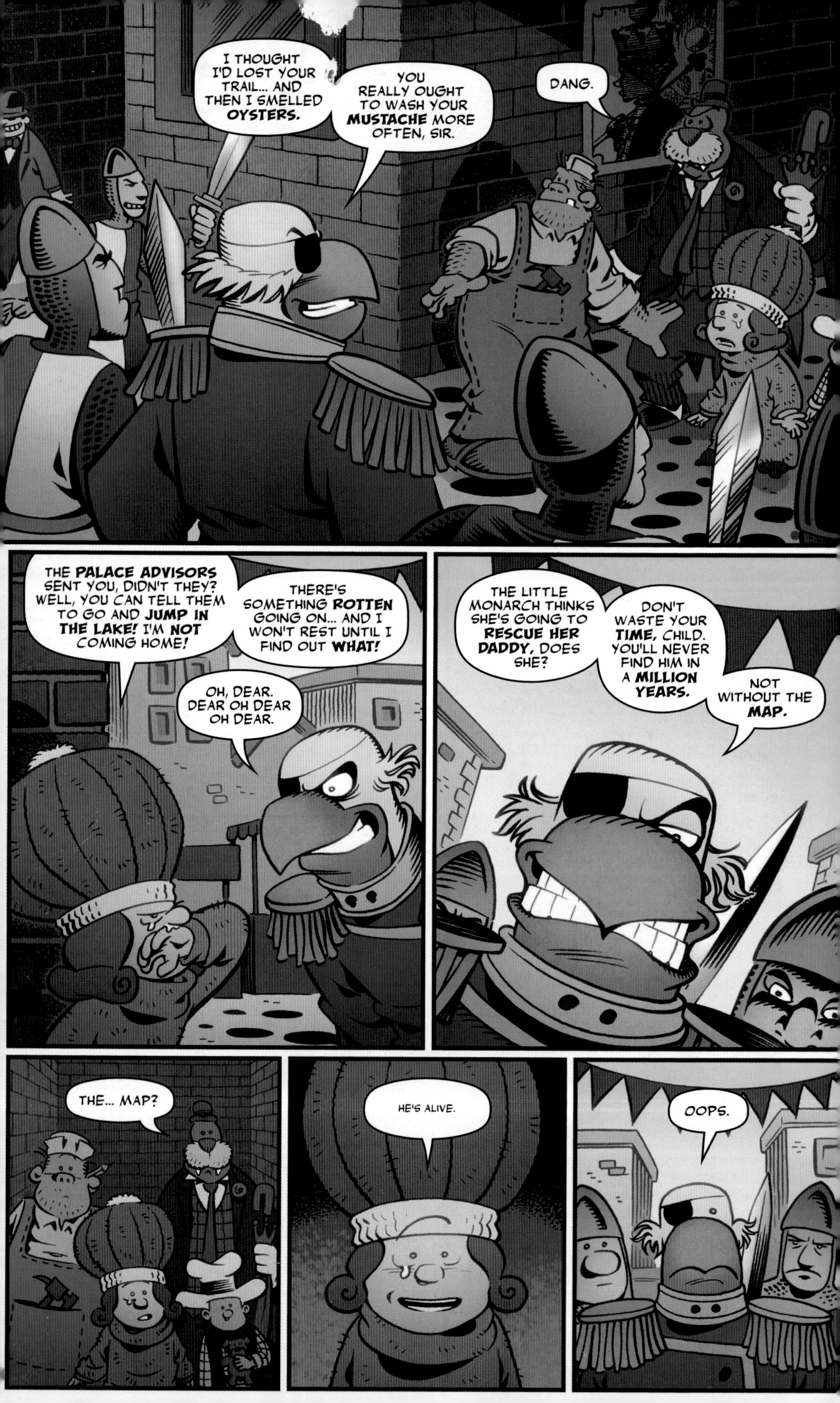
I THOUGHT I'D LOST YOUR TRAIL... AND THEN I SMELLED **OYSTERS.**
YOU REALLY OUGHT TO WASH YOUR **MUSTACHE** MORE OFTEN, SIR.
DANG.
THE **PALACE ADVISORS** SENT YOU, DIDN'T THEY? WELL, YOU CAN TELL THEM TO GO AND **JUMP IN THE LAKE!** I'M **NOT** COMING HOME!
THERE'S SOMETHING **ROTTEN** GOING ON... AND I WON'T REST UNTIL I FIND OUT **WHAT!**
OH, DEAR. DEAR OH DEAR OH DEAR.
THE LITTLE MONARCH THINKS SHE'S GOING TO **RESCUE HER DADDY,** DOES SHE?
DON'T WASTE YOUR **TIME,** CHILD. YOU'LL NEVER FIND HIM IN A **MILLION YEARS.**
NOT WITHOUT THE **MAP.**
THE... MAP?
HE'S ALIVE.
OOPS.

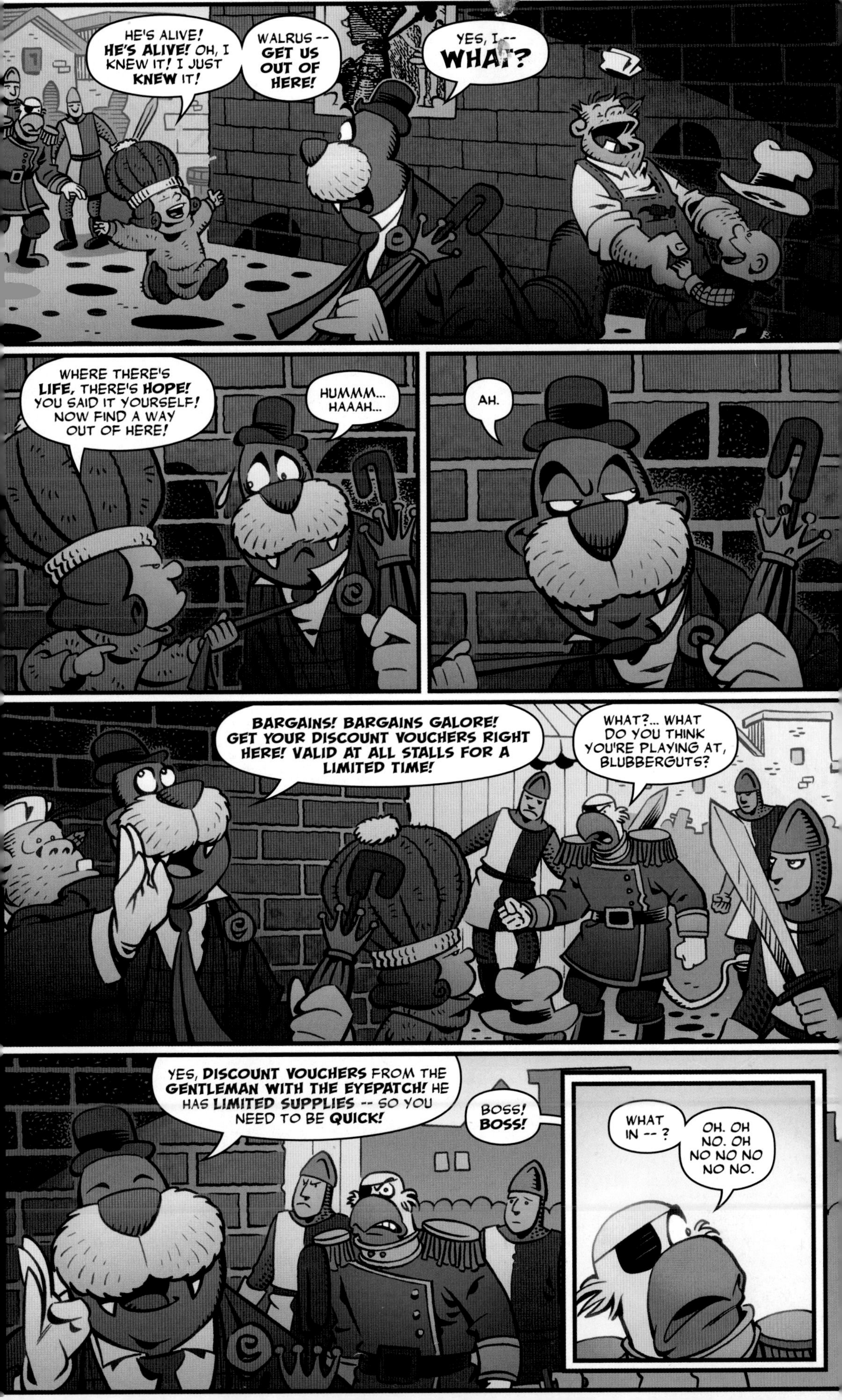
HE'S ALIVE! HE'S ALIVE! OH, I KNEW IT! I JUST KNEW IT!
WALRUS -- GET US OUT OF HERE!
YES, I -- WHAT?
WHERE THERE'S LIFE, THERE'S HOPE! YOU SAID IT YOURSELF! NOW FIND A WAY OUT OF HERE!
HUMMM... HAAAH...
AH.
BARGAINS! BARGAINS GALORE! GET YOUR DISCOUNT VOUCHERS RIGHT HERE! VALID AT ALL STALLS FOR A LIMITED TIME!
WHAT?... WHAT DO YOU THINK YOU'RE PLAYING AT, BLUBBERGUTS?
YES, DISCOUNT VOUCHERS FROM THE GENTLEMAN WITH THE EYEPATCH! HE HAS LIMITED SUPPLIES -- SO YOU NEED TO BE QUICK!
BOSS! BOSS!
WHAT IN -- ?
OH. OH NO. OH NO NO NO NO NO.

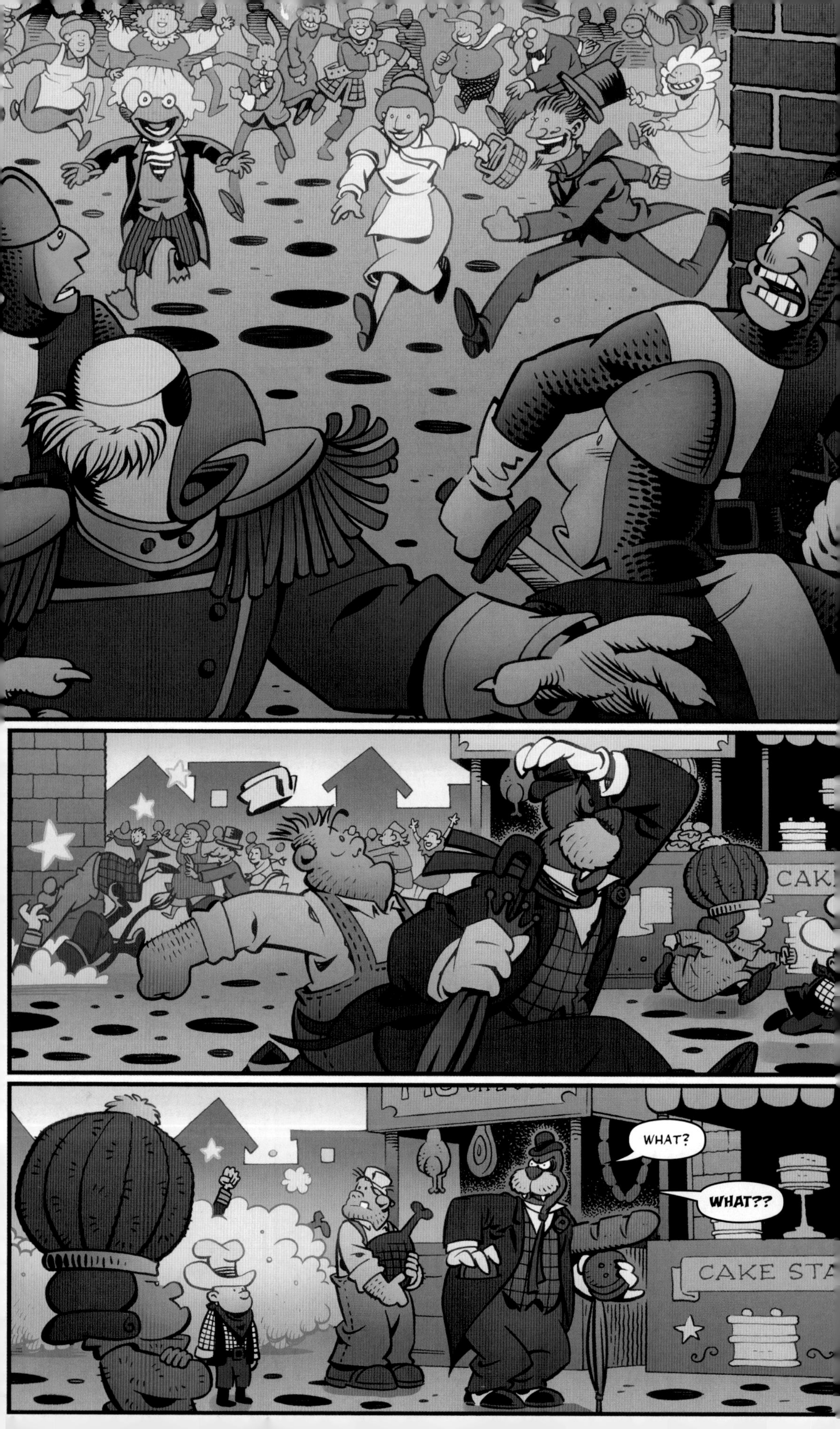
CAK
WHAT?
WHAT??
CAKE STA

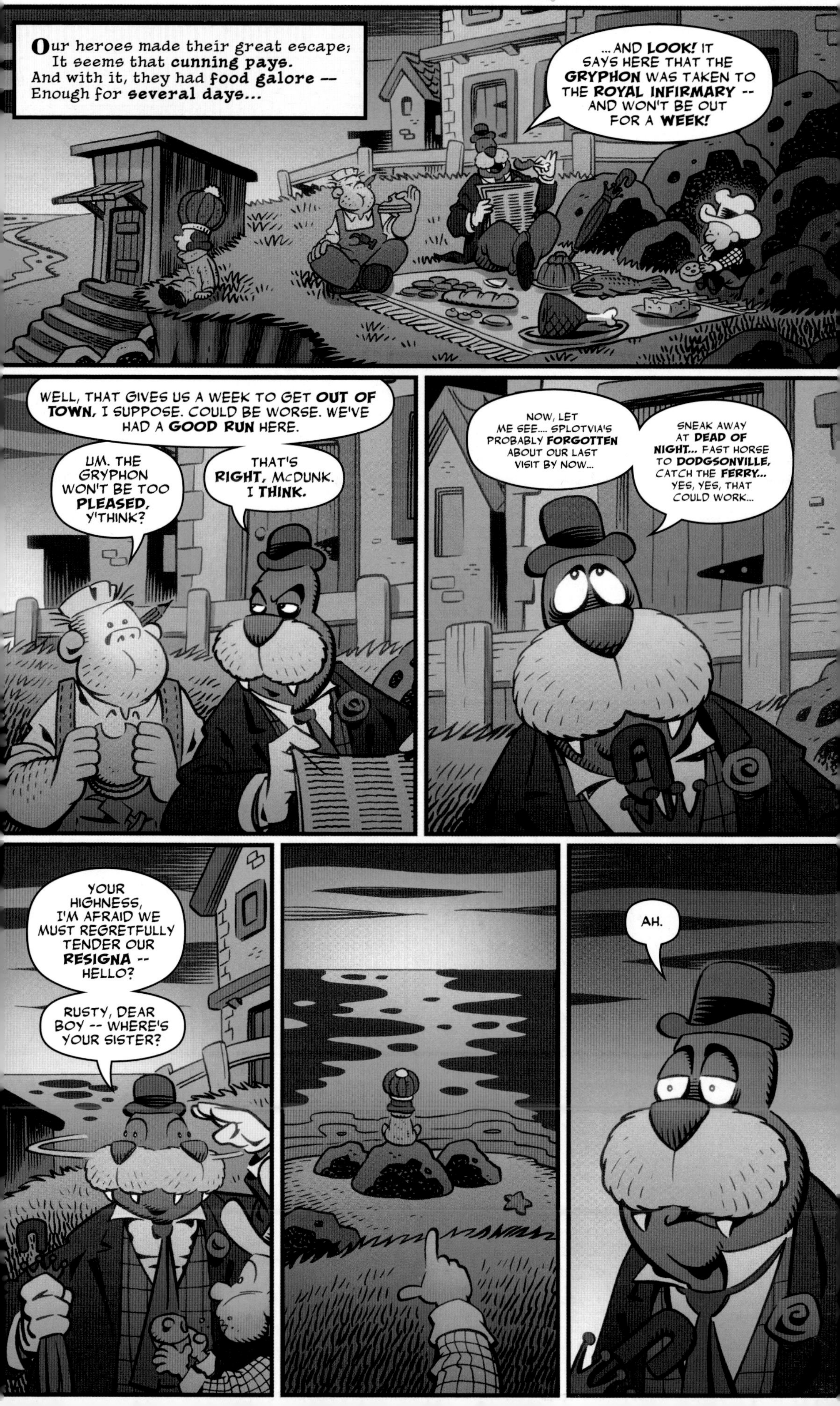
Our heroes made their great escape;
It seems that cunning pays.
And with it, they had food galore --
Enough for several days...
...AND LOOK! IT SAYS HERE THAT THE GRYPHON WAS TAKEN TO THE ROYAL INFIRMARY -- AND WON'T BE OUT FOR A WEEK!
WELL, THAT GIVES US A WEEK TO GET OUT OF TOWN, I SUPPOSE. COULD BE WORSE. WE'VE HAD A GOOD RUN HERE.
UM. THE GRYPHON WON'T BE TOO PLEASED, Y'THINK?
THAT'S RIGHT, McDUNK. I THINK.
NOW, LET ME SEE.... SPLOTVIA'S PROBABLY FORGOTTEN ABOUT OUR LAST VISIT BY NOW...
SNEAK AWAY AT DEAD OF NIGHT... FAST HORSE TO DODGSONVILLE, CATCH THE FERRY... YES, YES, THAT COULD WORK...
YOUR HIGHNESS, I'M AFRAID WE MUST REGRETFULLY TENDER OUR RESIGNA -- HELLO?
RUSTY, DEAR BOY -- WHERE'S YOUR SISTER?
AH.

HE'S ALIVE.

AND HE'S **OUT THERE** SOMEWHERE.

YES. UM, YOUR HIGHNESS... McDUNK AND I, WE FEEL IT WOULD BE BETTER FOR OUR **HEALTH** TO --

WE FEEL THAT **SPLOTVIA** MIGHT BE RATHER *CONGENIAL* AT THIS TIME OF YEAR...

ONLY WE THINK WE OUGHT TO BE **GONE** BEFORE THE **GRYPHON** GETS OUT OF --

⸎sigh⸎

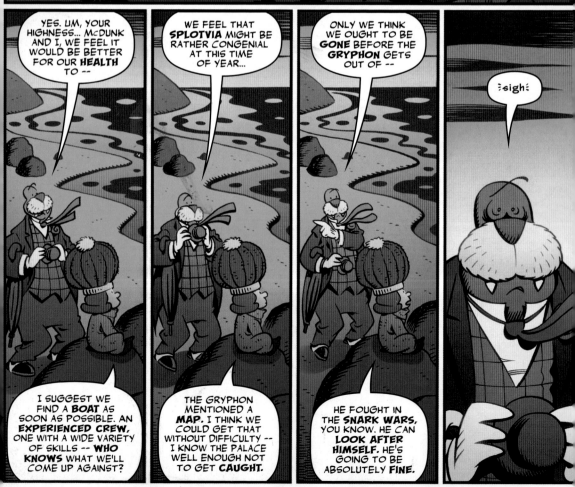

I SUGGEST WE FIND A **BOAT** AS SOON AS POSSIBLE. AN **EXPERIENCED CREW**, ONE WITH A WIDE VARIETY OF SKILLS -- **WHO KNOWS** WHAT WE'LL COME UP AGAINST?

THE GRYPHON MENTIONED A **MAP.** I THINK WE COULD GET THAT WITHOUT DIFFICULTY -- I KNOW THE PALACE WELL ENOUGH NOT TO GET **CAUGHT.**

HE FOUGHT IN THE **SNARK WARS,** YOU KNOW. HE CAN **LOOK AFTER HIMSELF.** HE'S GOING TO BE ABSOLUTELY **FINE.**

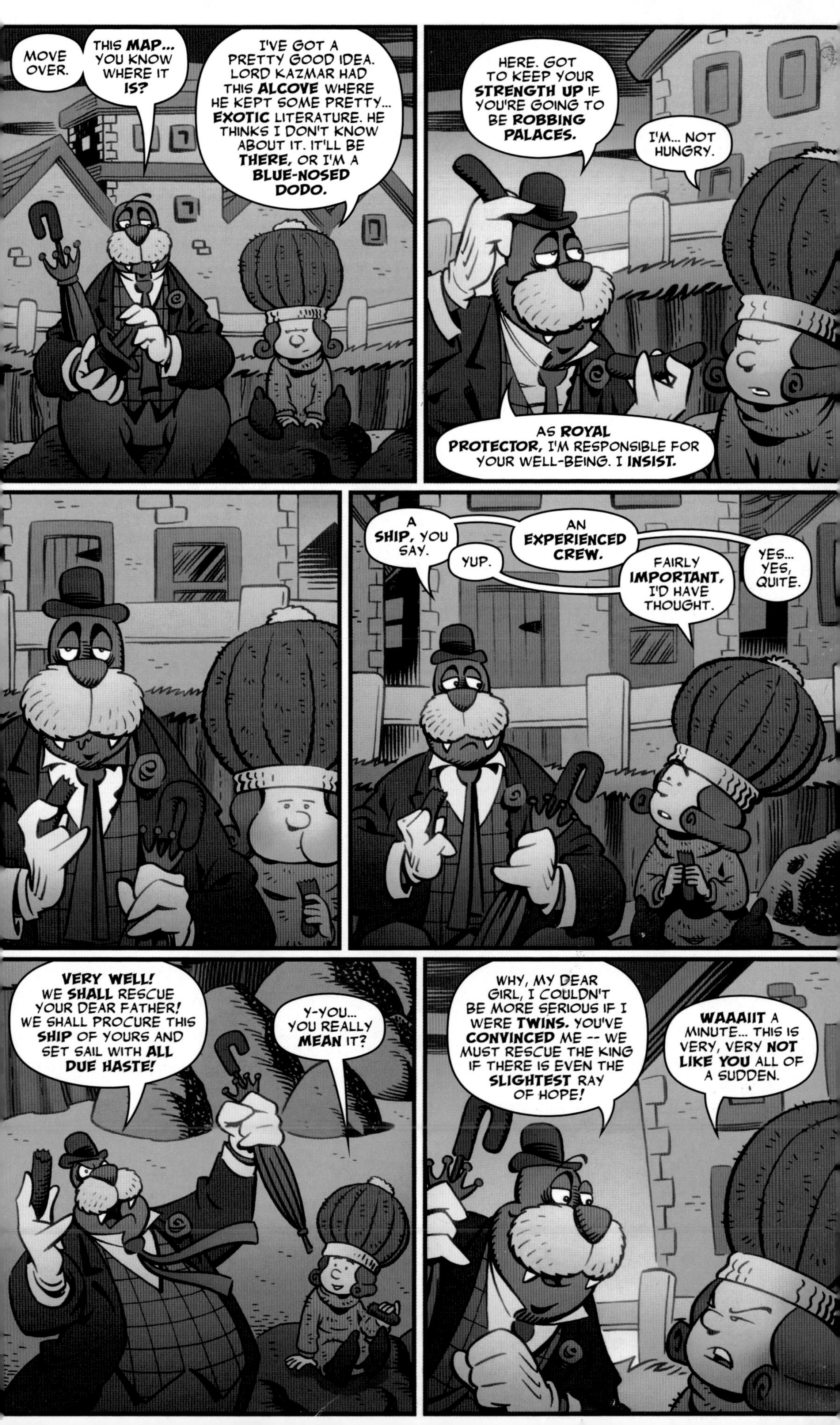
MOVE OVER.
THIS MAP... YOU KNOW WHERE IT IS?
I'VE GOT A PRETTY GOOD IDEA. LORD KAZMAR HAD THIS ALCOVE WHERE HE KEPT SOME PRETTY... EXOTIC LITERATURE. HE THINKS I DON'T KNOW ABOUT IT. IT'LL BE THERE, OR I'M A BLUE-NOSED DODO.
HERE. GOT TO KEEP YOUR STRENGTH UP IF YOU'RE GOING TO BE ROBBING PALACES.
I'M... NOT HUNGRY.
AS ROYAL PROTECTOR, I'M RESPONSIBLE FOR YOUR WELL-BEING. I INSIST.
A SHIP, YOU SAY.
YUP.
AN EXPERIENCED CREW.
FAIRLY IMPORTANT, I'D HAVE THOUGHT.
YES... YES, QUITE.
VERY WELL! WE SHALL RESCUE YOUR DEAR FATHER! WE SHALL PROCURE THIS SHIP OF YOURS AND SET SAIL WITH ALL DUE HASTE!
Y-YOU... YOU REALLY MEAN IT?
WHY, MY DEAR GIRL, I COULDN'T BE MORE SERIOUS IF I WERE TWINS. YOU'VE CONVINCED ME -- WE MUST RESCUE THE KING IF THERE IS EVEN THE SLIGHTEST RAY OF HOPE!
WAAAIIT A MINUTE... THIS IS VERY, VERY NOT LIKE YOU ALL OF A SUDDEN.

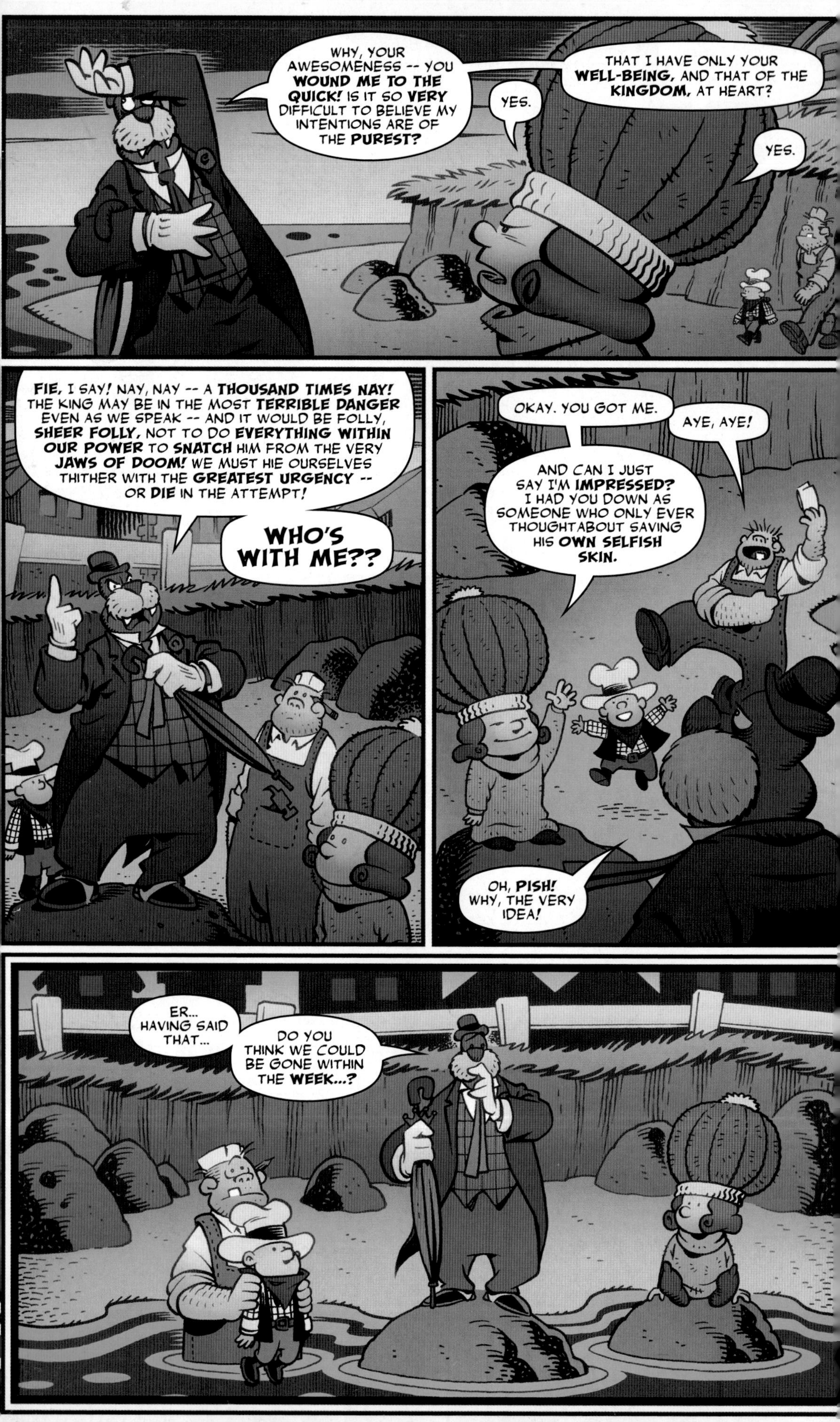
WHY, YOUR AWESOMENESS -- YOU WOUND ME TO THE QUICK! IS IT SO VERY DIFFICULT TO BELIEVE MY INTENTIONS ARE OF THE PUREST?
YES.
THAT I HAVE ONLY YOUR WELL-BEING, AND THAT OF THE KINGDOM, AT HEART?
YES.
FIE, I SAY! NAY, NAY -- A THOUSAND TIMES NAY! THE KING MAY BE IN THE MOST TERRIBLE DANGER EVEN AS WE SPEAK -- AND IT WOULD BE FOLLY, SHEER FOLLY, NOT TO DO EVERYTHING WITHIN OUR POWER TO SNATCH HIM FROM THE VERY JAWS OF DOOM! WE MUST HIE OURSELVES THITHER WITH THE GREATEST URGENCY -- OR DIE IN THE ATTEMPT!
WHO'S WITH ME??
OKAY. YOU GOT ME.
AYE, AYE!
AND CAN I JUST SAY I'M IMPRESSED? I HAD YOU DOWN AS SOMEONE WHO ONLY EVER THOUGHTABOUT SAVING HIS OWN SELFISH SKIN.
OH, PISH! WHY, THE VERY IDEA!
ER... HAVING SAID THAT...
DO YOU THINK WE COULD BE GONE WITHIN THE WEEK...?

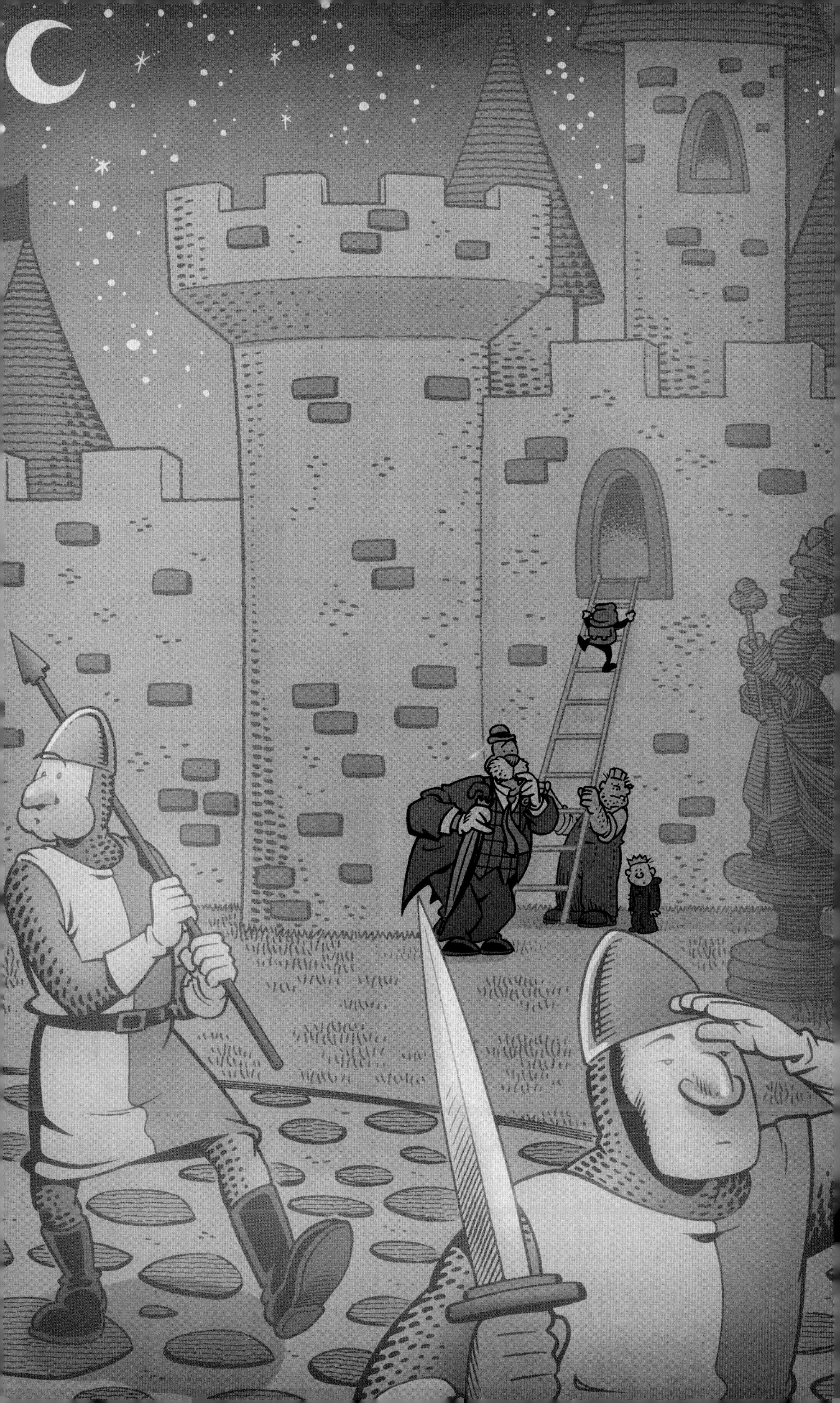

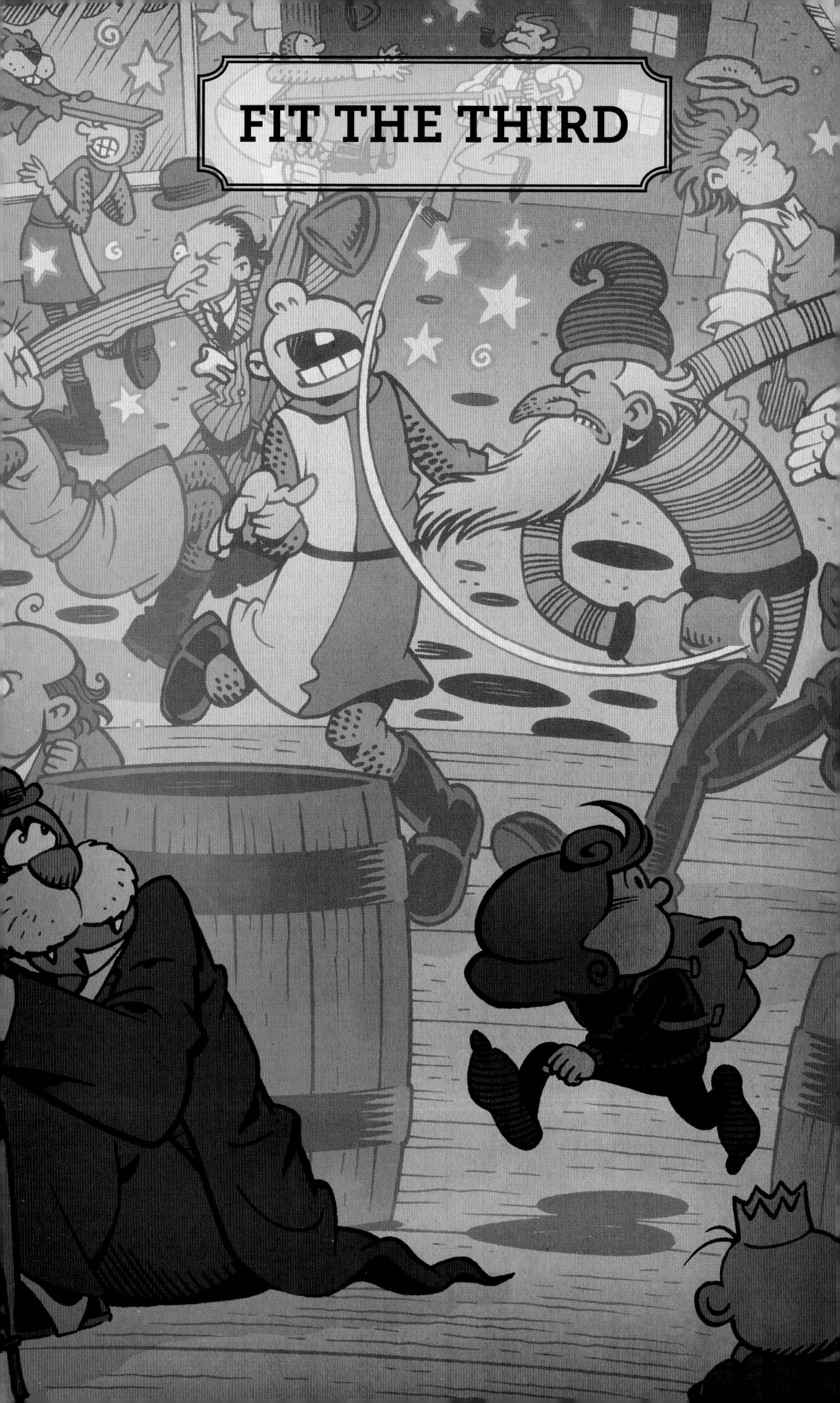
FIT THE THIRD

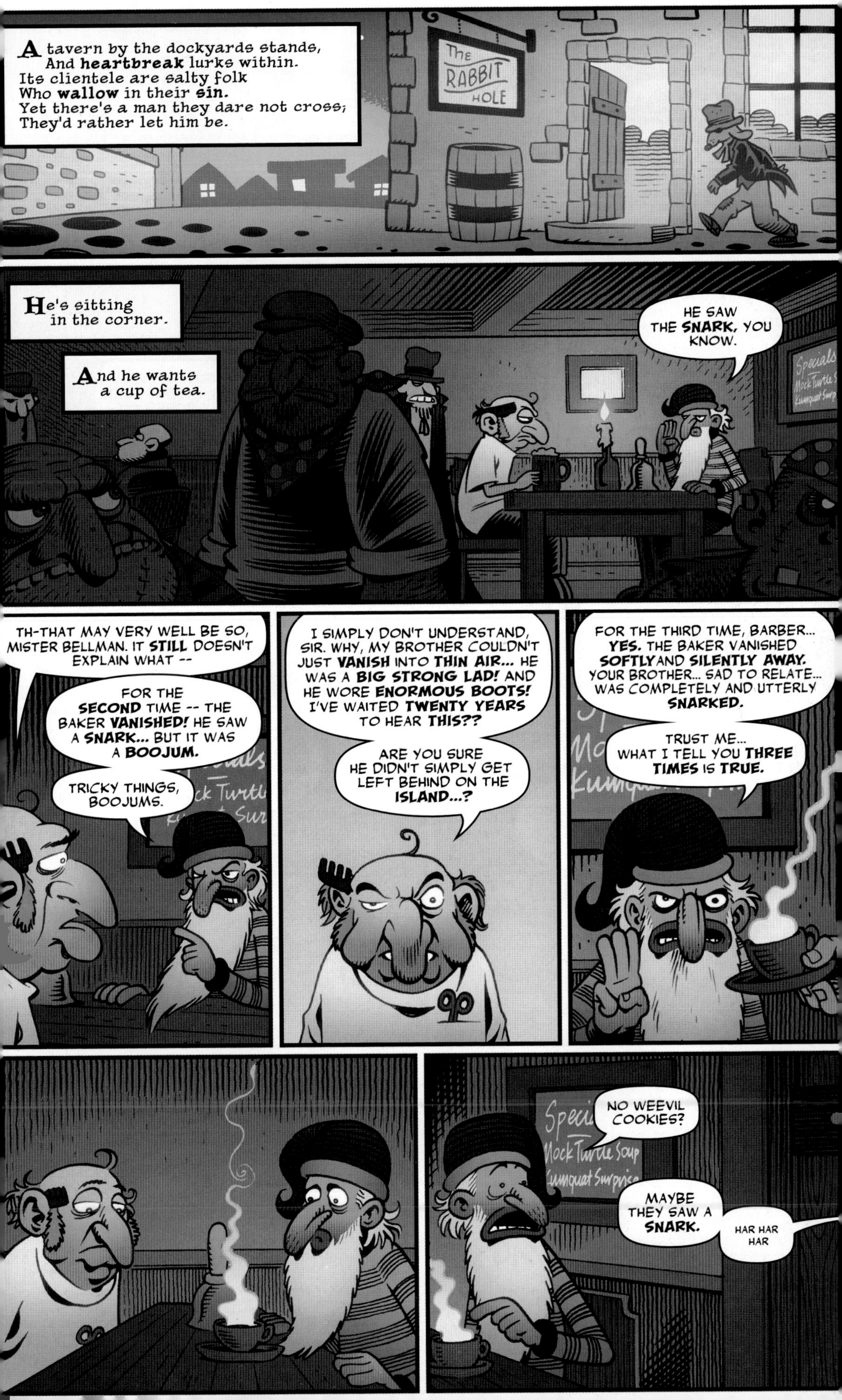
A tavern by the dockyards stands,
And heartbreak lurks within.
Its clientele are salty folk
Who wallow in their sin.
Yet there's a man they dare not cross;
They'd rather let him be.
THE RABBIT HOLE
He's sitting in the corner.
And he wants a cup of tea.
HE SAW THE SNARK, YOU KNOW.
Specials
TH-THAT MAY VERY WELL BE SO, MISTER BELLMAN. IT STILL DOESN'T EXPLAIN WHAT --
FOR THE SECOND TIME -- THE BAKER VANISHED! HE SAW A SNARK... BUT IT WAS A BOOJUM.
TRICKY THINGS, BOOJUMS.
I SIMPLY DON'T UNDERSTAND, SIR. WHY, MY BROTHER COULDN'T JUST VANISH INTO THIN AIR... HE WAS A BIG STRONG LAD! AND HE WORE ENORMOUS BOOTS! I'VE WAITED TWENTY YEARS TO HEAR THIS??
ARE YOU SURE HE DIDN'T SIMPLY GET LEFT BEHIND ON THE ISLAND...?
FOR THE THIRD TIME, BARBER... YES. THE BAKER VANISHED SOFTLY AND SILENTLY AWAY. YOUR BROTHER... SAD TO RELATE... WAS COMPLETELY AND UTTERLY SNARKED.
TRUST ME... WHAT I TELL YOU THREE TIMES IS TRUE.
NO WEEVIL COOKIES?
Mock Turtle Soup
Kumquat Surprise
MAYBE THEY SAW A SNARK.
HAR HAR HAR

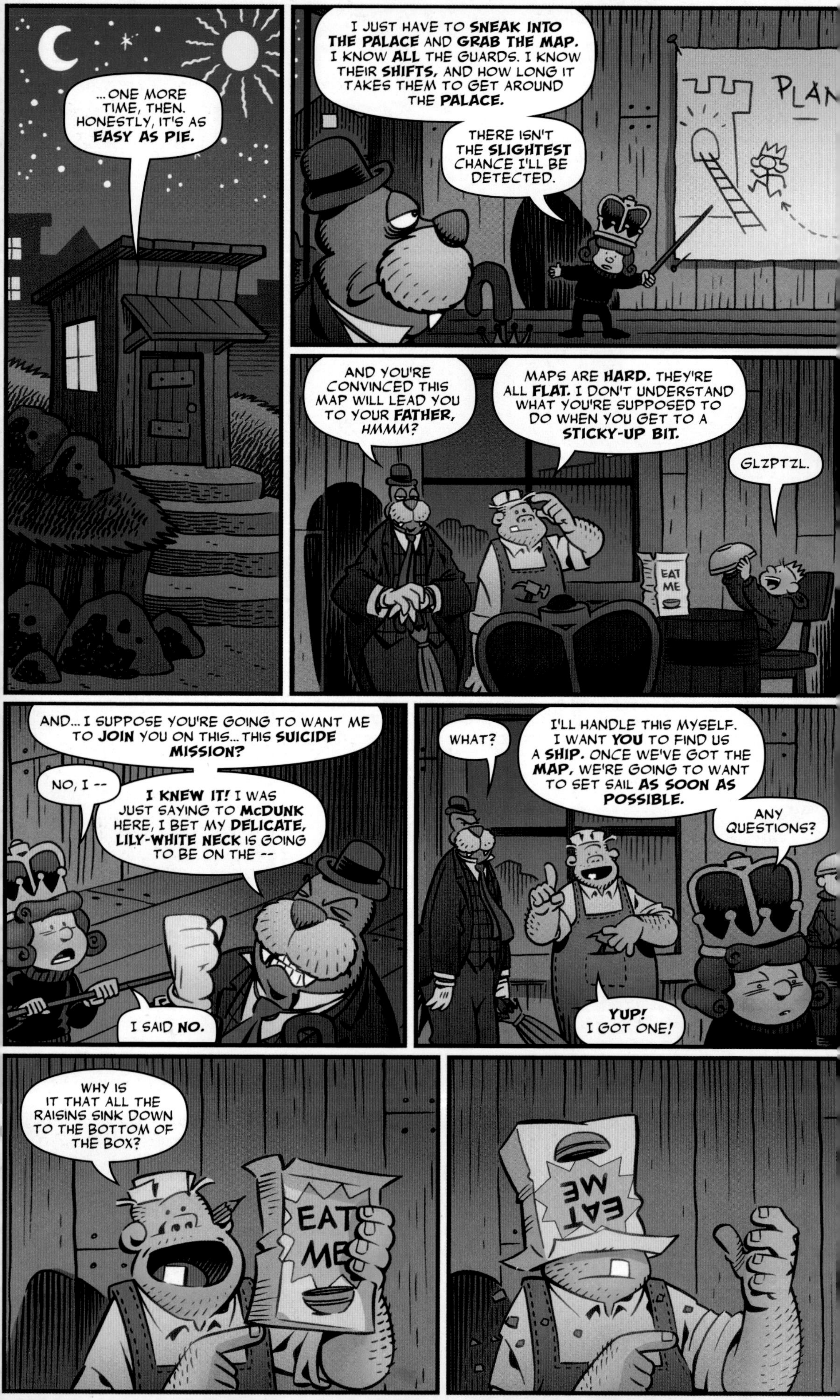
...ONE MORE TIME, THEN. HONESTLY, IT'S AS EASY AS PIE.
I JUST HAVE TO SNEAK INTO THE PALACE AND GRAB THE MAP. I KNOW ALL THE GUARDS. I KNOW THEIR SHIFTS, AND HOW LONG IT TAKES THEM TO GET AROUND THE PALACE.
THERE ISN'T THE SLIGHTEST CHANCE I'LL BE DETECTED.
PLAN
AND YOU'RE CONVINCED THIS MAP WILL LEAD YOU TO YOUR FATHER, HMMM?
MAPS ARE HARD. THEY'RE ALL FLAT. I DON'T UNDERSTAND WHAT YOU'RE SUPPOSED TO DO WHEN YOU GET TO A STICKY-UP BIT.
GLZPTZL.
EAT ME
AND... I SUPPOSE YOU'RE GOING TO WANT ME TO JOIN YOU ON THIS... THIS SUICIDE MISSION?
NO, I --
I KNEW IT! I WAS JUST SAYING TO McDUNK HERE, I BET MY DELICATE, LILY-WHITE NECK IS GOING TO BE ON THE --
I SAID NO.
WHAT?
I'LL HANDLE THIS MYSELF. I WANT YOU TO FIND US A SHIP. ONCE WE'VE GOT THE MAP, WE'RE GOING TO WANT TO SET SAIL AS SOON AS POSSIBLE.
ANY QUESTIONS?
YUP! I GOT ONE!
WHY IS IT THAT ALL THE RAISINS SINK DOWN TO THE BOTTOM OF THE BOX?
EAT ME
EAT ME

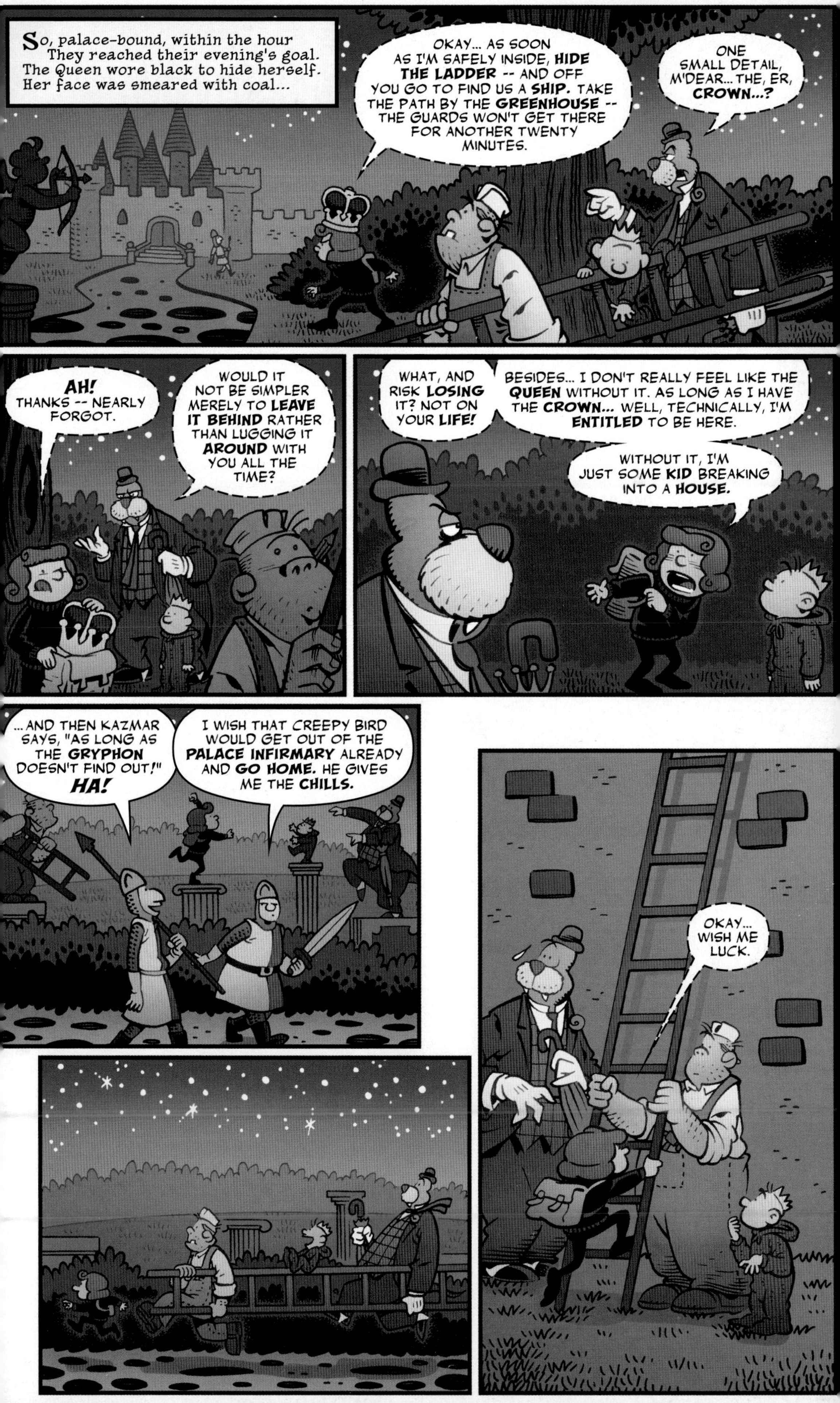

So, palace-bound, within the hour They reached their evening's goal. The Queen wore black to hide herself. Her face was smeared with coal...
OKAY... AS SOON AS I'M SAFELY INSIDE, HIDE THE LADDER -- AND OFF YOU GO TO FIND US A SHIP. TAKE THE PATH BY THE GREENHOUSE -- THE GUARDS WON'T GET THERE FOR ANOTHER TWENTY MINUTES.
ONE SMALL DETAIL, M'DEAR... THE, ER, CROWN...?
AH! THANKS -- NEARLY FORGOT.
WOULD IT NOT BE SIMPLER MERELY TO LEAVE IT BEHIND RATHER THAN LUGGING IT AROUND WITH YOU ALL THE TIME?
WHAT, AND RISK LOSING IT? NOT ON YOUR LIFE!
BESIDES... I DON'T REALLY FEEL LIKE THE QUEEN WITHOUT IT. AS LONG AS I HAVE THE CROWN... WELL, TECHNICALLY, I'M ENTITLED TO BE HERE.
WITHOUT IT, I'M JUST SOME KID BREAKING INTO A HOUSE.
...AND THEN KAZMAR SAYS, "AS LONG AS THE GRYPHON DOESN'T FIND OUT!" HA!
I WISH THAT CREEPY BIRD WOULD GET OUT OF THE PALACE INFIRMARY ALREADY AND GO HOME. HE GIVES ME THE CHILLS.
OKAY... WISH ME LUCK.

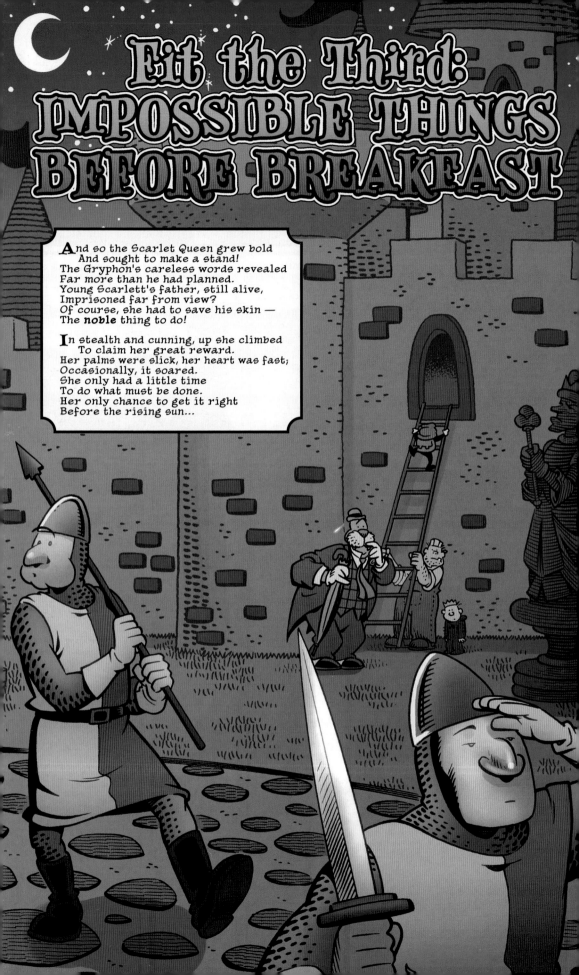

Fit the Third: IMPOSSIBLE THINGS BEFORE BREAKFAST

And so the Scarlet Queen grew bold
And sought to make a stand!
The Gryphon's careless words revealed
Far more than he had planned.
Young Scarlett's father, still alive,
Imprisoned far from view?
Of course, she had to save his skin —
The **noble** thing to do!

In stealth and cunning, up she climbed
To claim her great reward.
Her palms were slick, her heart was fast;
Occasionally, it soared.
She only had a little time
To do what must be done.
Her only chance to get it right
Before the rising sun...

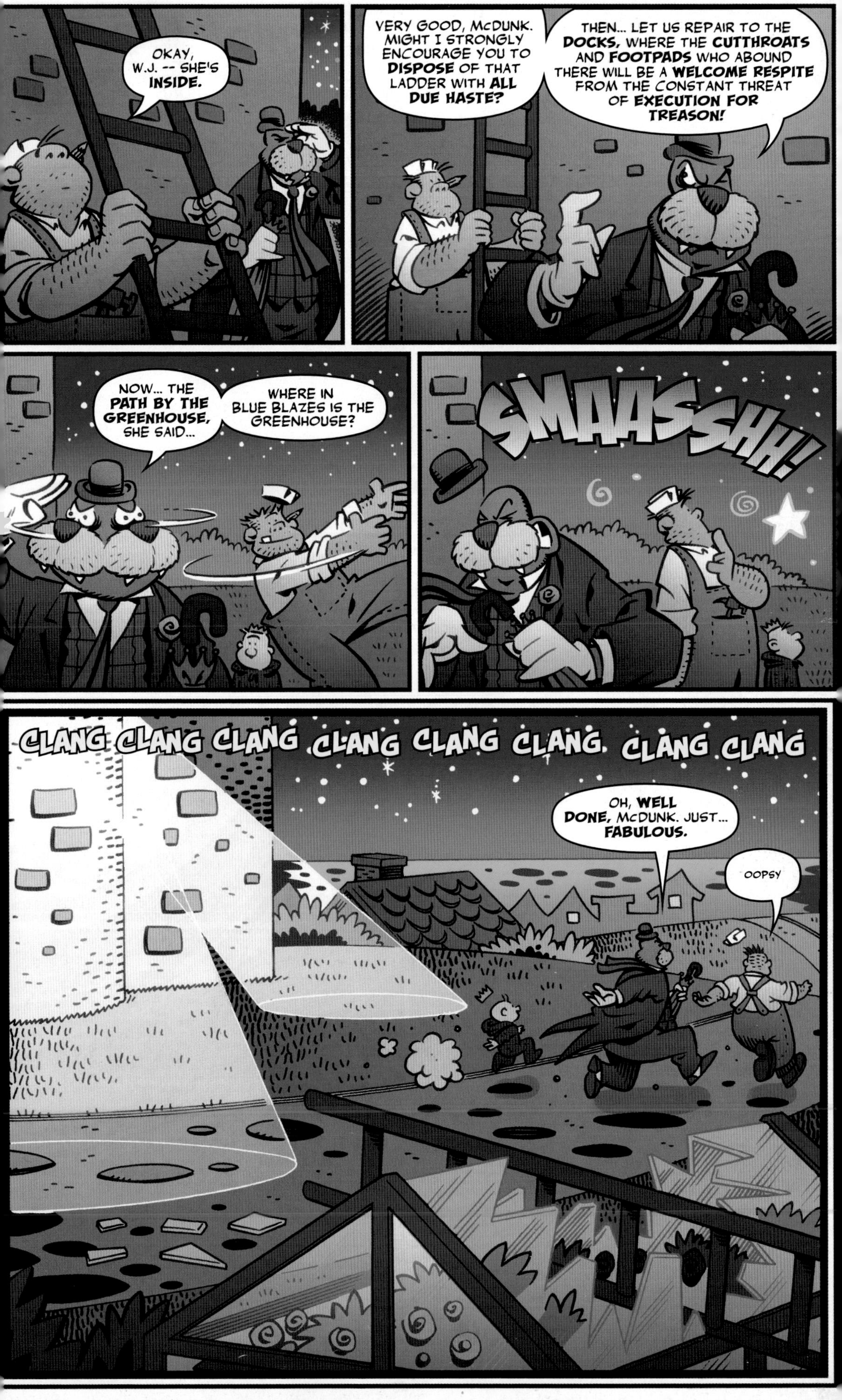
OKAY, W.J. -- SHE'S INSIDE.
VERY GOOD, McDUNK. MIGHT I STRONGLY ENCOURAGE YOU TO DISPOSE OF THAT LADDER WITH ALL DUE HASTE?
THEN... LET US REPAIR TO THE DOCKS, WHERE THE CUTTHROATS AND FOOTPADS WHO ABOUND THERE WILL BE A WELCOME RESPITE FROM THE CONSTANT THREAT OF EXECUTION FOR TREASON!
NOW... THE PATH BY THE GREENHOUSE, SHE SAID...
WHERE IN BLUE BLAZES IS THE GREENHOUSE?
SMAASSHH!
CLANG CLANG CLANG CLANG CLANG CLANG CLANG CLANG
OH, WELL DONE, McDUNK. JUST... FABULOUS.
OOPSY

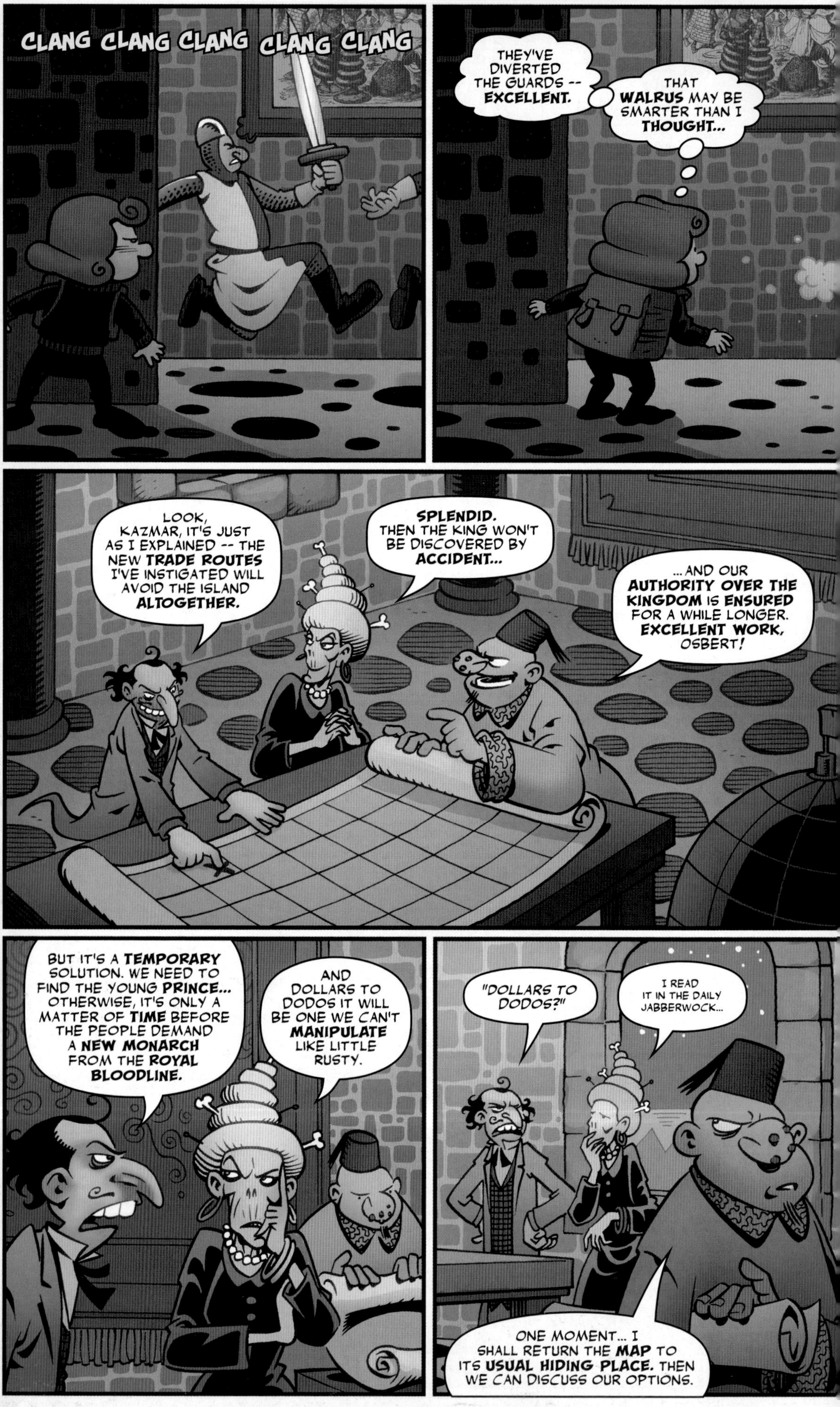
CLANG CLANG CLANG CLANG CLANG
THEY'VE DIVERTED THE GUARDS -- EXCELLENT.
THAT WALRUS MAY BE SMARTER THAN I THOUGHT...
LOOK, KAZMAR, IT'S JUST AS I EXPLAINED -- THE NEW TRADE ROUTES I'VE INSTIGATED WILL AVOID THE ISLAND ALTOGETHER.
SPLENDID. THEN THE KING WON'T BE DISCOVERED BY ACCIDENT...
...AND OUR AUTHORITY OVER THE KINGDOM IS ENSURED FOR A WHILE LONGER. EXCELLENT WORK, OSBERT!
BUT IT'S A TEMPORARY SOLUTION. WE NEED TO FIND THE YOUNG PRINCE... OTHERWISE, IT'S ONLY A MATTER OF TIME BEFORE THE PEOPLE DEMAND A NEW MONARCH FROM THE ROYAL BLOODLINE.
AND DOLLARS TO DODOS IT WILL BE ONE WE CAN'T MANIPULATE LIKE LITTLE RUSTY.
"DOLLARS TO DODOS?"
I READ IT IN THE DAILY JABBERWOCK...
ONE MOMENT... I SHALL RETURN THE MAP TO ITS USUAL HIDING PLACE. THEN WE CAN DISCUSS OUR OPTIONS.

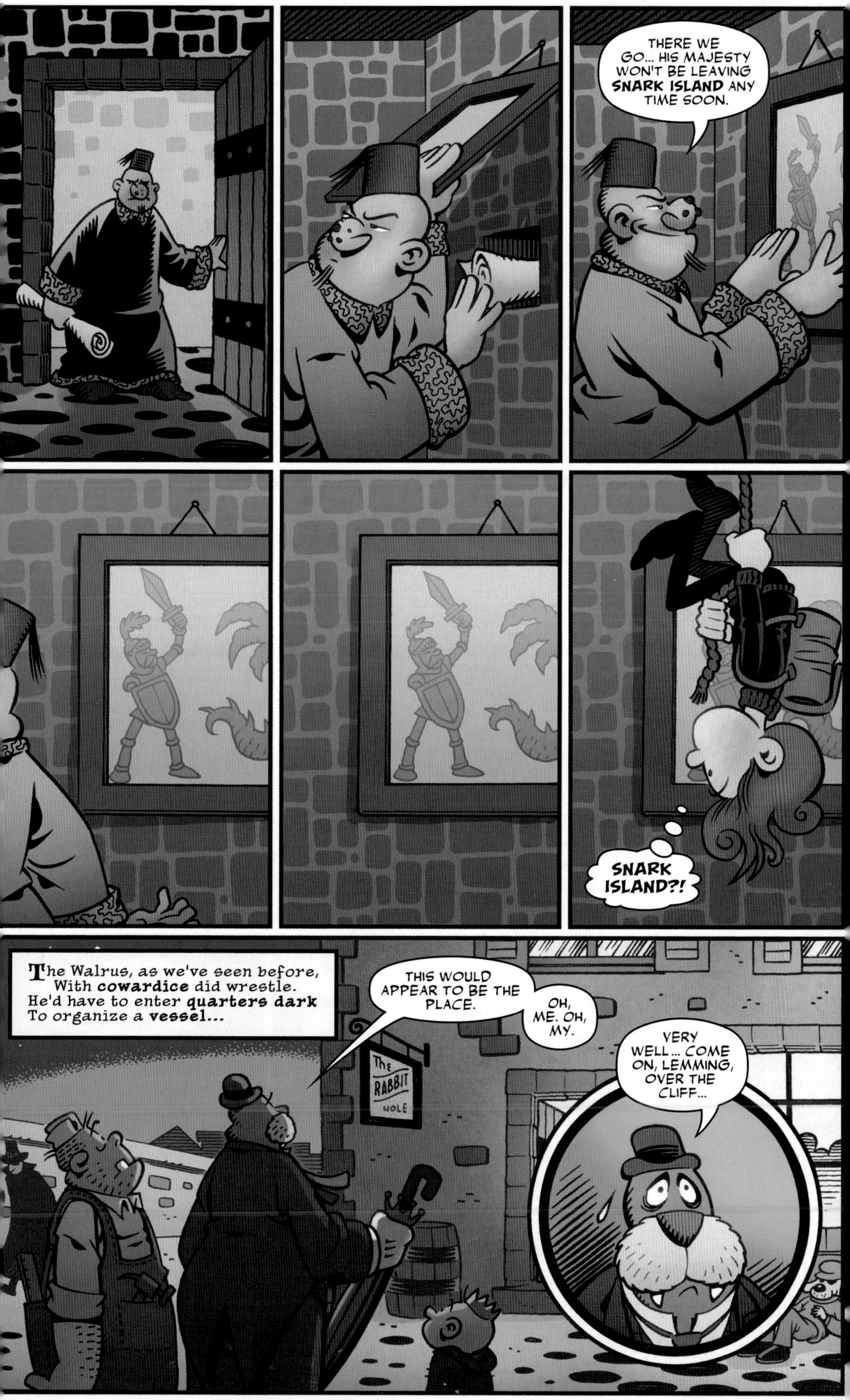
THERE WE GO... HIS MAJESTY WON'T BE LEAVING **SNARK ISLAND** ANY TIME SOON.
SNARK ISLAND?!
The Walrus, as we've seen before, With **cowardice** did wrestle. He'd have to enter **quarters dark** To organize a **vessel...**
THIS WOULD APPEAR TO BE THE PLACE.
OH, ME. OH, MY.
THE RABBIT HOLE
VERY WELL... COME ON, LEMMING, OVER THE CLIFF...

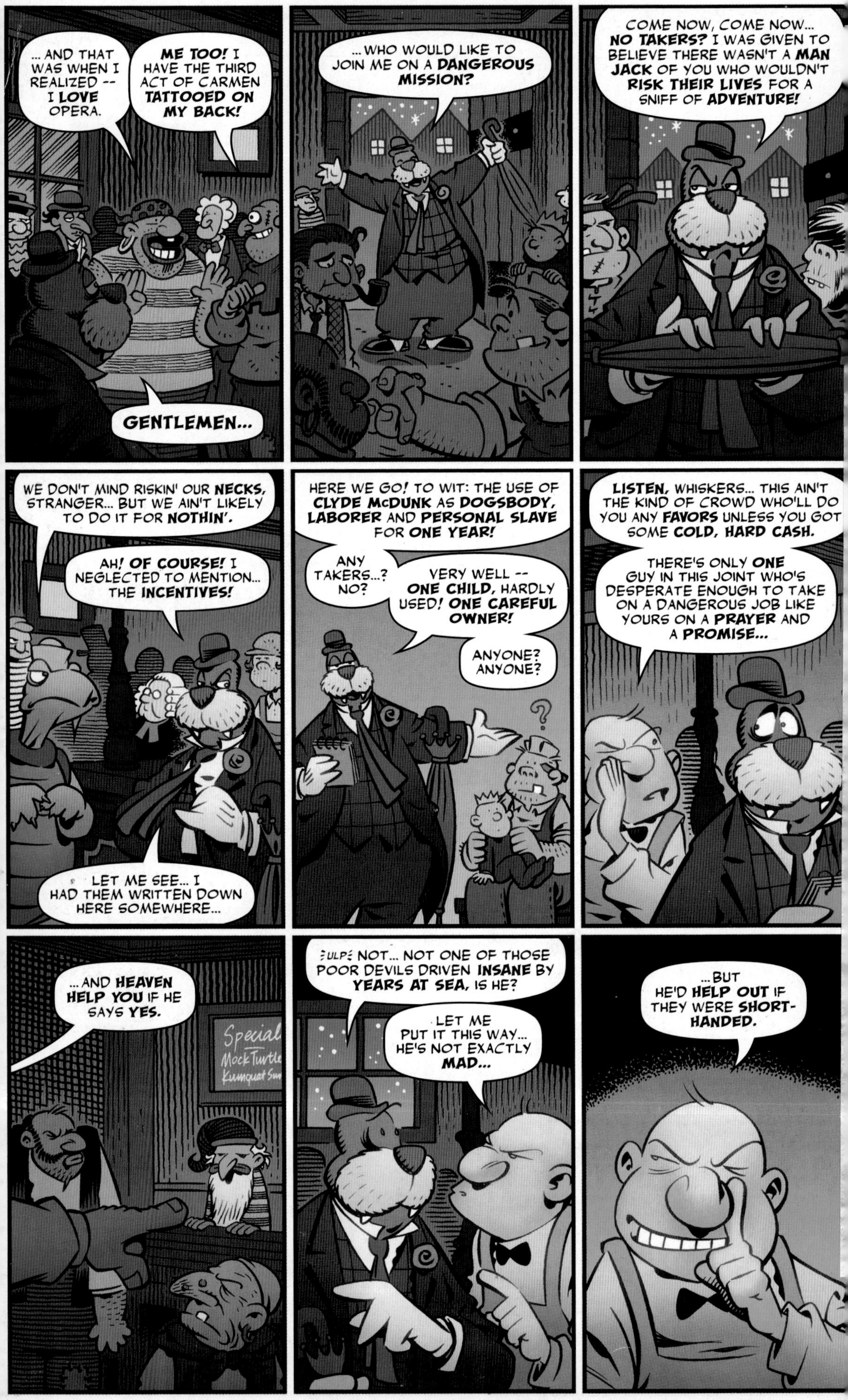

... AND THAT WAS WHEN I REALIZED -- I LOVE OPERA.
ME TOO! I HAVE THE THIRD ACT OF CARMEN TATTOOED ON MY BACK!
GENTLEMEN...
... WHO WOULD LIKE TO JOIN ME ON A DANGEROUS MISSION?
COME NOW, COME NOW... NO TAKERS? I WAS GIVEN TO BELIEVE THERE WASN'T A MAN JACK OF YOU WHO WOULDN'T RISK THEIR LIVES FOR A SNIFF OF ADVENTURE!
WE DON'T MIND RISKIN' OUR NECKS, STRANGER... BUT WE AIN'T LIKELY TO DO IT FOR NOTHIN'.
AH! OF COURSE! I NEGLECTED TO MENTION... THE INCENTIVES!
LET ME SEE... I HAD THEM WRITTEN DOWN HERE SOMEWHERE...
HERE WE GO! TO WIT: THE USE OF CLYDE McDUNK AS DOGSBODY, LABORER AND PERSONAL SLAVE FOR ONE YEAR!
ANY TAKERS...? NO?
VERY WELL -- ONE CHILD, HARDLY USED! ONE CAREFUL OWNER!
ANYONE? ANYONE?
?
LISTEN, WHISKERS... THIS AIN'T THE KIND OF CROWD WHO'LL DO YOU ANY FAVORS UNLESS YOU GOT SOME COLD, HARD CASH.
THERE'S ONLY ONE GUY IN THIS JOINT WHO'S DESPERATE ENOUGH TO TAKE ON A DANGEROUS JOB LIKE YOURS ON A PRAYER AND A PROMISE...
... AND HEAVEN HELP YOU IF HE SAYS YES.
Special
Mock Turtle
Kumquat
GULP NOT... NOT ONE OF THOSE POOR DEVILS DRIVEN INSANE BY YEARS AT SEA, IS HE?
LET ME PUT IT THIS WAY... HE'S NOT EXACTLY MAD...
... BUT HE'D HELP OUT IF THEY WERE SHORT-HANDED.

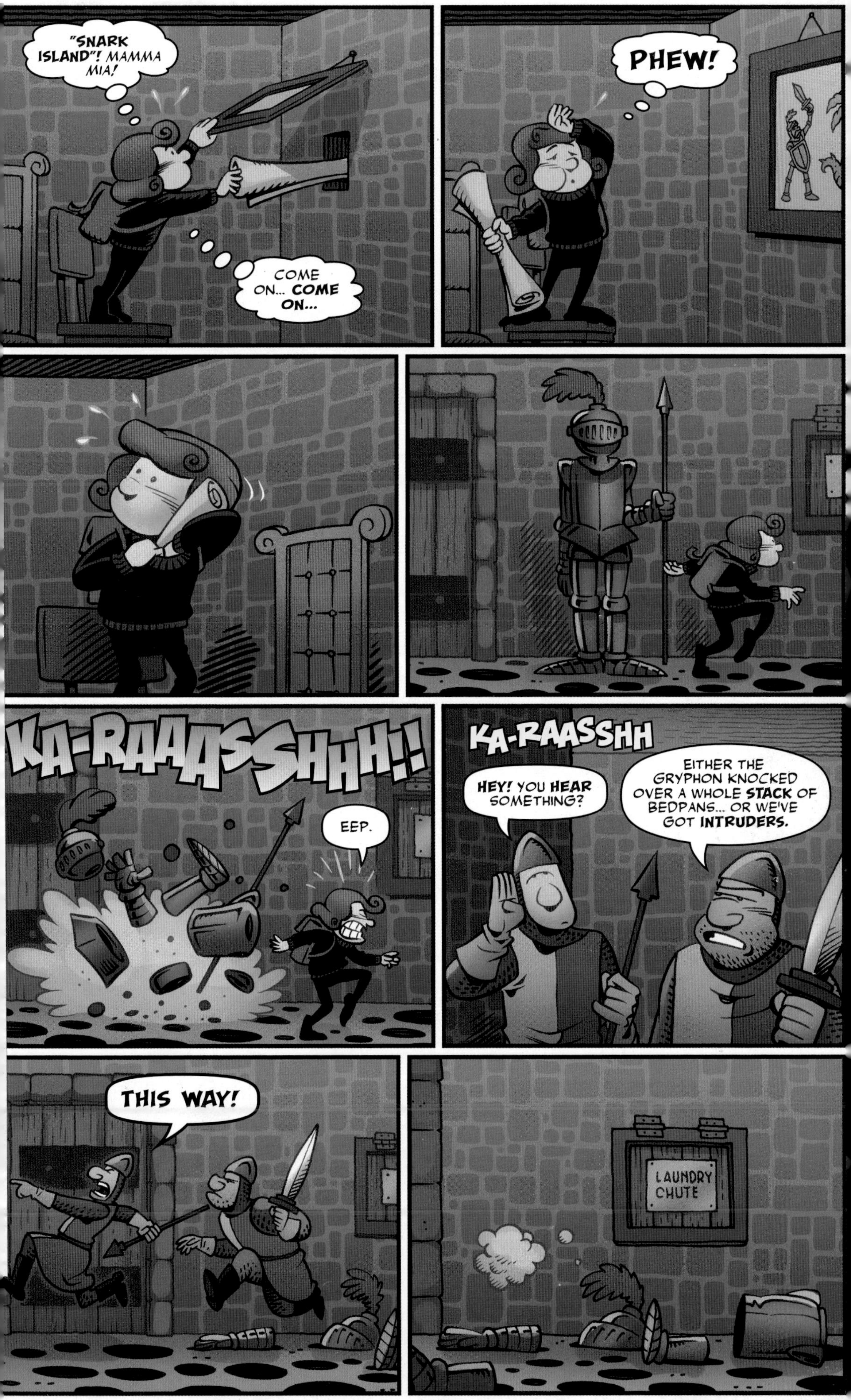
"SNARK ISLAND"! MAMMA MIA!
COME ON... COME ON...
PHEW!
KA-RAAASSHHH!!
EEP.
KA-RAASSHH
HEY! YOU HEAR SOMETHING?
EITHER THE GRYPHON KNOCKED OVER A WHOLE STACK OF BEDPANS... OR WE'VE GOT INTRUDERS.
THIS WAY!
LAUNDRY CHUTE

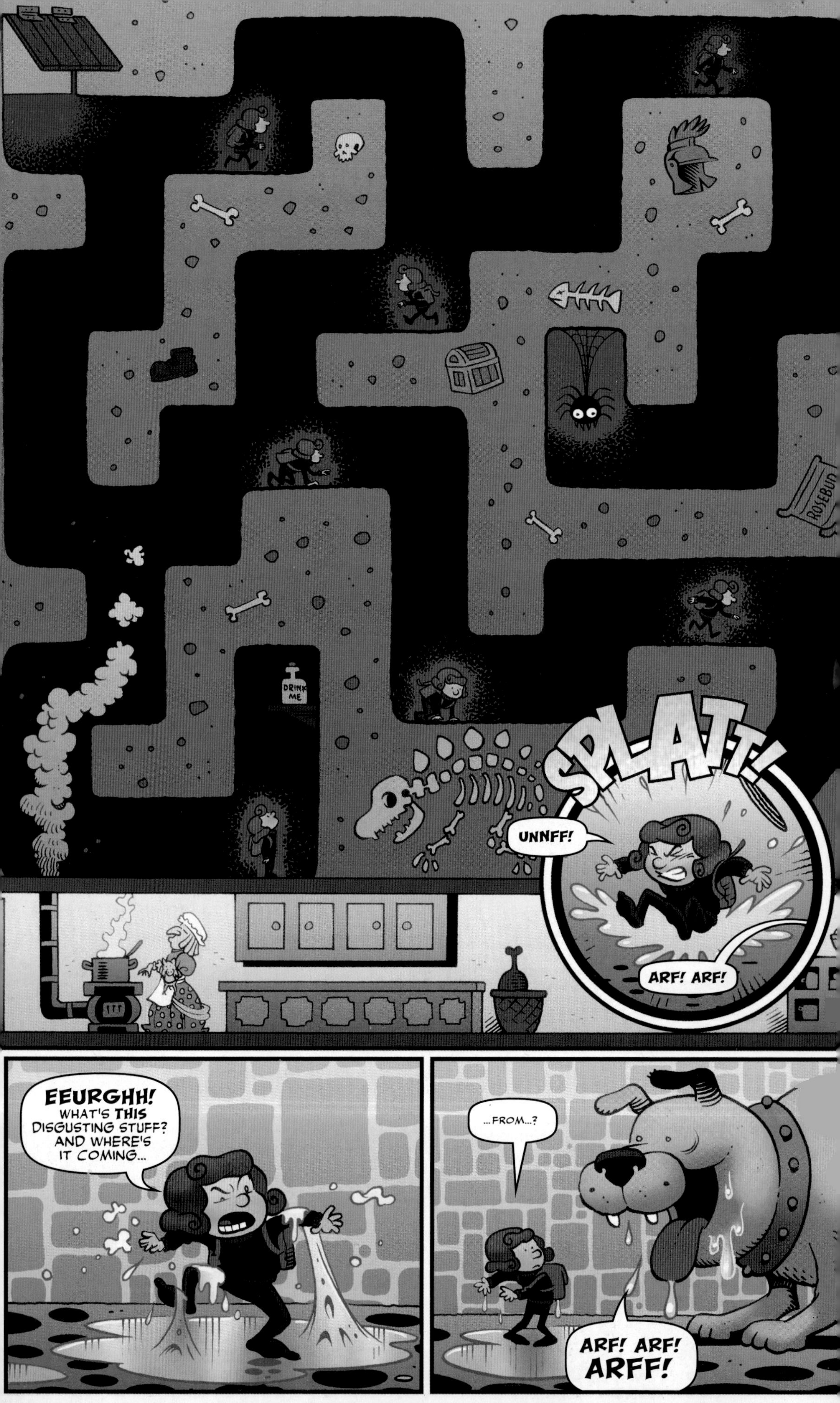
DRINK ME
ROSEBUD
SPLATT!
UNNFF!
ARF! ARF!
EEURGHH! WHAT'S THIS DISGUSTING STUFF? AND WHERE'S IT COMING...
...FROM...?
ARF! ARF! ARFF!

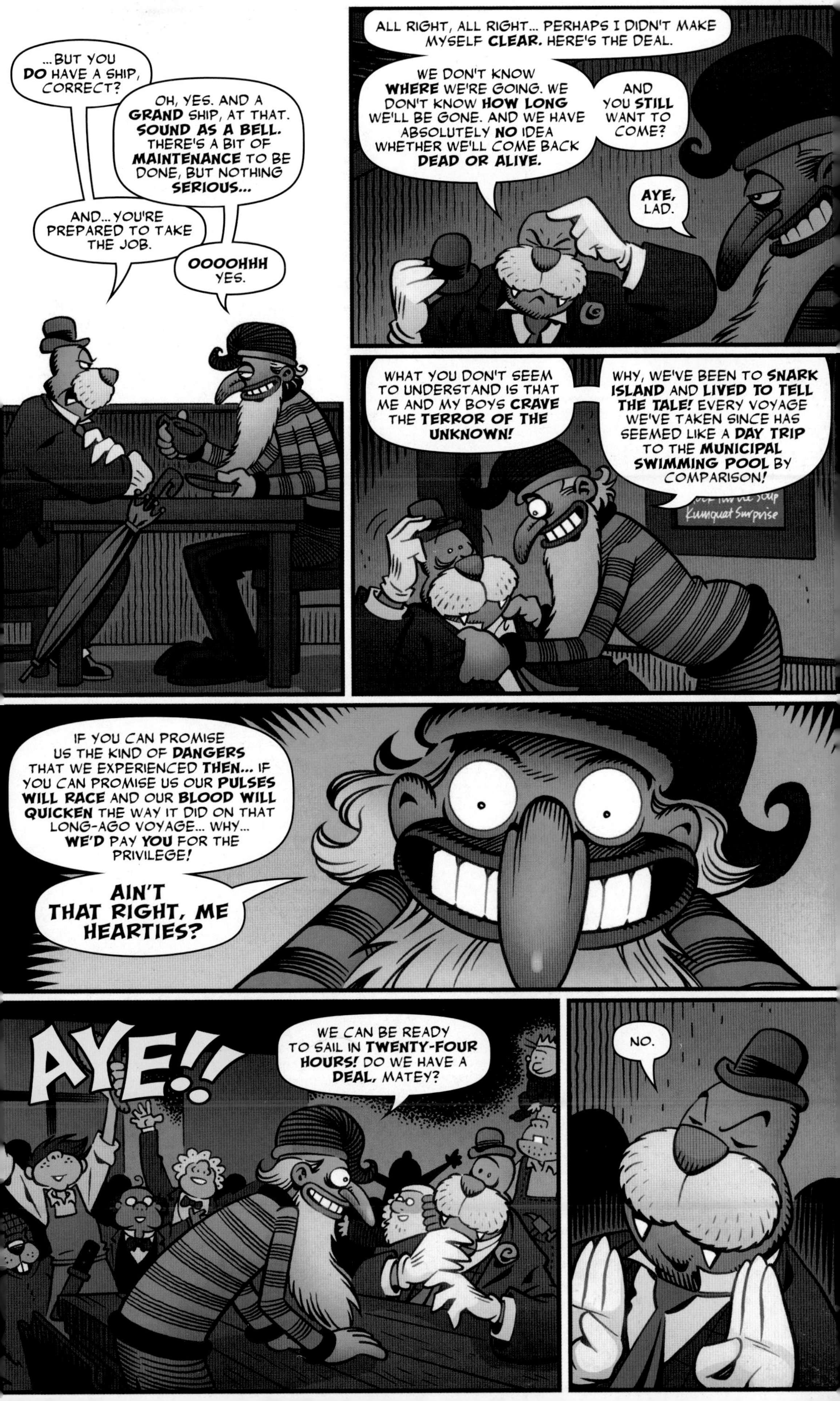
...BUT YOU DO HAVE A SHIP, CORRECT?
OH, YES. AND A GRAND SHIP, AT THAT. SOUND AS A BELL. THERE'S A BIT OF MAINTENANCE TO BE DONE, BUT NOTHING SERIOUS...
AND... YOU'RE PREPARED TO TAKE THE JOB.
OOOOHHH YES.
ALL RIGHT, ALL RIGHT... PERHAPS I DIDN'T MAKE MYSELF CLEAR. HERE'S THE DEAL.
WE DON'T KNOW WHERE WE'RE GOING. WE DON'T KNOW HOW LONG WE'LL BE GONE. AND WE HAVE ABSOLUTELY NO IDEA WHETHER WE'LL COME BACK DEAD OR ALIVE.
AND YOU STILL WANT TO COME?
AYE, LAD.
WHAT YOU DON'T SEEM TO UNDERSTAND IS THAT ME AND MY BOYS CRAVE THE TERROR OF THE UNKNOWN!
WHY, WE'VE BEEN TO SNARK ISLAND AND LIVED TO TELL THE TALE! EVERY VOYAGE WE'VE TAKEN SINCE HAS SEEMED LIKE A DAY TRIP TO THE MUNICIPAL SWIMMING POOL BY COMPARISON!
Kumquat Surprise
IF YOU CAN PROMISE US THE KIND OF DANGERS THAT WE EXPERIENCED THEN... IF YOU CAN PROMISE US OUR PULSES WILL RACE AND OUR BLOOD WILL QUICKEN THE WAY IT DID ON THAT LONG-AGO VOYAGE... WHY... WE'D PAY YOU FOR THE PRIVILEGE!
AIN'T THAT RIGHT, ME HEARTIES?
AYE!!
WE CAN BE READY TO SAIL IN TWENTY-FOUR HOURS! DO WE HAVE A DEAL, MATEY?
NO.

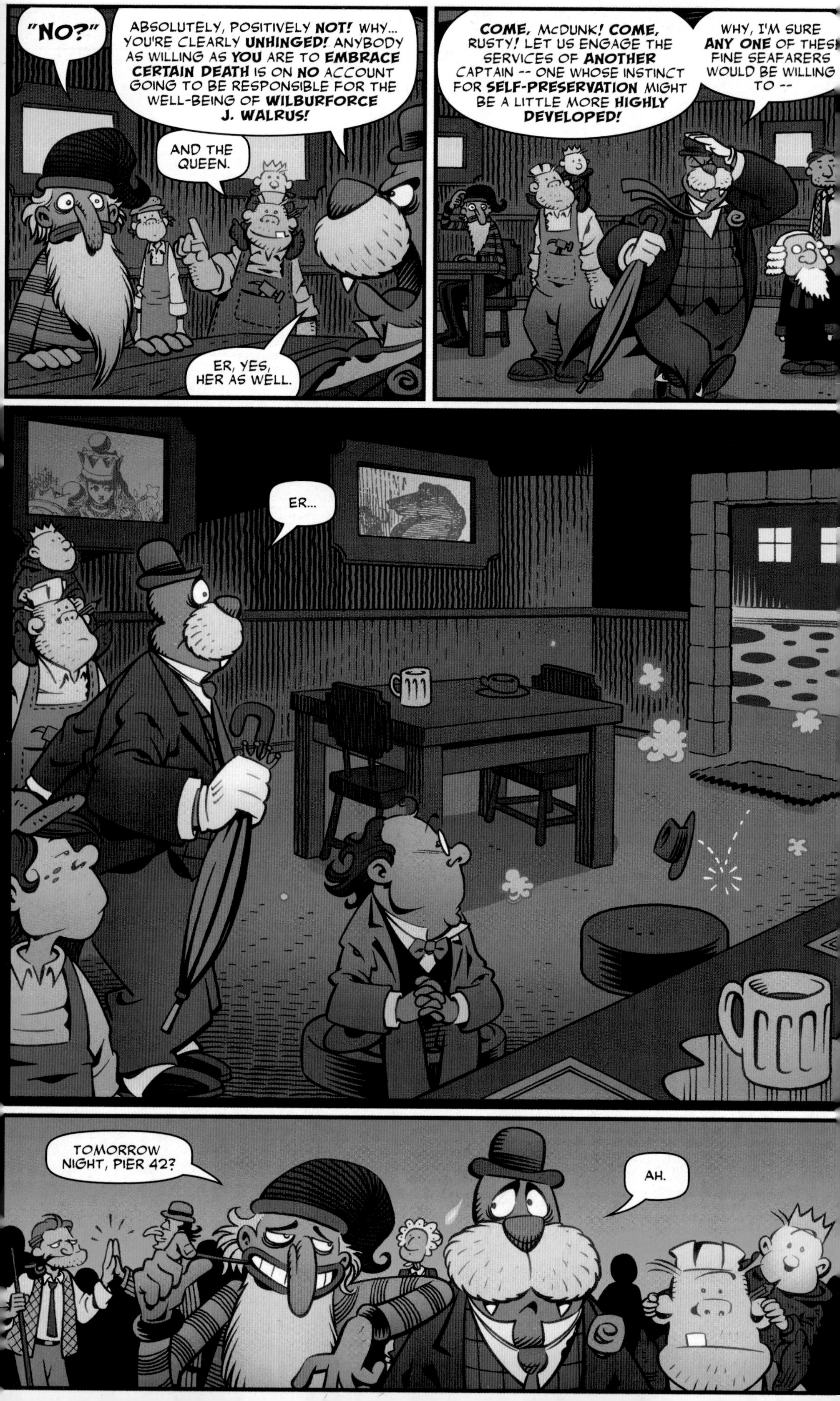
"NO?"
ABSOLUTELY, POSITIVELY NOT! WHY... YOU'RE CLEARLY UNHINGED! ANYBODY AS WILLING AS YOU ARE TO EMBRACE CERTAIN DEATH IS ON NO ACCOUNT GOING TO BE RESPONSIBLE FOR THE WELL-BEING OF WILBURFORCE J. WALRUS!
AND THE QUEEN.
ER, YES, HER AS WELL.
COME, McDUNK! COME, RUSTY! LET US ENGAGE THE SERVICES OF ANOTHER CAPTAIN -- ONE WHOSE INSTINCT FOR SELF-PRESERVATION MIGHT BE A LITTLE MORE HIGHLY DEVELOPED!
WHY, I'M SURE ANY ONE OF THESE FINE SEAFARERS WOULD BE WILLING TO --
ER...
TOMORROW NIGHT, PIER 42?
AH.

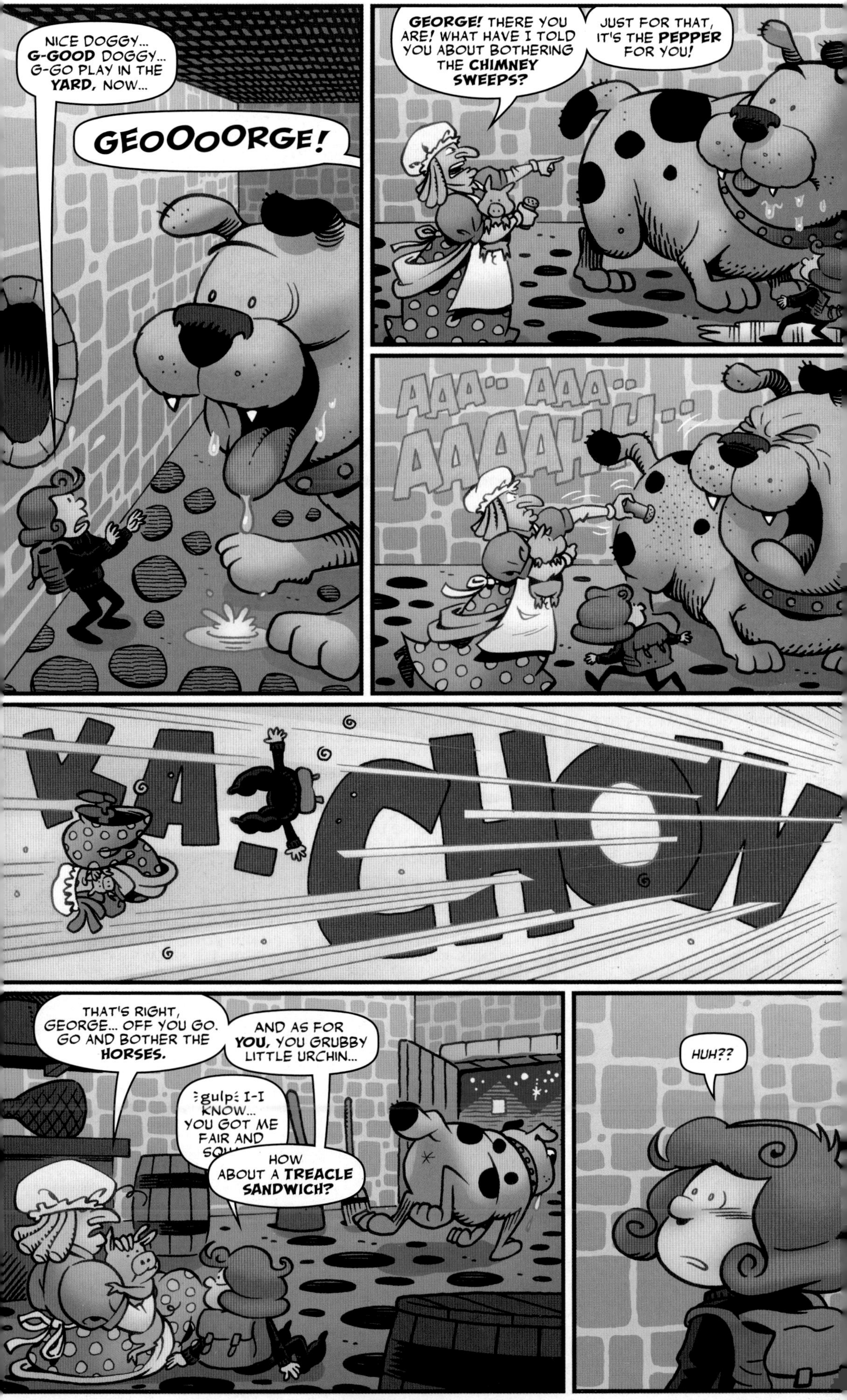
NICE DOGGY... G-GOOD DOGGY... G-GO PLAY IN THE YARD, NOW...
GEOOOORGE!
GEORGE! THERE YOU ARE! WHAT HAVE I TOLD YOU ABOUT BOTHERING THE CHIMNEY SWEEPS?
JUST FOR THAT, IT'S THE PEPPER FOR YOU!
AAA.. AAA.. AAAAHHH..
KA-CHOW
THAT'S RIGHT, GEORGE... OFF YOU GO. GO AND BOTHER THE HORSES.
AND AS FOR YOU, YOU GRUBBY LITTLE URCHIN...
gulp I-I KNOW... YOU GOT ME FAIR AND
HOW ABOUT A TREACLE SANDWICH?
HUH??

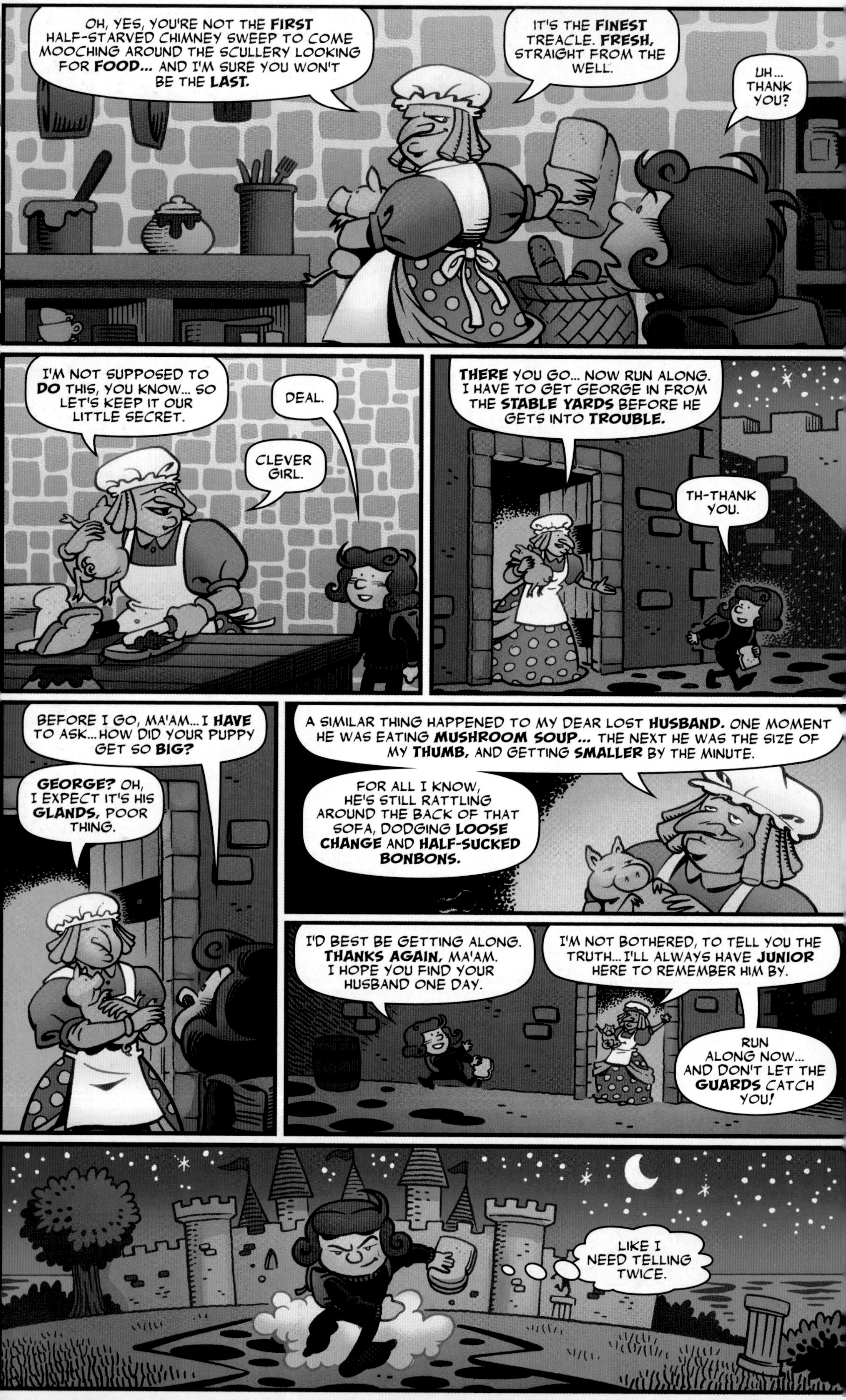

OH, YES, YOU'RE NOT THE FIRST HALF-STARVED CHIMNEY SWEEP TO COME MOOCHING AROUND THE SCULLERY LOOKING FOR FOOD... AND I'M SURE YOU WON'T BE THE LAST.
IT'S THE FINEST TREACLE. FRESH, STRAIGHT FROM THE WELL.
UH... THANK YOU?
I'M NOT SUPPOSED TO DO THIS, YOU KNOW... SO LET'S KEEP IT OUR LITTLE SECRET.
DEAL.
CLEVER GIRL.
THERE YOU GO... NOW RUN ALONG. I HAVE TO GET GEORGE IN FROM THE STABLE YARDS BEFORE HE GETS INTO TROUBLE.
TH-THANK YOU.
BEFORE I GO, MA'AM... I HAVE TO ASK... HOW DID YOUR PUPPY GET SO BIG?
GEORGE? OH, I EXPECT IT'S HIS GLANDS, POOR THING.
A SIMILAR THING HAPPENED TO MY DEAR LOST HUSBAND. ONE MOMENT HE WAS EATING MUSHROOM SOUP... THE NEXT HE WAS THE SIZE OF MY THUMB, AND GETTING SMALLER BY THE MINUTE.
FOR ALL I KNOW, HE'S STILL RATTLING AROUND THE BACK OF THAT SOFA, DODGING LOOSE CHANGE AND HALF-SUCKED BONBONS.
I'D BEST BE GETTING ALONG. THANKS AGAIN, MA'AM. I HOPE YOU FIND YOUR HUSBAND ONE DAY.
I'M NOT BOTHERED, TO TELL YOU THE TRUTH... I'LL ALWAYS HAVE JUNIOR HERE TO REMEMBER HIM BY.
RUN ALONG NOW... AND DON'T LET THE GUARDS CATCH YOU!
LIKE I NEED TELLING TWICE.

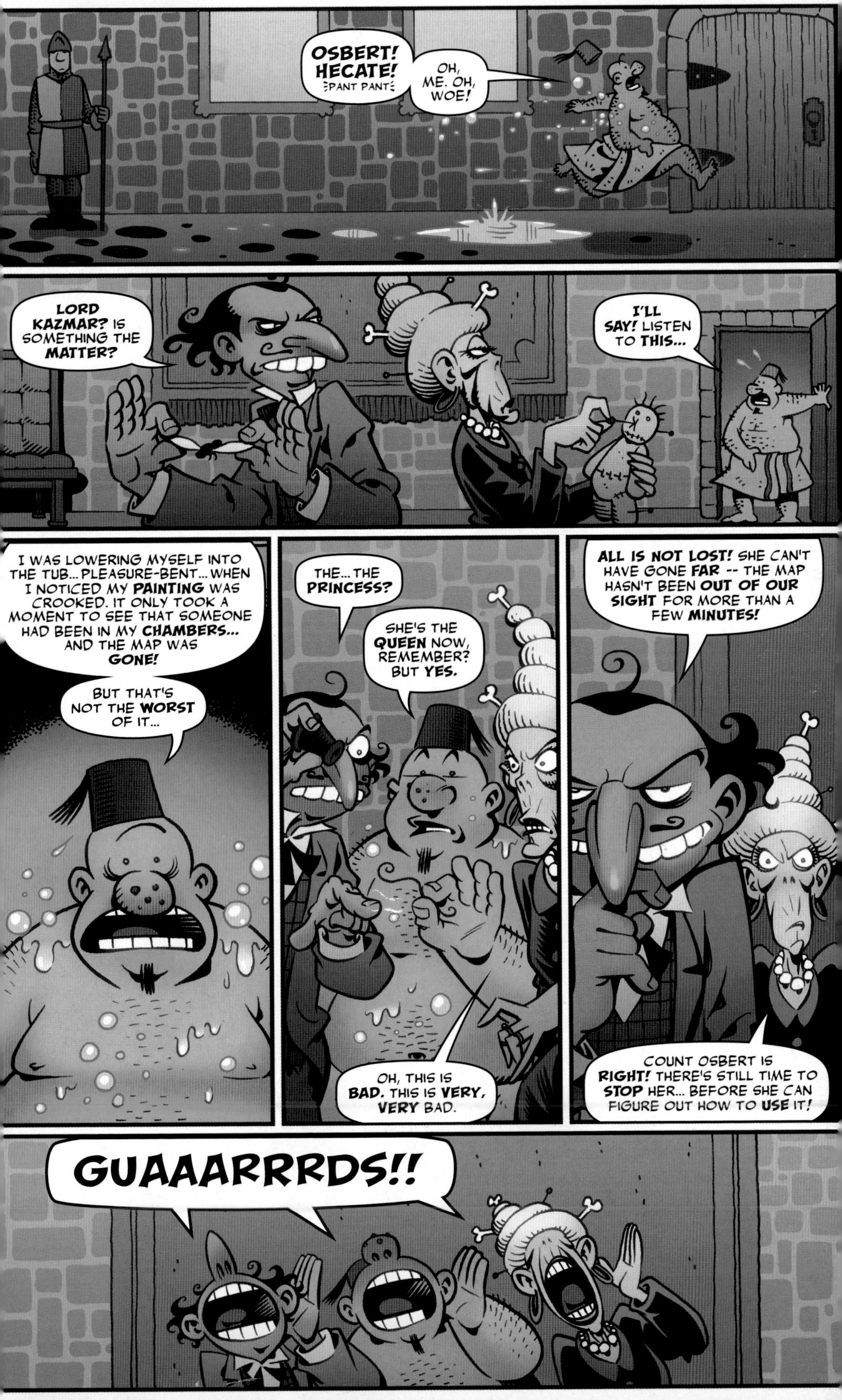
OSBERT! HECATE! PANT PANT
OH, ME. OH, WOE!
LORD KAZMAR? IS SOMETHING THE MATTER?
I'LL SAY! LISTEN TO THIS...
I WAS LOWERING MYSELF INTO THE TUB... PLEASURE-BENT... WHEN I NOTICED MY PAINTING WAS CROOKED. IT ONLY TOOK A MOMENT TO SEE THAT SOMEONE HAD BEEN IN MY CHAMBERS... AND THE MAP WAS GONE!
BUT THAT'S NOT THE WORST OF IT...
THE... THE PRINCESS?
SHE'S THE QUEEN NOW, REMEMBER? BUT YES.
OH, THIS IS BAD. THIS IS VERY, VERY BAD.
ALL IS NOT LOST! SHE CAN'T HAVE GONE FAR -- THE MAP HASN'T BEEN OUT OF OUR SIGHT FOR MORE THAN A FEW MINUTES!
COUNT OSBERT IS RIGHT! THERE'S STILL TIME TO STOP HER... BEFORE SHE CAN FIGURE OUT HOW TO USE IT!
GUAAARRRDS!!

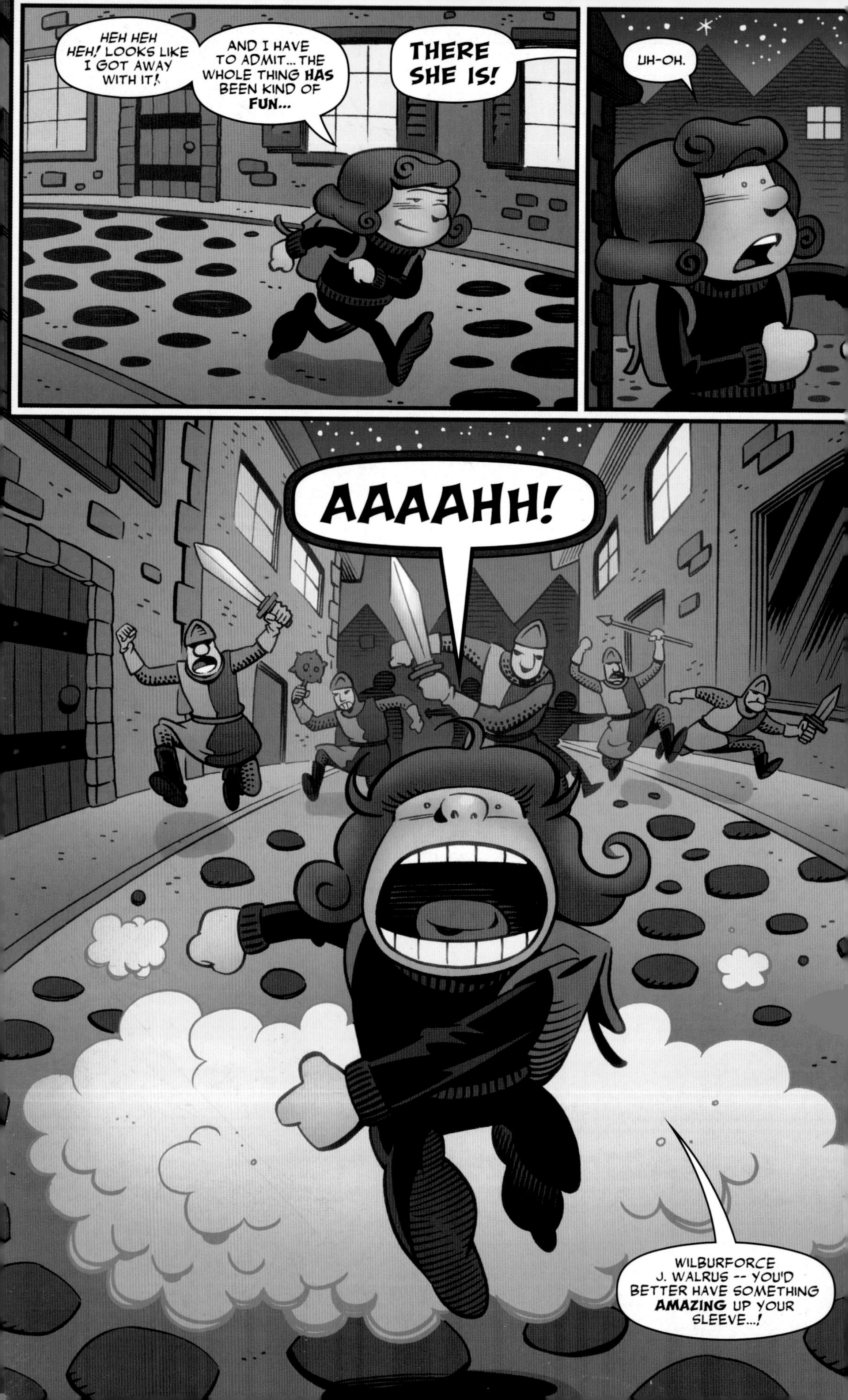
HEH HEH HEH! LOOKS LIKE I GOT AWAY WITH IT!
AND I HAVE TO ADMIT... THE WHOLE THING HAS BEEN KIND OF FUN...
THERE SHE IS!
UH-OH.
AAAAHH!
WILBURFORCE J. WALRUS -- YOU'D BETTER HAVE SOMETHING AMAZING UP YOUR SLEEVE...!

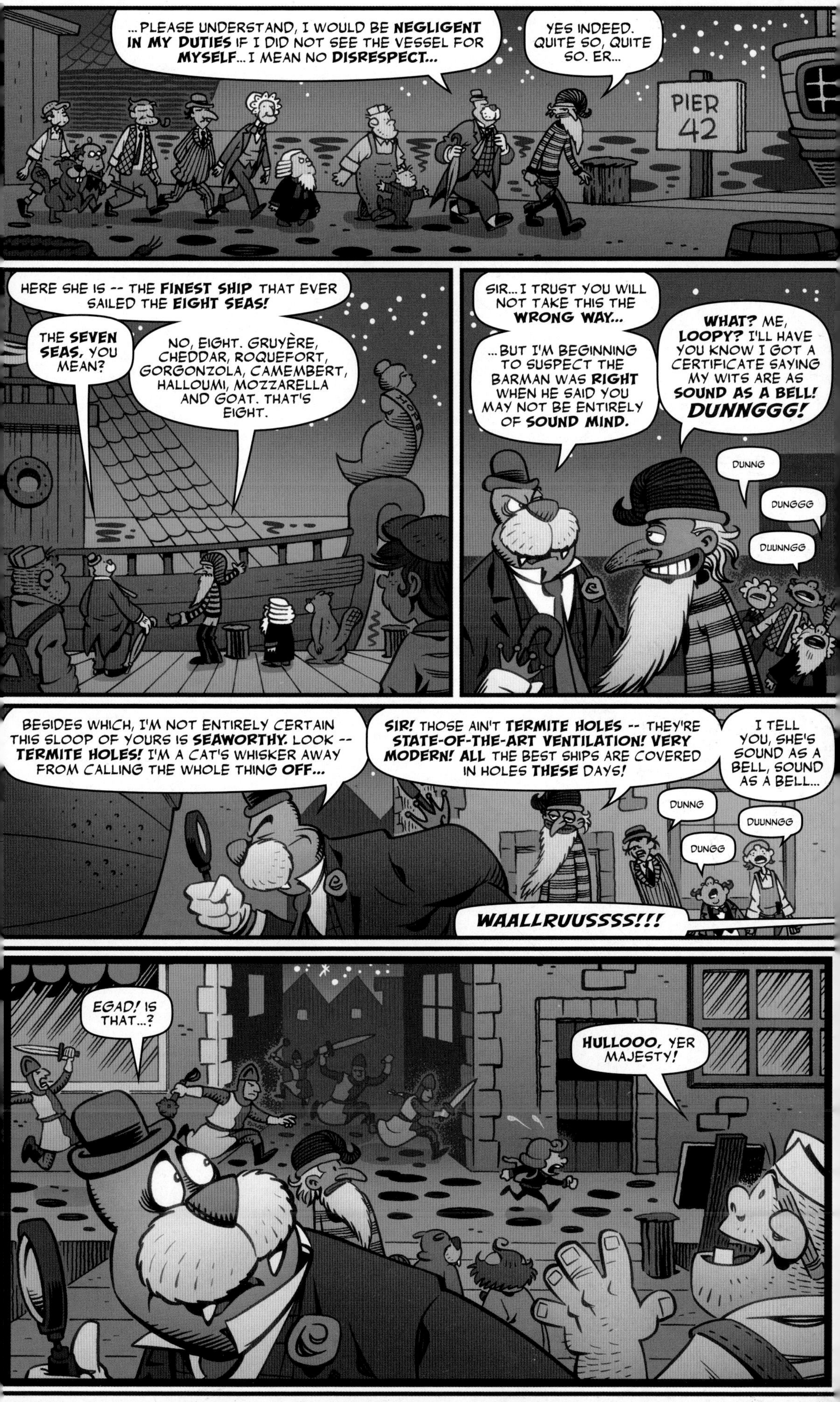
...PLEASE UNDERSTAND, I WOULD BE NEGLIGENT IN MY DUTIES IF I DID NOT SEE THE VESSEL FOR MYSELF... I MEAN NO DISRESPECT...
YES INDEED. QUITE SO, QUITE SO. ER...
PIER 42
HERE SHE IS -- THE FINEST SHIP THAT EVER SAILED THE EIGHT SEAS!
THE SEVEN SEAS, YOU MEAN?
NO, EIGHT. GRUYÈRE, CHEDDAR, ROQUEFORT, GORGONZOLA, CAMEMBERT, HALLOUMI, MOZZARELLA AND GOAT. THAT'S EIGHT.
SIR... I TRUST YOU WILL NOT TAKE THIS THE WRONG WAY...
...BUT I'M BEGINNING TO SUSPECT THE BARMAN WAS RIGHT WHEN HE SAID YOU MAY NOT BE ENTIRELY OF SOUND MIND.
WHAT? ME, LOOPY? I'LL HAVE YOU KNOW I GOT A CERTIFICATE SAYING MY WITS ARE AS SOUND AS A BELL! DUNNGGG!
DUNNG
DUNGGG
DUUNNGG
BESIDES WHICH, I'M NOT ENTIRELY CERTAIN THIS SLOOP OF YOURS IS SEAWORTHY. LOOK -- TERMITE HOLES! I'M A CAT'S WHISKER AWAY FROM CALLING THE WHOLE THING OFF...
SIR! THOSE AIN'T TERMITE HOLES -- THEY'RE STATE-OF-THE-ART VENTILATION! VERY MODERN! ALL THE BEST SHIPS ARE COVERED IN HOLES THESE DAYS!
I TELL YOU, SHE'S SOUND AS A BELL, SOUND AS A BELL...
DUNNG
DUNGG
DUUNNGG
WAALLRUUSSSS!!!
EGAD! IS THAT...?
HULLOOO, YER MAJESTY!

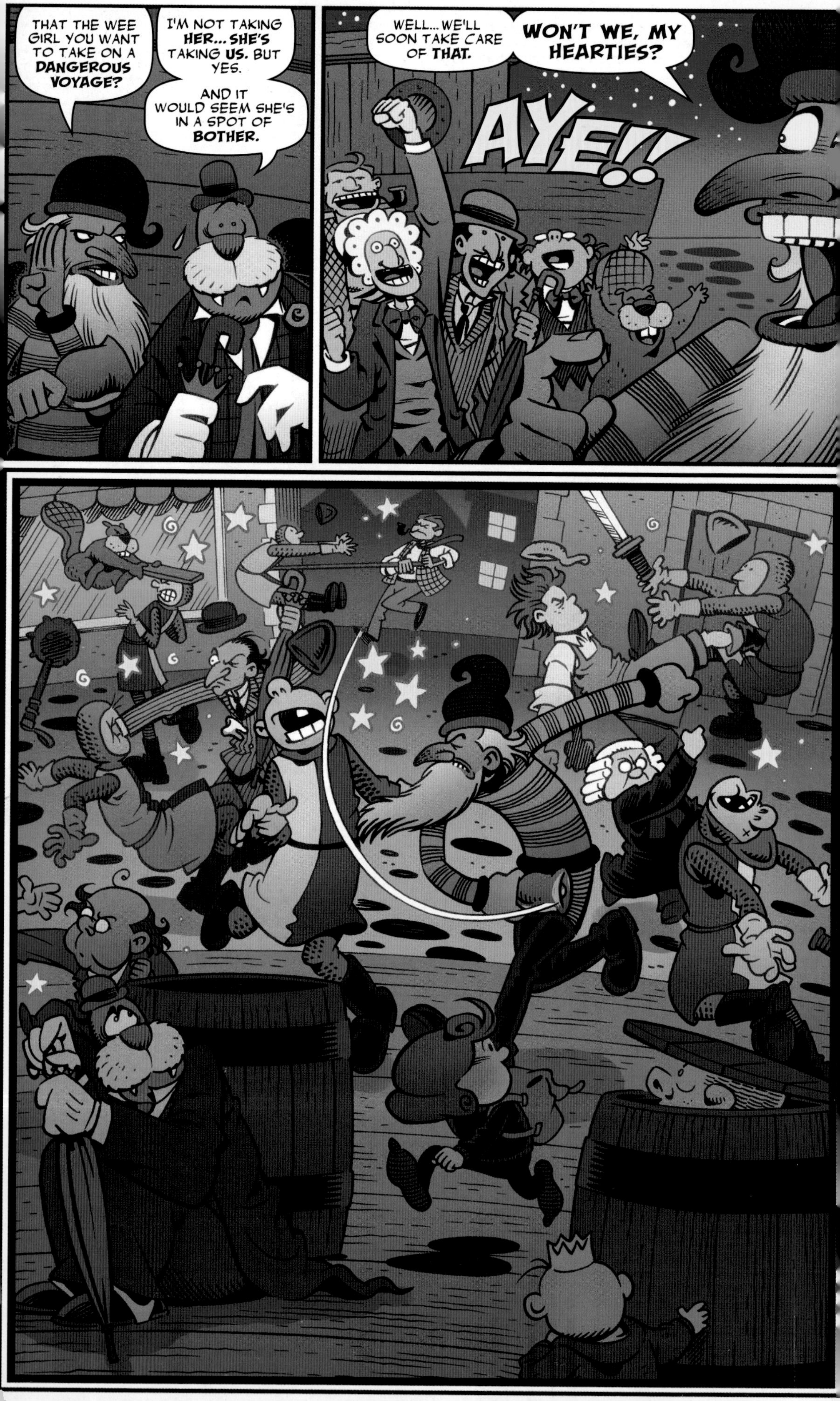
THAT THE WEE GIRL YOU WANT TO TAKE ON A DANGEROUS VOYAGE?
I'M NOT TAKING HER... SHE'S TAKING US. BUT YES.
AND IT WOULD SEEM SHE'S IN A SPOT OF BOTHER.
WELL... WE'LL SOON TAKE CARE OF THAT.
WON'T WE, MY HEARTIES?
AYE!!

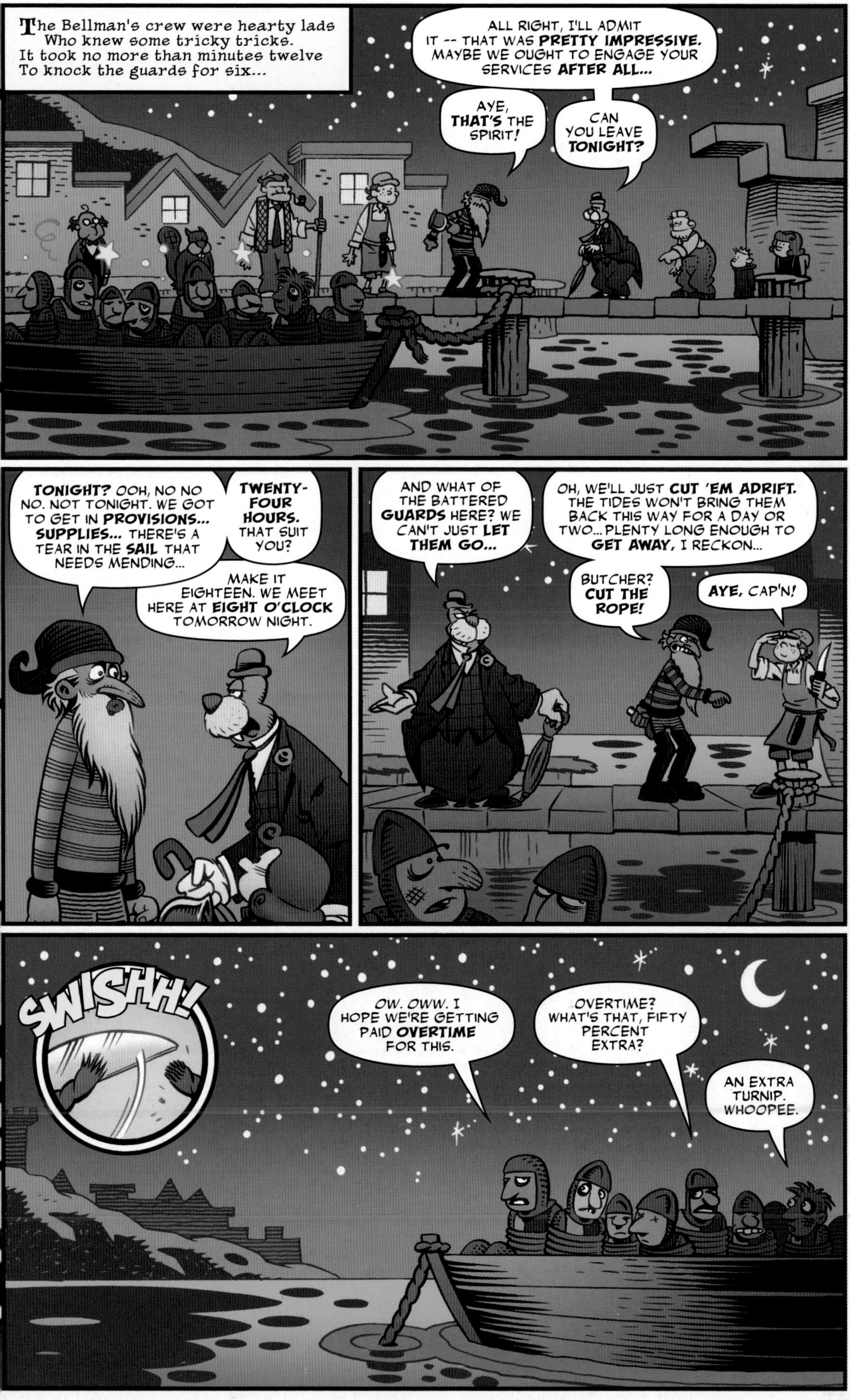
The Bellman's crew were hearty lads
Who knew some tricky tricks.
It took no more than minutes twelve
To knock the guards for six...
ALL RIGHT, I'LL ADMIT IT -- THAT WAS PRETTY IMPRESSIVE. MAYBE WE OUGHT TO ENGAGE YOUR SERVICES AFTER ALL...
AYE, THAT'S THE SPIRIT!
CAN YOU LEAVE TONIGHT?
TONIGHT? OOH, NO NO NO. NOT TONIGHT. WE GOT TO GET IN PROVISIONS... SUPPLIES... THERE'S A TEAR IN THE SAIL THAT NEEDS MENDING...
TWENTY-FOUR HOURS. THAT SUIT YOU?
MAKE IT EIGHTEEN. WE MEET HERE AT EIGHT O'CLOCK TOMORROW NIGHT.
AND WHAT OF THE BATTERED GUARDS HERE? WE CAN'T JUST LET THEM GO...
OH, WE'LL JUST CUT 'EM ADRIFT. THE TIDES WON'T BRING THEM BACK THIS WAY FOR A DAY OR TWO... PLENTY LONG ENOUGH TO GET AWAY, I RECKON...
BUTCHER? CUT THE ROPE!
AYE, CAP'N!
SWISHH!
OW. OWW. I HOPE WE'RE GETTING PAID OVERTIME FOR THIS.
OVERTIME? WHAT'S THAT, FIFTY PERCENT EXTRA?
AN EXTRA TURNIP. WHOOPEE.

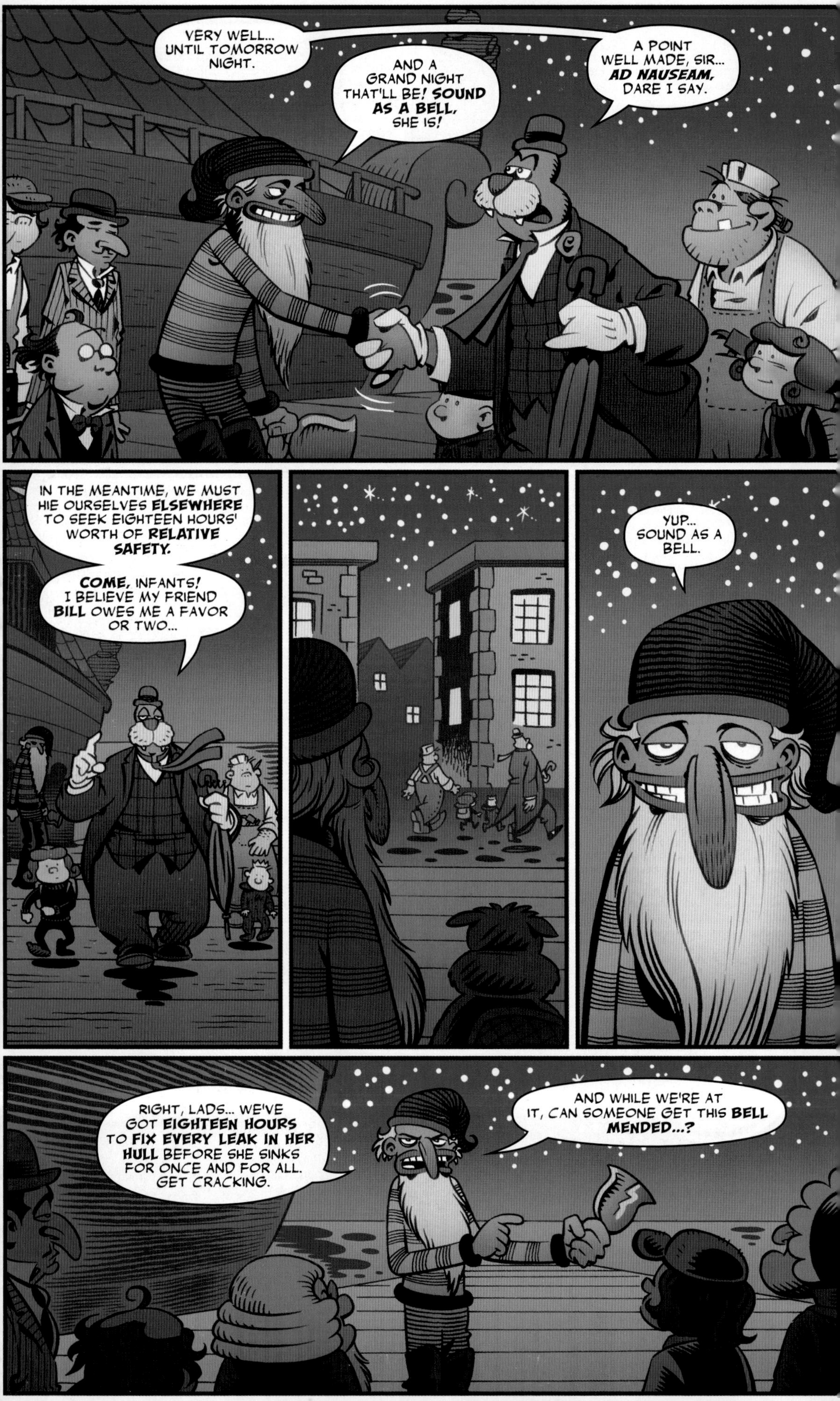
VERY WELL... UNTIL TOMORROW NIGHT.
AND A GRAND NIGHT THAT'LL BE! **SOUND AS A BELL,** SHE IS!
A POINT WELL MADE, SIR... ***AD NAUSEAM,*** DARE I SAY.
IN THE MEANTIME, WE MUST HIE OURSELVES **ELSEWHERE** TO SEEK EIGHTEEN HOURS' WORTH OF **RELATIVE SAFETY.**
COME, INFANTS! I BELIEVE MY FRIEND **BILL** OWES ME A FAVOR OR TWO...
YUP... SOUND AS A BELL.
RIGHT, LADS... WE'VE GOT **EIGHTEEN HOURS** TO **FIX EVERY LEAK IN HER HULL** BEFORE SHE SINKS FOR ONCE AND FOR ALL. GET CRACKING.
AND WHILE WE'RE AT IT, CAN SOMEONE GET THIS **BELL MENDED...?**

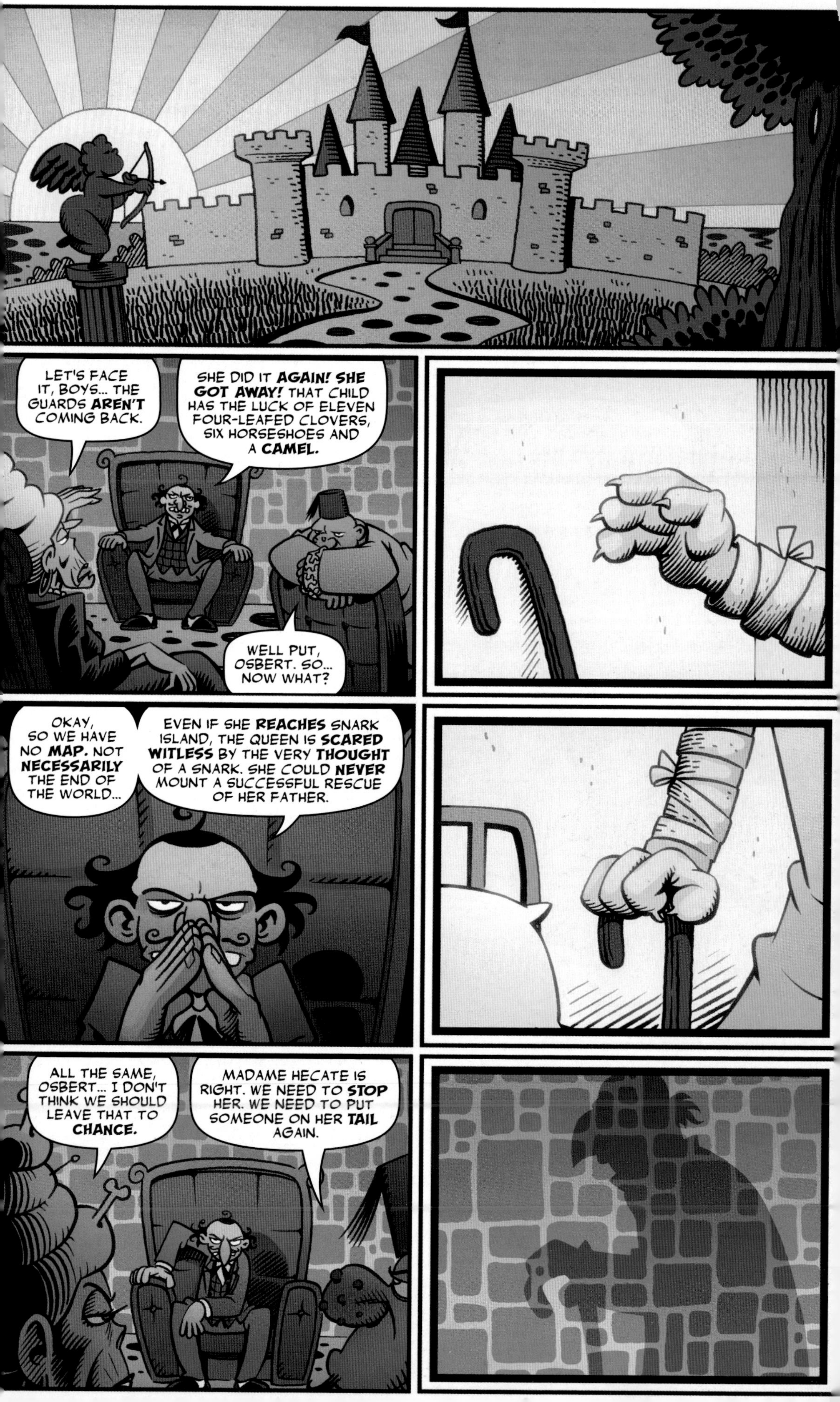
LET'S FACE IT, BOYS... THE GUARDS AREN'T COMING BACK.
SHE DID IT AGAIN! SHE GOT AWAY! THAT CHILD HAS THE LUCK OF ELEVEN FOUR-LEAFED CLOVERS, SIX HORSESHOES AND A CAMEL.
WELL PUT, OSBERT. SO... NOW WHAT?
OKAY, SO WE HAVE NO MAP. NOT NECESSARILY THE END OF THE WORLD...
EVEN IF SHE REACHES SNARK ISLAND, THE QUEEN IS SCARED WITLESS BY THE VERY THOUGHT OF A SNARK. SHE COULD NEVER MOUNT A SUCCESSFUL RESCUE OF HER FATHER.
ALL THE SAME, OSBERT... I DON'T THINK WE SHOULD LEAVE THAT TO CHANCE.
MADAME HECATE IS RIGHT. WE NEED TO STOP HER. WE NEED TO PUT SOMEONE ON HER TAIL AGAIN.

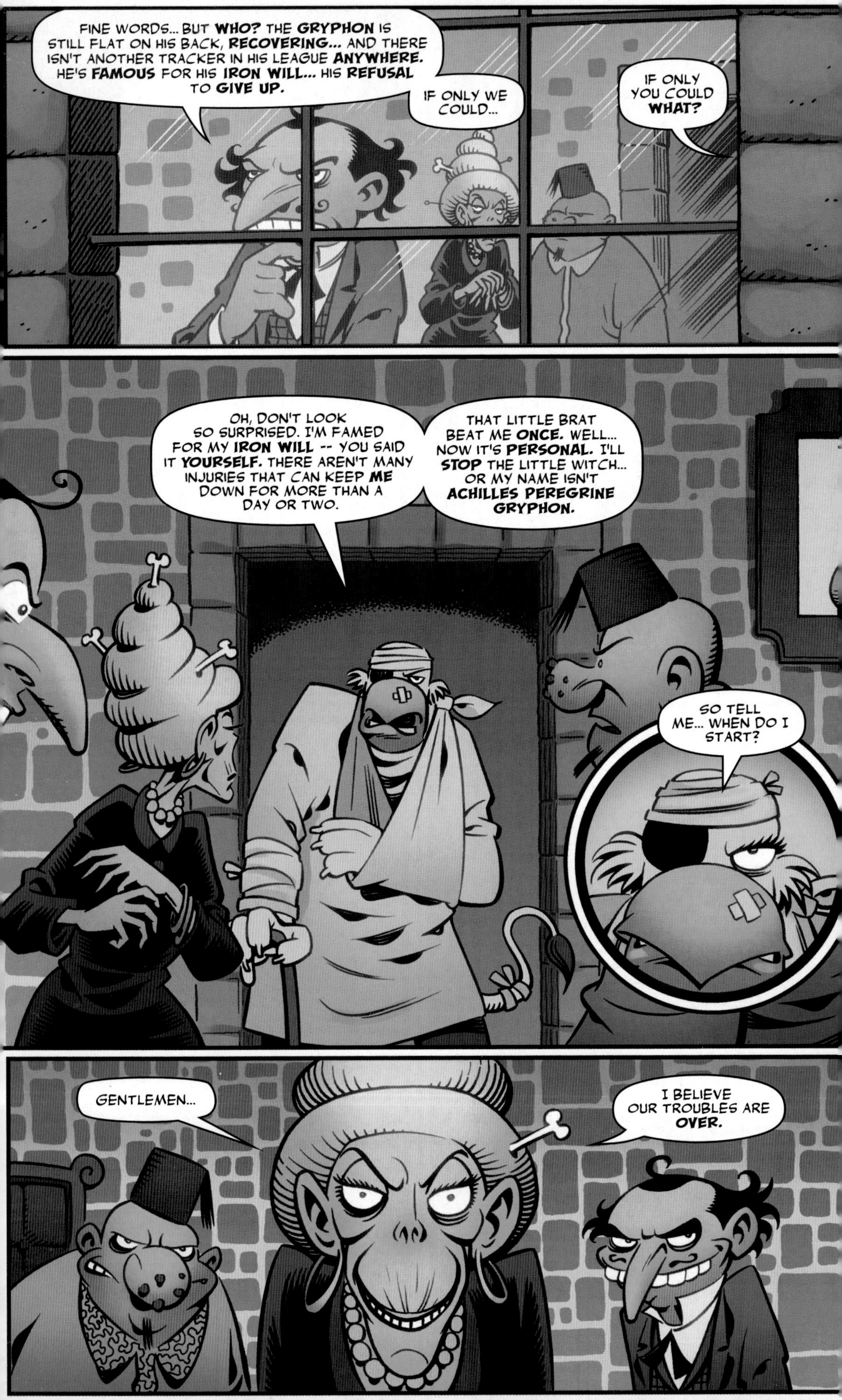
FINE WORDS... BUT WHO? THE GRYPHON IS STILL FLAT ON HIS BACK, RECOVERING... AND THERE ISN'T ANOTHER TRACKER IN HIS LEAGUE ANYWHERE. HE'S FAMOUS FOR HIS IRON WILL... HIS REFUSAL TO GIVE UP.
IF ONLY WE COULD...
IF ONLY YOU COULD WHAT?
OH, DON'T LOOK SO SURPRISED. I'M FAMED FOR MY IRON WILL -- YOU SAID IT YOURSELF. THERE AREN'T MANY INJURIES THAT CAN KEEP ME DOWN FOR MORE THAN A DAY OR TWO.
THAT LITTLE BRAT BEAT ME ONCE. WELL... NOW IT'S PERSONAL. I'LL STOP THE LITTLE WITCH... OR MY NAME ISN'T ACHILLES PEREGRINE GRYPHON.
SO TELL ME... WHEN DO I START?
GENTLEMEN...
I BELIEVE OUR TROUBLES ARE OVER.

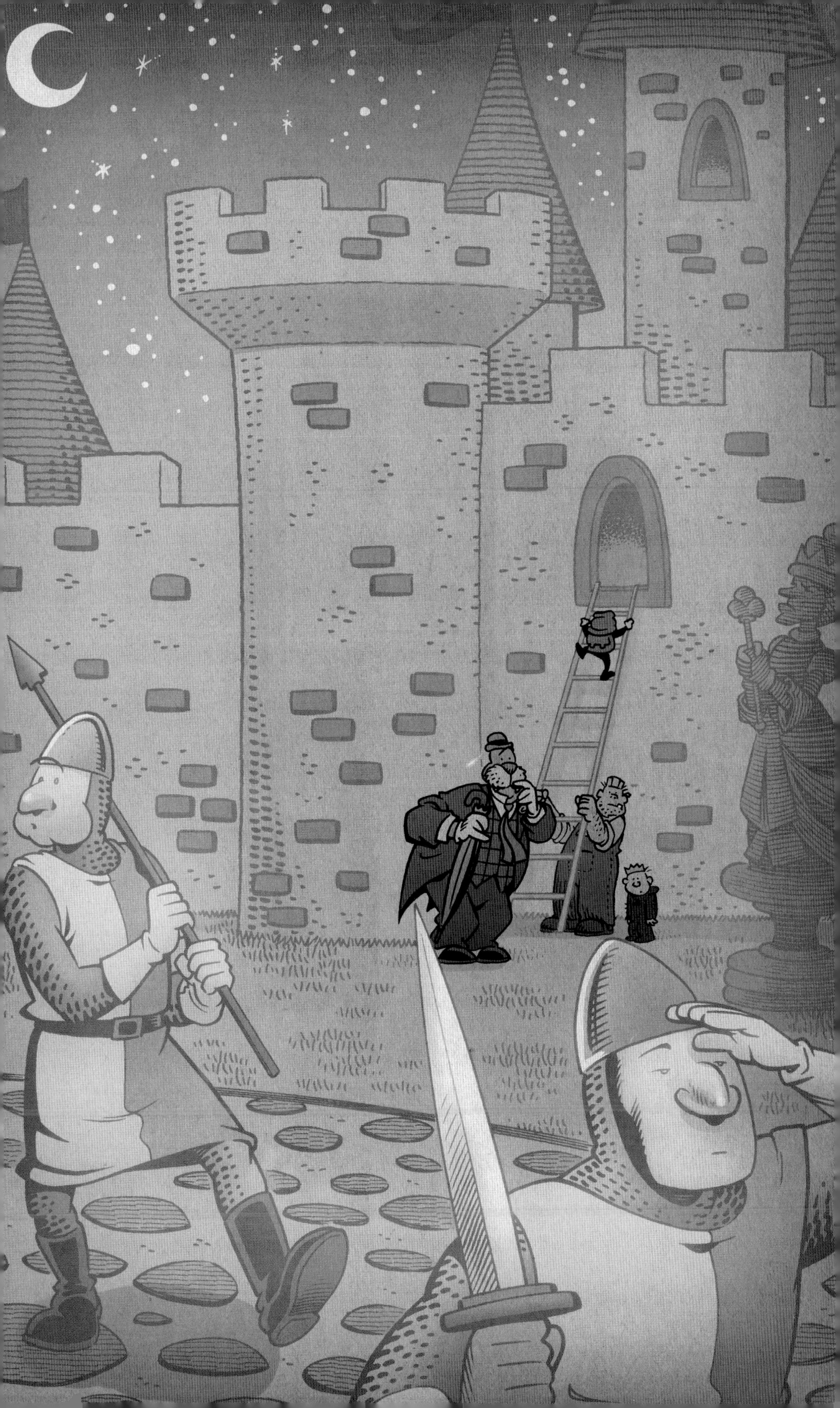

FIT THE FOURTH

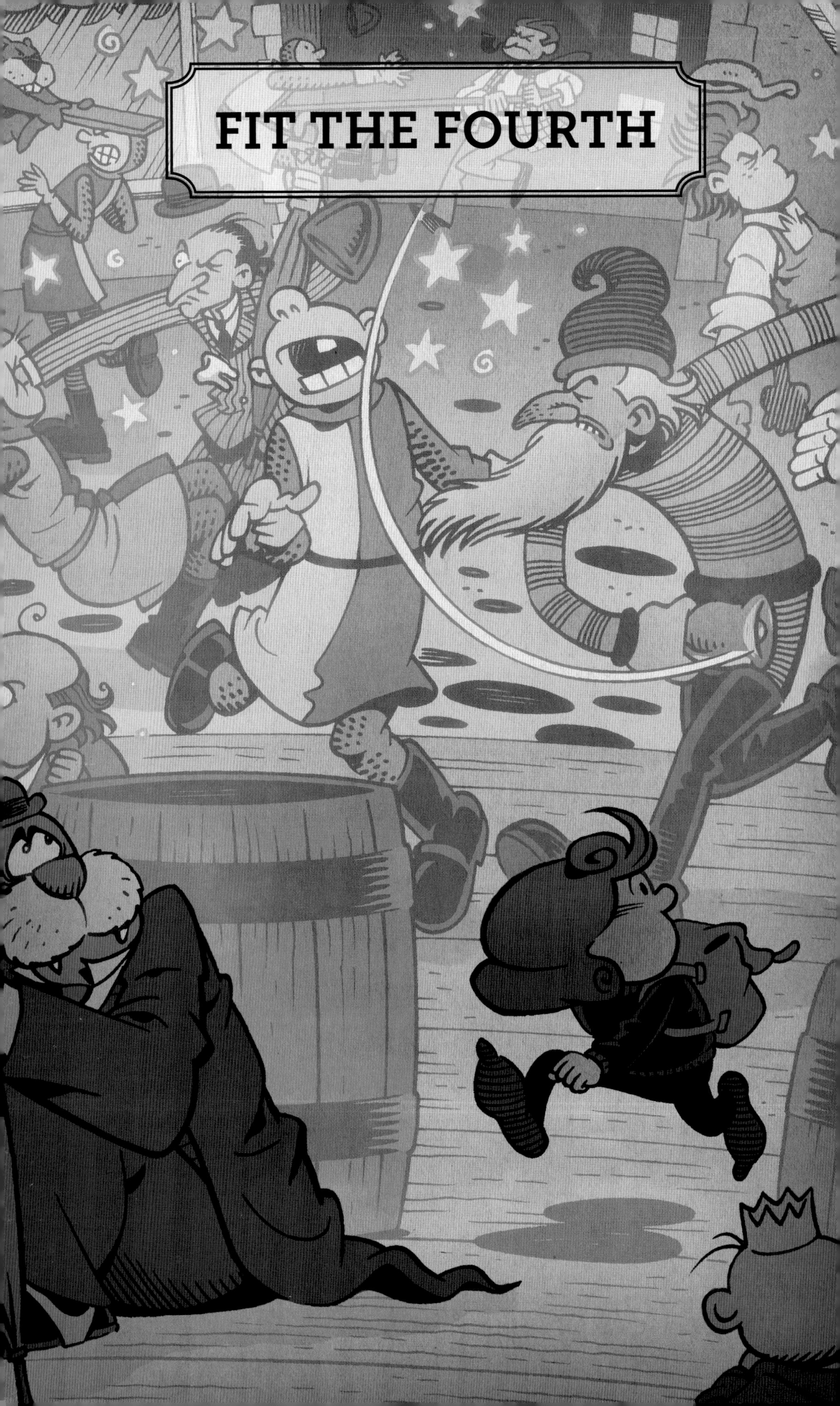

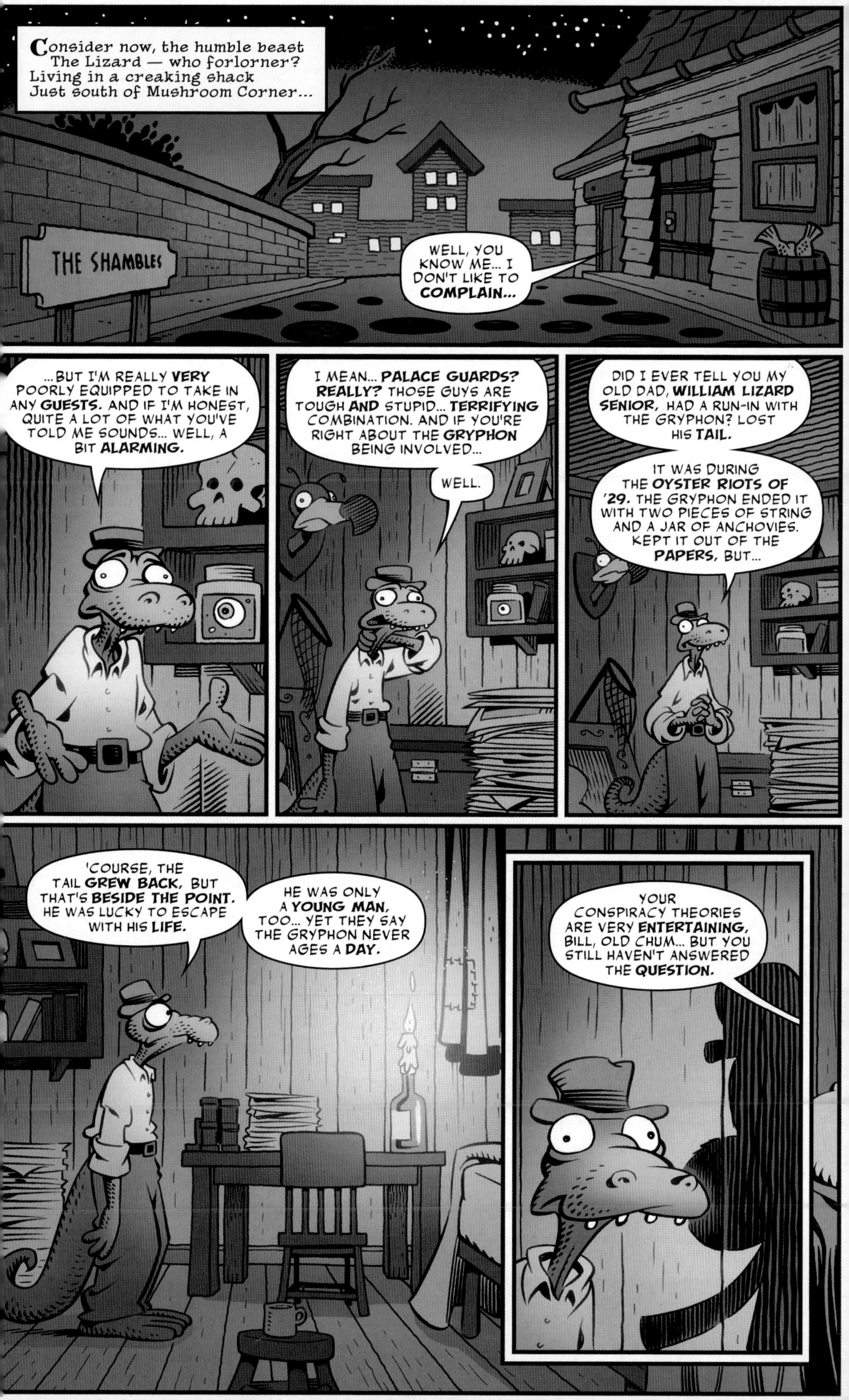

Consider now, the humble beast The Lizard — who forlorner? Living in a creaking shack Just south of Mushroom Corner...
THE SHAMBLES
WELL, YOU KNOW ME... I DON'T LIKE TO COMPLAIN...
...BUT I'M REALLY VERY POORLY EQUIPPED TO TAKE IN ANY GUESTS. AND IF I'M HONEST, QUITE A LOT OF WHAT YOU'VE TOLD ME SOUNDS... WELL, A BIT ALARMING.
I MEAN... PALACE GUARDS? REALLY? THOSE GUYS ARE TOUGH AND STUPID... TERRIFYING COMBINATION. AND IF YOU'RE RIGHT ABOUT THE GRYPHON BEING INVOLVED...
WELL.
DID I EVER TELL YOU MY OLD DAD, WILLIAM LIZARD SENIOR, HAD A RUN-IN WITH THE GRYPHON? LOST HIS TAIL.
IT WAS DURING THE OYSTER RIOTS OF '29. THE GRYPHON ENDED IT WITH TWO PIECES OF STRING AND A JAR OF ANCHOVIES. KEPT IT OUT OF THE PAPERS, BUT...
'COURSE, THE TAIL GREW BACK, BUT THAT'S BESIDE THE POINT. HE WAS LUCKY TO ESCAPE WITH HIS LIFE.
HE WAS ONLY A YOUNG MAN, TOO... YET THEY SAY THE GRYPHON NEVER AGES A DAY.
YOUR CONSPIRACY THEORIES ARE VERY ENTERTAINING, BILL, OLD CHUM... BUT YOU STILL HAVEN'T ANSWERED THE QUESTION.

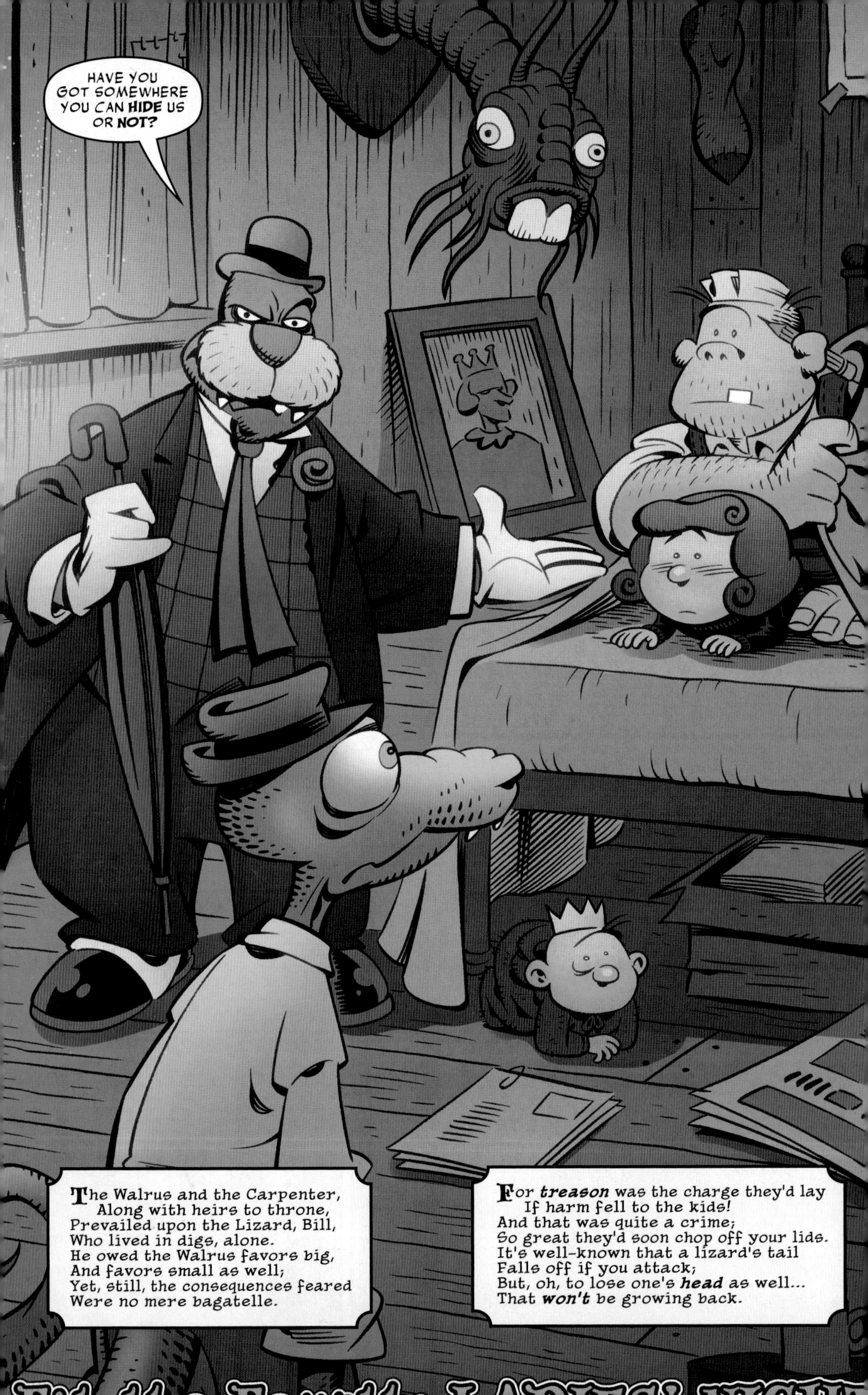
HAVE YOU GOT SOMEWHERE YOU CAN **HIDE** US OR **NOT?**
The Walrus and the Carpenter,
Along with heirs to throne,
Prevailed upon the Lizard, Bill,
Who lived in digs, alone.
He owed the Walrus favors big,
And favors small as well;
Yet, still, the consequences feared
Were no mere bagatelle.
For *treason* was the charge they'd lay
If harm fell to the kids!
And that was quite a crime;
So great they'd soon chop off your lids.
It's well-known that a lizard's tail
Falls off if you attack;
But, oh, to lose one's *head* as well...
That *won't* be growing back.

Fit the Fourth: LADIES' NIGHT

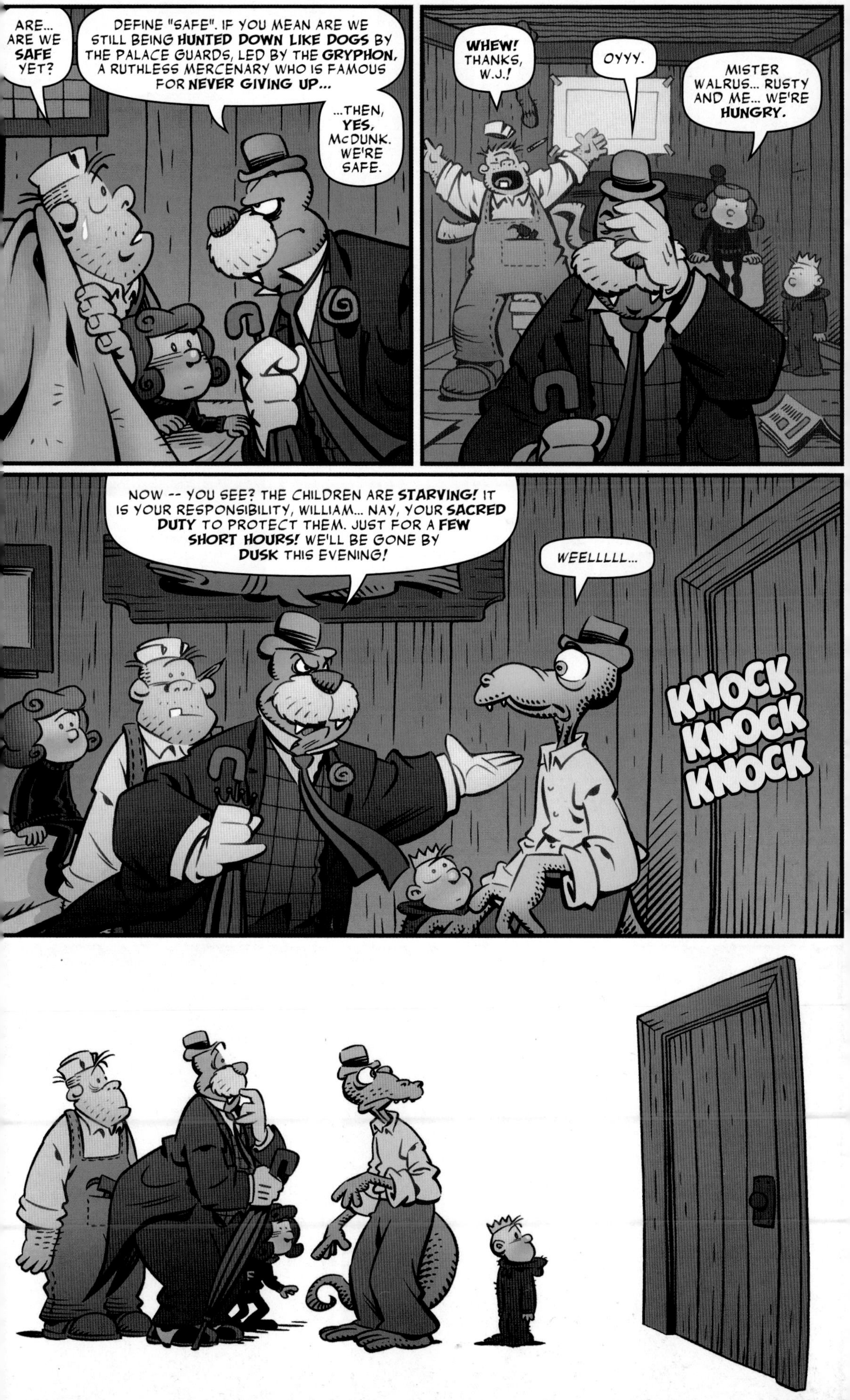
ARE... ARE WE SAFE YET?
DEFINE "SAFE". IF YOU MEAN ARE WE STILL BEING HUNTED DOWN LIKE DOGS BY THE PALACE GUARDS, LED BY THE GRYPHON, A RUTHLESS MERCENARY WHO IS FAMOUS FOR NEVER GIVING UP...
...THEN, YES, McDUNK. WE'RE SAFE.
WHEW! THANKS, W.J.!
OYYY.
MISTER WALRUS... RUSTY AND ME... WE'RE HUNGRY.
NOW -- YOU SEE? THE CHILDREN ARE STARVING! IT IS YOUR RESPONSIBILITY, WILLIAM... NAY, YOUR SACRED DUTY TO PROTECT THEM. JUST FOR A FEW SHORT HOURS! WE'LL BE GONE BY DUSK THIS EVENING!
WEELLLLL...
KNOCK KNOCK KNOCK

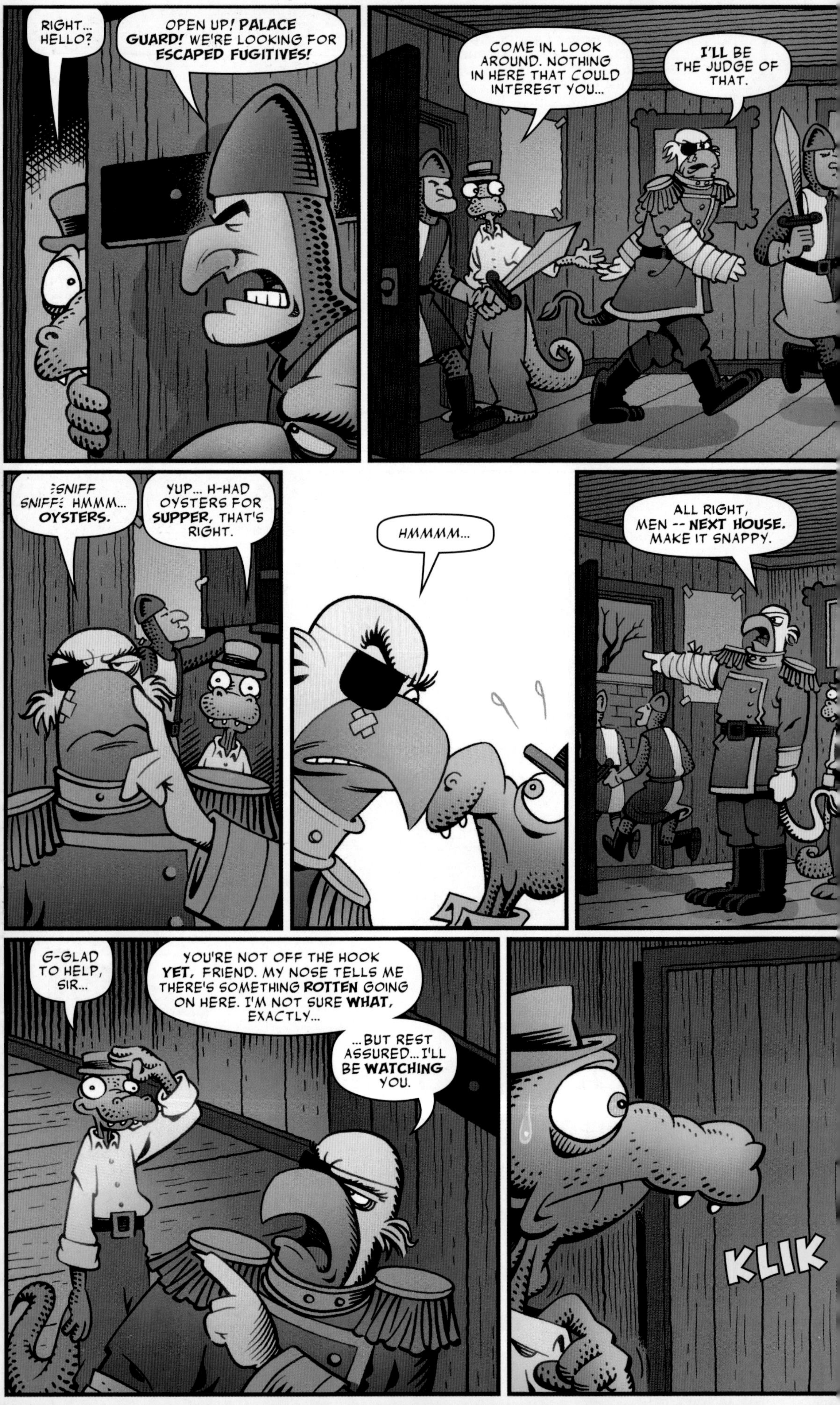
RIGHT... HELLO?
OPEN UP! **PALACE GUARD!** WE'RE LOOKING FOR **ESCAPED FUGITIVES!**
COME IN. LOOK AROUND. NOTHING IN HERE THAT COULD INTEREST YOU...
I'LL BE THE JUDGE OF THAT.
SNIFF SNIFF HMMM... **OYSTERS.**
YUP... H-HAD OYSTERS FOR **SUPPER**, THAT'S RIGHT.
HMMMM...
ALL RIGHT, MEN -- **NEXT HOUSE.** MAKE IT SNAPPY.
G-GLAD TO HELP, SIR...
YOU'RE NOT OFF THE HOOK **YET**, FRIEND. MY NOSE TELLS ME THERE'S SOMETHING **ROTTEN** GOING ON HERE. I'M NOT SURE **WHAT**, EXACTLY...
...BUT REST ASSURED... I'LL BE **WATCHING** YOU.
KLIK

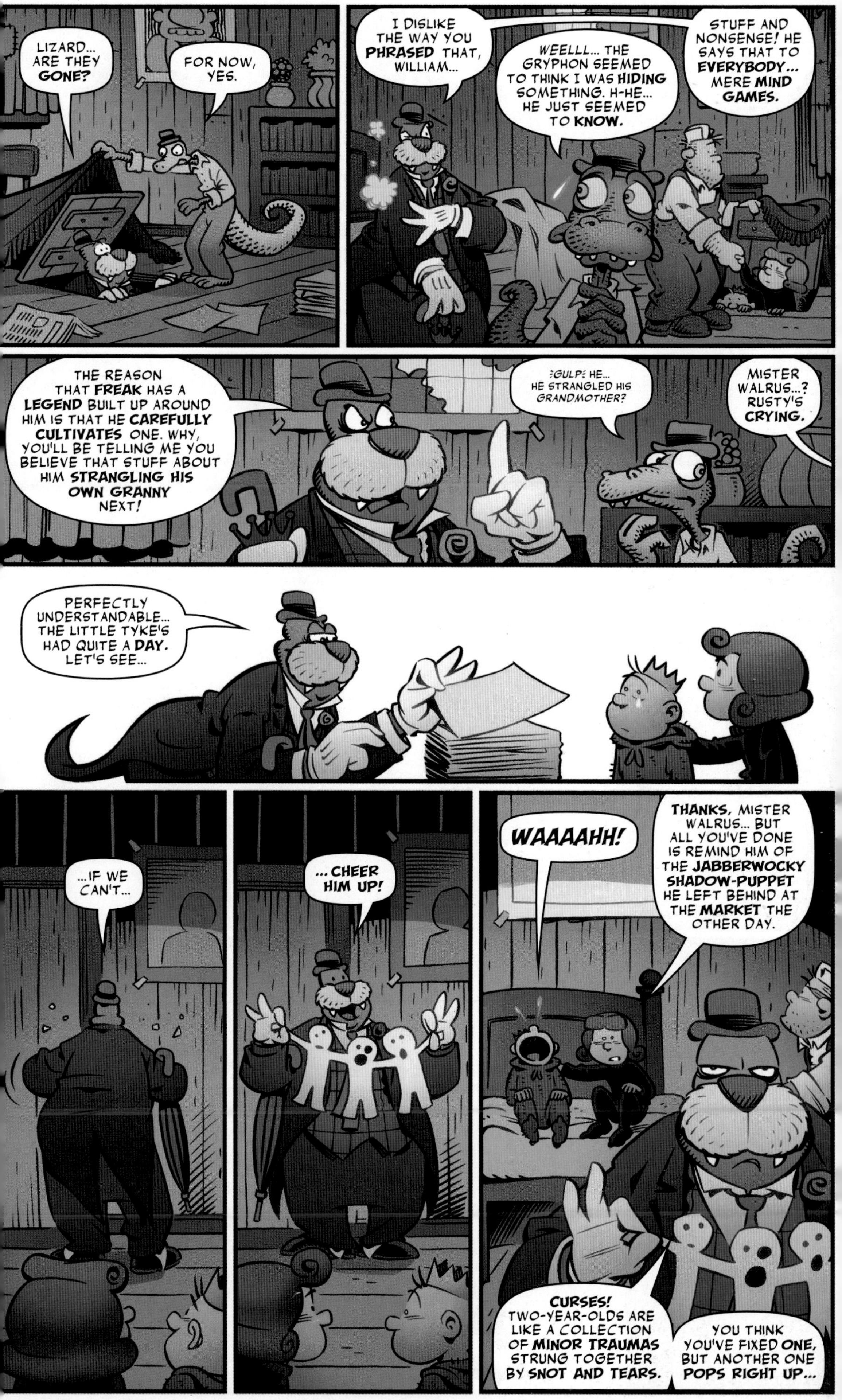
LIZARD... ARE THEY GONE?
FOR NOW, YES.
I DISLIKE THE WAY YOU PHRASED THAT, WILLIAM...
WEELLL... THE GRYPHON SEEMED TO THINK I WAS HIDING SOMETHING. H-HE... HE JUST SEEMED TO KNOW.
STUFF AND NONSENSE! HE SAYS THAT TO EVERYBODY... MERE MIND GAMES.
THE REASON THAT FREAK HAS A LEGEND BUILT UP AROUND HIM IS THAT HE CAREFULLY CULTIVATES ONE. WHY, YOU'LL BE TELLING ME YOU BELIEVE THAT STUFF ABOUT HIM STRANGLING HIS OWN GRANNY NEXT!
:GULP: HE... HE STRANGLED HIS GRANDMOTHER?
MISTER WALRUS...? RUSTY'S CRYING.
PERFECTLY UNDERSTANDABLE... THE LITTLE TYKE'S HAD QUITE A DAY. LET'S SEE...
...IF WE CAN'T...
...CHEER HIM UP!
WAAAAHH!
THANKS, MISTER WALRUS... BUT ALL YOU'VE DONE IS REMIND HIM OF THE JABBERWOCKY SHADOW-PUPPET HE LEFT BEHIND AT THE MARKET THE OTHER DAY.
CURSES! TWO-YEAR-OLDS ARE LIKE A COLLECTION OF MINOR TRAUMAS STRUNG TOGETHER BY SNOT AND TEARS.
YOU THINK YOU'VE FIXED ONE, BUT ANOTHER ONE POPS RIGHT UP...

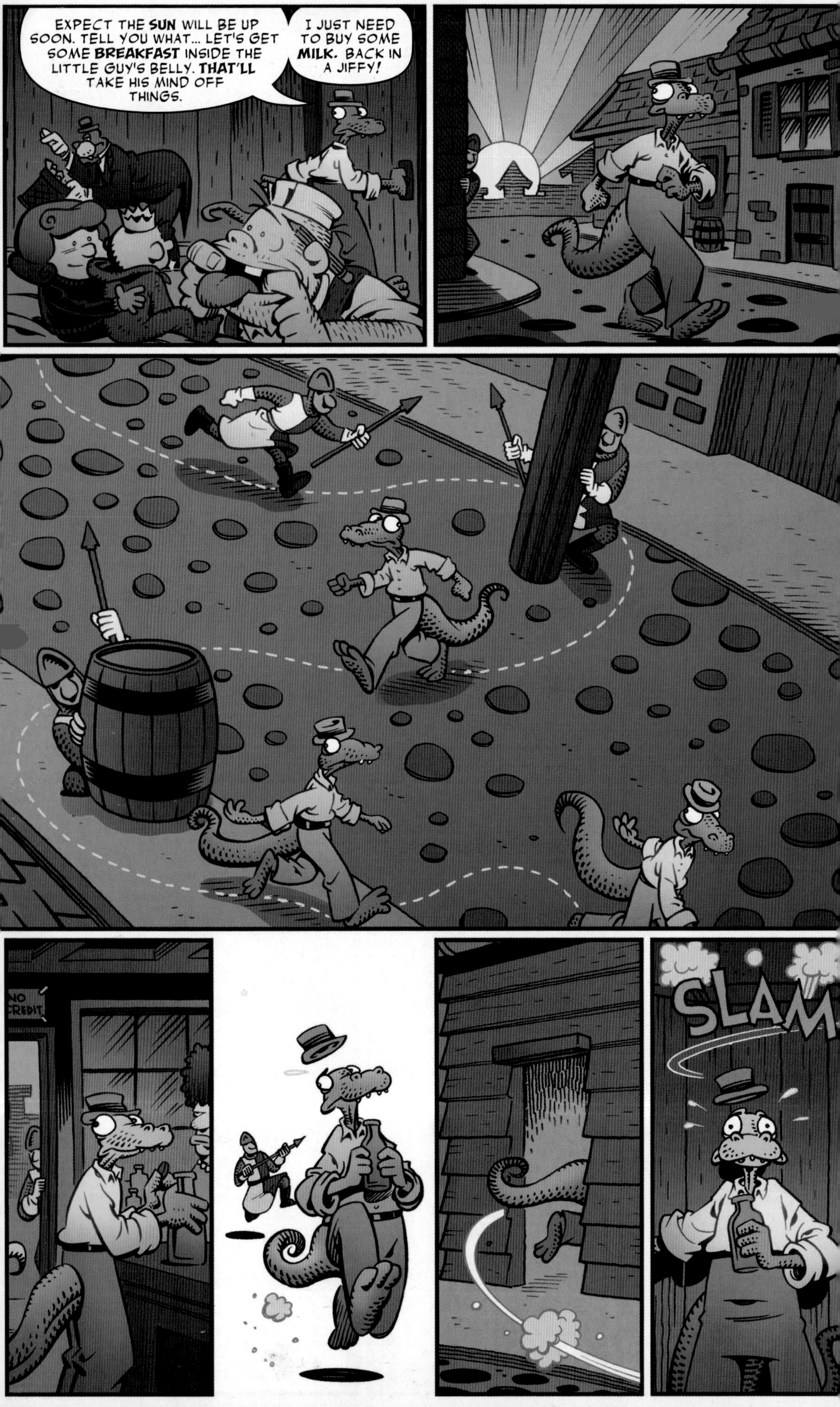
EXPECT THE SUN WILL BE UP SOON. TELL YOU WHAT... LET'S GET SOME BREAKFAST INSIDE THE LITTLE GUY'S BELLY. THAT'LL TAKE HIS MIND OFF THINGS.
I JUST NEED TO BUY SOME MILK. BACK IN A JIFFY!
NO CREDIT
SLAM

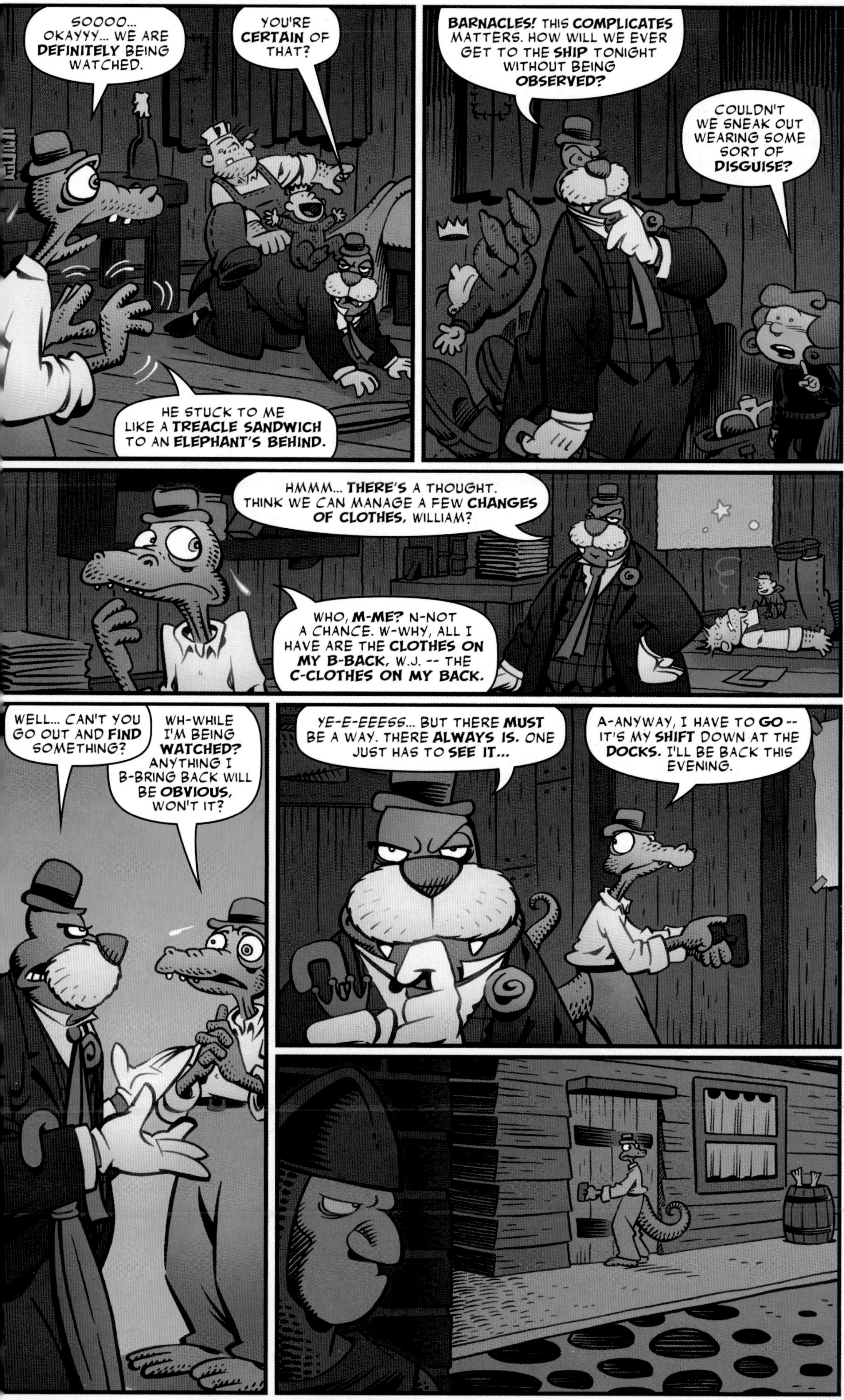
SOOOO... OKAYYY... WE ARE DEFINITELY BEING WATCHED.
YOU'RE CERTAIN OF THAT?
HE STUCK TO ME LIKE A TREACLE SANDWICH TO AN ELEPHANT'S BEHIND.
BARNACLES! THIS COMPLICATES MATTERS. HOW WILL WE EVER GET TO THE SHIP TONIGHT WITHOUT BEING OBSERVED?
COULDN'T WE SNEAK OUT WEARING SOME SORT OF DISGUISE?
HMMM... THERE'S A THOUGHT. THINK WE CAN MANAGE A FEW CHANGES OF CLOTHES, WILLIAM?
WHO, M-ME? N-NOT A CHANCE. W-WHY, ALL I HAVE ARE THE CLOTHES ON MY B-BACK, W.J. -- THE C-CLOTHES ON MY BACK.
WELL... CAN'T YOU GO OUT AND FIND SOMETHING?
WH-WHILE I'M BEING WATCHED? ANYTHING I B-BRING BACK WILL BE OBVIOUS, WON'T IT?
YE-E-EEESS... BUT THERE MUST BE A WAY. THERE ALWAYS IS. ONE JUST HAS TO SEE IT...
A-ANYWAY, I HAVE TO GO -- IT'S MY SHIFT DOWN AT THE DOCKS. I'LL BE BACK THIS EVENING.

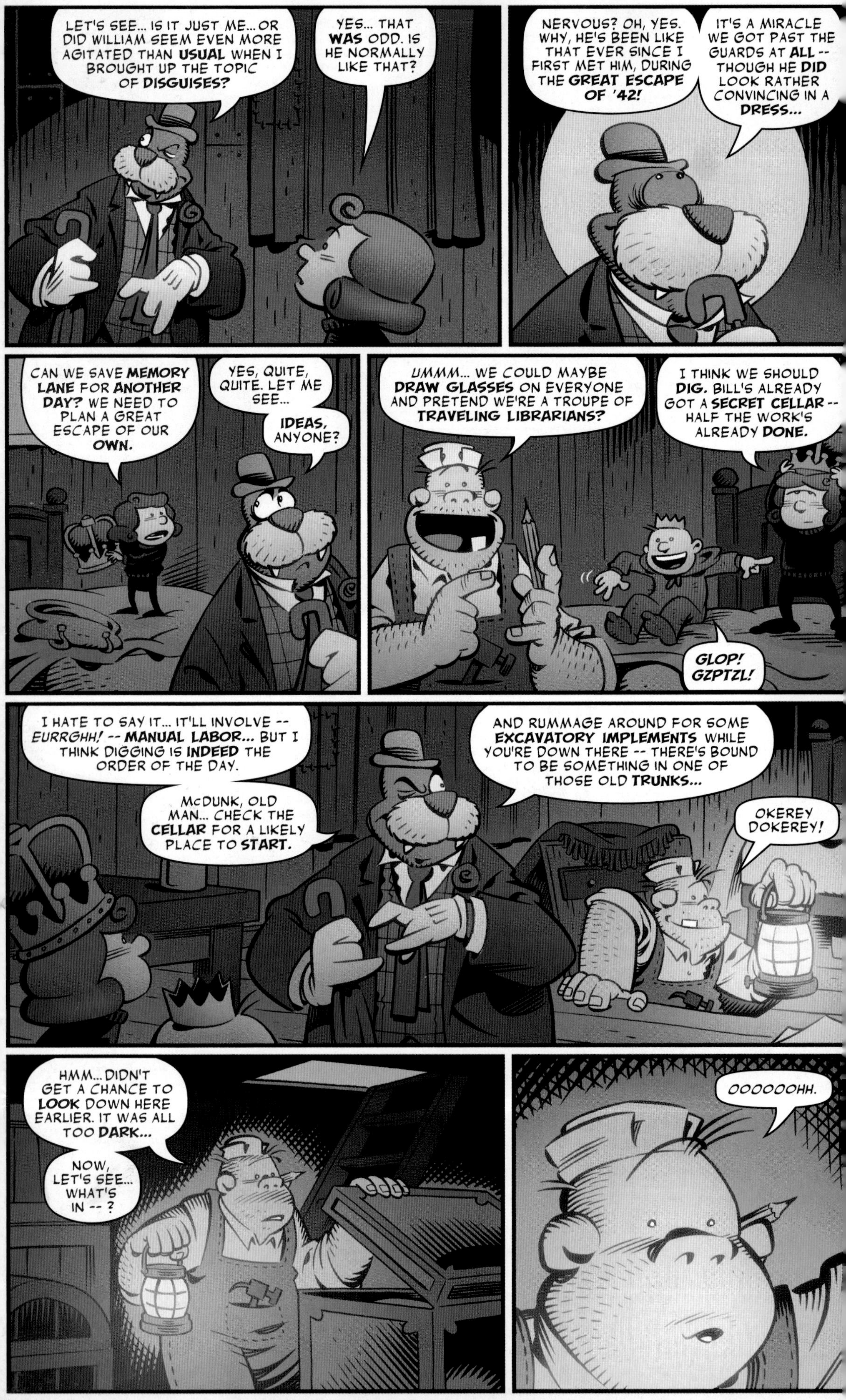
LET'S SEE... IS IT JUST ME... OR DID WILLIAM SEEM EVEN MORE AGITATED THAN USUAL WHEN I BROUGHT UP THE TOPIC OF DISGUISES?
YES... THAT WAS ODD. IS HE NORMALLY LIKE THAT?
NERVOUS? OH, YES. WHY, HE'S BEEN LIKE THAT EVER SINCE I FIRST MET HIM, DURING THE GREAT ESCAPE OF '42!
IT'S A MIRACLE WE GOT PAST THE GUARDS AT ALL -- THOUGH HE DID LOOK RATHER CONVINCING IN A DRESS...
CAN WE SAVE MEMORY LANE FOR ANOTHER DAY? WE NEED TO PLAN A GREAT ESCAPE OF OUR OWN.
YES, QUITE, QUITE. LET ME SEE...
IDEAS, ANYONE?
UMMM... WE COULD MAYBE DRAW GLASSES ON EVERYONE AND PRETEND WE'RE A TROUPE OF TRAVELING LIBRARIANS?
I THINK WE SHOULD DIG. BILL'S ALREADY GOT A SECRET CELLAR -- HALF THE WORK'S ALREADY DONE.
GLOP! GZPTZL!
I HATE TO SAY IT... IT'LL INVOLVE -- EURRGHH! -- MANUAL LABOR... BUT I THINK DIGGING IS INDEED THE ORDER OF THE DAY.
McDUNK, OLD MAN... CHECK THE CELLAR FOR A LIKELY PLACE TO START.
AND RUMMAGE AROUND FOR SOME EXCAVATORY IMPLEMENTS WHILE YOU'RE DOWN THERE -- THERE'S BOUND TO BE SOMETHING IN ONE OF THOSE OLD TRUNKS...
OKEREY DOKEREY!
HMM... DIDN'T GET A CHANCE TO LOOK DOWN HERE EARLIER. IT WAS ALL TOO DARK...
NOW, LET'S SEE... WHAT'S IN -- ?
OOOOOOHH.

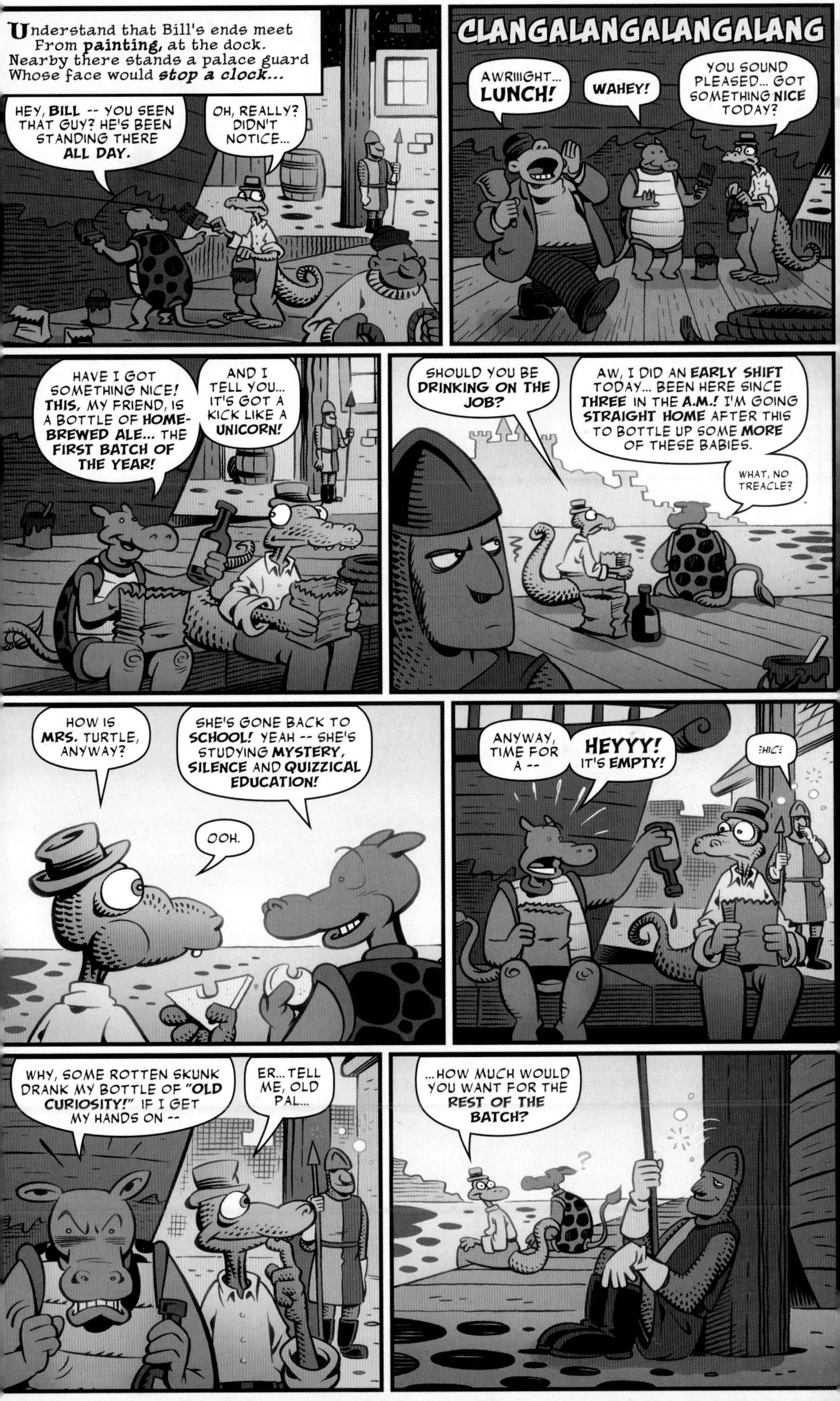
Understand that Bill's ends meet
From **painting**, at the dock.
Nearby there stands a palace guard
Whose face would ***stop a clock...***
HEY, **BILL** -- YOU SEEN THAT GUY? HE'S BEEN STANDING THERE **ALL DAY.**
OH, REALLY? DIDN'T NOTICE...
CLANGALANGALANGALANG
AWRIIIGHT... **LUNCH!**
WAHEY!
YOU SOUND PLEASED... GOT SOMETHING **NICE** TODAY?
HAVE I GOT SOMETHING NICE! **THIS**, MY FRIEND, IS A BOTTLE OF **HOME-BREWED ALE... THE FIRST BATCH OF THE YEAR!**
AND I TELL YOU... IT'S GOT A KICK LIKE A **UNICORN!**
SHOULD YOU BE **DRINKING ON THE JOB?**
AW, I DID AN **EARLY SHIFT** TODAY... BEEN HERE SINCE **THREE** IN THE **A.M.!** I'M GOING **STRAIGHT HOME** AFTER THIS TO BOTTLE UP SOME **MORE** OF THESE BABIES.
WHAT, NO TREACLE?
HOW IS **MRS.** TURTLE, ANYWAY?
SHE'S GONE BACK TO **SCHOOL!** YEAH -- SHE'S STUDYING **MYSTERY, SILENCE** AND **QUIZZICAL EDUCATION!**
OOH.
ANYWAY, TIME FOR A --
HEYYY! IT'S **EMPTY!**
HIC
WHY, SOME ROTTEN SKUNK DRANK MY BOTTLE OF **"OLD CURIOSITY!"** IF I GET MY HANDS ON --
ER... TELL ME, OLD PAL...
...HOW MUCH WOULD YOU WANT FOR THE **REST OF THE BATCH?**

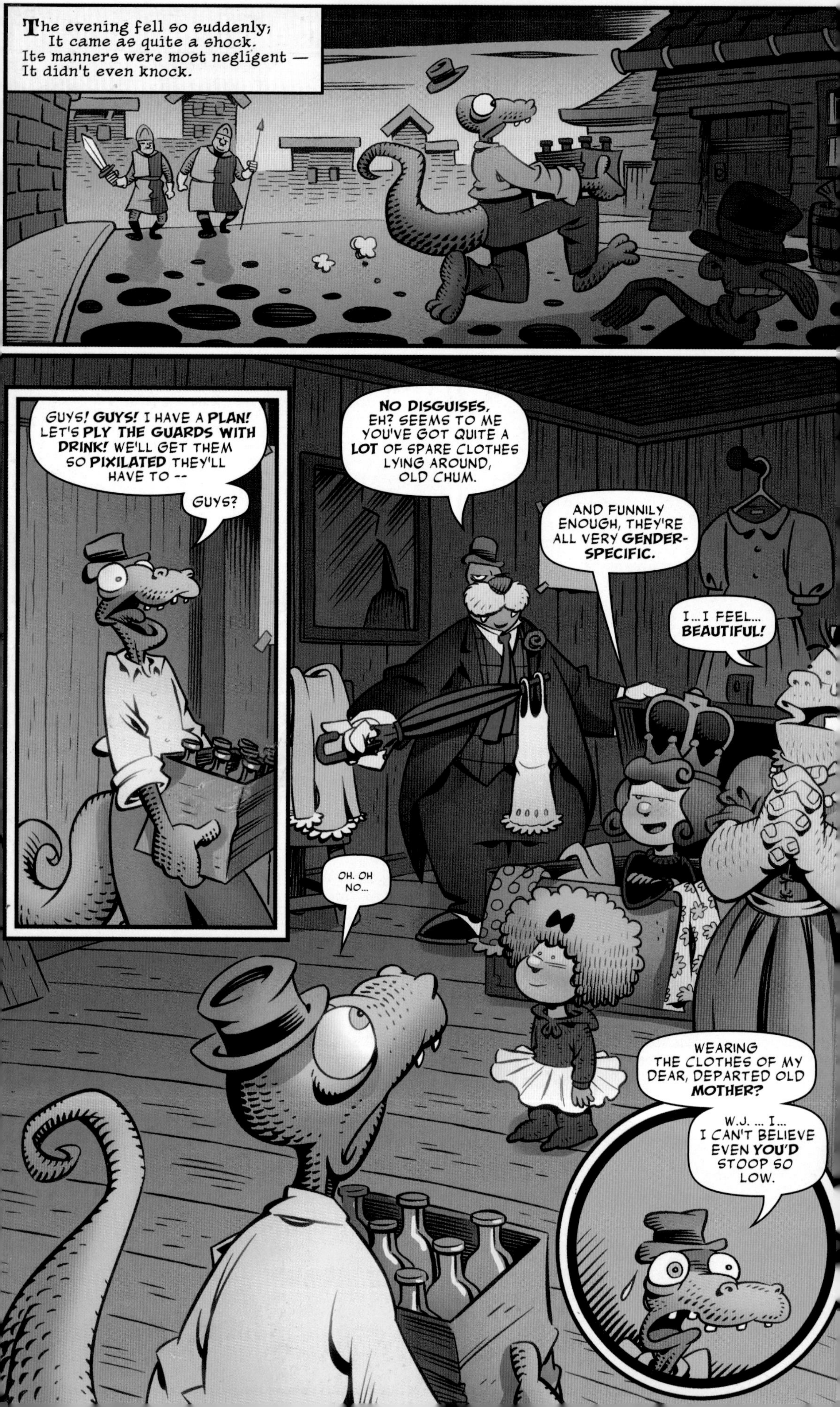

The evening fell so suddenly;
It came as quite a shock.
Its manners were most negligent —
It didn't even knock.
GUYS! GUYS! I HAVE A PLAN! LET'S PLY THE GUARDS WITH DRINK! WE'LL GET THEM SO PIXILATED THEY'LL HAVE TO --
GUYS?
NO DISGUISES, EH? SEEMS TO ME YOU'VE GOT QUITE A LOT OF SPARE CLOTHES LYING AROUND, OLD CHUM.
AND FUNNILY ENOUGH, THEY'RE ALL VERY GENDER-SPECIFIC.
I... I FEEL... BEAUTIFUL!
OH. OH NO...
WEARING THE CLOTHES OF MY DEAR, DEPARTED OLD MOTHER?
W.J. ... I... I CAN'T BELIEVE EVEN YOU'D STOOP SO LOW.

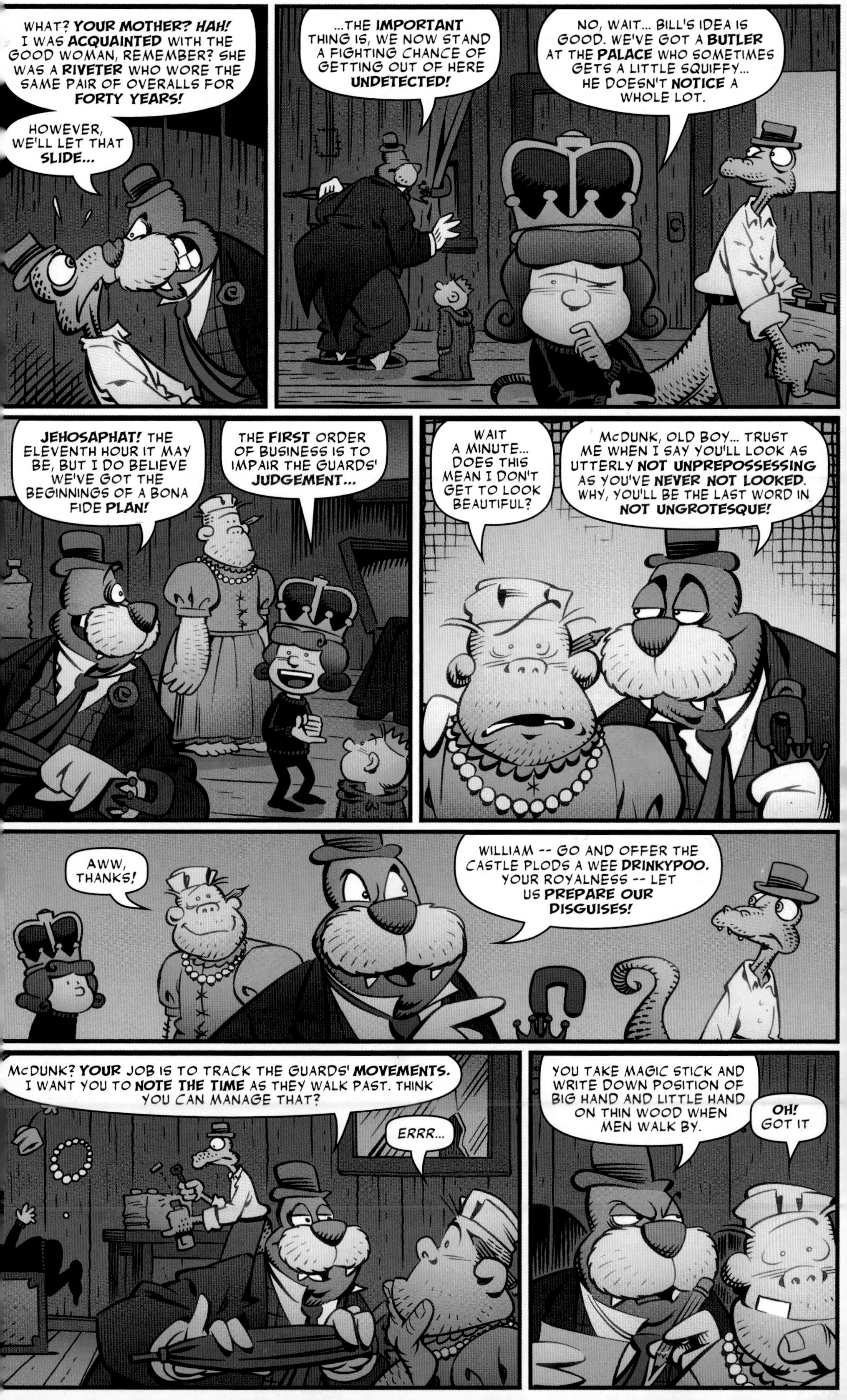

WHAT? YOUR MOTHER? HAH! I WAS ACQUAINTED WITH THE GOOD WOMAN, REMEMBER? SHE WAS A RIVETER WHO WORE THE SAME PAIR OF OVERALLS FOR FORTY YEARS!
HOWEVER, WE'LL LET THAT SLIDE...
...THE IMPORTANT THING IS, WE NOW STAND A FIGHTING CHANCE OF GETTING OUT OF HERE UNDETECTED!
NO, WAIT... BILL'S IDEA IS GOOD. WE'VE GOT A BUTLER AT THE PALACE WHO SOMETIMES GETS A LITTLE SQUIFFY... HE DOESN'T NOTICE A WHOLE LOT.
JEHOSAPHAT! THE ELEVENTH HOUR IT MAY BE, BUT I DO BELIEVE WE'VE GOT THE BEGINNINGS OF A BONA FIDE PLAN!
THE FIRST ORDER OF BUSINESS IS TO IMPAIR THE GUARDS' JUDGEMENT...
WAIT A MINUTE... DOES THIS MEAN I DON'T GET TO LOOK BEAUTIFUL?
McDUNK, OLD BOY... TRUST ME WHEN I SAY YOU'LL LOOK AS UTTERLY NOT UNPREPOSSESSING AS YOU'VE NEVER NOT LOOKED. WHY, YOU'LL BE THE LAST WORD IN NOT UNGROTESQUE!
AWW, THANKS!
WILLIAM -- GO AND OFFER THE CASTLE PLODS A WEE DRINKYPOO. YOUR ROYALNESS -- LET US PREPARE OUR DISGUISES!
McDUNK? YOUR JOB IS TO TRACK THE GUARDS' MOVEMENTS. I WANT YOU TO NOTE THE TIME AS THEY WALK PAST. THINK YOU CAN MANAGE THAT?
ERRR...
YOU TAKE MAGIC STICK AND WRITE DOWN POSITION OF BIG HAND AND LITTLE HAND ON THIN WOOD WHEN MEN WALK BY.
OH! GOT IT

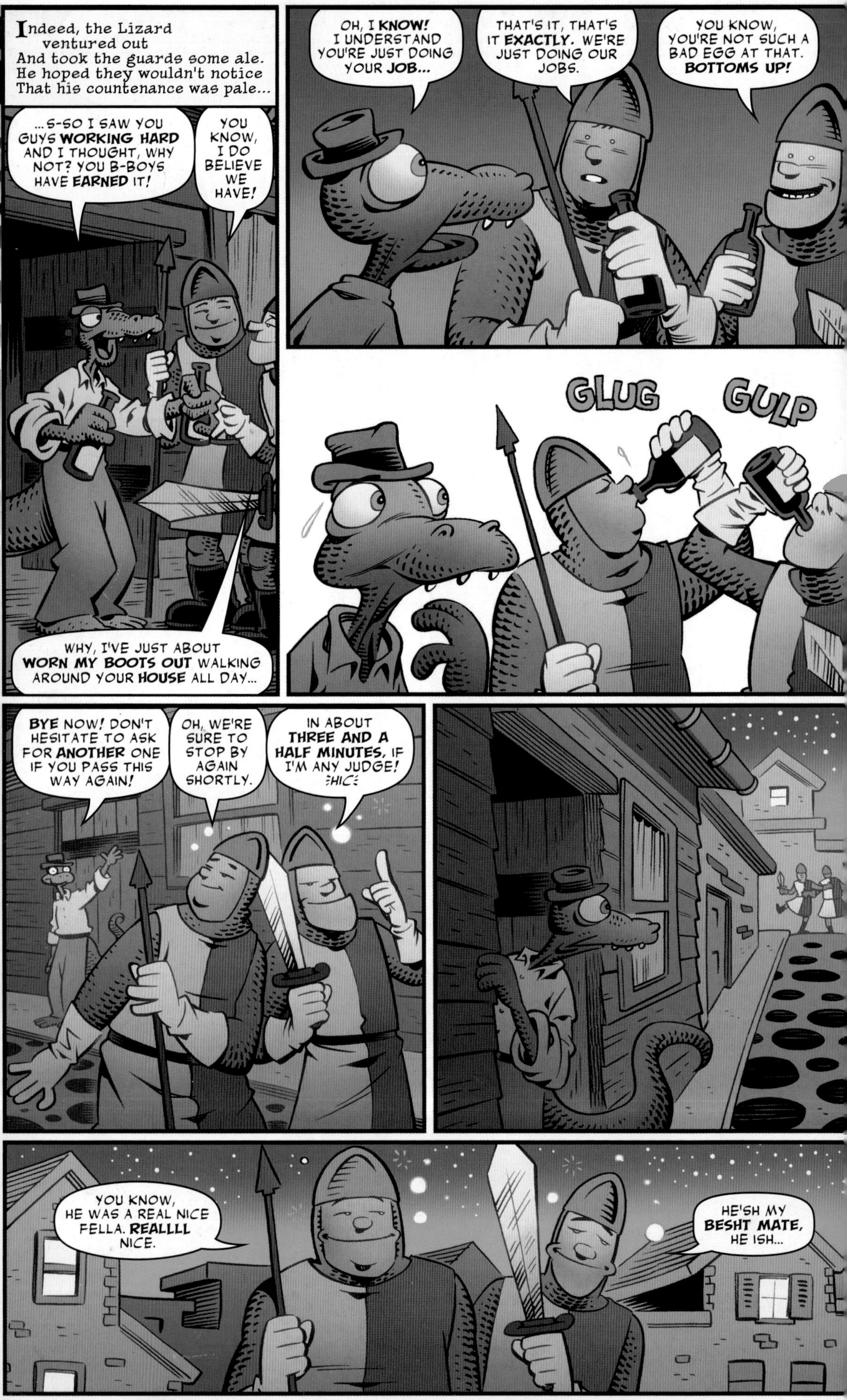

Indeed, the Lizard ventured out
And took the guards some ale.
He hoped they wouldn't notice
That his countenance was pale...
...S-SO I SAW YOU GUYS WORKING HARD AND I THOUGHT, WHY NOT? YOU B-BOYS HAVE EARNED IT!
YOU KNOW, I DO BELIEVE WE HAVE!
WHY, I'VE JUST ABOUT WORN MY BOOTS OUT WALKING AROUND YOUR HOUSE ALL DAY...
OH, I KNOW! I UNDERSTAND YOU'RE JUST DOING YOUR JOB...
THAT'S IT, THAT'S IT EXACTLY. WE'RE JUST DOING OUR JOBS.
YOU KNOW, YOU'RE NOT SUCH A BAD EGG AT THAT. BOTTOMS UP!
GLUG
GULP
BYE NOW! DON'T HESITATE TO ASK FOR ANOTHER ONE IF YOU PASS THIS WAY AGAIN!
OH, WE'RE SURE TO STOP BY AGAIN SHORTLY.
IN ABOUT THREE AND A HALF MINUTES, IF I'M ANY JUDGE! HIC
YOU KNOW, HE WAS A REAL NICE FELLA. REALLLL NICE.
HE'SH MY BESHT MATE, HE ISH...

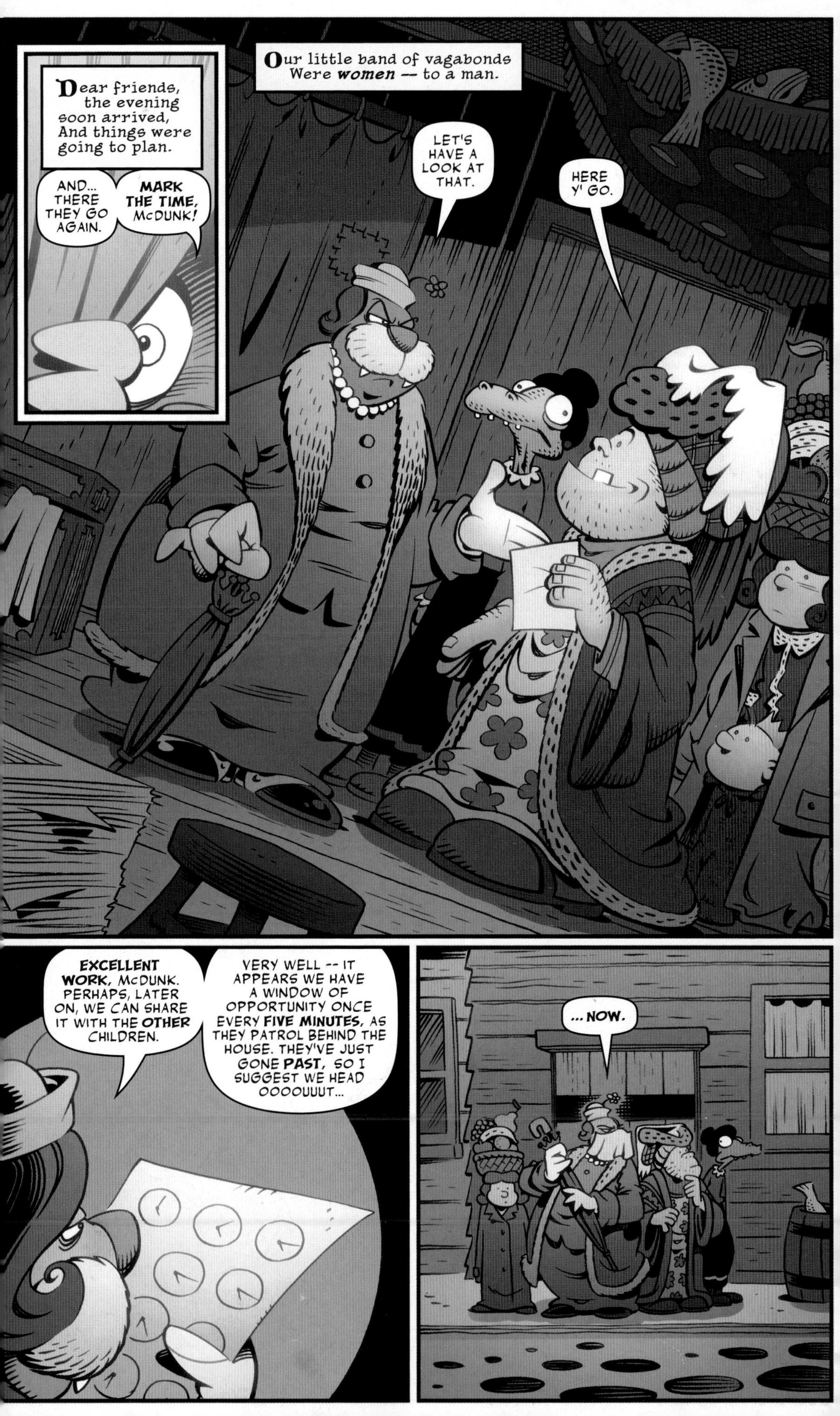
Dear friends, the evening soon arrived, And things were going to plan.
AND... THERE THEY GO AGAIN.
MARK THE TIME, McDUNK!
Our little band of vagabonds Were women -- to a man.
LET'S HAVE A LOOK AT THAT.
HERE Y' GO.
EXCELLENT WORK, McDUNK. PERHAPS, LATER ON, WE CAN SHARE IT WITH THE OTHER CHILDREN.
VERY WELL -- IT APPEARS WE HAVE A WINDOW OF OPPORTUNITY ONCE EVERY FIVE MINUTES, AS THEY PATROL BEHIND THE HOUSE. THEY'VE JUST GONE PAST, SO I SUGGEST WE HEAD OOOOUUUT...
... NOW.

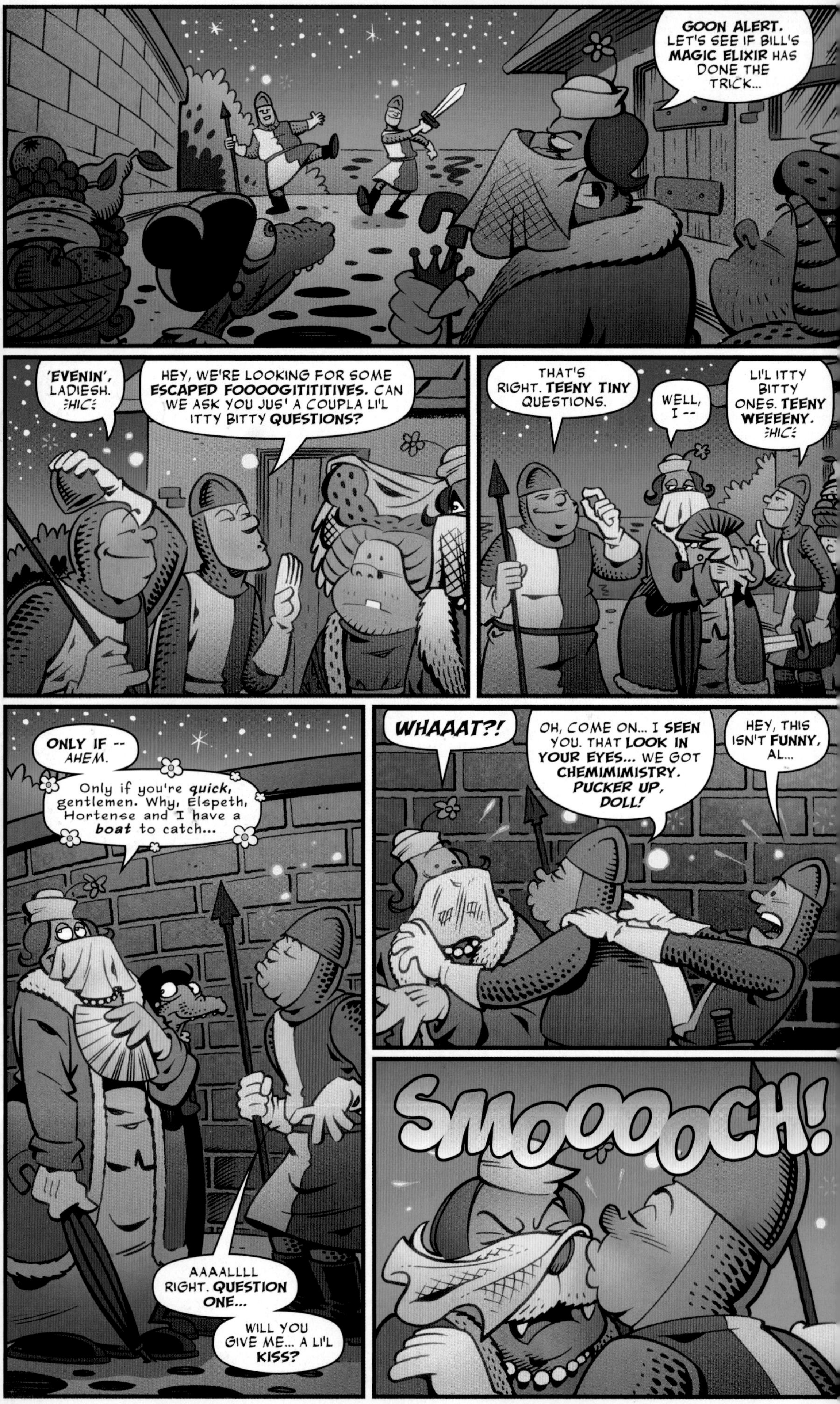
GOON ALERT. LET'S SEE IF BILL'S MAGIC ELIXIR HAS DONE THE TRICK...
'EVENIN', LADIESH. HIC
HEY, WE'RE LOOKING FOR SOME ESCAPED FOOOOGITITITIVES. CAN WE ASK YOU JUS' A COUPLA LI'L ITTY BITTY QUESTIONS?
THAT'S RIGHT. TEENY TINY QUESTIONS.
WELL, I --
LI'L ITTY BITTY ONES. TEENY WEEEENY. HIC
ONLY IF -- AHEM.
Only if you're quick, gentlemen. Why, Elspeth, Hortense and I have a boat to catch...
AAAALLLL RIGHT. QUESTION ONE...
WILL YOU GIVE ME... A LI'L KISS?
WHAAAT?!
OH, COME ON... I SEEN YOU. THAT LOOK IN YOUR EYES... WE GOT CHEMIMIMISTRY. PUCKER UP, DOLL!
HEY, THIS ISN'T FUNNY, AL...
SMOOOOOCH!

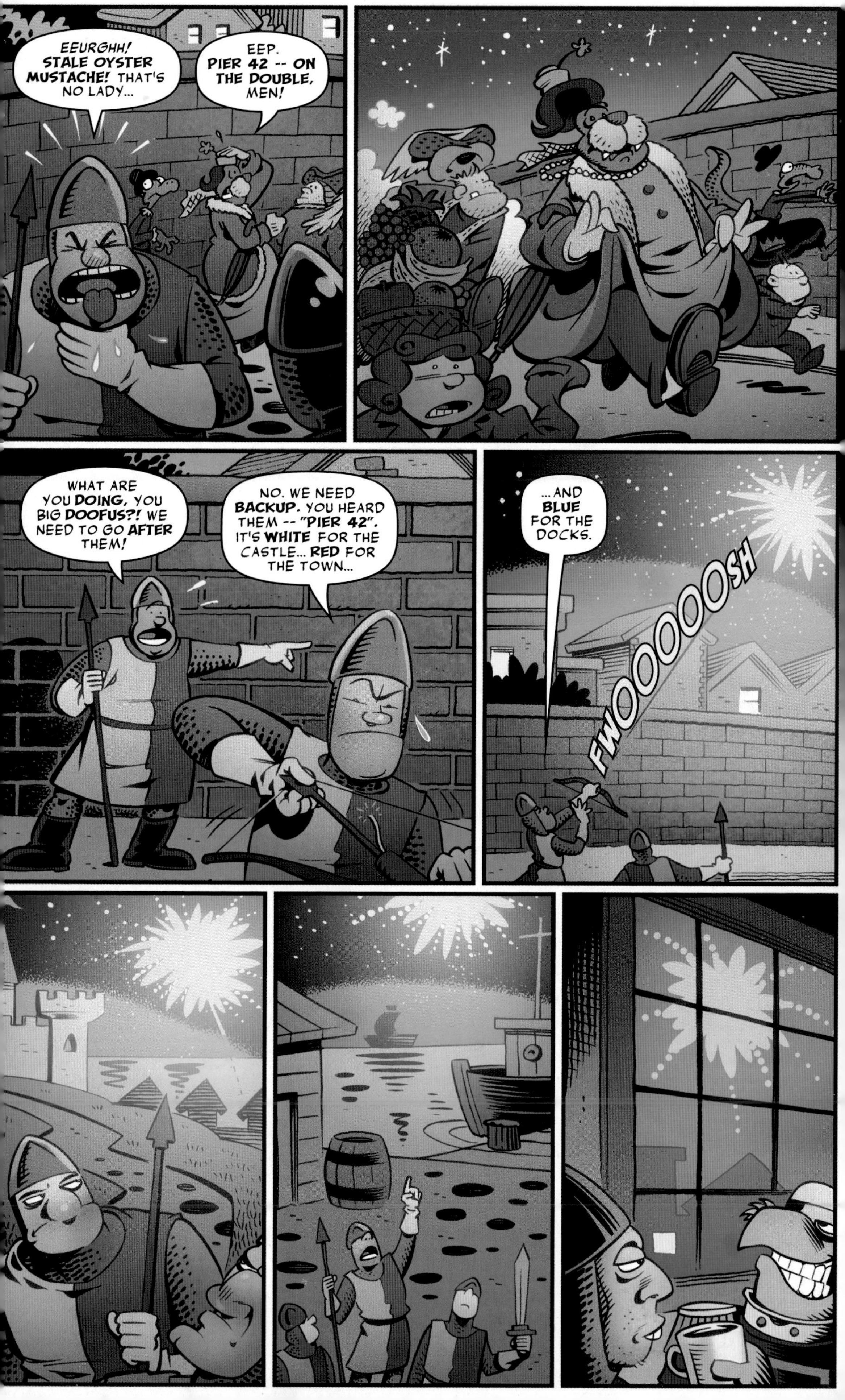
EEURGHH! STALE OYSTER MUSTACHE! THAT'S NO LADY...
EEP. PIER 42 -- ON THE DOUBLE, MEN!
WHAT ARE YOU DOING, YOU BIG DOOFUS?! WE NEED TO GO AFTER THEM!
NO. WE NEED BACKUP. YOU HEARD THEM -- "PIER 42". IT'S WHITE FOR THE CASTLE... RED FOR THE TOWN...
...AND BLUE FOR THE DOCKS.
FWOOOOOOSH

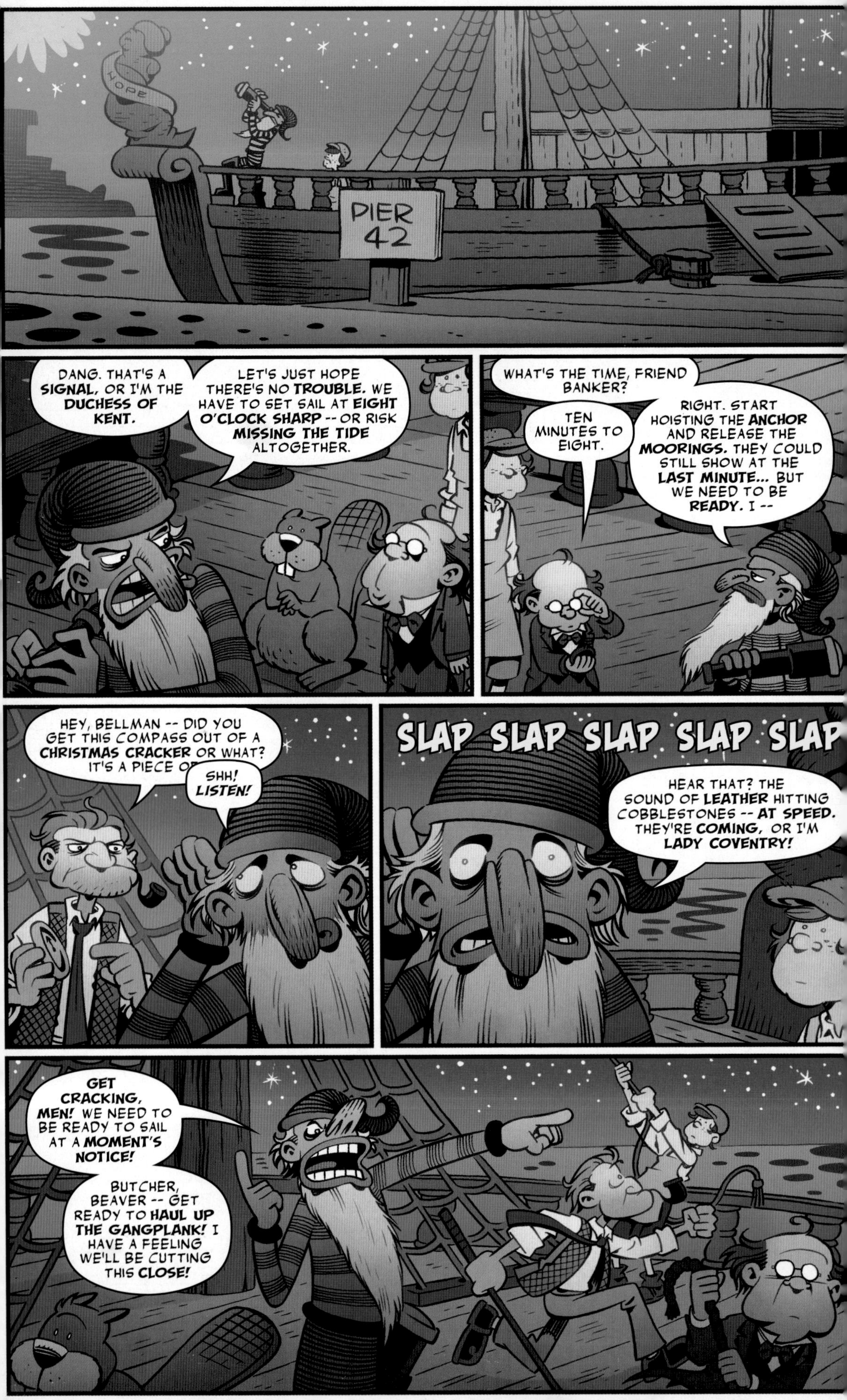

HOPE
PIER 42
DANG. THAT'S A SIGNAL, OR I'M THE DUCHESS OF KENT.
LET'S JUST HOPE THERE'S NO TROUBLE. WE HAVE TO SET SAIL AT EIGHT O'CLOCK SHARP -- OR RISK MISSING THE TIDE ALTOGETHER.
WHAT'S THE TIME, FRIEND BANKER?
TEN MINUTES TO EIGHT.
RIGHT. START HOISTING THE ANCHOR AND RELEASE THE MOORINGS. THEY COULD STILL SHOW AT THE LAST MINUTE... BUT WE NEED TO BE READY. I --
HEY, BELLMAN -- DID YOU GET THIS COMPASS OUT OF A CHRISTMAS CRACKER OR WHAT? IT'S A PIECE OF
SHH! LISTEN!
SLAP SLAP SLAP SLAP SLAP
HEAR THAT? THE SOUND OF LEATHER HITTING COBBLESTONES -- AT SPEED. THEY'RE COMING, OR I'M LADY COVENTRY!
GET CRACKING, MEN! WE NEED TO BE READY TO SAIL AT A MOMENT'S NOTICE!
BUTCHER, BEAVER -- GET READY TO HAUL UP THE GANGPLANK! I HAVE A FEELING WE'LL BE CUTTING THIS CLOSE!

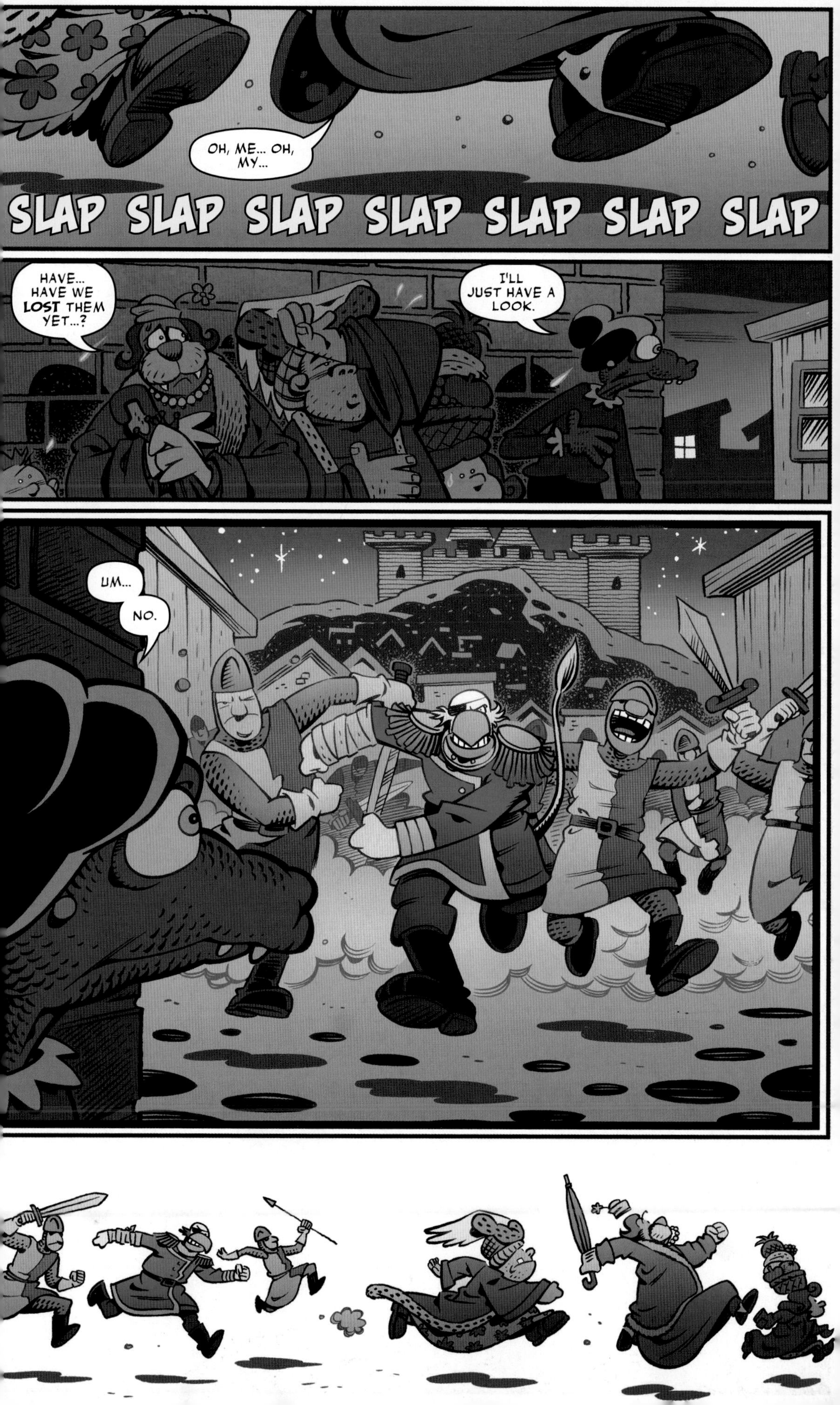
OH, ME... OH, MY...
SLAP SLAP SLAP SLAP SLAP SLAP SLAP
HAVE... HAVE WE **LOST** THEM YET...?
I'LL JUST HAVE A LOOK.
UM...
NO.

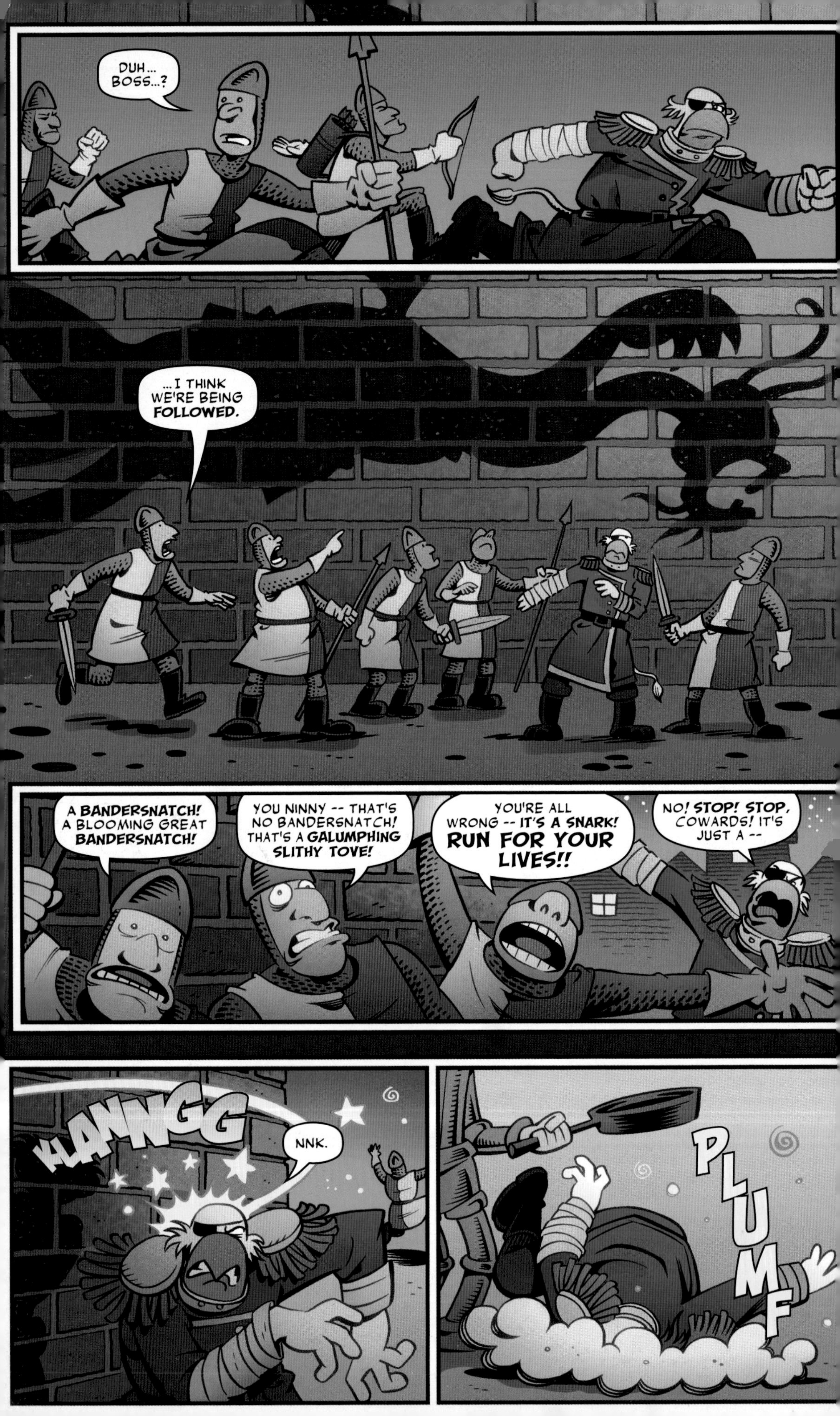
DUH... BOSS...?
...I THINK WE'RE BEING **FOLLOWED.**
A **BANDERSNATCH!** A BLOOMING GREAT **BANDERSNATCH!**
YOU NINNY -- THAT'S NO BANDERSNATCH! THAT'S A **GALUMPHING SLITHY TOVE!**
YOU'RE ALL WRONG -- **IT'S A SNARK! RUN FOR YOUR LIVES!!**
NO! **STOP! STOP,** COWARDS! IT'S JUST A --
KLANNGG
NNK.
PLUMF

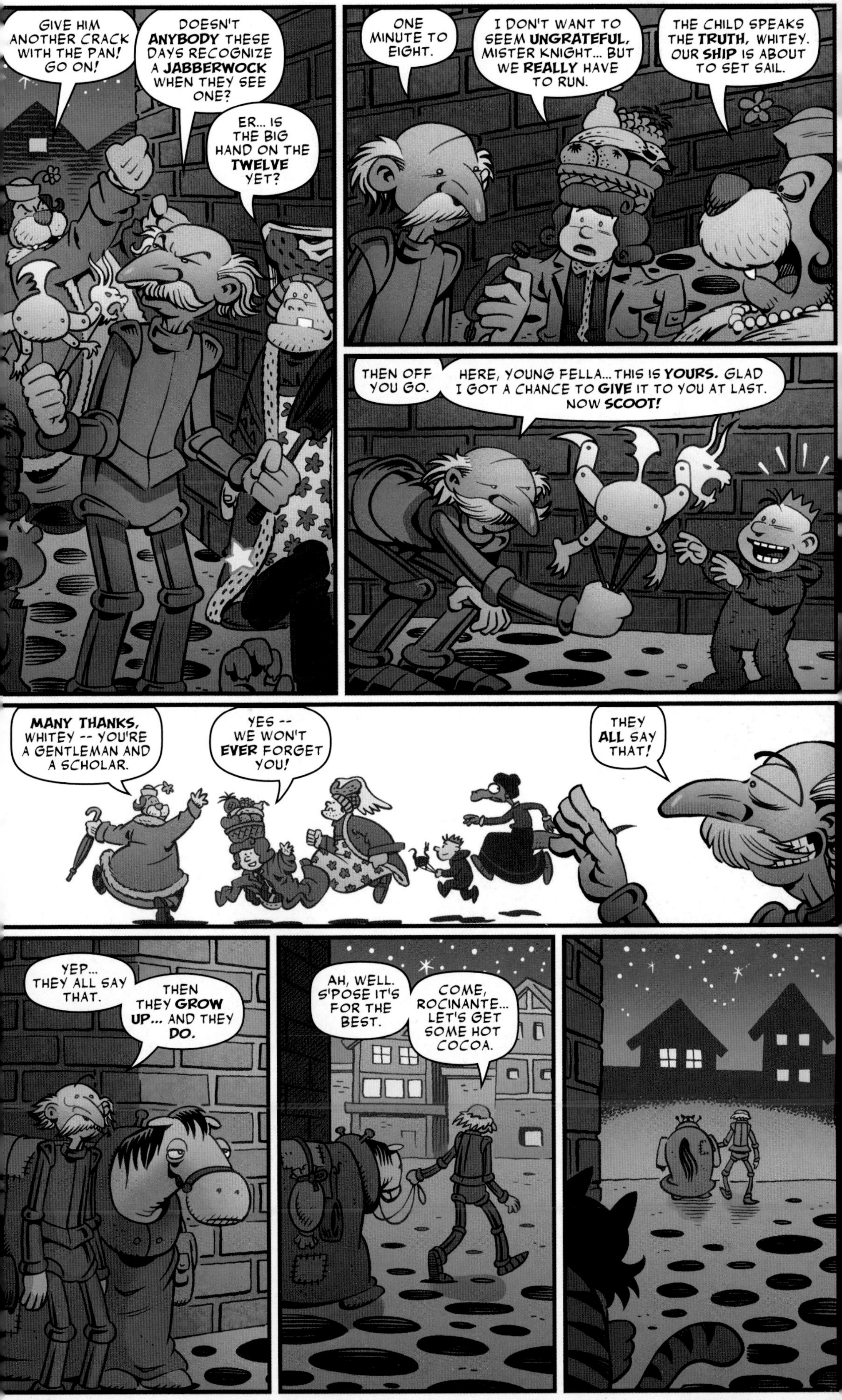
GIVE HIM ANOTHER CRACK WITH THE PAN! GO ON!
DOESN'T ANYBODY THESE DAYS RECOGNIZE A JABBERWOCK WHEN THEY SEE ONE?
ER... IS THE BIG HAND ON THE TWELVE YET?
ONE MINUTE TO EIGHT.
I DON'T WANT TO SEEM UNGRATEFUL, MISTER KNIGHT... BUT WE REALLY HAVE TO RUN.
THE CHILD SPEAKS THE TRUTH, WHITEY. OUR SHIP IS ABOUT TO SET SAIL.
THEN OFF YOU GO.
HERE, YOUNG FELLA... THIS IS YOURS. GLAD I GOT A CHANCE TO GIVE IT TO YOU AT LAST. NOW SCOOT!
MANY THANKS, WHITEY -- YOU'RE A GENTLEMAN AND A SCHOLAR.
YES -- WE WON'T EVER FORGET YOU!
THEY ALL SAY THAT!
YEP... THEY ALL SAY THAT.
THEN THEY GROW UP... AND THEY DO.
AH, WELL. S'POSE IT'S FOR THE BEST.
COME, ROCINANTE... LET'S GET SOME HOT COCOA.

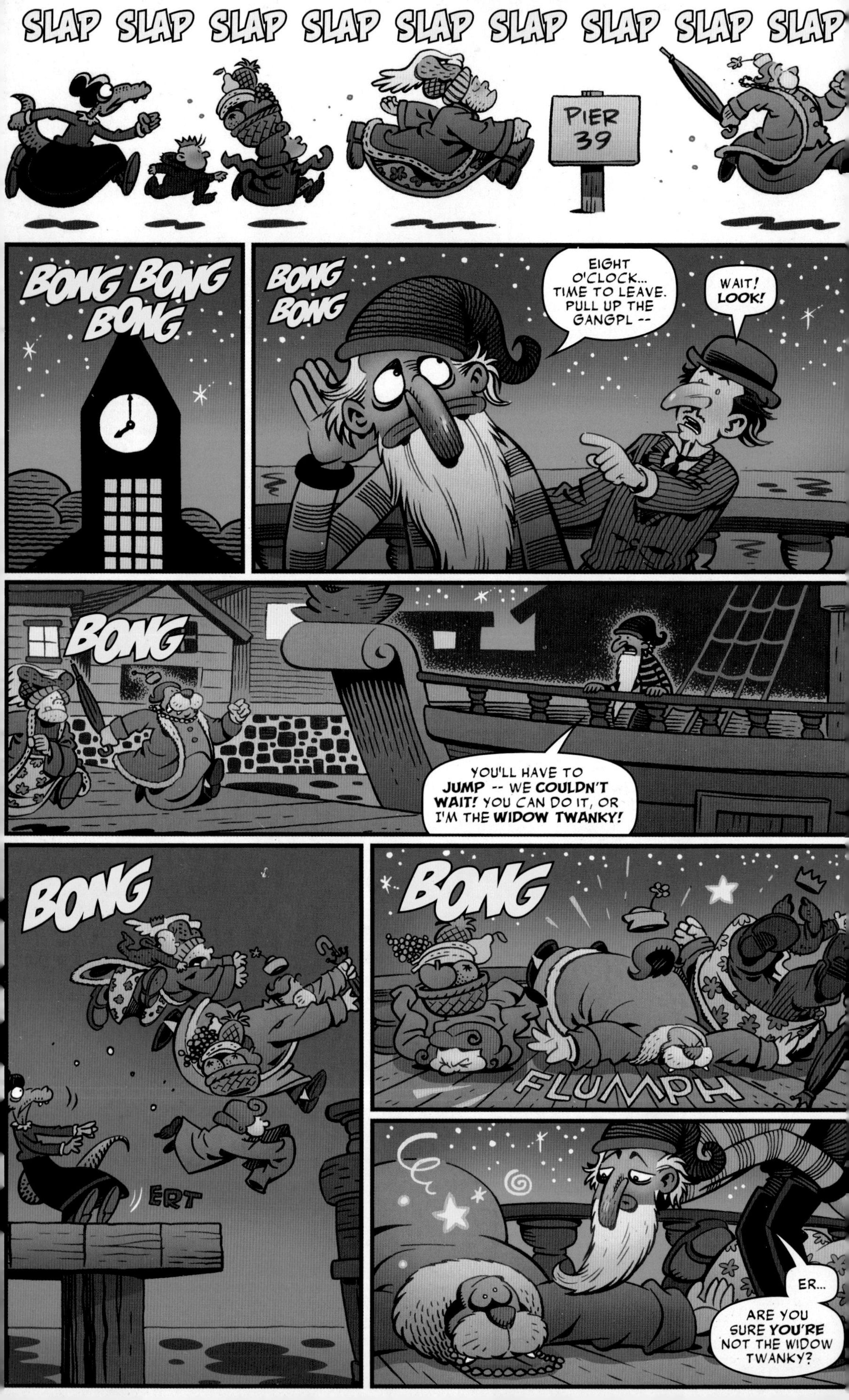
SLAP SLAP SLAP SLAP SLAP SLAP SLAP SLAP SLAP
PIER 39
BONG BONG BONG
BONG BONG
EIGHT O'CLOCK... TIME TO LEAVE. PULL UP THE GANGPL --
WAIT! LOOK!
BONG
YOU'LL HAVE TO JUMP -- WE COULDN'T WAIT! YOU CAN DO IT, OR I'M THE WIDOW TWANKY!
BONG
ERT
BONG
FLUMPH
ER...
ARE YOU SURE YOU'RE NOT THE WIDOW TWANKY?

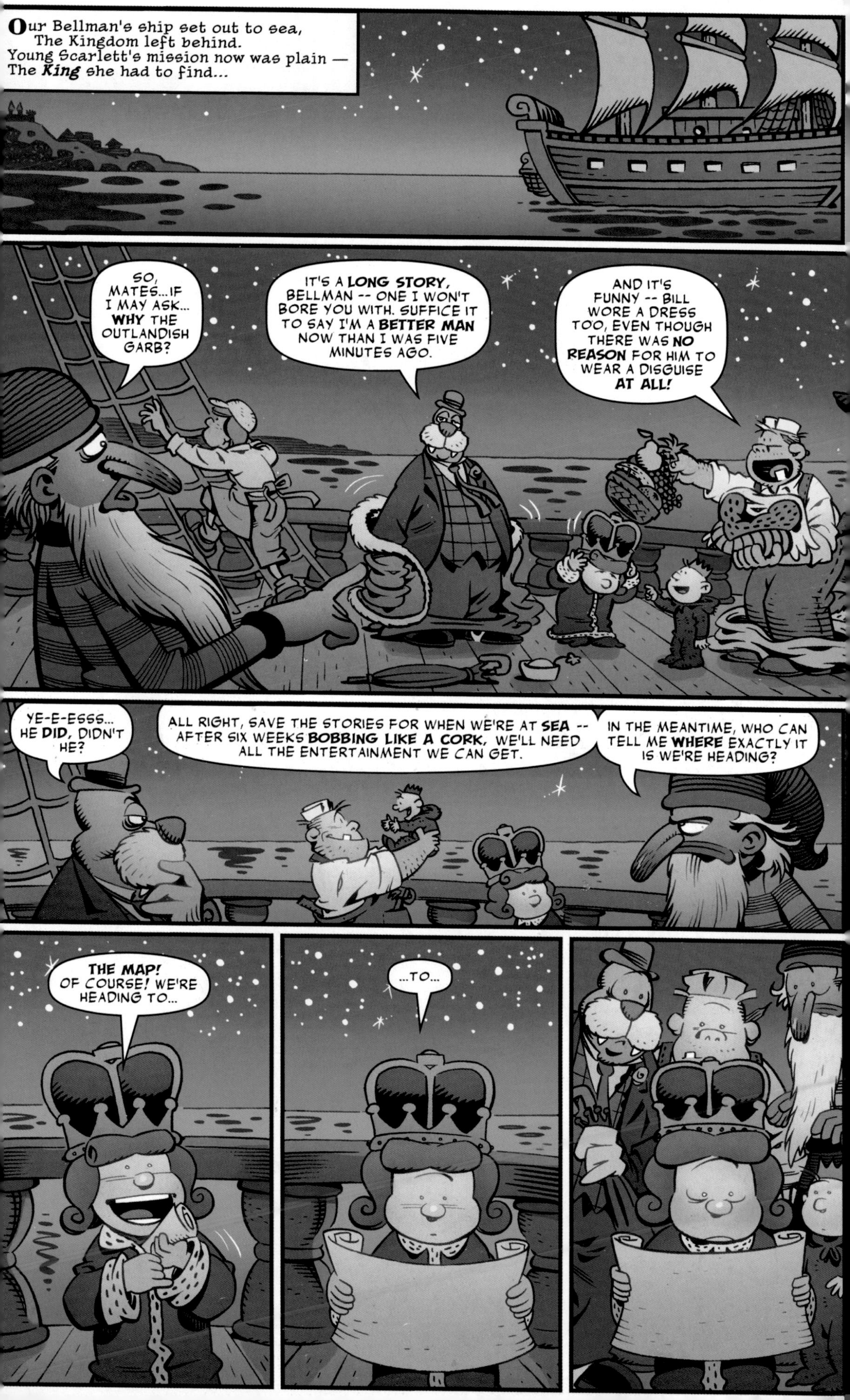
Our Bellman's ship set out to sea,
The Kingdom left behind.
Young Scarlett's mission now was plain —
The *King* she had to find...
SO, MATES...IF I MAY ASK... WHY THE OUTLANDISH GARB?
IT'S A LONG STORY, BELLMAN -- ONE I WON'T BORE YOU WITH. SUFFICE IT TO SAY I'M A BETTER MAN NOW THAN I WAS FIVE MINUTES AGO.
AND IT'S FUNNY -- BILL WORE A DRESS TOO, EVEN THOUGH THERE WAS NO REASON FOR HIM TO WEAR A DISGUISE AT ALL!
YE-E-ESSS... HE DID, DIDN'T HE?
ALL RIGHT, SAVE THE STORIES FOR WHEN WE'RE AT SEA -- AFTER SIX WEEKS BOBBING LIKE A CORK, WE'LL NEED ALL THE ENTERTAINMENT WE CAN GET.
IN THE MEANTIME, WHO CAN TELL ME WHERE EXACTLY IT IS WE'RE HEADING?
THE MAP! OF COURSE! WE'RE HEADING TO...
...TO...

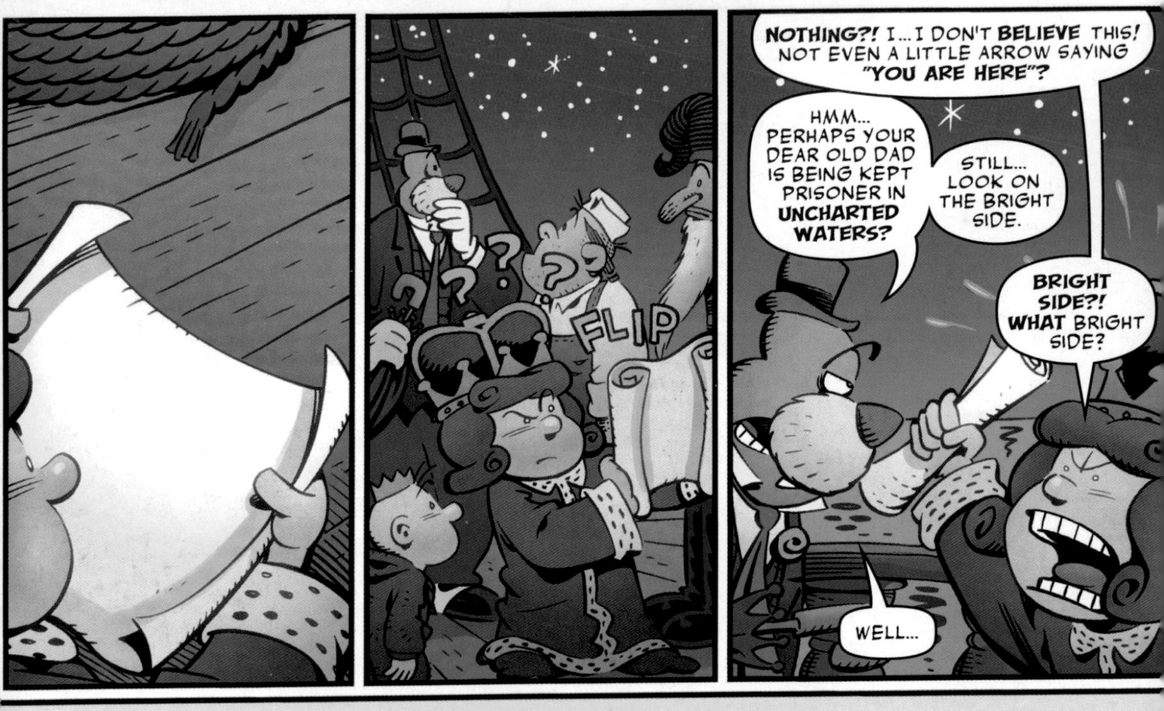
FLIP
NOTHING?! I... I DON'T BELIEVE THIS! NOT EVEN A LITTLE ARROW SAYING "YOU ARE HERE"?
HMM... PERHAPS YOUR DEAR OLD DAD IS BEING KEPT PRISONER IN UNCHARTED WATERS?
STILL... LOOK ON THE BRIGHT SIDE.
BRIGHT SIDE?! WHAT BRIGHT SIDE?
WELL...

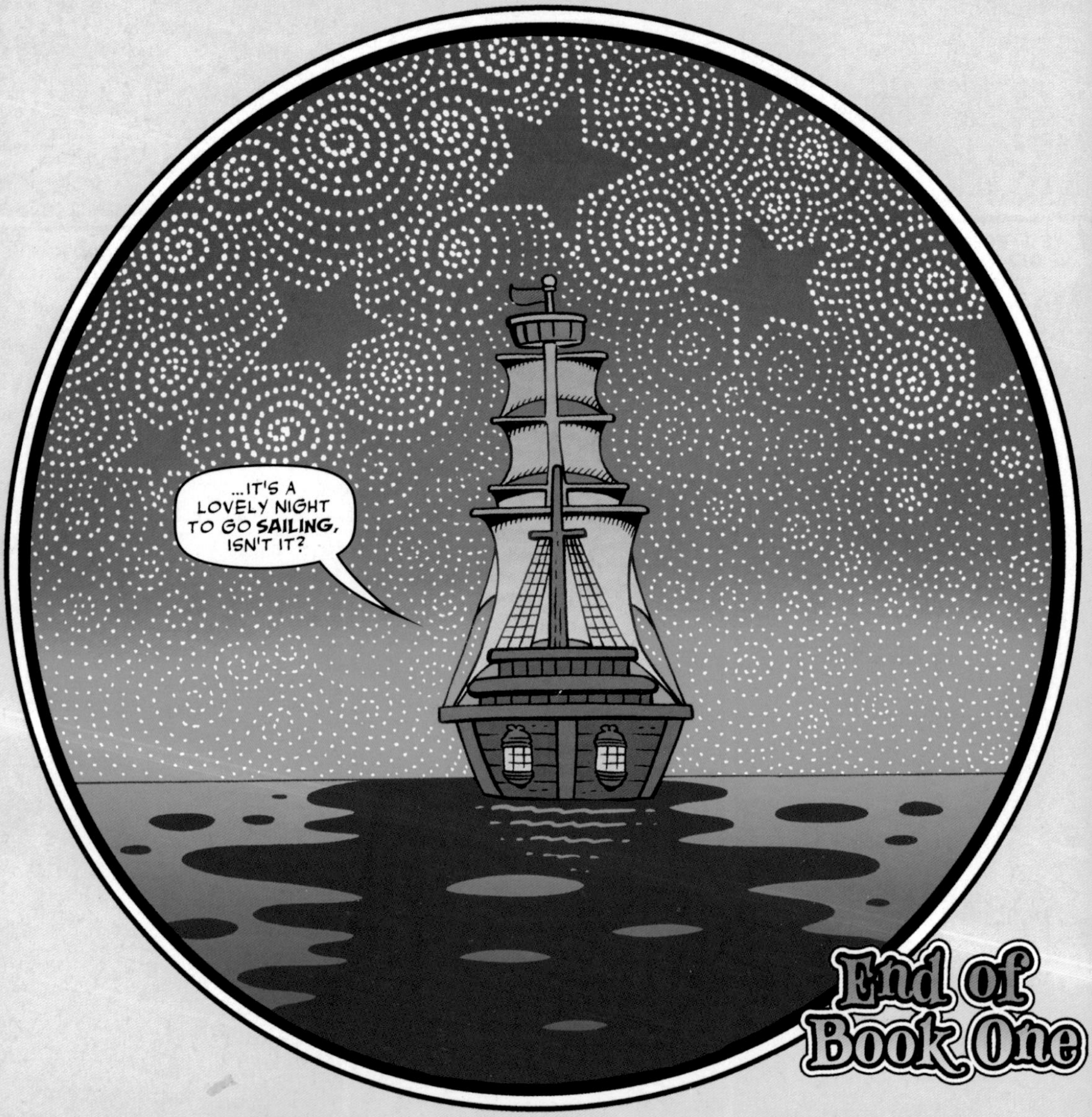
...IT'S A LOVELY NIGHT TO GO SAILING, ISN'T IT?
End of Book One

COMING SOON

BOOK TWO

SHIPS AND SEALING WAX

COVER GALLERY

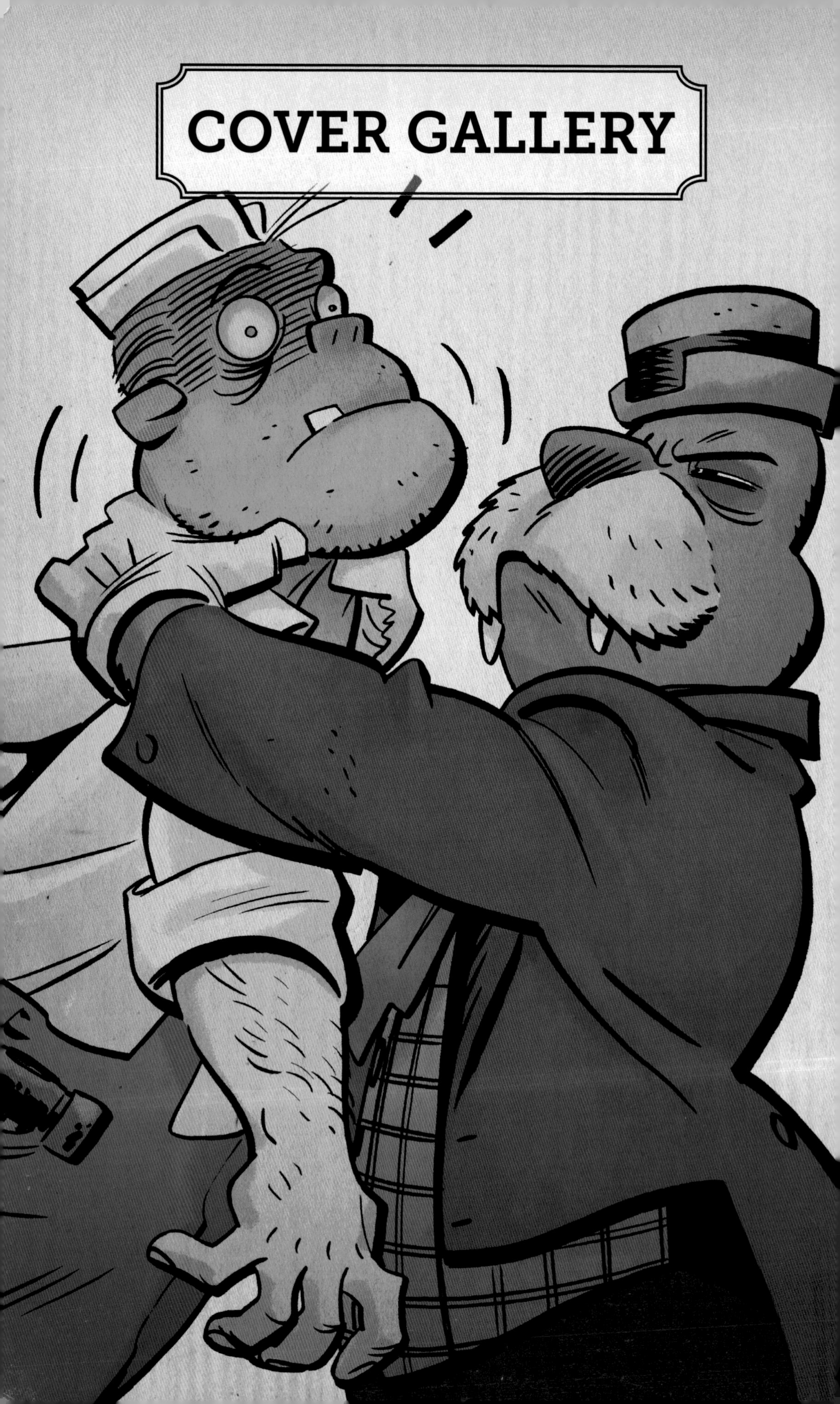

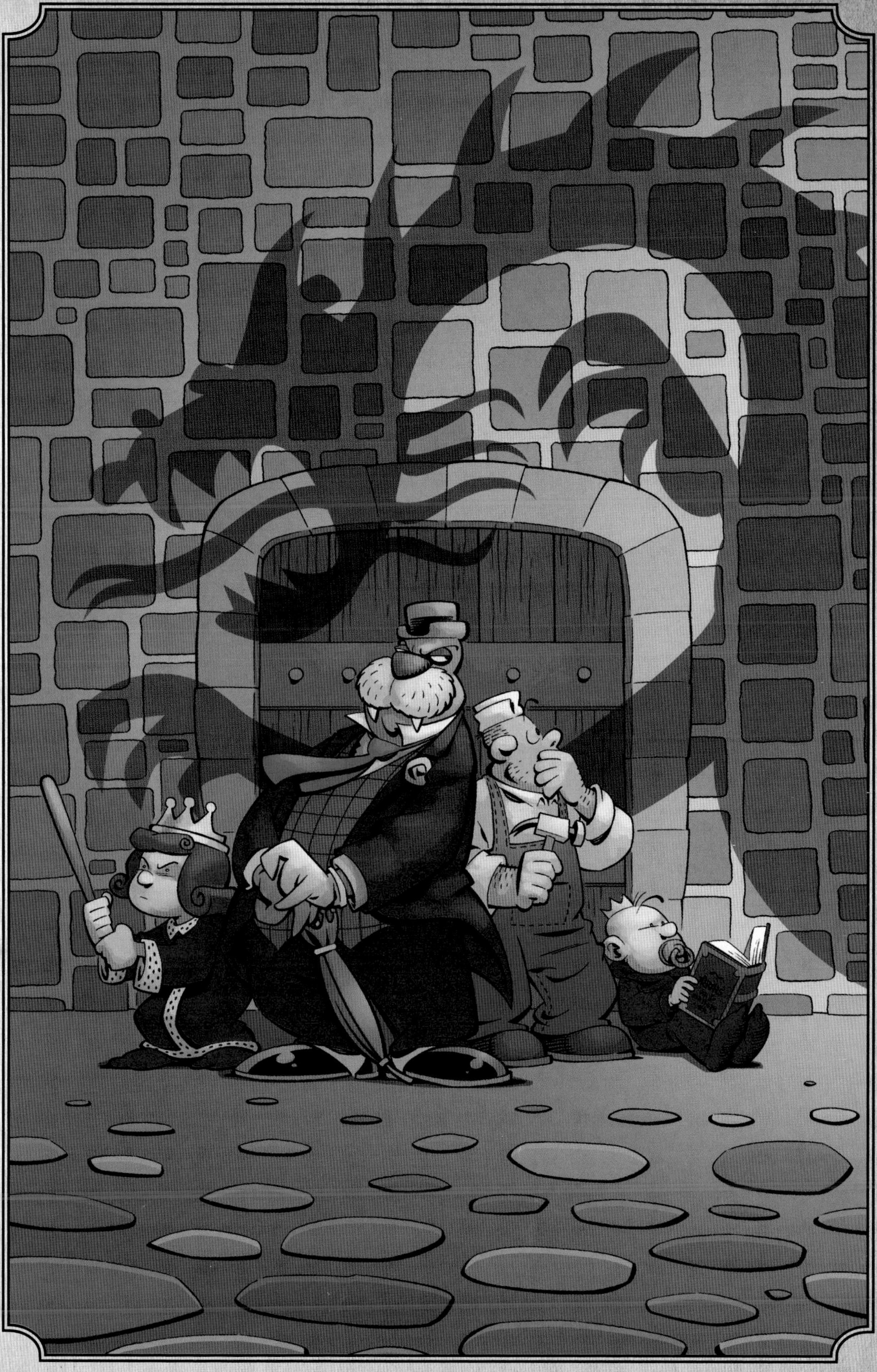

ISSUE ZERO COVER BY **ROGER LANGRIDGE**
WITH COLORS BY **MATTHEW WILSON**

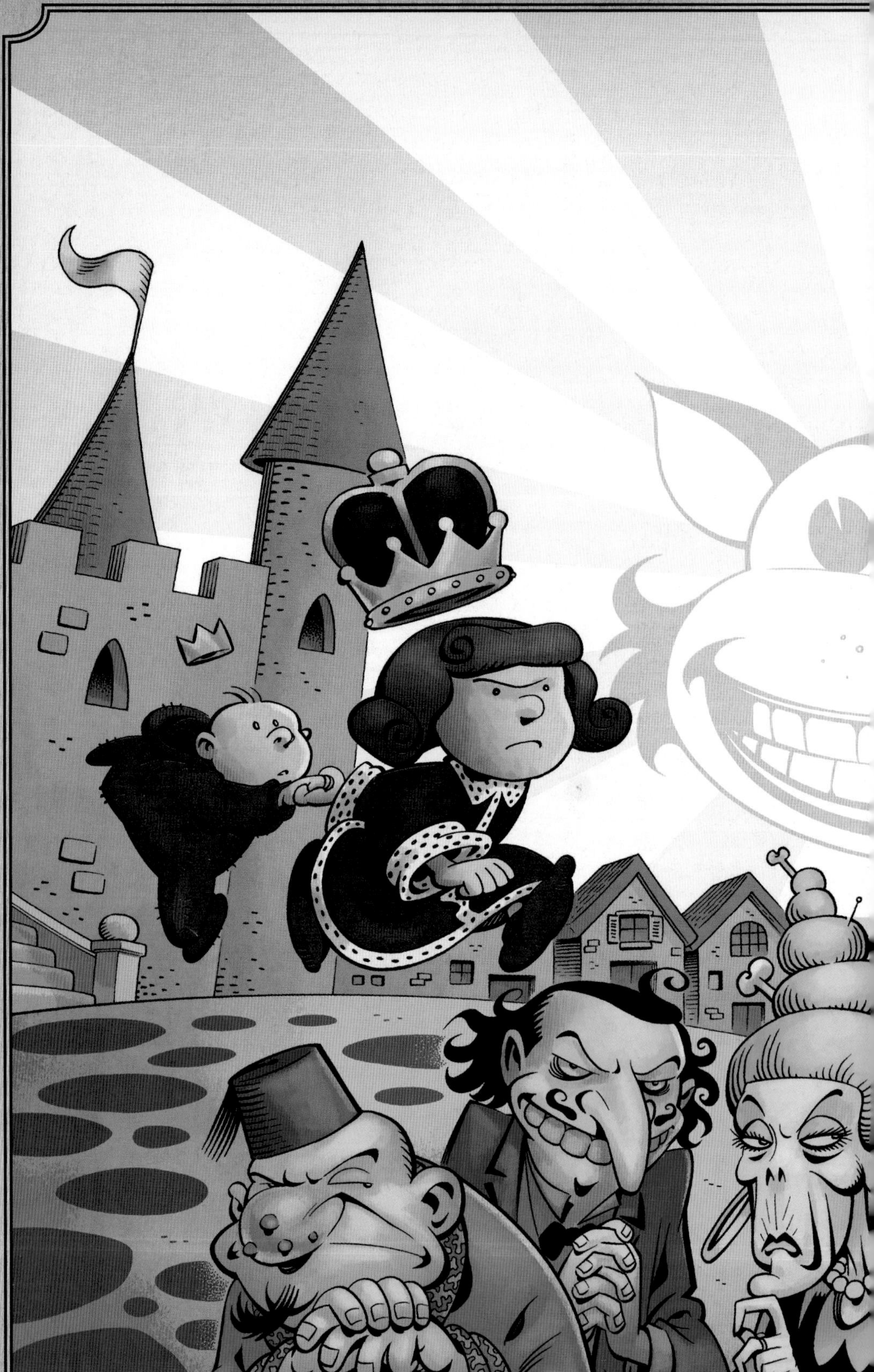

ISSUE ONE COVER BY **ROGER LANGRIDGE**
WITH COLORS BY **MATTHEW WILSON**

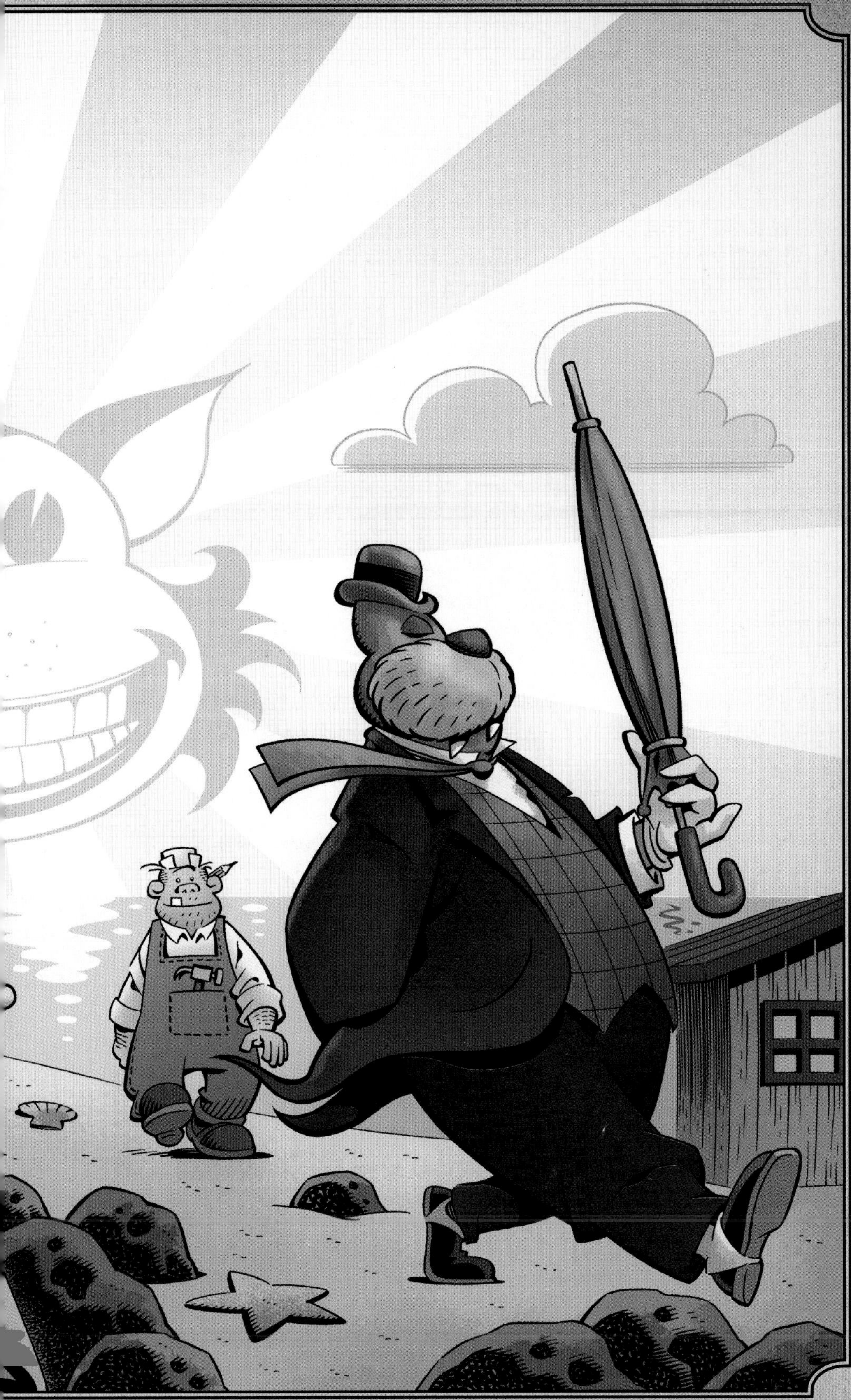

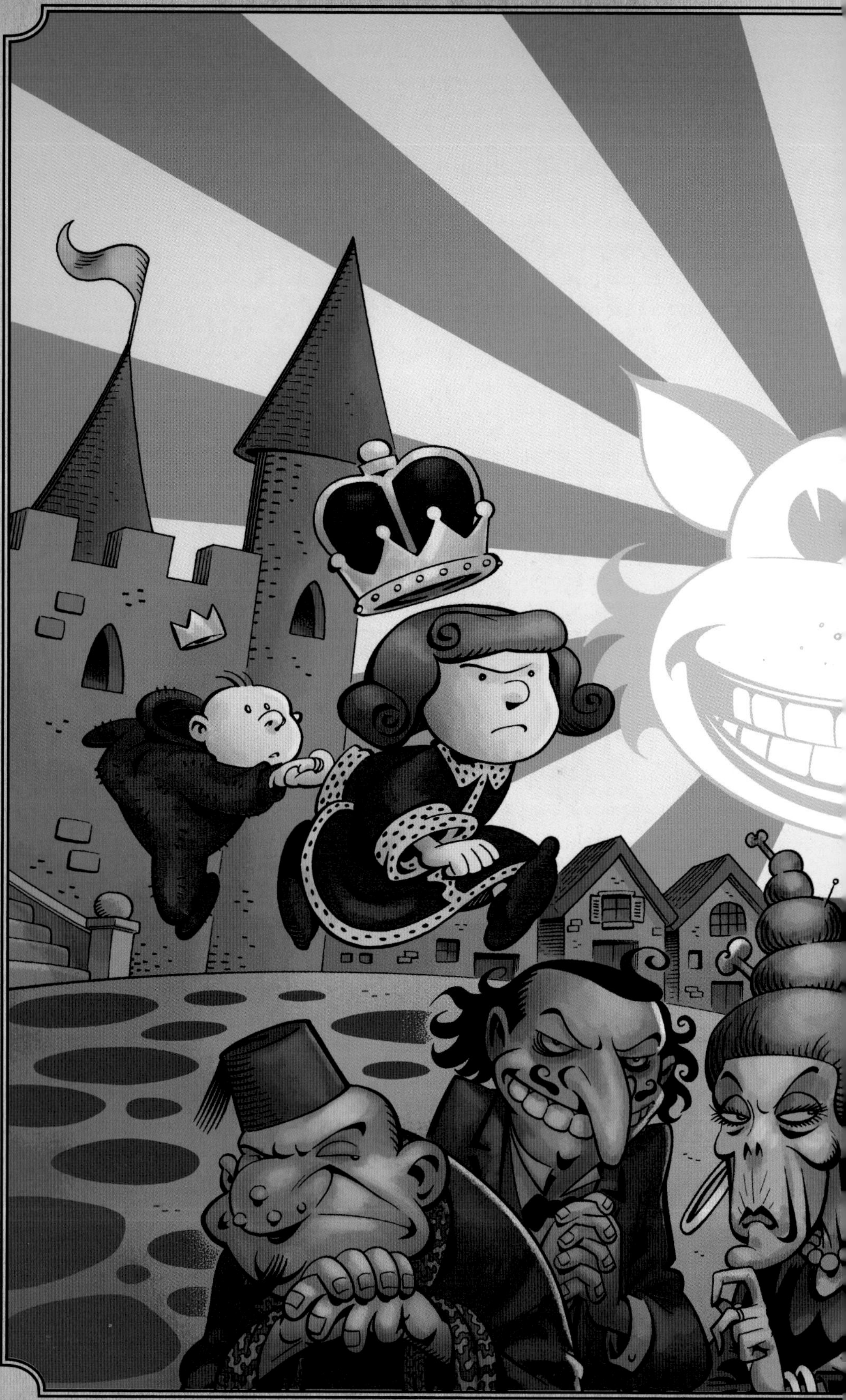

ISSUE ONE 2ND PRINT COVER BY **ROGER LANGRIDGE**
WITH COLORS BY **MATTHEW WILSON**

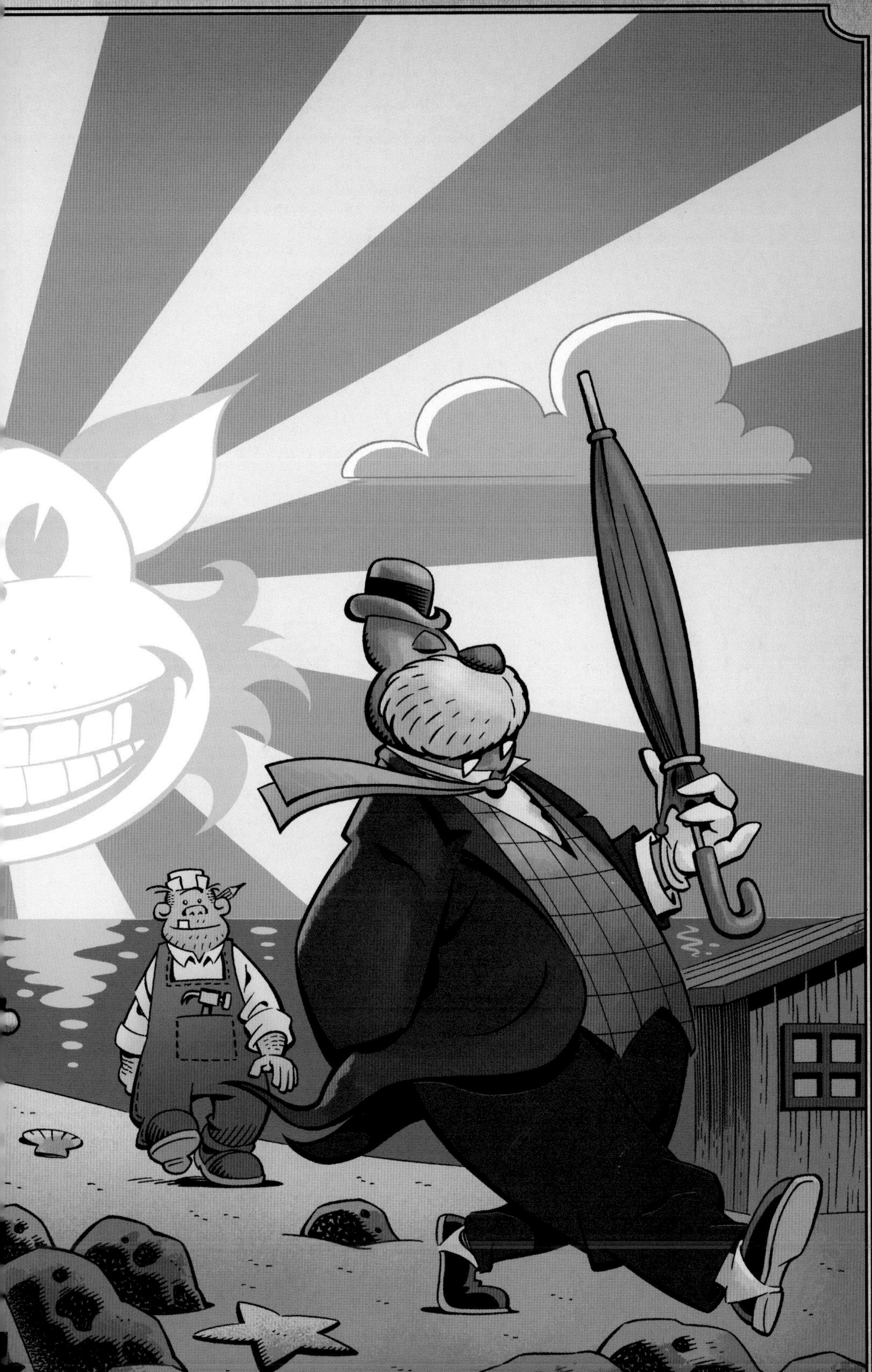

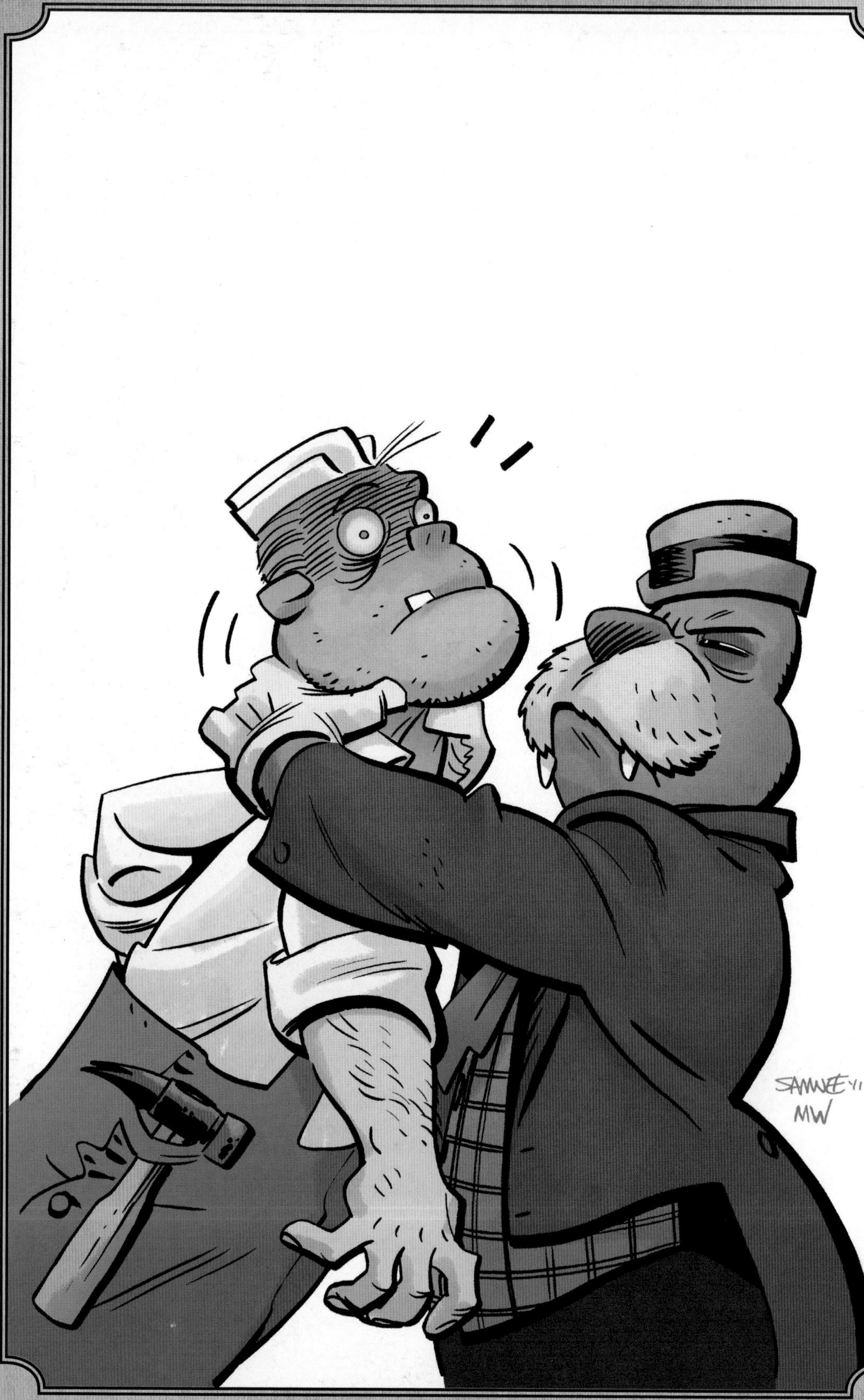
SAMNEE '11
MW

ISSUE ONE VARIANT COVER BY **CHRIS SAMNEE**
WITH COLORS BY **MATTHEW WILSON**

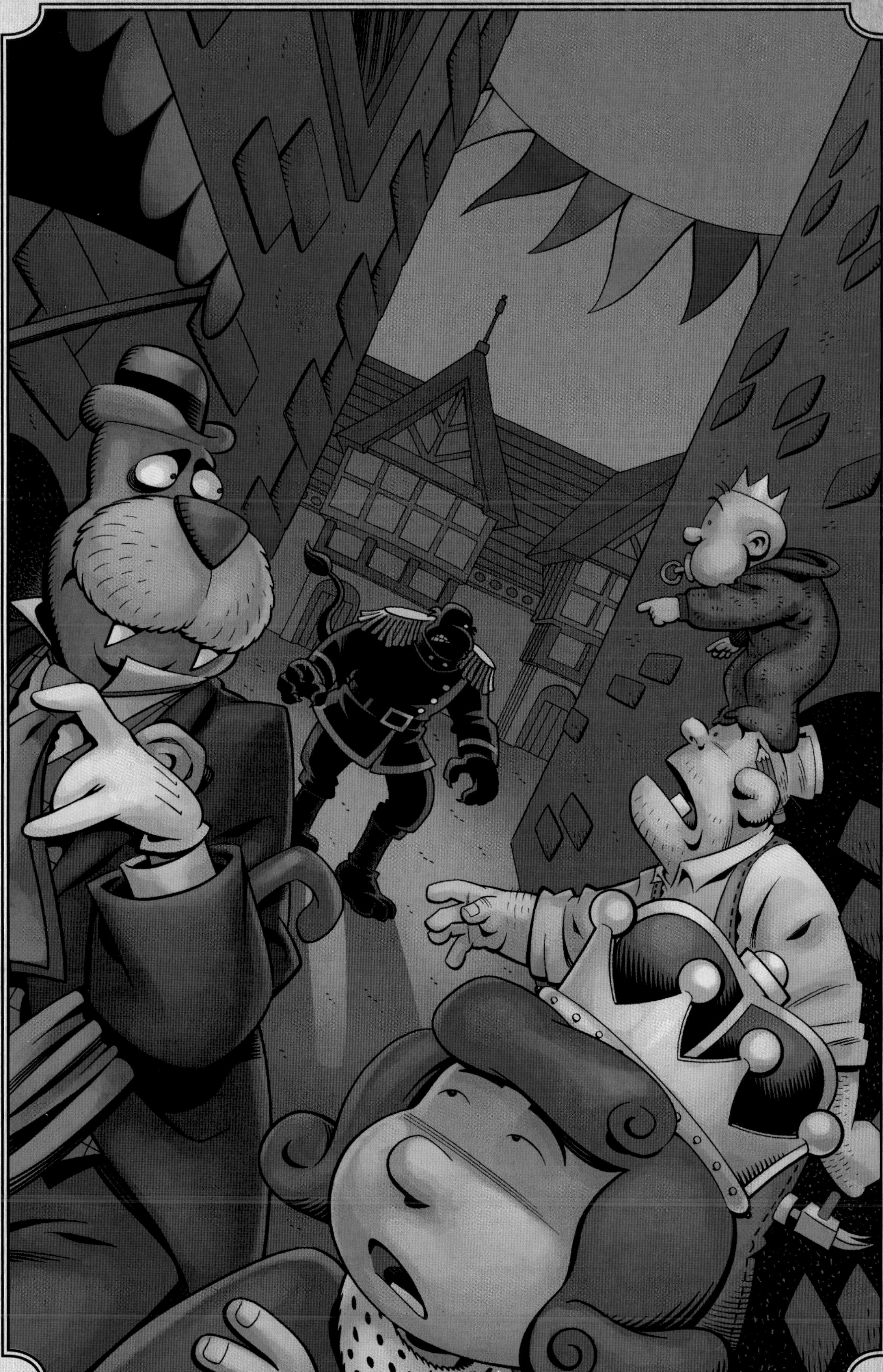

ISSUE TWO COVER BY **ROGER LANGRIDGE**
WITH COLORS BY **MATTHEW WILSON**

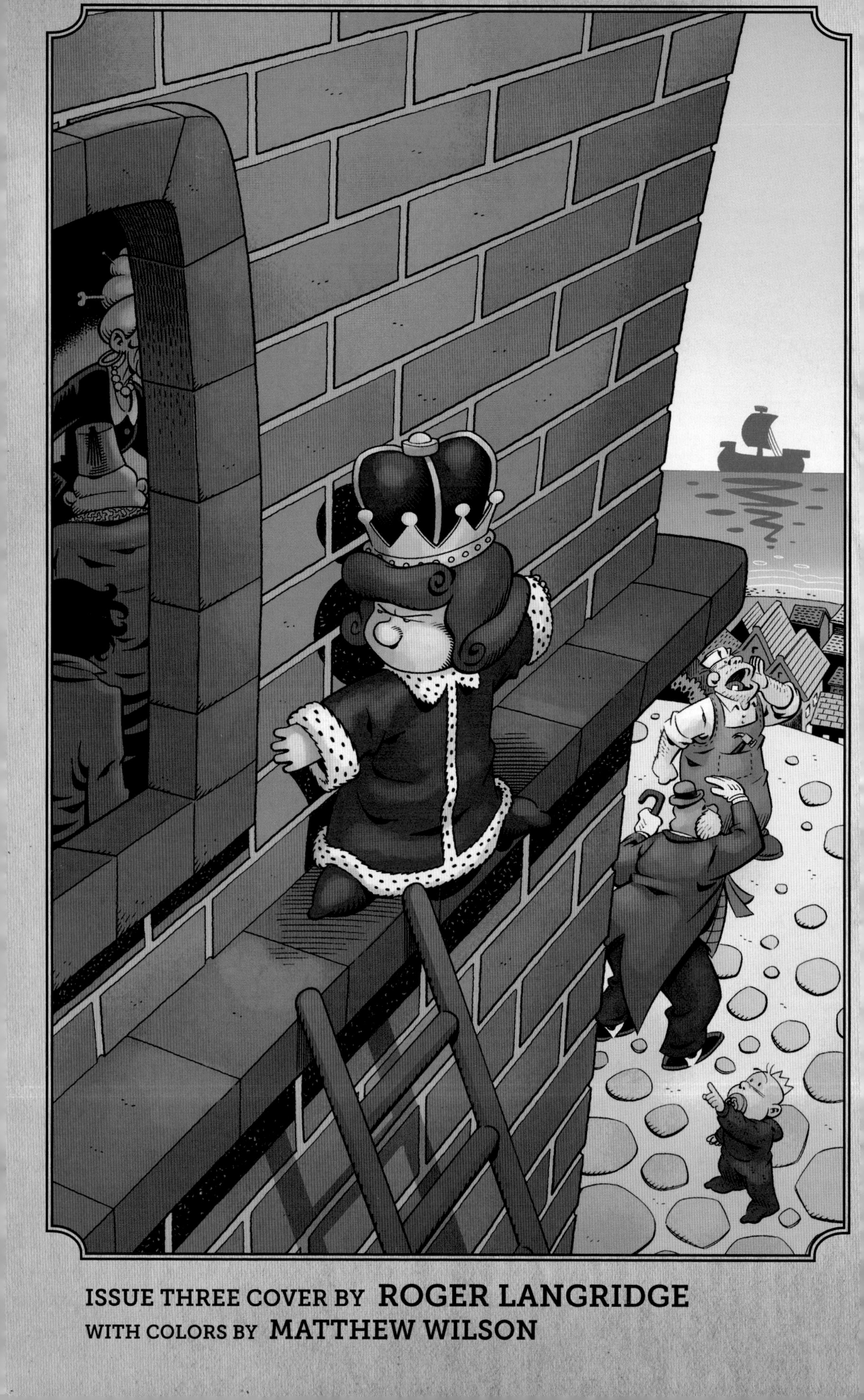

ISSUE THREE COVER BY **ROGER LANGRIDGE**
WITH COLORS BY **MATTHEW WILSON**

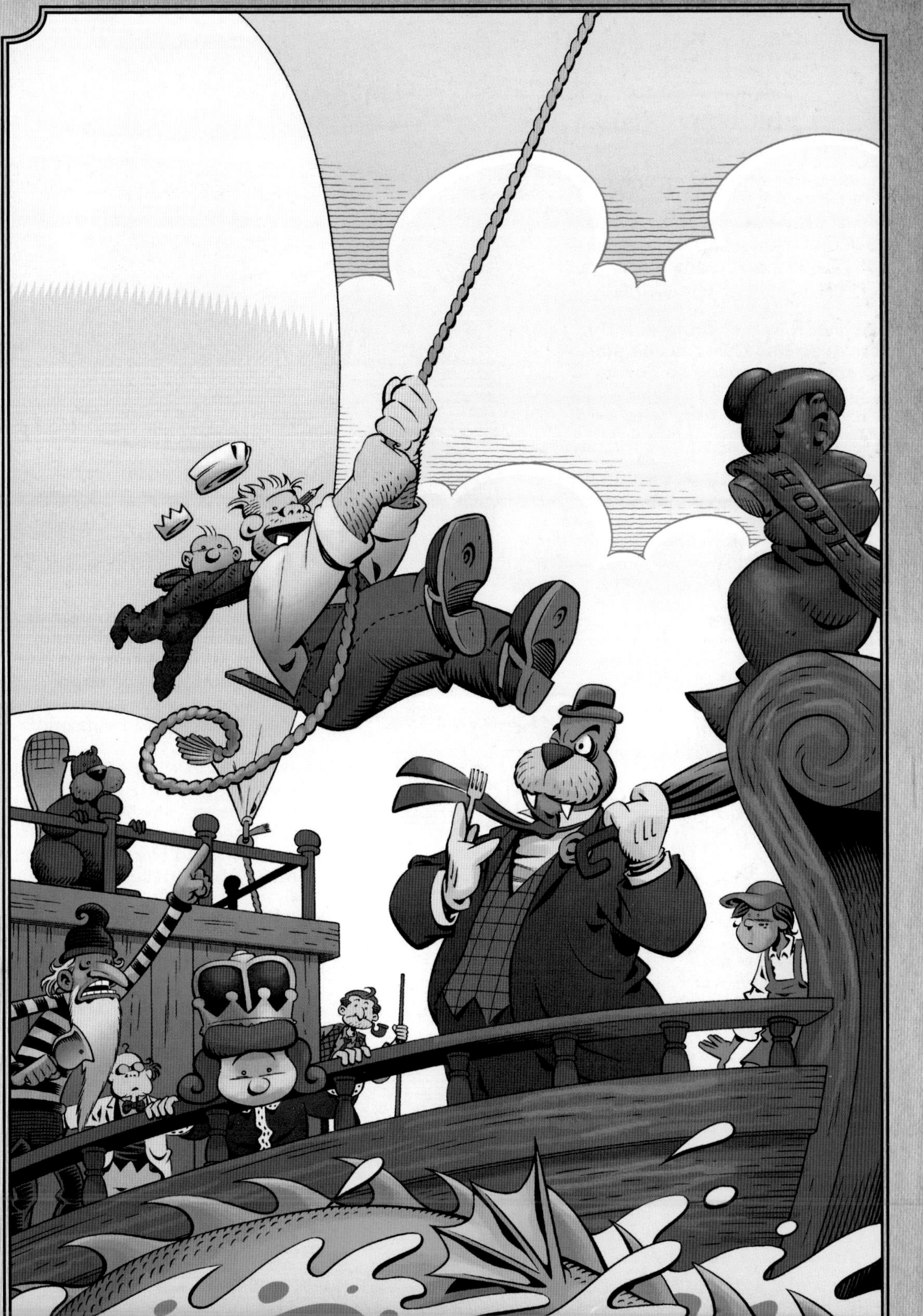
HOPE

ISSUE FOUR COVER BY **ROGER LANGRIDGE**
WITH COLORS BY **MATTHEW WILSON**

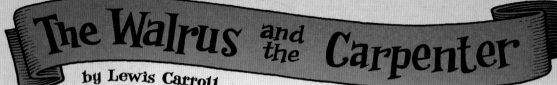

The Walrus and the Carpenter

by Lewis Carroll
Illustrations by Roger Langridge

The sun was shining on the sea,
Shining with all his might:
He did his very best to make
The billows smooth and bright —
And this was odd, because it was
The middle of the night.

The moon was shining sulkily,
Because she thought the sun
Had got no business to be there
After the day was done —
"It's very rude of him," she said,
"To come and spoil the fun!"

The sea was wet as wet could be,
The sands were dry as dry.
You could not see a cloud, because
No cloud was in the sky:
No birds were flying overhead —
There were no birds to fly.

The Walrus and the Carpenter
Were walking close at hand;
They wept like anything to see
Such quantities of sand:
"If this were only cleared away,"
They said, "it would be grand!"

"If seven maids with seven mops
Swept it for half a year.
Do you suppose," the Walrus said,
"That they could get it clear?"
"I doubt it," said the Carpenter,
And shed a bitter tear.

"O Oysters, come and walk with us!"
The Walrus did beseech.
"A pleasant walk, a pleasant talk,
Along the briny beach:
We cannot do with more than four,
To give a hand to each."

The eldest Oyster looked at him,
But never a word he said:
The eldest Oyster winked his eye,
And shook his heavy head —
Meaning to say he did not choose
To leave the oyster-bed.

But four young Oysters hurried up,
All eager for the treat:
Their coats were brushed,
their faces washed,
Their shoes were clean and neat —
And this was odd, because, you know,
They hadn't any feet.

Four other Oysters followed them,
And yet another four;
And thick and fast they came at last,
And more, and more, and more —
All hopping through the frothy waves,
And scrambling to the shore.

The Walrus and the Carpenter
Walked on a mile or so,
And then they rested on a rock
Conveniently low:
And all the little Oysters stood
And waited in a row.

"The time has come,"
the Walrus said,
"To talk of many things:
Of shoes, and ships,
and sealing-wax —
Of cabbages, and kings —
And why the sea is boiling hot —
And whether pigs have wings."

"But wait a bit," the Oysters cried,
"Before we have our chat;
For some of us are out of breath,
And all of us are fat!"
"No hurry!" said the Carpenter.
They thanked him much for that.

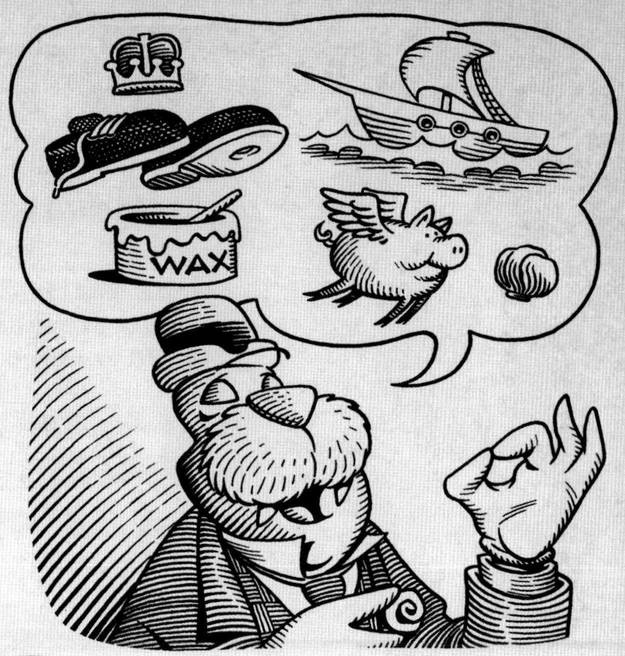
WAX

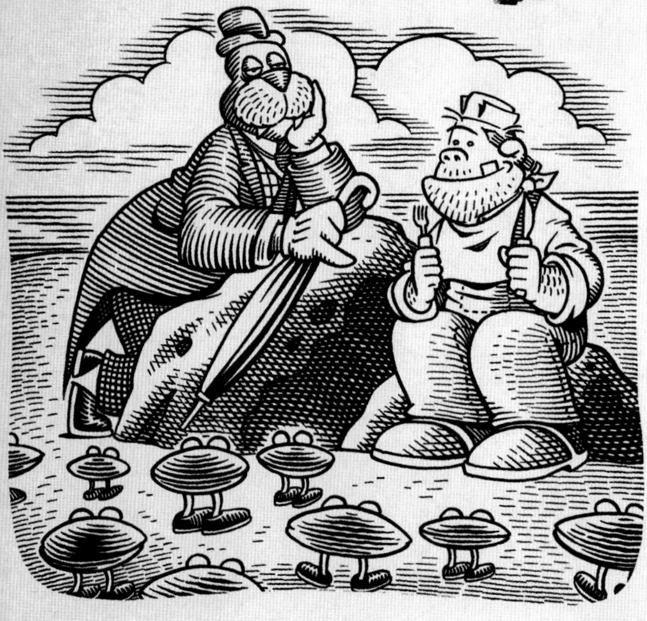

"A loaf of bread,"
the Walrus said,
"Is what we chiefly need:
Pepper and vinegar besides
Are very good indeed —
Now if you're ready, Oysters dear,
We can begin to feed."

"But not on us!" the Oysters cried,
Turning a little blue.
"After such kindness, that would be
A dismal thing to do!"
"The night is fine,"
the Walrus said.
"Do you admire the view?

"It was so kind of you to come!
And you are very nice!"
The Carpenter said nothing but
"Cut us another slice:
I wish you were not quite so deaf —
I've had to ask you twice!"

"It seems a shame," the Walrus said,
"To play them such a trick,
After we've brought them out so far,
And made them trot so quick!"
The Carpenter said nothing but
"The butter's spread too thick!"

"I weep for you," the Walrus said:
"I deeply sympathize."
With sobs and tears he sorted out
Those of the largest size,
Holding his pocket-handkerchief
Before his streaming eyes.

"O Oysters," said the Carpenter,
"You've had a pleasant run!
Shall we be trotting home again?"
But answer came there none —
And this was scarcely odd, because
They'd eaten every one.

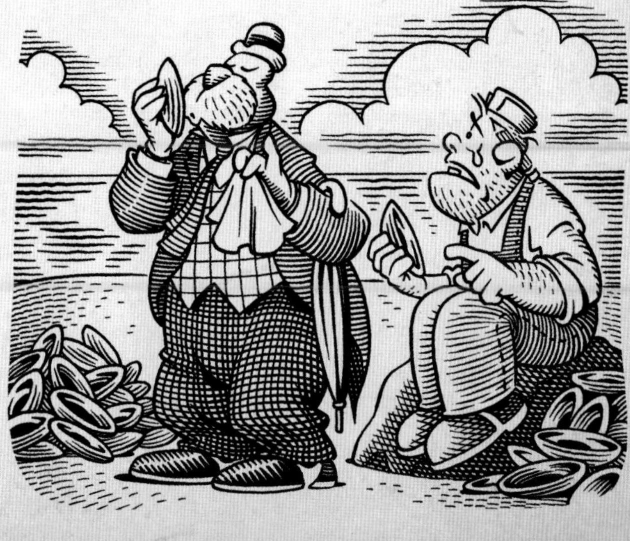

PUZZLES

The Walrus and the Carpenter have to flee the palace at speed! Find them a safe barrel to hide in!

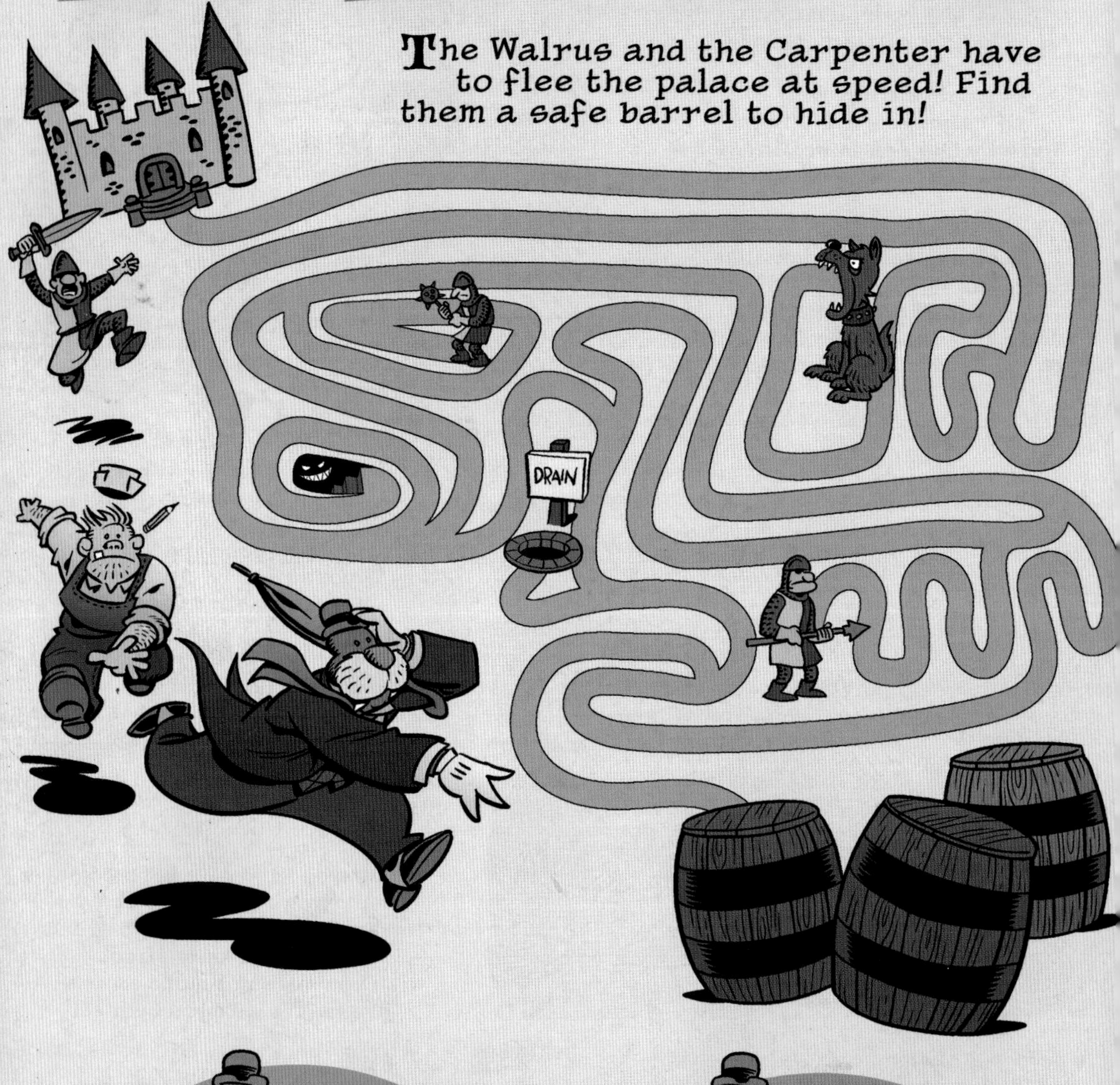
DRAIN

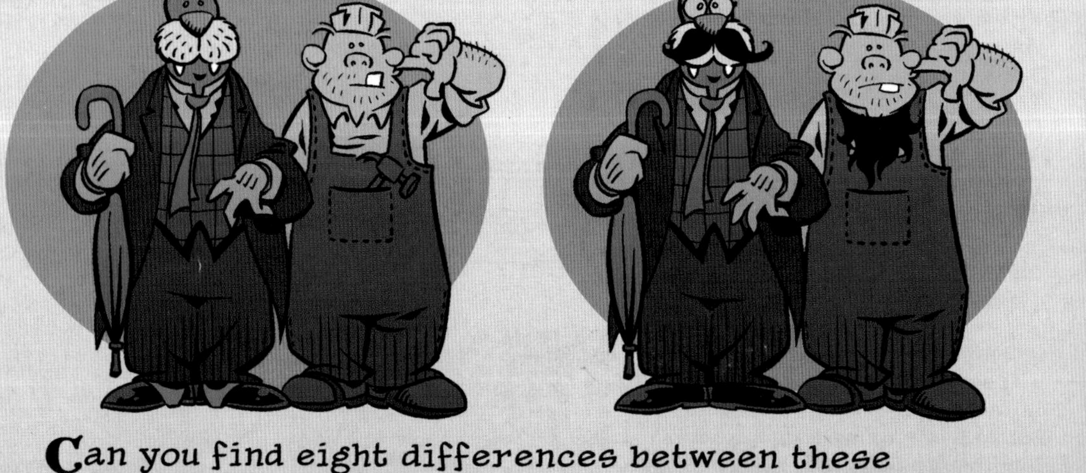

Can you find eight differences between these two pictures of the Walrus and the Carpenter?

AND GAMES

```
O S T R E T S Y O Z O
Y B X Z R O R Q Y O Y
S F R I E E U I S Y S
T L R E T S Y O T S T
E O P S S H Y R E T E
R L Y O Y S T E R E R
E O Y S O Y S T E R E
T O Y S T E R S T O T
S D Q O T B G Y S I S
Y O Y S T E R O Y A Y
O S T R E T S Y O Z O
```

How many occurrences of the word "oyster" can you find in the sand?

Can you change "FORK" into "HOPE" in four steps or less, altering just one letter at a time?

FORK

_____

_____

_____

HOPE

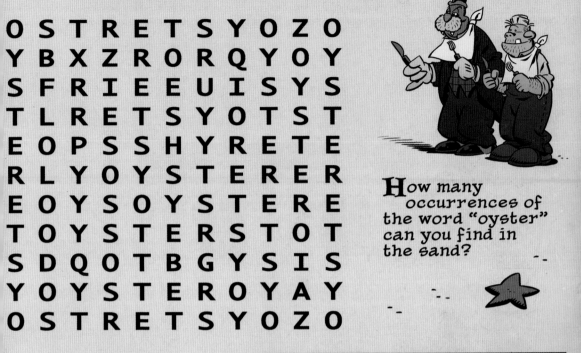

JOIN THE DOTS

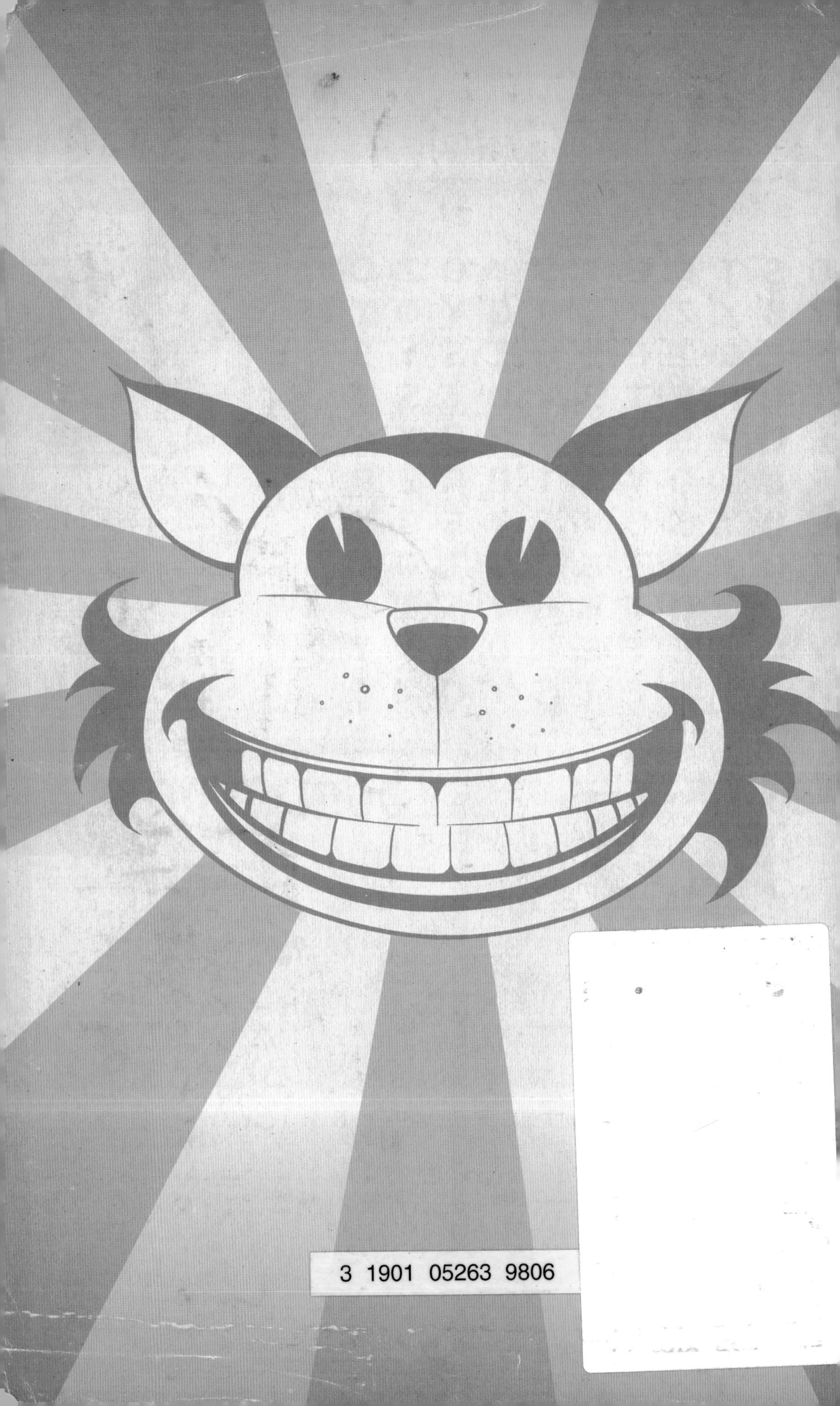